WITHIN OBSESSION AND LIES

A COURT OF GILT AND SHADOW

STACY JONES
HARPER WYLDE

Copyright 2021 © Stacy Jones and Harper Wylde.
All rights reserved.

WITHIN OBSESSION AND LIES
(A Court of Gilt and Shadow Series Book One)
by Stacy Jones and Harper Wylde

Edited by 34 Editing
Cover Design by Trif Cover Designs
Formatted by Harper Wylde
Artwork by Anna Sassi

This book is protected under Copyright laws. Any unauthorized reprint or use of this material is prohibited. No part of this publication may be reproduced, distributed, or transmitted in any form or by any means, including photocopying, recording, or other electronic or mechanical methods without the prior written permission of the author, except in the case of brief quotations embodied in critical reviews and certain other noncommercial uses permitted by copyright law. For permission requests, please contact the authors.

This is a work of fiction. All of the characters, organizations, and events portrayed in this story are either products of the author's imagination or are used fictitiously, and any resemblance to actual events, business establishments, locales, or persons, living or dead, is entirely coincidental.

POWER. OBSESSION. LIES.

Other people dream of being special. They wouldn't, if they knew what a nightmare it is.

Arawyn would give anything to be ordinary and rid herself of the power that lives inside her. Dangerous and alluring, it's caused nothing but pain and horror, making her the dark obsession of anyone who gets too close.

After years of barely containing it, Arawyn thought she had control... until the night it bursts free and pulses like a beacon.

As threats emerge from the shadows, each one more fixated on her than the last, she finds her life infiltrated by three mysterious men.

A mafia boss, a psychopath, and a killer.

Rathe, Viper, and Fear are much more than they seem. They taste of power and feel impossibly familiar. They call to her soul in a way she's never experienced and might have answers to questions she's been asking her entire life.

But, darkness and secrets surround them, ones covered in blood and mire.

When the monsters stalking her endanger not only her power but her life, she'll have to make a decision: take a risk and let these dangerous men in, or do what she's always done —walk away and try to survive on her own.

Trusting them would be a mistake. Yet, she may not have a choice.

The monsters hunting her aren't human, and they're out for blood. Rathe, Viper, and Fear might be her only chance of making it through this alive.

There's only one problem. They aren't human either...

"And above all, watch with glittering eyes the whole world around you because the greatest secrets are always hidden in the most unlikely places. Those who don't believe in magic will never find it."

-Roald Dahl

Chapter One

Arawyn

Arawyn swayed to the hard beat of the music playing on repeat in her earbuds, falling into the familiar, seductive trance that always came when she found the perfect song to match whatever weapon on which she was working.

This one was about playing with fire, about dancing with your demons and feeling at home in your nightmares, even as they haunted you. It made her think of sex with a dangerous, golden-eyed stranger and sweat-slicked bodies moving together in the darkness.

Arawyn let those fantasies fuel her as she drew by the faint light of the moon shining through the single, high window, her pencil a blur across the page, bringing to life the image of a twisted dagger.

Her eyes felt gritty and her body longed for sleep, but this wasn't the first time a dream for a new weapon design had awoken her in the middle of the night, and it wouldn't be the last. She knew from experience she wouldn't be able to get any rest until she had at least drawn the image in her mind, so she ignored the discomfort.

The silver lining to being alone was there was no one to bother her when she worked odd hours. The downside was there was no warm body waiting for her to come back to bed, and no one to care if she exhausted herself on a new project.

No one to bring me a robe either, she thought with a shiver.

Cool air whispered across her exposed skin from the vent in the ceiling as she meticulously drew every detail of the incredibly complex design. The soft silk of her lingerie glided across her bare thighs, tickling her as she shifted position to lean farther over the sketchbook.

To an outsider looking in, she was sure she made a strange picture: a curvy, yet delicate-looking, woman in a black silk and lace teddy sitting in a room full of power tools and instruments of death.

Thankfully, her closest neighbor was over a mile away, and no one knew where she lived, so there were no outsiders to catch a glimpse of her—one of the selling points of the rustic farmhouse when she bought it a couple of years ago. That it came with twenty-five acres of land was another, but the room in which she sat decided it.

The nondescript space looked more like an archaic dungeon than the 'addition' it was touted as, but what would have deterred most buyers had been a selling point for her. The moment she saw it, she knew it'd make the perfect workshop, complete with concrete floors and sheet metal walls. It was love at first sight, and she'd soon turned it into a refuge.

Even after two years, the rest of her house was still littered in boxes waiting to be unpacked, but this space was immaculate, a safe haven away from the world into which she rarely allowed herself to venture.

Adorning the walls, weapons in various shapes and sizes glinted and glittered, the sharp blades catching the moonlight in an array of dazzling color, the custom-ordered metal from which they were made appearing as though it were crafted from thousands of tiny stars. Each one told a story, another sleepless night that bore its creation.

These weapons were for her own private stash while the ones encapsulated in the stacks of boxes by the door were for the clients who funded her small business.

Straightening, she absently twirled a lock of her platinum blonde hair around her finger as she studied the flowing lines of the design she'd drawn.

It was the most complex weapon she'd ever attempted and was going to be hell to make. The twisted blade wasn't one piece, as it appeared in the first sketch, but three that fit together seamlessly. A turn of the hilt would separate the large dagger into individual throwing knives, each perfectly weighted and balanced.

Glancing from the second sketch back to the first, Arawyn frowned. When apart, the design etched into the metal was abstract, but when the three pieces came together, the image of a deadly snake formed, slithering around the hilt and up the blade.

Huh. That's unexpected.

Lifting her head, she scanned the weapons decorating the walls. She knew each one better than the delicate white tattoos inked into her skin, and still, she looked to see if any boasted an animal in the design.

None did.

All of them had images carved into them, but they were nonsensical symbols—strange, meaningless things she didn't understand, yet, couldn't resist engraving into every creation.

Dropping her gaze back to the sketchbook in front of her, she tapped her pencil against the edge of the paper.

You're different, aren't you, handsome?

There was something almost intimate about this piece, something... captivating.

She knew without question the serpent was just as important as the shape of the blade itself. It would be incomplete without every last sculpted feature. Wrong. Useless.

Her lips curved in anticipation of the challenge, her fingers already twitching to start shaping metal. Knowing she was too tired to work safely, she resisted the urge to jump up and get started and, instead, traced her fingers over the finished design.

The moment she skimmed across the snake's head, the power she kept such a tight hold on burst out of her, pulsing in waves with enough force to rattle the walls and window.

Shocked, she doubled over and squeezed her eyes shut as a low, ragged moan slipped from her lips, audible even over the pounding music in her earbuds. The erotic image of the golden-eyed stranger became more vivid as molten need set her alight.

The flood of power felt like one hundred hands stroking her all at once, overwhelming her with a nearly forgotten pleasure. Panting, her entire body shaking, she tried to stop the flood and pull the electric waves of power back into herself.

Minutes that felt like hours passed as she worked to reverse the torrent, until finally, she assumed control once more, coiling the power deep within her chest and trapping it in the confines of a tight fist.

"What the fuck... " she gasped, wiping away the sweat gliding down her temples before pulling the earbuds out and tossing them onto her workbench.

Nothing but silence greeted her as she caught her breath and looked around for an explanation she knew she wouldn't find.

Arawyn wasn't... normal.

There was a force inside her—power like a bottomless ocean just waiting to rise up and drown her.

She'd been normal, once. A regular kid with regular worries: keeping her grades up to stay on the honor roll. Volleyball practice. Fretting about not having the nice, name-brand things her friends had.

But, those days were long gone. Her worries now were much more grave.

She began to notice small differences the day she turned sixteen. Her parents were the first to show signs that something had changed. She'd thought they were just being extra attentive, at first. Even when their attention turned to fixation, and that fixation turned to obsession, she'd tried to ignore the signs, to find logical reasons for their strange behavior.

When her mother took her out of school and stopped letting her leave the house, denial turned to alarm. But, it wasn't until her father began sneaking into her room at night to watch her sleep that she became truly frightened.

It got progressively worse until one night, when her father snuck into her room, it wasn't to watch her sleep.

She ran away that night and never looked back. She'd been on her own ever since. And, still, she hadn't understood. Arawyn had thought they were sick or maybe possessed. It took almost a year of living on the streets to realize they weren't the problem.

She was.

Arawyn couldn't explain the well of power inside herself, nor did she understand why she had it or where it came from. What she did know was everyone she spent too much time around *changed*.

People were drawn to her like moths to a flame, and the longer she was in their presence, the deeper their infatuation grew.

That *magnetism* was only the first power to emerge and, unfortunately, it was only the beginning of the changes to come.

Shortly after, all her senses began to sharpen. Her night vision became almost perfect. She could smell impossible things: far-off storms, water, and sickness. It felt like she'd been living her entire life wrapped in cotton which muffled the world around her, and then, suddenly, the dampening blanket began to fall away.

Then, the physical changes started.

Her hair lost its color until it was nearly white. Her eyes, once a normal, soft green, were now a green so pale they were nearly silver.

She'd hated those changes. The magnetism already made her a target, but with them, she became striking. Noticeable. Easy to spot in a crowd.

But, with the bad came the good. Alongside those physical changes also came strength, speed, and stamina. Alcohol and drugs had only a mild effect on her, something for which she came to be endlessly grateful.

When she turned eighteen, more powers began to surface.

She could forge weapons as if she'd been doing it all her life. Somehow, she'd just known how to shape and hone the metal into the intricate designs that came to her in dreams.

The problem was those abilities flickered in and out. Sometimes they worked perfectly, sometimes not at all. And sometimes, a power would escape. There was no predicting what would happen, no telling what kind of damage would be caused.

She'd burned buildings to the ground, frozen people to death where they stood, brought on tornadoes and thunderstorms, and accidentally made entire crowds of people obsessed with her.

It took years to understand all those abilities came from the same deep well, and years more until finally, at twenty-six, she felt like she had a modicum of control.

At first, it had been like trying to hold back a raging river with a dam made of gossamer, but as the years progressed, she'd learned to contain it, bit by bit, clenching the metaphorical fist in her chest.

Now, if she concentrated hard enough, she could relax that tight grip and let the slightest trickle of power slip through.

Just these past two weeks, she'd been practicing her control. She'd been proud of herself when she'd been able to call forth small tendrils of power, handling them with ease before locking them away again. Slowly, she'd gained trust in her control, but all her progress shattered the moment her power erupted from her tonight.

Leaning back on her stool, Arawyn pressed a hand to her chest. She hadn't had a surge like this in years, not since before she moved here. This was supposed to be her fresh start, the place where things finally went right for her after years of struggling with her powers.

What the hell just happened?

Staring at the dark lines of her sketch, she had to fight the urge to touch it again. Even knowing it wasn't wise, the temptation to try once more, to see if the same reaction happened a second time, dared her to reach out until her hand hovered a scant inch above the paper.

The buzz of her smartwatch broke through the spell, startling her and making her jump guiltily. Glancing down, she blew out a breath when she saw 'Perimeter Alert' flashing across the small screen.

Still reeling, she slid off the stool on autopilot, legs shaking, and scanned the array of security monitors mounted on the far wall, looking at each live video feed for anything out of the ordinary. Most likely, it was her little nightly friend who'd tripped her system, but given how her evening had gone, thus far, she gave each screen a second pass before relaxing marginally when nothing seemed unusual.

Unsurprised by now he'd tripped her motion sensors, but somehow managed to evade her high-tech security cameras, she shook her head. A small grin pulled at one corner of her mouth, and her heart slowed its rapid beat. There was a reason she'd named him 'Sneaks.' The adorable raccoon was better at avoiding detection than a cat burglar.

While she always loved when he visited, she was especially thankful for the distraction tonight. She needed something to help her focus, so she could figure out why her power had surged so suddenly. Busying her hands always cleared her mind and helped her to think better.

Padding barefoot to the kitchen, she rounded the corner and saw her cat, Asshole, cleaning himself by the sink, his silky black fur gleaming in the soft light of the moon shining through the window. He paused to hiss at her, and for some reason, the normalcy of his perpetually rude behavior helped settle her.

As she bent to scoop his food into a bowl, she tried to figure out why her power had suddenly exploded. It had been years since she'd experienced a surge. They'd never been that strong before, but what worried her the most was there hadn't been any warning this time.

In the past, she'd always been able to feel the well rising and had known she was about to lose control. She hadn't been able to stop it, but those signs let her at least try to mitigate it. This time, it came out of nowhere. No warning, no buildup.

"And here I thought I was getting better at this," she muttered with a sigh.

She'd been proud of herself for daring to work with her power these past two weeks instead of trying to keep it restrained all the time. She'd truly thought she was making progress—beginning to gain more control and understand it, if only a little.

Realizing Asshole was still glaring at her, she arched a brow in response. Four years ago, she found him as a kitten living on the streets, starving and near death. He hated her on sight, but she hadn't been able to leave him to die. Arawyn hoped he would come around eventually. He hadn't. In fact, his animosity toward her only seemed to grow as the years passed.

"Someday you're going to stop hating me."

As though to show how he felt about the sentiment, he bent and began cleaning his unmentionables.

Arawyn made a face at the show. "Really? That's disgusting."

Looking deeply offended, he straightened and jumped off the counter, sauntering away with his tail lifted high in a feline 'fuck you.'

"And this is why I named you 'Asshole,'" she called after him.

Pausing with the full bowl of food, she drew in a slow, deep breath, then concentrated on very carefully unclenching the metaphorical fist in her chest, letting the tiniest slip of power through.

Nerves shot through her when she felt the first tendril slip free, but she shook them away. She'd come so far in the last few weeks, and she refused to let herself fall back into the bad habit of keeping that part of herself locked away, of hiding from it in fear. Arawyn had spent the last ten years afraid of that well inside her, and she wouldn't go back to that.

You have to use it to understand it.

Arawyn repeated the mantra to fortify her nerves, and let out a huge sigh of relief when it cooperated, the barest trickle searching outward as she focused on locating her nocturnal visitor.

It was a strange sensation, using her power to check places she couldn't physically see. Those ghostly wisps extended out from the well in her chest to touch and explore. They could sense energy by how bright it felt, the intensity of the glow helping her distinguish between animals and plants, as well as giving her a sense of their size..

What she found running toward her home, however, was way too fucking big to be Sneaks.

Adrenaline poured through her in a rush, destroying every effort she'd made to relax. Her free hand flew to her hip, meeting nothing but smooth silk before she remembered she'd left her gun in her workshop.

"Shit!"

Absently tossing the bowl of food on the counter, she raced on soundless feet, running so fast her hair flew behind her and everything became a blur.

Skidding to a stop, she grabbed the gun and pulled the slide back just enough to make sure there was a bullet in the chamber. Seeing there was, she released it and gripped the gun with both hands, the anxiety racing through her easing slightly at the familiar feel of the cool metal in her palms.

Giving her full attention to the monitors, her gaze flitted from screen to screen as she waited for a flash of movement to confirm what she already knew.

She'd fucked up—or at least her power had.

Chapter Two

Arawyn

The faint whisper of silk and lace across her thighs was the only audible sound as Arawyn prowled toward the foyer, avoiding the creaky floorboards with ease.

Who the fuck had she lured to her? A camper in the woods beyond her house? Someone driving by on the road a mile away? How far had her power pulsed this time?

And how the fuck did they evade being picked up by my security system? Sneaks making it past undetected is one thing. A person? That doesn't make any sense...

Faster than should have been possible from how far away she'd sensed the person, three loud thuds pounded against her reinforced front door. Her stomach dropped even as her lip curled in a snarl.

Goddamnit, this is why I live in the middle of nowhere. So shit like this doesn't happen anymore.

"Open the door!" a distinctly masculine voice called from outside, the loud thump of his fist echoing through the dark, empty hallway once more.

This wasn't her first rodeo. She knew better than to answer or make any noise. There was a chance whoever it was would leave soon, but if he knew she was inside, he wouldn't stop until he'd forced his way in.

Gun raised, but not aimed, she crept on silent feet, trying to listen past the pulse pounding in her ears. No matter how much she trained, no matter how hard she worked to be able to protect herself, the memory, the fear of what could—had—happened never went away.

"Open the door! I know you're in there. I can *feel* you... "

Just before she rounded the corner into the foyer, she caught the sound of the doorknob jiggling. A hard spike of fear shot through her, making her steps falter.

The door was locked. She knew it was. She triple-checked it every time she got home and again before she went to sleep each night.

She *knew* it was locked... but the minuscule possibility that, this time, she might've forgotten had alarm skittering up her spine like icy fingers.

The last time one of them got inside...

Her most recent scars—long, jagged things crisscrossing her shoulder blades—pulsed with remembered pain. A flashback of what she'd lived through, and what she'd had to do to escape the last time someone caught her unprepared, made her flinch.

The moment the door came into view, Arawyn quickly scanned the multitude of locks. A shaky sigh left her when she saw they were all secure, but the relief was short-lived. Peering at the security monitor set into the wall beside the door, nausea rolled through her.

She didn't know the man scratching at the metal, painting it in streaks of blood from his torn fingernails, but she recognized the effects of her power all too well.

The magnetism wasn't always harmless. How long it lasted, and in what way it affected people, differed depending on how much of her power they'd been exposed to... and who they were at their core.

It could bring out the darkest parts of a person, twisting their fascination into a destructive kind of obsession.

Sometimes, people wanted to destroy the very thing they craved.

Feeling as though she was trapped in one of her nightmares, Arawyn padded silently to the monitor and made herself look at the crazed stranger outside, made herself see what she'd done to him.

Dark memories from her past assaulted her, pounding against her mind like steady rain assaulting a tin roof—relentless and deafening. Memories of hands grabbing, hurting. Memories of being taken, trapped in the dark, of being caged. Memories of blood and pain.

Not again. Never again.

Her hand involuntarily tightened around the gun, a reminder she wasn't a victim... not anymore.

As though he could see the images playing out in her head, the man's voice filtered through the door, full of false promises. "I don't want to hurt you. I just need to see you."

Ignoring his plea, she pulled in a steadying breath and scanned what she could see of his body. The mess of dark hair offsetting his tanned skin and his brawny build matched the few brief glimpses she'd seen of her closest neighbor.

His house is more than a mile away...

That the surge had reached such a distance and still been strong enough to affect him like this stunned her.

His feet were bare and covered in dirt, telling her he'd trekked through the woods in his haste to reach her. Mud caked the hem of his rumpled pajama pants, and blood stained the sleeves from the scratches on his arms and torn nails. If that didn't make him appear unhinged enough, his eyes were bright, almost feverish in their intensity.

Through the riot of emotions pelting her, something niggled at the back of her mind. There was something... different about this man, something eerie about the light in his eyes.

For a moment, Arawyn felt trapped in that stare. The unnerving sense he could see her through the thick metal had goosebumps rising on her arms before she shook it off.

After two more, open-palmed bangs against her door, the man stopped, turned, and began pacing agitatedly across her small front porch. As he dove his hands through his hair, pulling roughly at the dark strands, moonlight glinted off a silver ring adorning his finger. The piece of jewelry was so ostentatious with its large, blue sapphire that she was momentarily distracted by it.

A class ring or family heirloom, perhaps? Neither were items Arawyn owned herself. Growing up, there'd never been any money for extra expenses beyond basic necessities, and the curse of her powers made school and graduation an impossible dream.

"Let me in, sweetheart," the man purred, trying to hide the desperate notes behind the seductive demand as he returned to the barrier between them. "I've come all this way to see you. So. Fucking. Far." Each word was punctuated by a thudding bang, making her flinch.

Right. Because a one-mile walk was really challenging.

She stopped herself short of rolling her eyes and returned her gaze to his face, taking in the dark bruises below his eyes that seemed to deepen as she stared. The tanned tone of his skin lost its color, becoming pale, and there was a visibly growing gauntness in his cheeks.

He looked unwell and seemed to be growing more so with every passing minute. She winced, guilt and concern adding to the emotions already twisting her stomach.

Anger hardened his features when she didn't respond. He straightened, and his whole demeanor changed in an instant. A sickening smile curled his mouth, and that feverish stare bored into her through the camera disguised as a peephole.

Without warning, he punched his fist into the door with more strength than she would've given him credit. She'd be surprised if there weren't a dent left from the impact. The harsh clang of the thick ring adorning his finger reverberated through the dark foyer, the melody of metal on metal accompanied by a furious growl.

A string of curses spoken so gutturally and with such vitriol they almost sounded as if they were in a different language flew from his lips. There was a confusing look of surprise in his bright eyes, like he'd genuinely expected that blow to knock the door down.

Arawyn tightened her hand around the gun, caressing the trigger with her finger. Some of the brittle tension in her shoulders eased with the reminder she could protect herself, even as her pulse raced.

Yet, just because she could, didn't mean she wanted it to come to that. Her chest tightened with the reminder of her sins. The lives she'd taken in self-defense marred her soul with scars that would never fade.

Killing wasn't for the weak. Every day she carried the weight of her decisions, and while she didn't want to add another name to her list of regrets, she wouldn't hesitate, if it came down to her life or someone else's.

He'll leave. It won't come to that, not this time.

The savage snarls continued, more animal than man, and Arawyn turned to brace her back against the cool metal of her door, sliding to the floor. The emotions she always kept tightly contained tried to break free and rise to the surface, making her eyes burn. Blinking away the tears before they could fall, she wondered if she was going to have to leave and uproot her life again.

Her heart sank with the notion.

The impulse to run, to start over, was strong, but those were old fears talking. She wasn't the same person—the same fragile, broken woman she once was. For the first time, Arawyn finally had some semblance of a life.

From the outside looking in, she was sure her existence seemed far from normal, small and isolated compared to most, but it was *her* normal, and she didn't want to give it up.

She couldn't do it. She *wouldn't* uproot her life and run. The effects of her power would wear off in a couple of hours or even in a few days' time. There was no reason to act rashly.

He'll go away. He will. *They always go away eventually.*

The litany repeated over and over again, both a promise and a plea.

But, he didn't leave.

One hour passed, then two, as she positioned herself near the door, gun trained, listening to him scream and rage and beat on the door. He circled her house, checking for another point of entry, trying to pry the windows open, then break the glass when that failed. Thankfully, she'd sprung for polycarbonate windows, and his efforts to shatter them were futile.

Another hour passed, and it became abundantly clear he wasn't going anywhere any time soon.

What if he really could sense her? She checked the well, but it didn't feel like anything was seeping out.

Still, it was possible putting distance between them would help diminish the effects quicker.

Weighing her choices, she finally decided leaving was worth the risk.

Arawyn walked silently away from the incensed man outside her house and into her darkened bedroom. Having a course of action helped steady her hands. She slipped out of the lingerie and into a pair of supple leather pants that molded to her curves like a second skin. Rifling through her closet, she quickly put on a long-sleeved, black shirt and her favorite knee-high motorcycle boots.

For just a moment, her gaze caught on the woman staring back at her from the standing mirror. On the surface, that woman was beautiful. Long, wavy, platinum blonde hair flowed to the small of her back. Large, glass-green eyes were framed by thick lashes and arching brows a couple of shades darker than her hair. Those eyes dominated a delicate face with an upturned nose and full lips. At only five foot three, she was petite, with just enough curves to round out her figure, make her look soft, and hide her true strength.

She looked ethereal. Dainty. Fragile.

It wasn't until you looked below the surface, into the depths of those eyes, that you saw the jagged edges sharpening and shaping her. A passerby wouldn't see the scars marring her small frame. They wouldn't notice the defined muscle or the callouses on her hands that spoke to dedication, training, and hard work, earning her freedom and relative safety. They wouldn't know the woman beyond the pretty face had lived through more horrors than most people could imagine.

They didn't know the phantom feeling of blood still coated her hands or that the scent of gunpowder both comforted and haunted her.

They couldn't hear the pained cries of those she'd killed that sometimes woke her up in the middle of the night.

And they would never know part of her didn't regret the lives she'd taken.

What did it say about her that she had to fight against this part of herself, to force a feeling of guilt that should've come naturally?

Arawyn turned away from the truth of her past reflecting back at her, even as she slid her gun into a hidden holster tucked within her boot.

Pulling open the old, carved wooden doors of her armoire, she paused for a moment to gaze at the assortment of weapons and jewelry displayed within.

With smooth, practiced movements, she adorned herself with a spiked ring and two bobby pins that worked as lock picks and were easily camouflaged by her hair.

Arawyn hadn't asked for this curse, didn't even fucking want it. In the ten years since it had emerged, she'd been assaulted and kidnapped, even tortured, more times than she could count.

Everyone always says to never blame the victim, but what her power did to people was her fault. Didn't that mean what they did to her was her fault, as well? It felt like it was.

And, yet, she knew, if it came down to it, she wouldn't hesitate to kill again, if her life was on the line.

Pausing to lovingly stroke her two favorite daggers—one light and the other dark—she strapped on her custom holster and slid them in, adjusting them until they sat flush on either side of her spine under her shirt.

Grabbing a backpack, she threw in a few basic supplies to last her a couple of days, in case she had to stay away for an extended period, though she hoped the effects of her power would wear off sooner rather than later.

Finished, she shrugged into a well-worn leather jacket and swiped her keys off the table. Pulling up the live feed of her security monitors on her phone, she quickly checked to ensure her neighbor was at the front of the house before silently slipping out the back door, closing it with barely a snick of the latch. Setting the alarm behind her, she moved swiftly to the run-down barn housing her motorcycle and SUV.

She made fast work of securing her helmet, then deftly swung her leg over and settled into the familiar seat. With a press of the ignition, the electric Harley LiveWire came silently to life beneath her.

Veering to the grass lining the driveway, she drove quietly away from her home, disappearing into the night like a ghost and leaving the moonlit silhouette of her latest mistake behind her.

The soft whine of the powerful machine between her legs and the wind whipping past her were intoxicating, seeping the tension from her, the feeling of freedom she always got when she was on the road washing away the remaining traces of fear and frustration.

Out here, she wasn't hunted. She wasn't craved. She wasn't cursed.

For a few blissful moments, she could almost forget...

Almost.

Chapter Three

Rathe

Rathe swirled the amber liquid in his tumbler, watching the way it sloshed against the sides of the crystal while steadfastly ignoring his brother. Or trying to.

"Been feelin' 'em for a week. Finally got a good taste. I'll find 'em if we go... somewhere. Where to go, where to go..." Viper mumbled to himself from where he'd been pacing the length of their loft for the last ten minutes.

Rathe's only response was to lift his glass and study the light playing off the honey-colored alcohol. It always reminded him of home, of the brightest sun and warm summer days. Unfortunately, it also reminded him of gilded cages and the responsibilities from which he'd spent the last seven years running.

He tipped the tumbler to his lips and took a healthy sip, enjoying the faint burn that trickled down his throat as he tried to drown out the grim call of duty and obligation.

"We need to go out tonight," Viper finally spoke up, oblivious to Rathe's souring mood. Or, perhaps, he was immune after so many years of living in close quarters.

Viper flipped the butterfly knife he was playing with through the air, the metal glinting in the low light before he deftly caught it and returned to flicking it open and closed, open and closed, while he mindlessly wore a path across the expensive hardwood flooring.

"Somewhere with alcohol..." Viper mumbled, shoving a hand through his blonde hair.

Shaved short on the sides and kept long enough on the top to fall into his eyes—something women universally seemed to love but would drive Rathe insane—it always seemed to stay styled, no matter how many times the man mussed it with his anxious habits.

"We have alcohol here," Rathe commented dryly, adjusting his position so he could stretch the span of his black, feathered wings out behind him. Having them free when they were so often contained sent a blissful ache through the muscles of his shoulders.

His brother ignored him and tilted his head, yellow eyes glowing and the slitted pupils constricting as he *saw* something beyond the brick walls before him.

"And dancing."

Rathe gestured with the clawed tip of a wing toward the elaborate sound system they could connect to using their phones. "Knock yourself out."

"I think it's a club." Viper gave a slow nod that got

progressively faster until he was enthusiastically agreeing with himself. "Yeah, definitely a club. If we go, they'll go." He snickered to himself, "I'm so good at this shit."

Rathe rolled his eyes.

Viper's free hand tapped a staccato rhythm against his thigh as he walked, his naturally black fingernails sharpening to claws as his true form peeked through. Every part of him was moving in some way. The man could rarely sit still, but this was different. He was practically vibrating with energy.

"No." The sharp command left no room for disagreement. Unfortunately, Rathe knew by now his brother would only listen if it suited him.

Viper jerked to a stop, ripped his knife out of the air, and pointed it toward Rathe in one smooth motion. "I'm serious."

Rathe narrowed his gaze. "So am I."

Viper went eerily still, eyeing him unblinkingly, the only movement that of his forked tongue toying with one of the rings piercing both corners of his lower lip—piercings referred to as 'snake bites,' an entirely intentional decision on his brother's part. Standing like that, the tip of his tongue slowly flicking, he looked unerringly like the animal from which he took his name. Finally, he relaxed, his eyes flashing golden yellow as he swiftly spun the butterfly knife closed.

Rathe knew this relaxed pose was deceptive and too often precipitated Viper doing, or saying, something he wouldn't like.

"It's been a week since we sent anyone for King Ehrendil to drain," his brother drawled tauntingly.

"And there it is," he murmured.

The long scar vertically bisecting Viper's left eye crinkled, the grin twisting his lips a little manic, because he knew he wasn't wrong. The mention of Rathe's overdue loyalty was the strongest tool in his brother's arsenal. It was the only argument Viper could've made to sway Rathe to change his mind, and he used it without remorse.

A muscle jumped in Rathe's jaw as he clenched his teeth tightly, barely holding back a sneer at the mention of his father, the High King of the Light Court. It also served as a further reminder of the very thing he strove to forget.

Their time in this realm was already limited, but it would come to a much swifter end, if he didn't do his father's bidding.

The King *graciously* allowed Rathe to live in the human realm with his bastard half-brother, Viper, and his official guard-turned-friend, Fearson. But, their temporary freedoms came at a cost: providing victims for the King to drain, feeding his insatiable hunger.

His father's most carefully guarded secret was his *gift*—if you could call it that—of *Devouring* another's power. For the first couple years Rathe was in the human realm, Ehrendil had been content with the *Fae* relics he and his friends sent back, items of power which had been lost or stolen over the millennia.

But, the King hadn't been satisfied with those little sips for long.

For the last five years now, Rathe had been under orders to send him bigger... *meals*.

Knowing his brother was right, he swallowed back his distaste and asked, "Can you sense if they're... deserving?"

"Does it matter?" Viper quipped.

"You know it does," he growled darkly.

Rathe's only consolation was the knowledge the rogue Fae he sent his father were twisted things, predators who preyed on the weak—both human and *other* alike—but it was cold comfort.

Those beings deserved punishment. Most had earned death, in some cases even slow, torturous ones. But, he'd seen his father feed.

No one deserved that horror.

Viper let out an almost soundless sigh, the apology in it imperceptible to anyone else, but he heard it. "I can sense they're... powerful."

Rathe got the feeling there was something he wasn't saying. Then again, there was always something Viper wasn't saying. Regardless, he was right. It had been too long since they sent the King fresh meat. If they didn't provide him a new victim, he would simply drain an innocent, discreetly preying on one of his own subjects under cover of darkness and disguise.

Rathe loathed his father and hated he was directly contributing to the growing strength the man used to keep his people enslaved. The fact that his father saw his efforts as a sign he was becoming a ruler who would follow in his notorious footsteps was the poison on the blade slowly slicing away pieces of Rathe's soul.

But, it was the lesser evil. For his people, if not for himself and his friends, anyway.

Realizing his desire for a quiet night at home had slipped away, he rolled his neck and forced some of the tension from his shoulders before giving Viper a terse nod.

The man—known to all in Faery as the Light King's most feared assassin—clapped like a child being given a treat, the sharp sound reverberating off the brick walls, then proceeded to rub his hands together like he'd just hatched a maniacal scheme instead of solidifying evening plans.

"What's going on?" came a low, rumbling voice from behind.

Rathe dropped a wing and glanced over his shoulder to find his guard, Fearson, standing in the doorway, the top of his head almost brushing the frame, observing the two of them with narrowed eyes.

Fearson had an uncanny ability to assess his surroundings. It wasn't a power, just a skill of his. So, Rathe wasn't surprised when he sighed resignedly, "We're going out, aren't we?"

It wasn't really a question, so Rathe didn't bother answering. Instead, he pushed to his feet, ruffled his wings, and tucked them tightly against his back before altering his appearance with a mere thought.

The magic of his glamour tingled over him, and his wings disappeared, ready and waiting for when he called them forth once more. He didn't need a mirror to know his pointed ears were now rounded like those of a human's, or that his ocean-blue eyes with their fiery orange sunbursts—a mark of his royal lineage—were now a normal blue. The golden shimmer of his skin dulled to something more natural for this realm, hiding his true form below a seemingly mortal and mundane exterior.

That done, he took a moment to draw the natural *Allure* all Fae gave off into himself so he could make it through the night without anyone becoming enthralled.

It was second nature, now, to keep it dampened, but it hadn't always been. When they first came to this realm, none of them had fully understood or experienced just how intensely it affected humans. Just remembering all the people, both women and men alike, trying to crawl all over him like *dust* addicts looking for a fix sent a grimace curling his lip.

Making quick work of his crisp button-down, he donned his suit jacket and slid his gun back into the holster hidden beneath.

"Apparently, we're to dress for dancing," Rathe quipped darkly, heading for the door.

Fearson stepped aside, his large frame barely leaving enough room for him to pass through the doorway. He could still smell the motor oil on the massive man, telling him he'd recently been downstairs working on their extensive collection of vehicles.

Grumbles followed him down the hallway, but in a matter of minutes they were all dressed and slipping into their vehicle of choice: him in his Aston Martin Vantage, Fearson in his rare 1970 Hemi Cuda, and Viper on his hideously bright orange Ducati Superleggera.

The sooner they left, the sooner they could return. He just hoped the latest target his brother sensed was easy to track... and had done something vile enough to even slightly deserve the fate that awaited them.

With a peel of his tires, Rathe steered the car out of the garage and followed Viper into late-night traffic.

ARAWYN

The empty, nighttime roads were freeing at first, but before long, the sense she was the only person in the world intensified the aching loneliness that was a constant, suffocating weight.

Whether it was her latest stalker, or the lack of social contact she'd had over the past month as she lost herself in her work, Arawyn didn't know, but suddenly the silence was stifling.

Arawyn lived as isolated as she could. She tried so hard, so fucking hard, to resist when the need for human contact and intimacy arose, not wanting to put anyone at risk.

But, eventually, she always broke.

When the need to be around other people grew to be too much, she allowed herself brief moments of normalcy: going to the cute downtown café for coffee, grocery shopping at the farmers' market instead of having her items delivered, bringing her packages to the Post Office instead of having them picked up. These outings seemed small and insignificant to most, but to Arawyn, they were everything.

Unfortunately, those outings were far too fleeting, hardly fulfilled her need to be around others, and never soothed the one thing she found herself craving the most: human touch.

When it got to the point she could barely breathe past the yearning, she caved to the temptation and sought out a one-night stand, but at best, those encounters only temporarily dulled the need.

Water, air, and food were essential for sustaining life, but no one ever mentioned touch was just as vital. Each night when she crawled into bed, she ached for companionship.

It had gotten so bad in the last few months that most mornings she'd wake from dreams of being held in strong arms, of being cradled against a warm, hard chest, only to open her eyes and find herself horribly, achingly alone. Always alone.

Those dreams were so painfully vivid, she could swear she smelled him on her sheets: a heady combination of smoke, warm cinnamon, and dark berries.

Maybe it was the ghost of her dream or the loneliness at fault, but suddenly, she felt a pulling sensation in her chest, like something was drawing her.

Wondering if her power was acting up again, she searched inside herself. Blowing out a breath when she found it calm and contained, she turned her focus back to that strange pull.

It felt different, unlike anything she'd ever experienced. It felt... good. Warm, comforting, exciting.

It felt like... home.

The compulsion to let it guide her, to see where it took her was strong, so strong she had to consciously stop her hand from torquing the throttle. A sense of familiarity, and an inexplicable knowing she would find someone on the other end of the draw washed over her, bringing with it a keen yearning.

A softly whispered thought hit her, a hidden longing that

had lived inside her from the moment she realized she was different...

What if it's someone like me?

It didn't matter that it was a remote possibility. It didn't matter that she thought she'd finally managed to accept she was alone. The chance, no matter how minute, there might be someone like her out there was enough to convince herself.

Wary, but unbearably curious, Arawyn resolutely followed the pull and let it guide her.

Chapter Four

Arawyn

Over an hour later, Arawyn found herself passing into city limits. With the realization there was a good chance she was being led somewhere with people, she tested the neverending well of power in her chest, making sure it was fisted tightly, while she weaved in and out of traffic between the tall buildings.

Jutting towers of glass and steel, along with the bright lights of the city, drowned out any view of the moon and stars above. It was one of the things she loved about living on the outskirts of the sprawling metropolis. For some reason, the view of the night sky had always soothed her.

Focusing on the pull as it grew stronger with every mile she drove, she let it guide her.

Even though driving into the city had guaranteed she'd

be around others, nervousness still slid through her when she pulled into the crowded parking lot of a night club. Eyeing the long line of people waiting to get into the building, she hesitated.

Being around so many people was never easy. It didn't matter how tightly she contained her power, there was something about her men and women alike found compelling. In a crowd this large, with inhibitions already lowered by alcohol, Arawyn knew she'd have to fend off far more than her fair share of attention.

She focused on the draw, hoping she was wrong and it was leading her somewhere less populated, but no, it was definitely pulling her in there.

Fuck it. I've come this far.

Arawyn paused once inside the club to scan the mass of writhing bodies on the immense, recessed dance floor—hypnotic strobes of light painting them in flashes of purple, pink, and blue.

The music was so loud it felt tangible, the bass pounding in her chest like a second heartbeat.

The darkened club offered her its own brand of freedom. In the shifting shadows, Arawyn could pretend to be just another face in the crowd. Below the colored lights and deafening music, there would be no questions to avoid, no small talk to tiptoe around. There was only dancing, drinking, and feeling.

The sense of anonymity that provided settled over her like a comforting blanket. It wouldn't last, but for just a moment, the sense of being invisible was intoxicating.

As she watched from the sidelines, the desire to join that writhing mass, to touch and be touched, had both longing and apprehension coiling inside her.

Looking away from the dance floor, she surreptitiously scanned the dark, cavernous interior of the club as she made her way through the tightly packed throng of people. A small thrill filled her with every accidental brush, every contact with another person, as she aimed for the long bar taking up the entire left wall.

Just how touch-starved have I let myself get?

Reaching for the well of power, she tightened her grip on it as firmly as she could to make sure nothing was leaking out, just in case the person on the other end of the pull didn't have the best intentions in mind. She didn't want to give herself away.

Of course, that would only work if they couldn't feel the same pull toward her, but better to err on the side of not getting kidnapped. Again.

The moment she reached the over-populated bar, the closest bartender turned to her like a flower turning its face to the sun, her expression brightening as if Arawyn was a best friend or lover instead of a complete stranger.

"What can I get you, beautiful?" the red-headed woman mouthed, not even attempting to shout over the rhythmic beat of the music.

The people on either side of her, who'd obviously been waiting a while to place their orders, turned to her, but the irritation on their faces lasted only a second. Even knowing they no longer cared she'd unintentionally cut the line, Arawyn still smiled apologetically in their directions before focusing her gaze on the bartender's upper cheek.

She didn't know if making direct eye contact made her influence worse, so she rarely did so, unwilling to risk it.

"Three shots, please," she mouthed back, holding up three fingers then making a quick motion of her hand to signal what she wanted, laying a bill on the counter with the other hand before one of the people bracketing her could.

"You got it, honey." She pushed the bill back at Arawyn with a wink. "It's on the house."

She knew better than to insist, so she just stuffed the money back in her pocket with a tight smile.

That it would take three shots to even feel the slightest buzz was annoying at times. While she liked to keep her wits about her, she also craved the blissfulness others seemed to have when they drank, like all their worries no longer mattered, at least while the effects lasted. After the night she'd had, and the nerves twisting her stomach into a knot at the thought of discovering who was on the other end of this unexplainable draw, trying to reach that kind of relaxation was too tempting to resist.

Faster than anyone could reasonably expect to be served in a place this crowded, the shots were placed in front of her, laid on a napkin with the woman's number scrawled on it. Slamming them back one after the other, Arawyn set the now-empty glasses back down, pretending she hadn't seen the writing.

Just as she started to turn away, the bartender laid a hand on Arawyn's forearm, halting her midmotion. Her heart skipped a beat, her body instantly beset with the conflicting urges to jerk away and lean closer.

She whipped a look up at the bartender's face, afraid she was one of those people who had no immunity to the magnetism Arawyn seemed to emit like perfume. Relaxing when, instead of the besotted expression she'd feared, she found the woman's gaze bouncing from the empty glasses to Arawyn's small frame, her expression concerned.

Smiling politely, Arawyn rubbed her stomach to signal

she'd eaten, not that she had, but it did as she wanted. With a nod of her head, the bartender let her go and turned to the next customer.

For any other woman of her size, taking three shots back to back would likely knock her on her ass.

For Arawyn, it was barely enough to get a buzz, but it at least took the edge off the nerves firing through her.

Alcohol, drugs, hell, even over-the-counter medication just didn't seem to work well on her. Though she often bemoaned that when trying to drown the loneliness, it had come in handy on too many occasions to count when someone tried to spike her drink or dose her with something.

Still, she knew better than to do anything that drew unnecessary attention, and that included downing shots like a college chick on a bender.

The mental lecture she was giving herself slowly quieted as the feeling of being pulled intensified to become all-consuming.

Eyes wide, almost walking on tiptoe, Arawyn searched every face, looking for whomever it was calling her, as she let it lead her to a thankfully less-packed section of the dance floor.

Allowing the hard beat of the music to guide her, she began swaying, even as she watched the people around her, senses heightened, alert for anyone paying her unusual amounts of attention.

Arawyn felt more than a few men trying to creep up behind her, but they weren't who she was looking for, so she gracefully sidestepped their reaching hands or slipped into a gap between bodies to escape their crudely thrusting hips.

She may be touch-starved, but she wasn't desperate enough to let some rude ass grind up against her.

Eluding another over-eager prick, she bit back a sigh and closed her eyes, concentrating on that inescapable feeling to pinpoint from which direction the draw was coming.

There.

Opening her eyes, she scanned the cavernous room, her movements slowing as she searched for that weighted stare in the strobing lights. In the darkened recess past the dance floor, she found not one, but two sets of eyes watching her steadily.

Their gazes felt like caresses against her skin, enticing lures shocking her with foreign intensity.

None of the men Arawyn had been with in the past had ever given her butterflies or made her pulse race. They'd been nothing but a means to a necessary end, a drop of water in the desert that was her hunger for touch. But this... staring into those eyes had her heart thundering and her stomach aflutter with excitement and fascination.

It felt how she imagined others felt toward her—attracted, intrigued, captivated.

Something inside her awakened, blossoming like a flower opening in spring, filling her with a heady warmth that unfurled in the center of her chest and spread outward.

Arawyn went still, a stone in the rushing river of heaving bodies around her, as the warmth filled her, suffusing every inch of her body until she could barely breathe past it.

Oh god, they feel... they feel like... me.

Chapter Five

Arawyn

She'd hoped, she'd yearned for it, dreamt of the possibility, but now that she was face to face with not one, but two men who felt like her...

It's not possible... is it?

As she held their gazes, the pull intensified, becoming such a persistent tug it drew on the deep well of power she had fisted tighter than ever before.

A sliver of wariness flared, reminding her not to trust too easily, to stay alert and wary, but every piece of her wanted to close the remaining distance and learn why she felt compelled to do so.

Instead, Arawyn buried the impulse and began swaying again to the rhythmic beat of the music, allowing herself to stare at them as they openly stared at her.

The two men were cloaked in shadow, the dark so thick it should've concealed them from view, but Arawyn had better night vision than most. She could make out enough to tell they were tall and broad, towering over the other men at the club.

Even from twenty feet away, she could sense the air of danger surrounding them. A quick glance told her she wasn't the only one who could feel it. Bodies were packed tightly together throughout the club, but a circle ringed them, as though no one dared get too close. It had the opposite effect on her, calling to her, beckoning her closer, inviting her to let their dark aura surround her like an embrace.

Arawyn's curiosity and interest deepened. Still resisting the urge to go to them, she looked from one to the other, not daring to blink. She was afraid if she did, these men and the feeling they inspired, might disappear.

Strobes of light flashed over them, teasing her with glimpses in the shifting darkness. The one on the right was indescribably handsome. Her breath caught in her chest at what she could see in the shadows.

Black hair, shaved close on the sides and left longer on the top, was slicked back, leaving his face starkly visible. Black brows and thick lashes framed eyes she yearned to learn the color of.

With each flash from the strobes, she could make out another defined feature. Sharp cheekbones, the hard cut of his jaw, and a kissable mouth set in a cruel line finished the dangerous perfection.

Beautiful and harsh, his was a face that could tempt an angel to sin.

Within the kaleidoscope of color, she saw him watching

her through slightly narrowed eyes, studying her with an intensity that sent tingles skating along her skin.

The first few buttons of his shirt were open, as though he'd undone them in an effort to relax, exposing a glimpse of bronzed skin and a chiseled, tattooed chest she wanted to trail her hands down.

Everything about him—from the confidence in his stance to the effortless style of his black hair and the expensive cut of his suit—screamed power and money.

Under that civilized veneer, however, she could sense a tightly leashed savagery, a beast hidden beneath a gorgeous exterior.

As he raised a glass to his mouth to take a sip of warm, golden alcohol, she bit her lip. He may have the face of a fallen angel, but he had the hands of a fighter. Strong and veined, Arawyn couldn't help but wonder what they would feel like against her skin, between her thighs, bringing her to a shattering release.

She didn't usually fantasize this strongly, but there was something about him, about the draw she felt pulling her in his direction, that increased her hunger for touch... for release.

A streak of red light momentarily blazed behind the dark stranger, casting his strong physique into a shadowed silhouette. Something about the way he held himself, like everyone else was beneath him and simply there to do his bidding, reminded her of a mafia boss with the world at his fingertips.

She imagined him as a man who got exactly what he wanted, and right now, she was the center of his attention.

Arawyn may be accustomed to that, but with everyone else it felt grasping, frantic, and needy. With him, it felt different. It felt... exhilarating.

He focused on her as if she were the only other person in the room, as if she were dancing for him, and him alone.

His slow perusal was full of wicked temptation, his gaze trailing down her body, pausing on the sway of her hips, then back up again to pin her with stunning blue eyes that flashed brilliantly in the beam passing over him. Despite the layers covering her, she felt positively bare. Sexy. Seductive.

A shiver tingled along her neck and down her spine, then settled low in her belly with tempting warmth before she moved her gaze to the second mysterious man.

His style was modern and much more laid back than that of his friend. Everything about this stranger was bright, almost ethereal, despite the bad-boy image he had in spades.

His blonde hair was trimmed short on the sides and longer on the top, falling into his eyes in a way that would drive her crazy, but on him, was sexy as hell. The desire to run her hands through the thick locks, to feel their silken texture against her palms, was so strong her fingers twitched.

A ray of light cut across the lower half of his face, revealing sun-kissed skin, a sharp jawline, and the silver glint of lip rings decorating both corners of his smirking mouth.

Her eyes lingered on that flash of metal, her tongue darting out to trace her own lips, wondering what it would feel like to kiss him.

For just a moment, Arawyn let herself imagine pulling one, or both, of them into a dark corner and let them soothe the ache that was her constant companion.

What would it be like to touch someone without fear of hurting them? To have a boyfriend or a long-term lover?

The gyrating bodies separating them parted again, letting her gaze linger on the white tee clinging lovingly to the hard muscle of the devilish blonde's abs and chest, then farther up to the colorful tattoos she could just see peeking out above the neckline.

Arawyn's gaze flashed upward when another bright beam revealed more of the golden bad boy. Everything inside her went still when she found herself trapped in amber eyes, the left bisected by a wicked scar that only served to intensify the attraction thrumming though her harder than the bass of the music.

God, but the way he was staring at her stole her breath—like she was air and he'd been suffocating.

Under the pulsing lights, she could've sworn those eyes changed color, flashing a predatory golden yellow. Arawyn's heart beat harder, and goosebumps rose on her arms as an impossible sense of familiarity washed over her in a knee-weakening wave at that flash of gold.

It's just a trick of the light.

Not daring to believe what she was sure she saw, her eyes flashed back and forth between both imposing men, trying to deny what she was sure she'd felt.

For the span of a breath, she'd felt... home. Like she belonged. Arawyn wasn't sure she'd ever experienced that, even before she became a freak, and was instantly addicted to the feeling.

The dream that haunted her sleep crashed over her. She could almost feel phantom arms wrapped around her, could almost smell the scents of smoke, warm cinnamon, and dark berries over the stench of sweat and alcohol.

Those tantalizing fragrances were almost tangible, hints of each swirling around her in an elaborate game of tag. They snuck up on her, only to disappear just as quickly, while she held the combined gazes of her steadfast admirers and immersed herself into the sinful beat of the music.

Her hands slid into the air, then back down her body as her hips moved. The atmosphere around her shifted as couples writhed together. She could nearly smell the sex in the air, the desire and lust pulsing with the music until she was heady with it. From afar, she performed for them, savoring their attention like forbidden fruit.

But, she didn't draw closer, and neither did they, both sides locked in a battle of will and fascination.

The dark one refused to look away, watching her over the rim of his glass as he sipped from his drink. With slow intention, he assessed her like she were a fine piece of art: priceless in value and highly sought after.

There was a glint of possession in his gaze, as though she were his and just didn't know it, yet. Instead of shying away, something in her rose at that look, something equally as possessive, something covetous and hungry.

That avidity spread from her, spanning the distance between them. She felt it brush along his hard frame, touching him in truth. Light slanted across his face, revealing a flash of surprise in his cerulean eyes and the intrigued curl of his lips.

She knew, somehow, he'd felt that invisible caress like a ripple against his skin.

Lowering his drink, he tilted his head and said something to his friend, never letting her out of his sight. A white flash caught her attention, and she dragged her gaze back to the devilish blonde whose smirk turned into a wide, dazzling grin.

His delight washed over her like the warm rays of the sun, making her own lips curve in response. Molten heat, and an energy she could feel all the way to the dance floor, brightened his amber eyes to something far more golden, the color almost unearthly.

Every piece of her yearned to close the distance between them, to succumb to the familiar, yet wholly foreign, feeling of home they inspired. To flirt and seduce. To touch. To *feel*.

The overwhelming intensity of the pull grew almost painful, the urge to give in becoming harder to deny.

Closing her eyes, she severed the connection between them.

These men felt different. They even *looked* different. But, Arawyn had suffered too many encounters like the one she'd left behind on her doorstep to make an impulsive decision. She'd spent too many years of her life being careful, and she wasn't about to throw caution to the wind and take a gamble unless she was sure… really sure.

An instant ache in her chest implored her to open her eyes again, to regain what she'd just broken, even as the magnetic pull urged her to cross the distance until she could feel their body heat, smell their cologne, touch the hard cut of their imposing bodies.

Fighting past the need, she quieted her mind and searched inside herself until she found the steady, reassuring intuition she'd been looking for. She wasn't sure if it was simply 'women's intuition' or something greater, something related to the power inside, but it rarely led her astray.

Surprisingly, there were no red flags, no blaring signals of warning telling her to turn back, to run, or to fight.

In fact, she felt almost…

A laugh bubbled up from Arawyn's chest, threatening to choke her as it caught in her throat.

Because the word she was going to use was 'safe.'

That she could still identify this feeling after all these

years stunned her, but it also made the decision to open her eyes and reclaim the connection between them easy.

Making the choice to trust that intuition and stop fighting the pull, she started to go to them. Before she'd managed a single step, she felt someone approaching from behind.

Someone who smelled like dark berries and felt like electricity...

Chapter Six

Arawyn

Arawyn could *feel* him behind her. Tingling warmth spread through her like a heated blanket on a cold winter's night as her body responded to his nearness. She wanted to curl up in that heat, wanted to let it soothe her to sleep at night... wanted to let it mend the broken pieces of her heart.

The intoxicating scents of cedar, oakmoss, and dark winter berries reached her, teasing her senses with the memory of her dream.

How...

Arawyn felt the touch coming and went perfectly still, anticipating, waiting for him to close the space between them.

Except he never did. Instead, a hand lightly skimmed

down her arm, the heat of it radiating through the layers of fabric separating them. The light touch was a question, instead of a demand, an invitation for more, if she wanted it.

Arawyn gasped, her lips parting and her lashes fluttered closed. In the sea of entitled men who thought it was their right to dance up against her, simply because she was there, his soft request had her entire body thrumming to life.

She made no effort to stop the sway of her body back into him, couldn't have even if she'd wanted to, and there wasn't a single part of her that wished to resist.

Sensing her acceptance, a massive, hard body warmed her back before pressing against her. Thickly muscled arms came around her, large hands settling on the curve of her hips in a light hold she could easily step out of.

Arawyn shivered. She'd never experienced anything as arousing as the feel of this man against her. She felt dwarfed by him, the top of her head barely reaching his chest. And, yet, despite towering over her, it seemed as though they fit together perfectly.

Being so close to someone so much larger than her should've unnerved her, it should have put her on high alert, but all she wanted to do was sink into him. She wanted him to cradle her against him, to hold her in those big arms.

Slowly, seductively, the man started to dance, guiding her in an erotic rhythm that drove her senseless. He moved like water—sinuous and graceful. Surprising for someone so tall and broad.

What would he be like in bed?

The temptation to find out sparked to life, teasing her with images of his body above hers, goading her with fantasies of feeling him buried inside her. Oh god, she wanted an answer to that question almost more than she wanted her next breath.

Every brush of their bodies felt electric. This close, his mouthwatering scent was stronger, enfolding her in a drugging cloud from which she never wanted to escape.

Arawyn didn't open her eyes, too entranced by the spell this man wove around her. Never in her life had she been this turned on, nor could she remember a time she'd been this affected by anyone, or felt this... safe.

He exuded a primal sense of security, a unique brand of protectiveness all his own. She became untouchable within his arms. The rest of the world could fall apart, go up in flames, burn to nothing but ash, and she would still be held safely against him, completely unharmed.

It wasn't a feeling she was familiar with, but *fuck* was it addictive.

Their bodies swayed closer and closer until they were pressed together tightly, her head resting back against his chest, his hands now circling her waist, hips flush against her, letting her feel she wasn't the only one affected.

Arawyn bit her lip when she realized he could feel the hard press of the daggers she had strapped to her lower back as surely as she could feel the hard press of his arousal.

Instead of recoiling or pulling away like most men would, he bent and purred in her ear, his chest rumbling like her Harley, "Mmm, beautiful and deadly."

Her breath hitched. His voice was deep, the bass notes rich and gravelly, shivering up her spine like distant thunder. She wanted to hear him speak again just to soak in the resonate sound once more.

Dancing with this man, who should feel like a stranger, yet didn't, was exhilarating, a breath of fresh air in lungs that had been starved for far too long. She was alive. She was thriving.

The desire to know his name, to see his face, became an aching need, but she refused to break the trance into which they'd fallen. Instead, Arawyn kept her eyes tightly shut and immersed herself in the moment, knowing somewhere in the back of her mind it would need to last her for when she was inevitably alone again.

The song changed, becoming something dark and primal. Their bodies moved together faster, harder, following the beat.

He bent over her until his nose hovered a bare inch above the column of her neck, his beard just tickling her skin, and inhaled deeply. He exhaled a low, hungry groan. The longing in that sound hit her like a shot of whiskey, settling low in her stomach. Biting her lip, she set her hands over his forearms, feeling the corded muscle beneath his sleeves, and guided his grip to her hips as she arched her ass back into him.

"You tempt, *moín Firláh*. By the Gods, do you tempt," he growled in her ear, making her pulse race and her nipples pebble.

She wanted to do more than tempt. She wanted to take, so badly her need turned visceral, lashing through her with the force of a lightning strike until she was sure she'd burn up from the intensity.

The rhythmic press of her thighs brushing together as they danced teased and tormented, creating just enough pressure where she was slick and swollen to magnify the ache.

She knew, if she asked, he would give her what she so badly craved. There was no doubt he would know exactly how to touch her to release the desperate need building inside her.

Opening her eyes before she gave in, she found herself staring directly into the intense amber gaze of the golden-haired bad boy. He'd moved closer, staring at her and the man dancing like he was entranced. Strangely, just knowing he was watching, excited her. Looking for the dark stranger, she found him still studying her from the deeper shadows.

Arawyn had the sudden sense they knew the man behind her. It was one of those deep, intuitive feelings she got that were rarely ever wrong.

Unable to resist the urge to see the one behind her any longer, but unwilling to turn and break eye contact with the devilish blonde, Arawyn lifted her arms above her head. Sliding her fingertips up his chest, she felt soft cotton stretched tightly over hard muscle, then higher to the soft brush of a beard covering his sharp jawline.

Gaze moving from one sexy stranger to the next, she watched them as she trailed higher still, tracing surprisingly full lips. The moment she touched his mouth, he stiffened, sucking in a hard breath she could feel against her fingers. She barely had time to wonder at his reaction before he opened for her, the movement both an invitation and a dare.

A hard thrill shot through her as she let just the tips of her fingers slide past his lips. Wet warmth and sharp teeth met her questing touch.

"Oh, god..." she panted, thighs clenching.

Whimpering at the light flick of his tongue, she shivered, her core tightening. Whether he heard her or just felt her reaction to him, she didn't know, but his hands flexed on her hips, pulling her harder against him, and he groaned, the sound so low she felt more than heard it.

Dizzy with want, Arawyn's hands shook slightly as she continued upward, tracing the straight line of his nose to a set of high cheekbones, then to thick, slashing brows.

Finally, burying her fingers in his hair, she let out a moan as the silken strands slid through her grip. Long and thick, they had to fall to at least his shoulders. Arawyn's lashes fluttered thinking about fisting that length while he moved above her. Her hands clenched involuntarily at the thought.

His hips immediately snapped forward at the tug, forcing a cry from her lips and a surge of wetness from her pussy.

Arawyn heard his guttural curse even over the deafening music. The knowledge that he liked it a little rough, enjoyed the way she pulled his hair, had heat rushing through her veins, heat that turned molten when she caught the flash of hunger tightening the fallen angel's features from beyond the dance floor. She saw his lips part on a hiss she swore she could almost hear.

The dark urges she kept such a tight leash on, urges that didn't give a fuck about what was wise or safe, urges that yearned to loose the power inside her and take what she wanted, rose up as if called by these men, swimming to the surface to fill her with a wicked kind of hunger.

She told herself she was testing them, experimenting to see if they were vulnerable to her power or if they really were like her, but that was only a partial truth.

Giving in, just for a second, she ever so slightly relaxed the metaphorical fist in her chest, allowing the barest wisp of power to leak out, and arched into the familiar stranger harder. Tightening a hand in his hair again, she pulled his mouth against her.

He went willingly, bending back over her, his teeth

grazing the sensitive skin of her throat before he rasped seductively low, "You need. I can taste it. Should I sate you, *moín Firláh*? Should I slip my hand between those thick thighs and stroke your pussy until you come for me?"

The thought of letting a stranger touch her like that in public should've appalled her. Maybe it was those sinful urges, maybe it was the impossible familiarity between them, or the intoxicating sense of safety he wrapped around her like a blanket.

Or maybe she was just hungry.

The voice that whispered from her lips barely sounded like her as she groaned, "Yesss."

"As you command, *moín Firláh*," he whispered.

Chapter Seven

Arawyn

Lips parting on a sharp exhale, Arawyn fought to keep her eyes open and on the devilish blonde still watching her from the sidelines as the man behind her slid a big hand over her hip, across her thigh, then between her legs.

Just that small amount of pressure where she throbbed so needily had her crying out softly, the sound drowned out by the din of the club. The expert way he circled his fingers over her, unerringly finding her swollen, throbbing bundle of nerves beneath the layers of leather and lace, had her knees going weak.

He caught her, holding her against him effortlessly, moving her body to the beat. Grinding together, they found a new rhythm, rocking forward and back, their hips in perfect sync as he pushed her against his hand before she pressed back against his cock, both giving as they took.

As if the cadence, that push and pull, was what it had been waiting for, the tiny wisp of power she'd released curled around him like a long-lost lover.

The warm feeling unfurling in her chest, seeking him out, was new and breathtaking, but it didn't shock her after the way she'd reacted to him, thus far.

No—what shocked her, what had her pulse hammering was when her power touched him, something drifted from him to touch her in return.

Those tendrils of power twinned together, touching and teasing in an electrifying dance that stunned her. The caress of his power against her own was unlike anything she'd ever felt, yet, it was everything she'd spent years waiting for. The pain of all those years spent alone, of all the time she'd searched for someone like her, broke apart as hope bloomed in her chest.

Heart in her throat, thighs slick with want, she moved with him, intoxicated with the feeling of his large body against her and the drugging power playing and mingling with hers. His hand never stopped, never slowed, and her pleasure coiled tighter and tighter.

She could barely focus past the heady bliss consuming her, but her gaze never strayed from the two men on the edge of the dance floor intently watching her fall apart one stroke at a time.

Her golden bad-boy flicked his tongue across his bottom lip in a slow, savory caress, as though he could taste her essence in the air. Amber eyes glittering, he captured his bottom lip between his teeth in a move that was full of pure, devious intent.

Behind him, the dark angel took a single step closer, his aura a menacing dare for any others in the club to glance her way. Even in the darkness, it would have been impossible for a bystander not to notice the sex in her eyes and the flush staining her cheeks, but he claimed that vision for himself and his friend, both devouring the sight of her writhing with the mysterious man at her back.

The familiar stranger behind her teased her mercilessly, alternating between whisper light touches and a steadier pressure that drove her wild. Each brush of his strong fingers brought her closer to the edge until she was panting for it. Each gasp, each mewl she made was met with an appreciative hum as the heat building low in her belly intensified.

"That's it, *moín Firláh*," he practically purred. "Let me give you what you need. Come for me. Come for *us*."

The deep, seductive cadence of his words rumbled through her, shooting straight to her center, adding to the unrelenting rhythm of his hand. His fingers worked magic over her needy flesh, and she ached for the feel of his skin on hers.

What would it feel like to have his fingers buried inside me?

Arawyn ground her pussy into his hand before rocking back into the thick length branding her lower back.

Or something much, much bigger?

Just the image of being bare before him, rocking against him in an entirely different way had her pussy fluttering, intensifying the ache inside of her.

As though he could sense she was right on the edge, he cupped her in his big hand, grinding the heel of his palm over her clit in tight, quick circles as he curled his fingertips directly over her opening.

Cursing the barrier of her clothes, she arched into his hand. The leather strained against his seeking fingers when he pressed against her, so hard it almost felt like he was inside of her.

It was too much, the sensation overwhelming.

"That's it, Baby, let go. I've got you."

Between one breath and the next, pleasure crashed over her in hard, shattering waves. Fingers curling into claws on his forearms, she threw her head back and let it drown her.

He held her tightly against him, his hold gentle but unwavering, as she trembled with release, his other hand covering her mouth to muffle the cries she made no effort to silence.

The waves were neverending, and his hand never stilled. Even as he tensed behind her, even as he curled his big body around her with a groan, he never slowed.

"Ah, fuck, Baby... I'm gonna... "

Through the pleasure engulfing her, she felt his big body jerk, felt the hard bar of his cock pulse through the layers separating them and knew he was following her over the edge.

Listening to him grunt with every hard, rhythmic buck of his hips against her ass, knowing it was her pleasure that broke his control, sent her straight into a second climax.

Nearly screaming behind the muzzle of his palm as the waves of bliss doubled, Arawyn clamped her thighs together, riding his hand. He ground his palm into her harder, letting her use him to wring every last drop of pleasure from her body.

When their pleasure began to ease, Arawyn nearly collapsed against him, leaning heavily into his large frame. Never in her life had she orgasmed so strongly. Her legs shook and her knees wobbled, making her unsure if she could stand on her own, not that she needed to. The man behind her was a rock, his warm chest a solid force she never wanted to leave. He held her steadily, tenderly, his grip never faltering as they both recovered.

Using the hand still covering her mouth, he turned her face toward him and pressed his forehead against hers. He was so close she couldn't make out anything but grey eyes that appeared almost lavender in the strobing lights.

"Give me your name, *moín Firláh*," he whispered hoarsely.

His request was both a gentle demand and a seeking question. Calloused fingers snuck under the hem of her shirt to trace over the soft skin of her stomach. The light touch was reverent, teasing her in the afterglow as he waited for her answer.

Her sole focus moved to his feather-light touch. The way he pet her, held her, doted on her...

She'd only been with one-night stands. The way this impossibly familiar man was touching her was so unlike those encounters it was staggering. He didn't touch as though he wanted to trap. He didn't hold like he wanted to own. He cradled. He soothed. He *cared*.

She knew it wasn't wise to give him her name. She knew if he tried, he would be able to find her.

But, maybe she wanted him to, because, despite knowing it was a bad idea, she found her lips parting...

"Arawyn." It was barely a breath, a whisper beneath the beat of the music, yet, she knew he heard it.

"Arawyn," he rumbled back, her name a deep, low melody rolling effortlessly off his tongue.

It shivered down her spine, sending tiny bumps rising

along her skin. She wanted to wrap herself up in his voice and listen to the lilting bass notes on repeat.

Gazing up into his eyes, she opened her mouth to ask him the same when some instinct had her turning in time to see the dark one prowling toward them. A flash of light skimmed over his cruelly beautiful features, revealing heat and hunger in his eyes warring with something colder, something menacing.

The fallen angel she'd compared him to was gone, leaving a far more dangerous devil in its place.

Her familiar stranger saw him coming half a second after she did, but instead of offering a greeting, he tightened his arms around her in a way that felt distinctly protective. The post-bliss haze cleared in an instant, replaced with wary tension.

Had she been wrong? Did they not know each other?

No, the sense they were friends, or at least friendly acquaintances, felt right. But, something had damn sure changed.

The man behind her spun them around, reinforcing what she'd already felt—the danger she could sense rolling off the dark one was directed at her, not the man at her back.

"You need to leave," he growled in warning.

"Why?" Her question had sharp, pointed edges, much like the weapons she crafted.

She wasn't asking why he wanted her to go. She was asking why they'd lured her there to begin with and why he'd suddenly changed his mind about whatever it was they'd planned for her.

"Trust me, *moín Firláh*. It's time for you to go," the man said again, this time softer than the first.

Trust.

It wasn't a word that came easily for Arawyn. How long had it been since she'd trusted anyone but herself? Yet, no matter how hard she tried to resist the foreign feeling squeezing her heart, she realized she did, in a way, trust the man who still held her like she was precious to him.

"Will you be okay?"

The dark devil who watched her like he owned her didn't seem like a man who would relish not getting what he wanted.

And he very clearly wanted her.

Her stranger made a noise of surprise at her question. "Would you stay and fight if I said 'no'?"

The smart answer was 'no.' Arawyn wasn't a risk taker. What she'd done tonight, following the insatiable pull that still, despite the danger, yearned for her to get closer to the other men, dancing with a stranger whose touch felt like home, letting herself fall apart in his arms with an audience watching every moan, every grind, every blissful second of her release, had been so far removed from the usual caution she used in everyday life.

Her mind told her to move, to run and not look back, but her heart...

"Yes, I would."

There was no ridicule in his voice, no mocking undercurrent that she was concerned about him when he bent and whispered, "Beautiful and deadly. I'll be fine, *moín Firláh*. But, you're out of time. You need to go. Now."

She knew she should leave. She didn't know what the dark one's intentions were, but if the man she'd danced with sensed a threat, she wasn't going to heedlessly ignore him and put herself in danger.

Better safe than sorry.

It was a motto to live by, one that had seen her out of more potentially shitty situations than she could count.

And still, she hesitated.

These three men were the first of her kind she'd ever come across. Leaving them now felt like leaving a piece of herself behind. She wanted to know them. Wanted answers. Wanted to finally understand the power that lived inside of her.

At the very heart of it... Arawyn didn't want to be alone any longer.

Her protector seemed to understand her reluctance.

The hard planes of his chest brushed along her shoulders, and his beard lightly tickled her neck as his nose skimmed intimately along the shell of her ear.

"Don't worry, Arawyn. I'll find you. That's a promise."

Those words coming from anyone else would have been a threat, but it wasn't dread or fear that followed her as she finally forced herself to step out of the protective haven of his arms.

It was the unadulterated desire to see him again that stayed with her as she slipped through the throng of dancers, using her small stature to her advantage as she quickly wove her way between bodies.

Arawyn glanced back only once to see all three men shoulder to shoulder, watching her as they stood supernaturally still among the writhing sea of people she'd placed between them, and then she was gone.

She barely noticed the soft purr of her Harley as she revved the engine and left the club behind. With each mile she placed between them, she battled the increasing need in her chest urging her to go back, to turn around and find them all over again.

A shuddering breath escaped her lips when she left the city and turned onto the familiar dark, lonely roads.

Arawyn drove for hours, taking a long, circuitous path home, only stopping to check her security system to make sure the coast was finally clear.

As she crawled into the comfort of her bed with dawn breaking on the horizon, she knew nothing would ever be the same again.

I'll find you.

That whispered promise lulled her into a restless sleep.

Chapter Eight

Fearson

Fearson watched her slipping through the crowd like water while he absently waved a hand to dissipate evidence of his release. Her movements were lithe and graceful, as if this weren't her first time having to escape.

Arawyn.

There was something strange about his little beauty, something undeniably mysterious, but equally alluring.

He hadn't realized his friends had already spotted her before he approached, but once he'd seen her, he couldn't have turned away, and they were just as spellbound.

Even through the humans packed tightly together on the dance floor, he'd noticed her pale blonde hair. Pure and luminous, it was as lightly colored as a pearl from the shores of the Azarian Kingdom, a color no human could attain naturally.

Then, the bodies parted for just a moment, and he saw her.

Once he laid eyes on her, he couldn't look away, stood frozen as he tried to catalogue every minute detail. Each movement she made was regal and elegant, containing a grace most humans could never master. Even dressed as she was, covered in a long-sleeved shirt and a pair of leather pants that hugged her ass deliciously, he could see the sun-kissed tone of her otherwise creamy skin.

He'd been drawn to her, so much so he hadn't fought the pull luring him closer. Enchanted, he moved behind her, asked permission to touch her. It would have killed him to pull away, had she refused, but when she'd let him...

There was no resisting. Like a man dying of thirst in the desert sands of Móirlhev, she was a refreshing drink of water, an oasis he was happy to lose himself in.

By the Gods, but the way she moved with him, against him. She made his blood simmer in a way no other ever had.

Maybe it should've shocked him that he was so immediately attracted to her, but it didn't. Everyone who glanced at her turned away with lust in their eyes, and he was no different.

What stunned him was feeling the tightly contained power she held. It was a small ripple in a pond, stretching to lap at his skin. He knew the tiny taste of her was just the surface, alluding to a vast well beneath, much like his own. That she'd somehow retained such power in the human realm was odd, to say the least.

There was something different about her, something special. It was the way she carried herself, the way her power felt, even locked so tightly away, as she had it. It was the weapons she wore, and how she seemed hunted, yet, not prey. She wasn't a victim.

She was a warrior, a fighter.

Arawyn reminded him of a woman from the Night Court, but her power didn't taste distinctly of Night or Light. Another oddity.

Still watching her slip away, he felt his friends come up beside him. Rathe's irritation was as palpable as Viper's manic energy. Fearson spared a brief moment to glance at his Prince, meeting his narrow, blue-eyed stare unflinchingly.

"Why?" Rathe asked with a calmness belying just how unhappy he was their mission just went sideways.

Looking toward where she'd disappeared, Fearson simply shook his head. He'd known the plan for the evening. Capture a powerful Fae, send them to the King, and buy themselves another month in the human realm.

That he'd let her go would be seen as treason in the King's eyes, if he ever found out, but he couldn't bring himself to regret his decision.

He found feeding Fae to the King repugnant. Despite his reservations, he understood why his friend—and Prince, ever since Fear's Clan fell to the power-hungry clutches of Ehrendil—followed orders.

Rathe was many things, but he was nothing like his odious father. The atrocities his friend commited, the very same offenses Fear and Viper helped him perpetrate, were done in an effort to keep not just the three of them, but Rathe's people safe from the King's brutality.

Yet, sending a woman to Ehrendil to be drained and discarded was beyond the crimes Fearson was willing to commit. Especially one as sweet and fierce as Arawyn.

He could sense a darkness within her, could feel the shadows dancing in her soul, but there was no question in his mind. He'd known the second he was close to her she wasn't deserving of the fate awaiting her, and it was only confirmed by her questioning if he'd be okay.

In the midst of danger, she'd cared enough to make sure he would be alright, would have dared to stay and face Rathe, if his answer were 'no.'

Despite that they'd just met, his feisty little temptress was loyal and protective, and it was undeniable that he felt the same in return. He wouldn't let anyone, not even his Prince, hurt her.

Fearson waited patiently as Rathe studied him, knowing his irritation would wane. Whether he would admit it or not, Rathe had been equally affected by the little beauty.

"What did you sense from her?" Rathe pressed, an edge of authority in his voice, though he didn't use any power behind his quiet demand.

They may be friends, nearly brothers, but Fearson knew, when it came down to it, there was a hierarchy that sometimes preceded their friendship.

First and foremost, Rathe was his Prince, the man Fearson had sworn fealty to when his own Clan had been taken from him, and again when the honor of being Rathe's guard was bestowed upon him in acknowledgement of his skill and power.

Regardless of the authority of his Prince's position, Rathe had never used it against him. The two of them shared a mutual respect for each other, one that had easily forged itself into a bond of brotherhood. Even now, as Rathe held his eyes, he didn't force an answer.

Although they were friends, and despite Fear's fierce

loyalty, he felt protective over Arawyn, and answered casually, careful with how much information he bestowed.

Shrugging, unrepentantly owning what he'd done, he said, "I couldn't sense what Court she's from."

Usually, he could detect a flavor of one or the other, a faint inkling as to the Court of power from which a Fae descended.

All Fae were either of the Night or of the Light. However, races that were now considered 'lesser'—any that weren't High Fae, beings once called *Ísledair*—were often harder to discern, thanks to years of interbreeding between Courts and shifting rulership.

With the mixed bloodlines many were born from, they didn't smell strictly of one Court or the other, making the flavor he ascertained from them potentially inaccurate. His own signature, for example, was full of mixed Fae bloodlines from his *Dragon, Giant,* and High Fae heritage. Add in that his own Night Clan fell to Ehrendil, High King of the Light Court, and he knew his signature would confuse the most trained tracker. It was something Viper liked to tease him about, but it also came with its own perks.

Fearson was harder to track, and that was one of his assets—one he'd learned to use to his advantage over the years.

But, Arawyn didn't feel like a 'lesser' Fae, nor one of diluted blood.

She was an enigma, and he wanted to figure her out.

That desire had only grown when their powers tangled together, mingling and dancing. When she let him slide his fingers between her shapely thighs, he was hooked.

Her confidence, as well as the small gasps and mewls, had turned him molten, making him burn for her as brightly as a pyre in the dead of night. The sweet scent of her—a tantalizing mix of moonlit lilies, springtime thunderstorms, and vanilla—saturated the air with her release, wrapping around him, pulling at his cock, and sending him careening over the damn cliff of release right alongside her.

Fuck.

A shiver raced through him just thinking of the moment they'd shared.

Who was she? What was she doing here? And how had they never crossed paths before now?

All he knew was he wanted time to learn the answers to those questions, and if Rathe had his way, she would've already been in the King's clutches.

The thought was enough to make him growl, the low, protective sound buried under the noise of the club.

The three of them watched as she peered back through the crowd, her gaze flicking from one to the next, before the tightly packed bodies filled in the small trail she'd created in her escape.

A connection, an undeniable thread, spanned between him and the little temptress, and it pulled taut, the sensation a tug in his chest as she left him behind.

Moín Firláh.

Those two little words whispered into the back of his mind. It'd been as natural as breathing to call her such, and that might have been the most surprising of all.

Could she truly be the other half of my soul?

She was small, so fucking small, but she'd fit against him as though they were made for each other. And the connection...

Fearson rubbed his chest, half expecting to feel a physical string tying them together, but his fingers grazed only the soft cotton of his shirt.

"What else did she say?" Rathe questioned, leaning slightly closer, his eyes glued to where they'd last seen her.

"Her name."

It was the only other piece of information he had, and as much as he wanted to keep it for himself, he wasn't that selfish.

While Rathe looked confused, irritated, and intrigued, Viper appeared to be vibrating with energy. The man's eyes glittered in the low light, the amber color teasing from beneath his *Glamor*, edging halfway to the golden yellow of his unglamored form. Already, his pupils looked misshapen, partly shifted into serpentine slits.

They were just as bewitched as he was, so when Rathe asked him to elaborate, he did.

"Her name is Arawyn."

Fearson looked back to the door, and the promise he'd made turned into fierce resolve.

He would definitely be finding his *Firláh*—his Fated.

And soon. Very, very soon.

Chapter Nine

VIPER

Viper leaned over, sniffing at Fearson's shirt where the woman had been pressed against him—the beautiful woman with the pretty, pretty eyes and the power that had been teasing him mercilessly for the last two weeks.

That first taste had been unlike any other power he'd experienced before, and he'd been immediately curious about who and where it came from. Every day for two whole weeks, he'd gotten small glimpses of a woman, her image always swimming just out of reach of his Sight.

Never before had he struggled to bring a premonition into focus, and it only served to torment him along with the unique flavor of her power that only seemed to grow in intensity as the weeks passed.

Drawing another lungful, his eyes rolled back at the

decadent scent of her. Being in her presence, feeling the tingle of her power against his skin like a caress, inhaling her sweet signature this closely only served to heighten what he'd been feeling for weeks. He groaned. She smelled like all his favorite things. Gods, but he wanted to wallow in her scent, wanted to bathe in it.

Finally found you.

That Fearson didn't know from which Court she hailed was frosting on the cookie. Viper hadn't been able to tell either, not from those little tastes he'd gotten of her.

Mmm, a mystery. I love mysteries.

When Fear said her name, Viper straightened sharply and gazed at the entrance of the club, savoring the sound of it.

Arawyn.

It both did and didn't feel like hers, but he loved it instantly.

"There wasn't even a small tell of which Court she's from?" Rathe asked sharply.

"No. She's powerful. Probably not of mixed blood, but that's all I was able to decipher."

With a peek at Rathe, Viper adopted a matching expression so he would look appropriately serious and brooding, then nodded slowly. "Hmm. That's weird. Yes, yes. Very weird. Suspicious, even." He glanced at Rathe again, then looked away and asked in what he thought was an admirably offhanded tone, "Want me to go after her?"

Rathe gazed assessingly at where she'd disappeared for so long Viper felt his patience fraying. After five, maybe even six seconds, his brother finally nodded once.

"Do it."

Viper grinned and immediately *Light Jumped*, riding the

strobing beams unseen to the door. Once outside, his eyes zeroed in on the motorcycle pulling into traffic, headed right.

His smile grew so wide it made his cheeks ache. He'd already been on the knife's edge of obsession, but learning she drove a motorcycle?

I think I'm in love.

Images of riding behind her, his body curled around her much smaller one, as they sped down dark roads flooded his mind. Or maybe she'd race him. Him on his Ducati, her on her Harley LiveWire. If she won, he'd make her pancakes. If he won, he'd claim her shirt as his prize and use it as a pillowcase.

Either way, he won, which was exactly how he liked it.

Viper tilted his head back and breathed deeply, basking in the lingering feel of her. Exhaling on a groan, he dropped his chin, flicking one of his lip rings with the tip of his tongue as he watched her taillight disappear around the bend.

Soon, my Pretty Little Loon. I'll be seeing you again very soon.

Strolling to his Ducati, he got on and started it up, then drove into traffic. He didn't wait for a gap, narrowly missing being run over, ignoring the blaring horns as he turned left.

Putting in his earbuds one-handed, he cranked up the music and sang along to the song as he let his mind wander back to her. Always back to her. The premonition he'd had weeks ago now—of glass-green eyes, of power like gilded shadows washing over him, through him—filled his mind.

Aside from his brother and best friend, Viper had never cared about anyone, had never felt protective of anyone. But, he felt protective of her, and had from his first, tiny vision. He wanted to hold her and keep her safe and help her.

He may not understand why, *yet*, but she was important to him—to all of them.

That he'd had to tell a little white lie tonight to get his brother and his friend to the club, luring them there under the pretense of capturing the little beauty, barely bothered him. It had worked, and she'd been drawn to them, just like his vision led him to believe.

When his premonition had finally alluded he'd meet the pretty lady from his visions tonight, he'd been unable to pass up the opportunity to get closer, to finally know *who* she was.

Those tiny glimpses of her had nearly driven him to obsession, and seeing her, tasting her power on his tongue and feeling it tingle against his skin had only sealed his devout interest.

He was almost giddy everything had played together so perfectly.

The only hiccup was they didn't have a meal to send to the King. A problem Viper planned to rectify.

Weaving recklessly fast in and out of traffic, he opened his senses, letting them stretch outward and guide him to his prey. He'd been catching glimpses of this being for days now and had planned to go after him before he got the taste of Arawyn's power.

Focused on those glimpses, he found himself pulling up in front of a spectacularly sketchy-looking house in a very questionable neighborhood. Popping the kickstand, he ambled up the walkway, bobbing his head along to the song.

Opening the door, he walked inside, took a moment to shake his ass at his favorite part of the chorus, then slammed it closed behind him. A rather ugly man appeared in the doorway ahead, just as the final notes played.

At the sight of Viper, the being instantly dropped its

Glamor. It grew two feet taller, and its limbs stretched out, long claws growing from its fingertips. Shark teeth bared, solid black eyes glittering menacingly, the *Wendigo* rattled a growl.

Unnaturally tall and emaciated to the point of looking skeletal, with skin the color of ash, it was a horrific sight to behold.

Viper smiled in greeting. "Hi! I'm looking for the person who's been eating people. That wouldn't be you, now, would it?"

The Wendigo didn't answer, not that he'd expected it to. With an eerie, eardrum-vibrating howl, it charged.

Using one of his elemental abilities, Viper smiled darkly and drew all the air in the room toward him with a thought, robbing the Wendigo of breath. When it stumbled, he raised both hands, his own black nails lengthening into claws. He released a bright beam of light from one, burning its desiccated skin. With the other, he forced it to feel every ounce of fear and horror it had inflicted upon its victims.

Mouth opened on a silent scream, long claws tearing at its throat, it dropped to its knees.

Viper kept going, mercilessly searing its flesh until the stench of it was thick enough to choke him, pouring terror into its mind, watching on coldly as it flayed its own throat open until black blood soaked its front.

Only when it tipped to the side, its body falling bonelessly to the floor, did he relent.

Viper walked past its unconscious form and peeked into the kitchen. At the sight of the blood-covered table and the gruesome remains of its latest victim, he gritted his teeth.

Raising his hands, he used his Light Bending ability to draw the illumination from the bulbs overhead, bending the light to his will and concentrating it into a focused beam strong enough to incinerate. It took him longer than it would've taken Rathe—his mixed blood making this particular power weaker than his brother's—but eventually the kitchen went up in flames. It spread quickly, fire crawling up the walls, curling the stained wallpaper and charring the ceiling.

Pausing a moment, he tapped an earbud, swaying to the beat as he watched the pretty show. When the fire was licking at his boots, he finally returned to the Wendigo and kicked it, hard, in the ribs. At the satisfying crack of bones, Viper smiled cruelly, then bent and hoisted it over his shoulder. Whistling merrily, he walked out of the blazing house and got back on his bike.

This was the kind of neighborhood where people turned a blind eye. He understood it was out of self-preservation, but it was also how the being had gotten away with its... *proclivities* for so long. At the moment, it worked to his advantage, meant he didn't have to be overly concerned about someone causing a ruckus that he had a body slung over his lap.

Taking the time that provided him, he let himself recover from using so much energy. Once on the outskirts of the neighborhood, he finally pulled an *Illusion*, hiding the body from sight.

By the time he got back to the warehouse, it was almost three in the morning. Yawning widely, Viper heaved the unconscious Wendigo back over his shoulder, then climbed the stairs to the second floor.

Fear was in the living room, seated in a chair by the floor-to-ceiling windows, soaking in the moonlight in his unglamored form while he cleaned his favorite shotgun. No one else would notice the way the big guy tensed, then relaxed, when he realized the body slung over Viper's shoulder wasn't Arawyn's. But, Viper did.

He tossed his bestie a wink and got a tiny smile and a subtle dip of horns in return. Hearing Rathe approach, they both smoothed their expressions. His brother glanced briefly at the body hanging over his shoulder, leaned to the side to look behind him into the stairwell, then raised a single, questioning brow.

"Where is she?"

"I lost her!" he said with wide eyes, feigning shock.

"You lost her," Rathe repeated slowly, sounding patently disbelieving, which was kind of flattering but, also, fair. Viper had never lost a target before.

"Mmhm, yep. I lost her. She's good."

Rathe stared at him silently for a long, long moment, his regard probing, but Viper kept his face expressionless. As close as they were, as well as Rathe knew him, he couldn't see through his mask unless he wanted him to. No one could. It was a point of pride.

Viper had never hidden anything like this before. Usually, it was just pain or the nightmares that haunted him, because his brother would blame himself for what he had endured.

He felt a little bad for lying, but only a little. Arawyn was worth this small betrayal.

Rathe still looked suspicious, but thoughtful now, too. Before his brother's mind could go further down the line of thinking Viper could see in his eyes, he smiled brightly and threw the unconscious Wendigo on the floor.

"Don't worry! I brought you a present!" he declared cheerfully. "This motherfucker, here, was eating people.

Can you imagine? Ew, am I right?" He blew a raspberry and waved the question away. "Of course, I'm right. It's powerful. I think it'll make a great meal for the King."

Still frowning, Rathe hummed but nodded. Lifting his arms, he closed his eyes and spread his wings, the black feathers rustling softly. Viper could feel him drawing power, could feel it building and coalescing around him.

With an audible pop that had Viper's ears ringing, Rathe channeled the power, opening a *Portal*. The swirling, golden haze grew wider and wider, clearing as it opened until the wet stone walls of a dungeon could be seen on the other side.

The sight of it sent dread down Viper's spine, had memories—awful, painful memories—trying to escape the box in which he kept them. Jolting slightly when a hand came down on his shoulder, he started to whip around, a blade already in his right hand, only to go still at the sight of Fear.

"Easy, Brother," Fear rumbled, his gaze soft and knowing. Cupping the back of his neck, Fear bent and pressed their foreheads together, repeating, "Easy. You're not there anymore." In a voice too low for Rathe to pick up, he murmured, "Think of her, not the memories."

Nodding a little jerkily, Viper closed his eyes when Fear moved away, picturing Arawyn instead of the memory of dank stone soaking up his blood. He remembered the interest in her eyes when she'd looked at him instead of leering faces watching him being beaten. He imagined she was standing before him.

Would she smile up at him? Would she look at him like he were a person, like he were an equal instead of a bastard, instead of the King's unwanted son and his brother's—the Prince's—whipping boy?

He would like that, very much. He wanted her smiles.

Ignoring the Wendigo's horrific screams as it awakened when Fear tossed it through the portal and into the cell, Viper let his mind build a fantasy. Making her pancakes. Her laughing at something he'd said, not *at* him, but *with* him. The sight of her glass-green eyes, warm and sparkling as she gazed up at him.

Soon, Pretty Loon. I'll see you again soon.

Chapter Ten

Arawyn

Arawyn let her head fall back against the seat, staring blankly at the night sky past her windshield and waited for the last few people to leave the gym.

The past five days had been exhausting, but she was more than ready to exert herself in the most physically taxing way possible.

Outside of sex, that was.

Releasing a sigh, she relished the peace and quiet sitting in her car allowed. Her neighbor, who the Internet told her was named Peter Harrison, was relentless in his determination to get to her.

The hope that her absence would help ease the effect her power had on him disappeared when he returned to her house a few hours after she got back from the club.

She thought about retreating to a hotel but dismissed it quickly.

Not only would there not be any reliable security measures there, but if her power surged again in such a populated place, she could have hundreds beating down her door instead of one. Add in the extra, potential threat of the dark man from the club, and she decided her safest bet was to remain in the home she had painstakingly reinforced and wait it out.

So, she'd spent the last few days listening to Peter alternate between trying to coax her outside and force his way in. After it became abundantly clear there was no way in hell she was going outside or letting him in, he'd decided to try a different tactic.

One that included scattering the carcass of a dead animal across her front porch.

Staring at the bloody mess through the security monitor, she'd thought, for a long, sickening minute, that it was Sneaks.

Thankfully for Peter, it wasn't, else she would've done something she probably, some day, might have come to regret.

Why the hell he thought that would make her go outside, she didn't know. Did she want to save more forest animals from him? Yes. Was she willing to kill him to do it? No. Because that's what it would come down to. He clearly wasn't able to shake off the effects of her power, and if she went out there, experience told her only one of them would walk away.

Arawyn thought about leaving again after that, but the memory of how her familiar stranger urged her away from his friend, clearly worried for her safety, solidified her decision. The threat she'd felt from the dark man at the club still outweighed the threat her neighbor presented.

Better the enemy you know than the one you don't.

Besides, she had no way of knowing which one of those men she'd felt drawn toward or if they could feel and follow it back to her. What she did know was she hadn't felt it until she was near city limits. It had grown more intense the closer she got to those men, and it had faded again with distance, so unless they made a habit of coming out to the country, which she doubted, she should be safe at her house.

And if they did find her, if they could track her so easily, nowhere she went would be safe.

Braven, the owner of the gym she was parked in front of, probably would've welcomed her staying there, and would have insisted on protecting her, but what if the threats followed her? Arawyn wasn't willing to bring that kind of insanity to his business. How would she have explained it, if she had?

Who's that crazed man breaking into your gym, you ask? That's just my neighbor, whom I cursed into being obsessed with me when the awful, magical power inside me burst out. Now, he's feeling compelled to get closer to me, maybe even kidnap and try to torture me to death. No biggie. Oh, and those three hot-as-fuck men that look like mafia? So sorry about them. I'm sure they won't actually *kill us. Probably. Nothing to worry about.*

Yeah. That would go over like a lead balloon.

It was better to deal with her problems herself, just like she'd been doing most of her life.

They'd known each other for a year and a half, and Braven was her only friend. From what she'd seen, she was probably his only friend, as well. The thought of jeopardizing the friendship with the shit show that was her life just wasn't something she could bring herself to do.

Once a week for a month, she sat outside the gym until the last person left, only to sneak in a quick workout before closing. He watched her but left her alone, until one night he finally approached and offered to spar with her. Wary and cautious, she hesitantly accepted.

Weeks passed, and with each workout she monitored him for signs of obsession, but they never came.

She didn't know why Braven was apparently immune to her. It gave her hope there were others out there like him who weren't affected by her, people she could be around, but she never let herself take the chance, unwilling to be selfish enough to ruin another's life to find out.

Unable to simply accept he was different, she tried to question him about small things such as where he was from, his family life, and his heritage, trying to uncover any piece of information from which she could glean answers. Every time she did, a shutter seemed to fall over his eyes, and he gave her vague responses that dissuaded further questioning.

Eventually, she stopped, worried he would shut down for good and she would lose the one good thing that had come her way. It wasn't fair for her to question him anyway when she wouldn't share about her own life, in return.

As if he could sense that fear, he never pried for information, never asked anything personal, like he knew it would make her feel uncomfortable or flighty.

An unspoken agreement settled over their friendship: no questions, no trying to uncover the many secrets they both kept.

Arawyn didn't know what would happen if she broke the

tacit understanding, if she brought the insanity of her life crashing into his.

So, she stayed home and spent that time locked in her workshop, losing herself in crafting the snake dagger and designing two new dream weapons: a long sword, and twin claymores.

And waiting. Waiting for her familiar stranger to find her. Waiting for the dark one or the golden devil to track her down. Waiting, waiting, waiting.

But, they hadn't come.

Her neighbor finally, blessedly, stopped harassing her that morning. That, and the creeping claustrophobia, were the only reasons she finally left the safety of her house to come here and work off some of her frustrations.

No, that wasn't entirely true.

There was a part of her—a foolish, lonely part—that wanted those men, any of them, to find her, even if it meant putting herself in danger.

Luckily, the draw she'd felt that day was mostly absent, only present as a faint tug toward the east, easing the foolish temptation and leaving her feeling relatively safe.

Drawn from her thoughts by the sudden sense someone was watching her, Arawyn tensed but contained any other outward reaction. As casually as she could, she rolled her head to the side so she was staring out her side window and scanned the dark parking lot.

It took only a moment to locate what looked like a homeless woman, standing in the shadows next to a dumpster at the edge of the lot.

Something about her had wariness skittering up Arawyn's spine. It took a moment to realize it wasn't that the woman was staring directly at her, or that she looked like a freshly turned zombie with feverish eyes. It was the way she was standing perfectly still, arms hanging limply at her sides, upper body leaning forward with her nose raised like she was trying to catch a scent in the air.

Thump, thump, thump.

Arawyn whipped around to face her passenger window and drew her gun in the same movement, aiming at the huge shadow of a person standing outside her SUV.

Moving slowly, the shadow put their hands up, but didn't make any other movements. Lowering the gun and blowing out a breath, Arawyn glared at Braven through the glass.

"Goddamnit, Brave! You know better than to sneak up on me like that!"

"I didn't sneak," he answered, his deep voice muffled through the window. "I called your name. Twice. You didn't answer."

"Oh." She grimaced and holstered the handgun. "Well, I didn't hear you."

He snorted. "Clearly."

Coming around to the driver's side, he scanned the parking lot where Arawyn had been staring. She followed his gaze, looking for the creepy-as-fuck woman, but she was gone.

Turning back to her, bright green eyes narrowed inquisitively, he asked, "What did you see?"

Arawyn grabbed her stuff and opened the door, answering as she hopped out of the SUV, "Some woman, homeless I think, was being a creeper. There was something weird about her."

Brave immediately turned, giving her his back as he swept the lot again, slower this time. "I haven't seen anyone hangin' around, but I'll keep an eye out for her. Let's go inside, hmm?"

Despite the life she'd lived, Arawyn wasn't known for being skittish. Braven might not know about her past, but he knew she didn't jump at shadows, so her saying something had been off about the woman was enough for him to take it seriously.

Clicking the remote to activate the alarm on her SUV, she led the way, Braven walking backward behind her.

Once inside, she turned the lock on the door, then smirked up at him. "Still overprotective, I see?"

He cut her a look, one rich brown eyebrow arched. "Still quick to draw, I see."

Arawyn shrugged. "Better safe—"

"Than sorry," he finished. They shared a grin before he jerked his chin to the side, indicating the flatscreens that were still on and droning softly in the background and the assortment of equipment scattered around. "I gotta finish closing up. You good?"

"Yeah, I'm headed for the bags."

"One of those days, hmm? Give me a few and I'll spar with you."

"Sounds good."

Arawyn watched him as he walked away. At six foot six and built like a boxer, with at least three hundred pounds of solid muscle, Braven was a scary looking fucker, but from the moment she met him, he'd been kind to her.

Narrowing her eyes on his back, something niggled at the back of her mind. The thought was slippery, falling through her fingers like sand... and then it hit her with the force of a sledgehammer.

He almost feels like them...

She didn't feel drawn to him, and it wasn't the same as what she felt from those men at the club—wasn't anywhere near as evident. But, now she'd been around them, she could identify a similar kind of familiarity from Brave.

It was vague, only strong enough to make her feel more at ease around him than she did around other people, but now that she recognized the feeling, it was unmistakable.

She'd noticed it before. How could she not? To find someone she felt instinctively comfortable around when most everyone else put her on edge wasn't something she would miss. He'd never acted toward her like most other people did, never got overly attached or clingy, never pushed to know more about her or her life than she was willing to share. He was an anomaly, even in a life that was anything but ordinary.

But, she'd thought he felt different because of his immunity to her.

Now that she'd met those men at the club, now that she'd felt it so strongly from them, so clearly, an entirely different possibility emerged.

Fuck me. Is Braven like me, too?

It was almost too outlandish to believe, but as she continued to stare at his back, the sense he was like her grew stronger.

Does he know?

He hadn't ever hinted he could sense her power, and she'd never sensed any from him, so it didn't seem likely. Questions spun in her mind almost faster than she could process.

Did this mean there were people like her that had different levels of power? Did it mean there were half-breeds or people with some of whatever the hell she was in their lineage?

In order for that to be possible, it would mean she wasn't strictly human and *that* wasn't something she was ready or able to consider just then.

Reeling from the epiphany, Arawyn made her way to the nearest punching bag on autopilot.

How long she worked the bag before the news anchor's voice filtered through the shock, she didn't know.

"In other news, the body of a man identified as Peter Harrison was found today. Authorities are still investigating the cause of death, but it is believed he was ill and..."

Arawyn turned slowly to face the flatscreen. What did it say about her that the first thing she felt was relief? Nothing good, she was sure, but that Peter had been ill explained so much.

The way he'd looked like he'd crawled out of his deathbed, and the severity with which he reacted to that surge of power—which thankfully hadn't happened again—made so much more sense now.

"You okay?"

Glancing at Brave, she nodded slowly. "Yeah." She swallowed and took a moment to truly assess how she was feeling. "Yeah, I'm good."

He frowned like he wasn't sure he believed her, but after a probing look, he shrugged. "You warmed up? Ready to get your ass kicked?"

His challenge was the dose of reality she needed. "Ha! You haven't managed to kick my ass in a year."

Brave didn't have an ounce of toxic masculinity in him, so she wasn't surprised when he grinned like a proud big brother instead of being bitter about repeatedly losing to a woman. Especially one so much smaller than him.

"I've still got a few tricks up my sleeve."

"Oh, yeah? Well, bring it, old man. Let's see what you've got."

"Old man! Oh ho ho, it's on now," he growled, green eyes sparkling.

Once gloved up and inside the ring, they circled, no longer smiling as they sized each other up, both looking for weaknesses and cracks in the other's defenses.

Arawyn lost patience first, as usual, and attacked, using speed and her small size to dart forward within his guard. Feinting with a jab, she tried to land a shot to his ribs.

Unfortunately, that left her face unguarded.

She saw the punch coming in time to twist and avoid most of the blow, but not all of it. He caught her at the corner of her mouth, splitting her lower lip on her teeth.

Darting away again before he could land another hit, Arawyn licked the blood off her lip and embraced the cold stillness that always came when she fought, letting it quiet her mind and sharpen her senses.

Brave winced but didn't apologize. "C'mon, Winner, you can do better than that," he taunted, using his favorite nickname for her.

One thing she loved about sparring with Brave was he didn't hold back. He loathed hitting her, but if she fucked up and gave him an opening, he took it without hesitation.

'Pain is an excellent teacher', as he liked to say.

Serious now first blood had been drawn, they went quiet, the only noises the meaty sound of fists and legs hitting flesh, grunts, and heavy breathing. They switched fluidly between traditional martial arts, boxing, and dirty street fighting styles, dancing across the ring.

For over an hour they sparred. Arawyn subtly began pushing herself to move faster, testing to see if Brave could keep up. For just shy of the year and a half she'd been training with him, her speed had increased to the point she had to hide it from him. Now, she let some of that speed loose, wanting to prove to herself her suspicions were correct.

When Brave wasn't fast enough to block two blows in a row, doubts filtered in. Realizing she was playing a dangerous game, one that could expose her carefully guarded secrets, if she were wrong and he wasn't like her, Arawyn slowed her movements back down.

Careful to keep her speed to something more normal, she took the upper hand when he made a mistake, executing a brutal spinning hook kick. The heel of her foot hit him square on the cheekbone with such force, it spun his body around. Sweeping his legs out from under him while he was off balance, she pounced.

Dropping down before he had a chance to spring up, she pressed her knee to the back of his neck, hooking his left arm with her calf and grabbing his right with both hands, butter-flying them so he couldn't get any leverage to throw her.

Brave looked up at her from the corner of his eye, the side of his face not squished to the mat lifting in a grin. "Nicely fucking done, Winner. God*damn*, does my cheek hurt."

Panting with exertion, Arawyn paused, still pinning him as she stared down at the side of his face. Even held to the mat and bleeding, those stunning, grass-green eyes, darker now with adrenaline, peered up at her warmly.

He was beautiful, inside and out. Aside from having the

face of a model and the body of a god, he was kind, protective, thoughtful, and a hundred other things she should want in a man.

Not for the first time, she tried to will herself into being attracted to him.

His blood-tinged smile slowly faded to a look of concern. "What's up, Winner?"

Shaking her head, she sighed, "Just thinking how much better my life would be if I saw you as... not a friend."

Brave snorted, the force of it moving her on top of him. "Don't I fucking know it. Don't think I haven't tried. You're smart, fierce, beautiful, hell... everything I love in women, but you feel like—"

Family. I know." Sighing again, she tipped to the side, letting herself flop onto the mats.

He turned, propping himself on an elbow to smirk mischievously down at her. "Should we make one of those pacts like they do in rom-coms?"

"Huh?" she questioned, expression scrunching with confusion.

"You know, where if we haven't met anyone by the time we're a thou- er, forty, we get married."

"Ahh!" Arawyn nodded like she were considering it. "And live sad, sexless lives like old spinsters." She widened her eyes in mock excitement. "We could even collect cats! Oh, Asshole would love that! We could start a cat farm—"

His expression twisted with genuine distaste. "I take it back. Fuck me, I'll just die single."

"Wait, wait, hold on... " He paused mid-pushup to eye her suspiciously. Fighting back a smile with everything she had, she asked, "You watch rom-coms?"

He narrowed his eyes to slits and sniffed haughtily. "I'll

have you know, rom-com is the most elite of all movie genres."

Unable to hold it in any more, she burst out laughing. By the time it died down, she felt better, lighter, as though a bit more of the stress and tension she'd been carrying for days had been released.

Chapter Eleven

Braven

B raven watched Arawyn pull out of the parking lot. Something had changed with her.

He'd always been able to sense the tightly leashed power in her—a deep, hidden thing like a *Leviathan* swimming unseen in the dark waters of the ocean. But, it felt different now; something or someone had woken it up.

He blew out a breath while he watched her taillights until they disappeared completely, then rescanned the parking lot for good measure.

She'd seen something earlier, something that had disturbed her enough to mention it to him. Had it truly just been a homeless woman? Or was there something more going on? His instincts told him something had changed in Arawyn's world, and the thought left him unsettled.

In the year and half he'd known her, she'd never, not once, voiced any concern over... fuck... anything. Seeing her on edge, first in the parking lot and again as she'd stared at the news anchor on the television, had him wishing for the millionth time he could question her.

Just as many times, he'd wondered if she truly knew what she was. No matter how badly he wanted to ask her outright, the curse placed upon him during his banishment from Faery wouldn't allow him to speak of anything relating to forbidden magic or the Fae, and all his subtle attempts to draw it out of her were futile. He'd never been able to figure Arawyn out, but that didn't stop him from befriending her. Unfortunately, the more time he spent with her, the more rooted his suspicion became that she had no idea what she was.

Since he couldn't ask, and she never shared, they'd settled into a mutual arrangement of don't ask, don't tell, which suited his own need for privacy, despite how curious he'd become about his sparring partner. Having someone in your corner, a friend you could count on, no questions asked, was a luxury not many—human or other—ever got to experience. He knew the importance of having someone in your life you could depend on through thick or thin. He wanted to be that person for Arawyn.

Besides, it wasn't like he was eager to tell her about his own past and why he'd been banished to the human realm.

Secrets and privacy went both ways.

He just hoped like fuck she'd open up to him, if she were truly in trouble, and instead, did what he was good at. Training. Sparring. Thankfully, Arawyn was strong and independent, and he knew she could take care of herself. She was a powerful machine in her own right, and he helped her hone and sharpen her skills so she was equipped to handle herself in a world full of monsters she didn't seem to know anything about.

If she used the power he could feel just below the surface, she'd be a lethal weapon, a warrior the likes of which he'd never seen.

The sharp ring of his phone pierced the night. He dug it out of his pocket as he headed back inside, turning the lock when he answered.

"I need you, Brother." The voice on the other end of the line was eerily similar to his own and needed no introduction.

Braven gritted his teeth and pinched the bridge of his nose.

Hearing from his twin brother after four years should be a good thing. Except it wasn't. It never was.

"What trouble are you in now, Breac?" he asked with a barely contained growl.

A dark chuckle reverberated back to him. "Ah, you know me so very well."

"Mm."

A sigh echoed down the line. "The *Blood Fae* are threatening me again. Asking for more of the magic…"

"You know you're not supposed to be fucking with that shit in the human realm," Braven hissed.

"I know you've been using it just as well as I have," his twin retorted sharply, his voice edged in condescension.

Braven couldn't deny he had, but his reasons were far more noble than those of his brother.

"It's serious, Brave," Breac said, the goading and anger leaving his voice.

That told him whatever his twin had gotten into, it was

worse than he was letting on. A rock sank into the pit of Braven's stomach, but he already knew his answer. His brother was the only other person he cared about this side of the realms, and he refused to leave him to fend for himself, if he were truly in trouble.

"Send me your coordinates. I'll leave tonight."

"This is why you're my favorite brother," Breac said, far too brightly for the worry that had infused his voice not a second earlier.

That was Breac. Jovial to a fault. So unlike Braven it was a wonder they'd ever shared a womb. The two could not be more different. Night and day, as different as the stars were from the moon.

"I'm your only brother," Brave drawled.

Hanging up, he scrubbed a hand down his face and climbed the stairs to his apartment above the gym. A message dinged before he'd reached the top. Glancing at it briefly, he bit back a grimace.

Of course he's in the fucking South. Godsdamn, I hate the heat.

How Breac could stand the temperatures down there, he would never know. They were Night Court, of *Chimera* blood. They were made for the cold.

Packing a bag, he made his way back down to pause at the front door, leaving a sign stating the gym would be closed for the next two weeks, hoping he wouldn't be gone longer than that. He then moved to the back door, where he left an entirely different, cryptic missive only Arawyn would understand.

The thought of leaving her didn't sit right with him. From what he'd gathered, she didn't have many other friends, if any at all. She never mentioned a family, and he knew she was single, no significant other in her life. As far as he could surmise, she was alone.

What if she needed him while he was gone?

She's never asked me for help before, he scolded himself.

Still, he couldn't quite shake the feeling something had changed, that she might need him, and he wouldn't be there.

But, even if she were willing, bringing her with him wasn't a choice. He wouldn't put her in more danger, and wherever Breac went, threats were sure to follow.

Hiding a key for her made him feel a little better, and again, when he eyed the note he'd left, letting her know the gym was hers, if she wanted to use it while he was out of town.

Throwing his bag in his truck, he went back inside and stuffed a duffle full of weapons, then strapped some more to his body. Lastly, he shoved twin wooden stakes into the holster on his belt, one on either side for convenience.

Of all the Fae banished to this realm, he hated the Blood Fae the most.

With only so much magic throughout the human realm, the banished Fae grew weaker, their power diminishing. Only their strongest ability remained, playing a large part in which Clan they joined.

Regardless of what they once were in Faery, the Blood Fae in the human realm were nothing more than leeches now, weaving their power and influence over humans in an effort to lure them in and feed off them in a futile effort to maintain their vitality.

The humans called them 'vampires,' romanticizing the dark Clan in movies and books. Unfortunately, the more the humans adored their species, the more magic was dispersed to them over others, creating wars between the 'vampires' and the other Clans, aptly the 'shifters,' 'witches,' and 'demons,' to name a few.

Just about every supernatural creature the humans fantasized about, from 'mermaids' to 'angels,' could be traced back to Faery and some watered-down sect of banished Fae.

Heaving a sigh, Braven locked up and climbed into his truck.

"It just had to be the bloodsuckers," he muttered as he threw one last look at the gym and his note to Arawyn before pulling out of the parking lot and hitting the road to save his brother's ass.

Again.

Chapter Twelve

ARAWYN

The lightness she felt from her workout with Braven lasted right up until she pulled into her driveway and saw something fluttering on her front door. Hitting the brakes, she scrunched down in the seat and drew her gun, scanning her property outside the windows and stretching her senses at the same time.

Not seeing or feeling anything, she, nevertheless, kept her head on a swivel as she parked in the barn and made her way back around the house. Nose wrinkling at the lingering stench of rotten meat and death, despite a thorough power wash, Arawyn breathed through her mouth and stepped onto the old wooden porch.

With her back to the door, she reached behind her and

tore the paper off, glancing at it quickly, only to do a double-take, her jaw dropping in shock.

Arawyn gaped at the photo in her hand, tracing every detail of the image. It was her, dancing with her familiar stranger at the club. Whoever snapped the picture had caught her mid-orgasm. Her face was flushed, his large hand clamped over her mouth to muffle her cries as she rode out an intense release with the massive man at her back. She looked positively sinful.

What the hell...

Brows drawn down, she glanced around quickly, assessing her property again for any immediate threat, only returning to the picture when she was sure the coast was clear. Exhaling a pent-up breath, she devoured the sight of the man behind her.

His hair was a deep mahogany, falling forward in loose waves to conceal most of his face. She remembered the soft feel of those strands between her fingers. Butterflies took flight in her stomach at the memory of his groan when she'd fisted them in her hand.

He looked even bigger than he'd felt. Pressed against him, they'd seemed to fit together perfectly, but gazing at the photo, she appeared tiny, like a doll dancing with a giant. He had to be at least six foot eight and built like a grizzly bear.

A hard knot of longing tightened her throat at seeing the way he held her. Bent nearly in half, arms wrapped around her, he surrounded her small form with his much, much bigger one, cradling her as though she were precious to him, whispering seductive commands in her ear.

If she closed her eyes, she could still hear them, still ached from the deep rumble of his voice.

The ghost of his touch haunted her, teasing her through the lonely nights.

Arawyn hadn't been able to get him out of her mind. Any of them, if she were being honest with herself. Each of those men had occupied her daydreams, her thoughts, even her fantasies. Those amber eyes and the rueful smirk of the devilish blonde, the addictive power and confident touch of her familiar stranger, and even the dark intensity and possessiveness of the fallen angel, despite the threat he posed.

Had one of them taken this picture of her when she'd been blissfully lost in pleasure? Was it possible this was her stranger's calling card? Had he finally found her, like he'd promised?

Leaving her an intimate picture didn't feel quite like him.

As soon as the thought crossed her mind, Arawyn scoffed at herself. Just because she'd let herself get intimate with that man didn't mean she knew a damn thing about him.

Just because she'd never felt so connected to anyone before didn't make him any less a stranger. And, yet...

Her rational mind warred with what she'd felt, what she *still* felt for him.

Undeterred by the shadowed night, she assessed her yard, long driveaway, and the tree line beyond more thoroughly for any sign of danger. Though she no longer had to fear her crazed neighbor, she knew she wasn't safe from the dark one.

Her finger caressed the trigger, every sense on high alert.

Carefully, so very carefully, unclenching that tight fist in her chest, she let power seep from her in tiny tendrils to search for any lingering intruders, or more hopefully, another taste of the familiar stranger's power.

What would it be like if he were here? If he'd truly found her?

She'd dreamt of that very moment more times than she cared to admit over the last so many days.

She let those threads crawl outward until she had searched every last inch outside of her home. Her hope wilted, even as her relief over her safety bloomed.

Staying vigilant, she unlocked the numerous locks on her front door and let herself inside.

The door creaked lightly, making her wince as the sound shattered the silence. Her power traced the floorplan, reassuring her it was, indeed, empty, but that didn't stop Arawyn from doing a full sweep herself.

After making sure the locks were secured, she crept on silent feet through each room, clearing the foyer, bedroom, workshop, kitchen, and living room. She went so far as to check below the bed, behind the shower curtain, and in every closet, making sure no spot was left untouched before allowing herself to relax.

There was no such thing as being too careful in her life. The control she held over her power was still a work in progress at best, and though she was growing more accustomed to using it, she couldn't—*wouldn't*—let go of old habits so easily.

Lowering her gun, she holstered it and silently crossed to the monitors of her security system. She sat on the hard wooden stool and searched through the footage once. Then twice.

What the fuck? That's... not possible.

The security cameras hadn't picked up anyone approaching her front door. One minute her door was blank.

In the next frame, there was a picture taped to it. There was nothing in between.

Heart beginning to pound, Arawyn checked her system for any evidence it had crashed or glitched, but it appeared to be working perfectly. Opening the logs from the night her neighbor first appeared, she watched the footage on fast forward. Still nothing.

"How in the hell?"

Thoughts racing, she tried to process what her mind told her was impossible.

Arawyn wondered again if this was supposed to be a display of her familiar stranger's power but dismissed it immediately. This didn't feel inviting, it felt invasive, almost threatening. She may not know the man who'd brought her such pleasure, but she trusted her instincts about him.

"The dark one, then?" she puzzled aloud.

That still didn't feel right, for some reason, but it seemed more plausible... if teleporting a fucking photo out of thin air and taping it to her door didn't feel like science fiction.

Torn between anger someone had invaded her space, alarm they managed to evade her security, and a flutter of excitement at the admittedly distant possibility she could learn to do that, as well, Arawyn just sat there for a long while.

Finally, she sighed and moved to pick up the picture she'd tossed on her desk. Her hand hovered over it as she noticed her sketchbook beneath.

Slowly, she lifted the picture, her gaze moving from the image of the man to her latest design: matching claymore swords.

The twin swords almost reminded her of her familiar stranger. Strong. Sure. Beautiful in their simplicity.

The pair was regal and deadly, the tools of a warrior. The double-edged blades would be longer and heavier than traditional swords, designed for someone very large to wield. The basket hilts were the only embellishment they boasted, appearing as intricately twisted branches forming the shape of a crown.

Arawyn tore her attention from the sketch before the compulsion to begin crafting them took over, the picture still clasped in her hand as she pivoted and left her workshop.

Padding to the living room, she toed off her shoes and scrubbed at the back of her neck, hoping to alleviate some of the tension that had built there. Her workout had helped her vent off her frustration, but the shock of realizing someone had found her home destroyed any semblance of relaxation.

As soon as he saw her, Asshole mewled from his perch on the back of the couch, the sound utterly annoyed.

"You try being me for a day," she snarked back, then blew out a tired breath.

The clock ticking steadily in her living room told her it was well after midnight, nearing one in the morning.

Arawyn grabbed a treat for her cat before settling on the massive, old couch that took up an entire wall in her living room, curling her legs under her and leaning back against the arm.

Laying the treat in front of her, she waited with a knowing smirk as Asshole leapt onto the seat cushions. He meowed, the sound wholly unhappy as he assessed her through narrowed eyes that conveyed he knew exactly what game she was playing.

And he didn't appreciate it one bit.

His steps slowed the closer he got to her, but eventually, he'd crossed the distance, bending his head to lap up the treat while she stole a few loving strokes across the soft, black fur of his back.

Even though Asshole barely tolerated her, he was still nice to have around, especially on nights like this.

As though he could hear her thought, he bristled at her touch, and Arawyn sighed heavily.

Just as quickly as he'd appeared, he ran from her, the tag on his collar jingling with each hasty step as he left her alone.

Alone. Always fucking alone.

The times she spent training with Braven at the gym were always the highlight of each passing week, but those small doses of human contact weren't enough to sustain her.

Arawyn glanced back to the picture in her hand.

But, she wasn't truly alone anymore, was she?

Jolting slightly at the distant ping of her laptop, she stood, crossed back into her workshop, and skimmed the email from the new metal supplier she'd been trying to get in touch with for the last three weeks.

The man was squirrely, anxious, and never answered her calls, but from her research, he was worth the effort. Since her old supplier disappeared, he was the only man on the entire Eastern seaboard who sold *dakaryian* steel.

It was expensive and damn near impossible to get ahold of, but it was the only metal that felt right. She'd tried dozens of other, more readily available kinds, but they all felt... dead, empty.

After a quick shower, she dressed in all black, strapped on her various weapons, then tucked a beanie into her jacket pocket, in case she needed to hide her very pale, very noticeable hair.

Being that this was an off-the-books deal at one in the

morning with a new supplier she'd never met, at a dock she'd never been to, she wanted to be able to disappear, should the situation call for it.

In the back of her closet, Arawyn pressed on a hidden latch in the floorboards, then lifted the section up. Squatting down, she opened her safe and pulled out stacks of bills, stuffing them into a small duffle bag before closing everything back up again.

Just as she was leaving her bedroom, she glimpsed the picture she'd stashed on her dresser and, without giving it any thought, folded it and shoved it into her back pocket.

Swiping her car keys from the hall table, she tossed some food in Asshole's dish and quickly slipped out the back door, making her way to the barn.

With only an hour to navigate through the city and get to the docks to meet with the supplier before he turned into a ghost once again, she'd have to drive like a bat out of hell.

Pulling into the night, she drove toward the city limits, the thrumming pull in her chest growing stronger with every passing mile.

Chapter Thirteen

Arawyn

The docks were dark and deserted at two in the morning. The only sounds piercing the night were the waves lapping against the concrete pillars and the distant horns of cargo ships. The stench of fuel, wet metal, and dead fish was so thick it felt tangible, overwhelming her sensitive nose.

Arawyn kept her ears perked and her eyes roving while she walked between the maze of stacked shipping crates and under towering cranes, avoiding the pools of sickly yellow light cast by industrial bulbs high above.

These weren't the same shipping docks at which she'd always met her last supplier. The unfamiliarity of being in a new place so late at night had tension building between her shoulder blades. The faint sense of being watched did nothing to ease it.

If she'd had more than an hour of warning before meeting her new dealer, she would've scouted this place out, mapped it so she knew where to go and how to escape if shit went south. She'd quickly looked up a satellite picture of the dock so she wasn't coming in totally blind, but those images were never perfectly accurate and were often outdated.

Containers got moved and rearranged, exits got blocked off.

Arawyn sucked in a steadying breath only to immediately regret that decision as the smell of rotting fish assaulted her.

Her nose wrinkled, and she had to swallow to chase down the bile threatening to crawl up her throat. It was almost as bad as the lingering stench of the rotting animal her neighbor had left on her porch, only slightly more tolerable.

Arawyn wasn't a princess. She'd lived in some pretty rough places that didn't smell like roses, but decaying sea life and sour seaweed was a particular brand of gross to which she had no desire to get accustomed.

She was still fighting back her gag reflex when she rounded the corner and saw someone standing in a circle of light a ways off. Steps slowing, she rested her hand on the gun holstered visibly on her hip, waiting for the signal.

The figure raised their arm and moved it in two clear circles. Returning the gesture, Arawyn picked up the pace, ready to get this over with and be on her way home.

The moment she was close enough to see the little man waiting for her next to the shipping container, Arawyn knew with absolute, shocking clarity he wasn't human.

It wasn't a sense, and she didn't need to release any of her power to tell. No one looking at him would mistake him for homo sapien. It wasn't that he was all of four feet tall, or that he looked like Gollum's less attractive, slightly less lanky cousin.

He had fucking horns.

They were just little nubs sprouting at his hairline, but they were unmistakably horns, and as much as she wished otherwise, they were undeniably real.

Blinking rapidly, it took everything she had to keep the shock off her face.

"Ar- are you Orin?" she asked, her voice coming out admirably steady considering, inside her head, she was freaking the fuck out.

He grunted, beady eyes narrowed to slits. "Mebbe. You Arawyn?"

Jolting slightly in surprise at hearing such a deep, rasping voice coming from such a small... *being*, she choked back hysterical laughter. Or maybe that was a scream she could feel building in her throat? Yeah, it was probably a scream.

"Well?" he barked.

"Yee- ahem, yeah. I'm Arawyn."

"You got the money?"

She nodded, and forced herself to breathe. "Yep."

"Lemme see it."

Pulling the bag forward, she unzipped it and showed him the stacks of bills tucked inside. When he leaned forward to peer into the duffle, Arawyn had to physically stop herself from mirroring the movement to try and get a better look at him.

What the- is his hair moving?

Having noticed her blatant staring, he glared. "Wrong wit' you? Ain't never seen a *Bauchan* before?"

Swallowing down another bubble of hysterical laughter, she waved her hand dismissively and lied through her teeth, "Of course I have. It's just been a while, is all."

He relaxed and nodded, letting out an almost mournful sigh. "Yea, don' see many my kind in this realm. Fekkin Ehren- er," he cut short and narrowed his eyes up at her. "What Court did ya say yer from?"

Realm?! Is he a fucking alien? Am I a fucking alien?

Inhaling slowly, she exhaled the hysteria. Now was not the time to try and make sense of all the information he was throwing at her. For whatever reason, he either thought she was like him or, at the very least, understood what the fuck he was talking about. Revealing otherwise was the last thing she needed to do, so instead of answering, she narrowed her eyes right back.

Intentionally threading her tone with suspicion, she drawled, "I didn't say."

That was either the right answer, or he'd skipped dinner and was feeling peckish, because a slow grin spread across his face, revealing sharp, pointed teeth like a piranha.

Oh my god, stop smiling. Please, stop smiling.

Chuckling, he nodded again, "Ah, smart lass. Can never be too careful. Well, c'mon then, let's get down ta business. Got other shit ta do tonight."

Turning, he threw open the doors of the shipping container, then pried the lid off one of the many wooden crates stacked inside. With a wave of his hand, he stepped back out.

"Go on then, give her a look-see. I only deal in the finest dakaryian. Purest you'll find on this side. None of that mixed shite like what ole Graeme was sellin' ya, may the Old Gods let him rise again. I otta be chargin' double what yer payin'."

Grasping onto the familiarity of a coming haggle with the desperation of a drowning woman being offered a life vest, instead of letting herself dwell on what he'd just said, Arawyn cut him a look.

"You don't mind if I check it, then, hmm?"

"A'course not."

Positioning herself so she could still see Orin from the corner of her eye, she reached into the crate and tested the steel, though to anyone watching, it wouldn't look that way.

Generally, she'd go through the motions of filing it and checking its magnetism to hide how she truly verified the metal, but with the horned, possible-alien three feet away, pretending like that seemed unnecessary.

Instead, she simply unclenched the fist in her chest just enough and touched the steel.

A blissful sigh slipped unbidden past her lips as soon as she stroked her fingers across the glittering surface of the top sheet, letting her power taste it. Pushing the top sheet to the side, she checked the next and the next.

Straightening, she turned back to Orin. "It's the same purity as what I was getting from Graeme, so I'll offer you the same price."

He gasped, offended. "This is much better quality than that shite. Why, I got three other buyers ready ta pay six hundred—"

"I'll give you four fifty."

"Oh no, way too low! Way too low! I couldn't take less than five seventy-five."

"Five hundred a pound. That's as high as I'm willing to go," she interrupted.

His beady eyes lit up and he grinned that shark grin. "Deal!"

Handing him the duffle bag of cash, she asked, "You have a cart—"

Sensing someone approaching, she cut off mid-word and whipped around in time to see three figures round the corner of the nearest warehouse. They were still far enough away that she couldn't make out any features, but the air of menace they radiated spanned the distance with ease.

Frowning darkly, she moved so she could see Orin and the three approaching men, gun half unholstered. "What the fuck is this, Orin? You gave me your word it would be just you."

"Easy now, lass. Them's my next appointment, s'all. Ain't nothin' to get squirrely about," he soothed, hands held up. To the advancing men, he yelled, "Yer early. I told ya three."

Arawyn didn't hear whatever it was they yelled back over the sudden pounding of her heart in her ears as that magnetic pull in her chest, which she'd been steadily ignoring, flared to life with new vengeance, almost rocking her forward with the force of it.

It's them...

Even without the unmistakable draw, they were close enough now for her to recognize, and it still took a frozen moment to believe what her eyes were seeing. The dark one was in the lead with her familiar stranger and the devilish blonde flanking him on either side.

Arawyn couldn't have been more stunned than if an octopus had just crawled up her leg and asked for a fucking cookie.

What the hell! Did they follow me?

On the heels of finding that picture taped to her front door, it seemed the most logical conclusion. Anger flickered to life. As much as she'd longed to see them, mostly the massive man currently staring straight at her, their timing was absolute shit. They were going to blow her deal with...

That was when Orin's words finally registered.

Glancing quickly at the little man who was still watching her like she were a feral animal about to attack, she repeated, "Next appointment?"

"That's right," he rasped nervously.

Eyeing the men who were now close enough for her to see clearly, Arawyn quickly catalogued the various weapons they wore, then allowed herself only a second to trace their features.

Damn. They're even sexier than I remember.

Her stranger was just as massive as he appeared in the photo. He had to be every bit of the six foot eight she'd estimated, but it wasn't his size that stole her breath. For the first time, she could see his face.

His facial features were harsher than she imagined from the gentle way he'd touched her. He was undeniably attractive, but it was a feral, untamed kind of beauty. Striking grey eyes seemed to pierce straight into her and stood out starkly against his dark mahogany hair currently gathered into a bun on the top of his head.

A thick beard covered his strong jaw and square chin, framing a set of full lips currently tipped up in a barely there smile she knew was just for her. If she closed her eyes, she could still feel the delicious scratch of it against her neck. Just the reminder of that night, of the way he brought her pleasure, sent butterflies fluttering wildly in her stomach.

Tracing her eyes down his body, she took in his burly

chest tapering to trim hips and muscular thighs straining against his jeans.

Her lips parted with surprise when she got to his forearms and saw the white tattoos covering them, visible with the sleeves of his black Henley pushed up.

Her fingers twitched to touch her own white designs as an odd sense of closeness swept through her. It may have been a silly reason to feel closer to him, but she couldn't help the warmth spreading through her chest.

He looked like a man who could kill, and had killed, people, but she had to consciously stop herself from going to him and snuggling into his massive chest. Hell, she was pretty sure the suspicion he'd taken lives only made the urge stronger, which probably said there was something seriously wrong with her mentally.

What was it about this guy that made her good sense want to take a vacation?

Returning her attention to his face, she got trapped in that silvery stare. There was a coldness in his eyes that spoke to an intimate familiarity with violence.

No, not cold. Ruthless.

This man was dangerous. She knew without question he could be absolutely merciless, that he could dispense brutality just as skillfully as he had bliss. But, there was a difference between being ruthless and cruel. There was no cruelty in him. She knew it as surely as she knew the intricate details of every weapon she'd created.

Tearing her eyes away before she lost the fight with herself and went to him, she peered at the golden devil next.

The moment she looked at him, she had to stop her lips from automatically curling. His smile was infectious, and he exuded a manic kind of energy she found bizarrely enticing.

There was something about him that just screamed 'mentally unstable.' Before that very moment, she would've sworn that wasn't her type. Why, then, did she so very badly want to taste his insanity?

He was the kind of man you knew would burn you, yet, you still wanted to dance in the flames.

His amber eyes almost seemed to glitter in the sickly yellow, industrial lighting and bored into her as if she were the only thing that existed. The scar slashing down the left side of his face from hairline to cheek, bisecting his left eye, was crinkled with the grin stretched across his lips, adding to the enticing air of crazy he gave off.

Straight white teeth, and canines that seemed a little longer than normal flashed at her. Arawyn hadn't realized she had a kink for biting, but the thought of him skimming those sharp teeth over her neck had her nipples tightening.

Flicking a quick look between him and the dark one, she realized there was a resemblance between them. It was in the shape of their faces, the sharply squared jawlines or the cut of their cheekbones, maybe.

Briefly, she wondered if they were related somehow before she looked back up at the golden devil. Her gaze caught on the silver hoops in his ears. Arawyn was pretty sure she had a pair just like them. She'd never seen a man wear earrings like that, but he wore them very, very well. Arawyn had the brief mental image of wearing hers and matching him like a couple.

Zeroing in on his mouth when movement caught her eye, she watched him play with one of the rings piercing the corners of his lower lip, flicking it back and forth with the tip of his tongue. Her brows rose with interest when a glint of silver caught her eye, and her thighs clenched when it dawned on her his tongue was pierced, as well.

At six foot four, he was taller than she'd thought and built like a street fighter, all brawn and hard, sculpted muscle. He moved like a panther—lithe and deceptively relaxed—but Arawyn could sense the coiled power in every defined muscle and knew he could lash out in the blink of an eye.

As though entirely unaffected by the cold night air, he wore a ripped, sleeveless, white shirt revealing broad shoulders and thickly corded arms, every inch of which were covered in brightly colored tattoos.

Doing a double take at his right forearm, she realized there were cookies tattooed among the colorful array of snakes, daggers, and skulls. Chocolate chip, if she wasn't mistaken.

Someone has a sweet tooth.

Completing his look were a pair of black jeans, motorcycle boots, and a chain that... Arawyn squinted.

It's got fucking barbs on it. Oh, I want one of those.

Of the three, he had the most weapons. They were well concealed, and she was positive she missed some, but she counted at least thirteen. Impressive, considering he was dressed for summer.

Last, but certainly not least, she let her gaze trail over the dark one. She took in the solid black, perfectly tailored suit that clung to his big frame like a lover. If it weren't for the black and grey tattoos she could see on his hands and peeking above the collar of his button up, he might look like a reputable businessman. Instead, they only reinforced the impression she'd had in the club of a mafia boss.

Tracing her way to his face, she had to clench her teeth to stop a lustful sigh from escaping.

She'd hoped the strobing lights made him appear more attractive than he actually was. Unfortunately, they'd apparently had the opposite effect, because he was even more handsome than she remembered.

Should be illegal for someone so obviously dangerous to be that good looking.

The contrast of those brilliantly blue eyes against his black hair and bronze skin was striking. Despite, or maybe because of, the glare he was sending her way, she had the ridiculous and decidedly ill-advised urge to bite that sharply squared jawline of his or lick those full lips currently pressed into a hard line.

He was the same height as the golden devil and had the same build, all that chiseled brawn visible even through the cut of his suit, but there was something more refined about him. He didn't have the same roughness as the blonde.

Or the same happy demeanor.

Unfortunately for her, she apparently found dark and dangerous just as attractive as she did cheerful and crazy.

When a full minute passed and she hadn't responded or relaxed, Orin tried to explain himself once more, "They're just early. I wouldn't do nothing—"

That was as far as he got before the devilish blonde broke formation with a low, somehow masculine giggle and beelined straight for her.

Chapter Fourteen

Arawyn

Arawyn watched as the golden devil came for her, knowing somehow he had no intention of stopping. And, yet, she made no move to evade him.

"Viper don't—" her familiar stranger started, but it was too late.

She stood perfectly still, like an idiot, as Viper, as was apparently his name, skipped—actually fucking skipped—up to her and wrapped her in a full body hug.

Her eyes popped wide, and her mind went perfectly blank, but that didn't stop her body from reacting.

Without consciously willing it, she had her gun drawn and pressed to his ribs before his arms were even fully wrapped around her.

Completely ignoring the weapon digging into his side,

the very large, very muscular man who smelled deliciously of blood oranges, honey, and cinnamon curled himself around her like a fucking anaconda and buried his face in her hair.

What the fuck! This is... this is... kind of nice, actually. No wonder people hug all the time. Oh god, he smells good.

It was the single most comprehensive embrace she'd ever experienced in her life. How, at over a foot taller than her, he managed to press himself to her from forehead to ankles defied the laws of physics.

I should shoot him. Wait. Sniff him some more, then *shoot him.*

Arawyn blinked at her stranger from over Viper's shoulder, catching his wince.

"Don't shoot him, please. He's not—"

Hoping desperately he'd read the thought on her face and not from her mind, she cut him off, "If you're about to say 'not dangerous', I'm going to shoot you first for lying."

That surprised a chuckle out of him, the low sound gliding up her spine like a caress. Shaking his head, he smirked, but his pale grey eyes were utterly serious when he murmured, "I'd never lie to you. I was going to say he's not going to hurt you."

The man still coiled around her like a lover inhaled deeply, then released it on a groan and murmured, "Mmm, I missed you. He's right, ya know. I'd never hurt my Pretty Loon."

Oh god...

Her nipples instantly tightened to hard points and her clit gave an excited little throb. His voice was pure fucking sin. Deep and smoky, he sounded like he'd just woken up. Or just had incredible sex.

Arawyn tried to hide her reaction to hearing him speak

for the first time, but knew he'd felt it when he hummed low in his throat and, somehow, wiggled himself even closer.

"You like me," he whispered in her ear, sounding absolutely delighted.

Arawyn opened her mouth to refute that—which would've been a lie, because apparently mentally unstable men with the voices of phone sex operators did it for her—but he kept going before she could.

"I like you, too. You're so fucking tiny and pretty and"—he inhaled deeply again—"by the Gods, you smell *good*. And the gun"—he shivered—"Godsdamn, that's hot."

Her clit pulsed a little harder with every word. She had the shocking realization she was in serious danger of having a miniature orgasm, if he didn't shut up. She should pull away or pry him off. She knew she should. But... she didn't.

"You're insane," she whispered.

He nuzzled his way past her hair until he was rubbing his face against her neck like a cat, making her lashes flutter with pleasure. "Mmhm, but it's a fun crazy, right?"

She couldn't help it, she smiled. "Yeah. It's a fun crazy. But, I'm pretty sure it's going to get you killed one day."

He skimmed his teeth across the sensitive skin of her neck, surprising a moan from her, before he purred, "Worth it, if I die with you in my arms."

Before she could respond to that, he tightened his hold on her, lifting her up on tiptoe and moving her with him as he twisted to address the men watching.

"We should keep her, Brother."

She knew with absolute surety who he was talking to, but it was confirmed when the dark angel answered, "We've spoken about this. You have to watch out for the pretty ones. They tend to have the worst bite." He gave her a knowing look, though what the hell he thought he knew was beyond her, and smirked coldly. "Besides, I'm sure this pet is already owned."

This motherfucker, here!

Arawyn contained her reaction to his deep, rich voice purely out of spite, because he was a fucking dick. Torn between confused indignation he'd called her a pet and just the *tiniest* sliver of pleasure he thought she was pretty, she almost gave into the urge to shoot him instead.

She settled for a look to convey how stupid it was to poke the bear holding the gun and pressed said gun against Viper's ribs harder.

Voice hard with warning, she drawled, "I would not recommend you try that."

Viper pulled back to peer down at her, looking genuinely confused. "Why? I'd take good care of you!"

Finally forcing herself to step out of his arms, she holstered her gun. "I take care of myself just fine. And I don't like cages."

She didn't even have time to regret how much she'd just given away with that one sentence before everything about the man in front of her changed.

In an instant, his animated expression twisted into something dark and knowing. He bent until they were almost nose to nose, letting her see the shadows behind those beautiful amber eyes.

Voice low, serious, and meant for only her to hear, he murmured, "I'd never cage you, Little Loon. But, I would keep you. Oh, yes, I'd keep you forever."

Fast as the snake he was named for, he darted forward and flicked just the tip of his tongue over her upper lip. Arawyn gasped, arousal igniting inside her in a rush that had her thighs slick and her heart racing. Groaning, his eyes went hooded as he rolled her flavor around in his mouth.

"By the Gods, you taste just as good as you smell," he whispered hoarsely.

She didn't know what possessed her to do it, but Arawyn wanted *more*. She chased him, leaning forward until her lips brushed his and held his gaze as she breathed, "So do you, Cookie Monster. But, I wont be 'kept' by anyone."

He was nearly panting, eyes wide with a fanatical kind of want, when she straightened away from him.

His voice was hoarse when he whispered, "How did you know I love cookies?"

"Lucky guess," Arawyn murmured, eyeing the cookie tattoos on his forearm, lips twitching.

He glanced to her mouth at the movement. Groaning, he made no effort to hide it when he reached down to adjust the prominent outline of his hard cock.

And she made no effort to pretend she wasn't looking.

"*Fuuuck* me. I got a better idea. You keep me." He smiled lopsidedly, his gaze going slightly unfocused as he agreed with himself, nodding slowly at first, then faster. "Oh, yeah, that's such a good idea. You can pet me and feed me treats, and I'll lick your puss—"

"Viper," the dark one snapped.

At the interruption, Viper cut him a look, eyes narrowed to slits and sparkling dangerously, violence rolling off him in such a tangible wave she was a little surprised the dark one didn't react other than to cock a black brow.

After a brief stare-off, Viper was the first to look away, grumbling under his breath, "It was a good idea. Killjoy."

Biting back a smile, she turned away to address Orin, only to hesitate at the expression on his face. It was an odd mix of horror, fascination, and morbid curiosity, kind of how she imagined someone would look at a person who'd just cuddled a rabid hyena.

Flicking a look at Viper, she had to admit that was fair.

To Orin, she asked, "Do you have a cart I can use to transport this?"

He blinked a couple of times, then nodded rapidly and darted around the side of the shipping container, returning a moment later with a small, hand-operated forklift.

Arawyn reached for the controller, only for a large hand to get there first. She felt him warm her back, the familiar feel of a large, defined chest brushing against her shoulder blades. That warmth crawled through her, settling low in her belly. She tipped her head back, resting it against his chest so she could peer up at her stranger with raised brows.

"May I?" he asked, chin almost touching his chest as he stared down at her with those intense grey eyes.

A smile tugged at the corner of her lips, and she started to respond but stopped abruptly, tensing at the sudden fury twisting her gorgeous stranger's face. Stepping away from him, she spun around.

He reached for her face but paused when she pulled back. Tearing his cold, wrathful glare from her lips, he met her eyes, waiting with his hand raised. Despite not knowing what the hell was going on, or why he was so intensely angry, Arawyn straightened.

Still wary, she, nevertheless, went still, letting him cup her cheek. His hand was so big it covered the entire side of her face, the tips of his fingers curling around the back of her neck.

Arawyn was so utterly entranced by the aching tenderness in his touch when he ever-so-gently brushed his thumb across the corner of her lip, the twinge of pain surprised her enough she made a soft noise.

He winced and started to hastily withdraw. Without thinking, she caught his hand before he could pull away entirely and brought it back to her face.

Striking grey eyes boring into hers, voice a rough growl, he asked simply, "Who?"

Everything inside her went warm and tingly. Arawyn couldn't stop her lips from lifting in a smile, even as she swallowed down a knot in her throat.

I'm not gonna cry that he cares I got a split lip.

She broke eye contact with her stranger when the other two came up on her left side. She felt irrationally touched at the murderous glint in Viper's eyes, but it was the look on the dark one's face that held her attention and had her heart fluttering in her chest.

He was staring unblinkingly at her mouth, his own parting as he slid his tongue across his lower lip like he wanted to taste her pain.

Goddamnit, that should not *be sexy.*

Turning back to her stranger before the dark one could see the lust in her eyes, she answered, "My sparring partner. It was my fault. If I'd moved faster, he wouldn't have clipped me."

He still looked pissed, like he wanted very badly to argue against that logic but couldn't. His teeth were clenched so tightly a muscle was jumping in his temple, but his touch was gentle as he dragged his thumb down the middle of her lips.

She could almost feel her pupils dilate with arousal. Her shuddering exhale was immediately echoed by his sharp inhale as if he were trying to breathe her in.

"Is this the only place he got you?"

She felt her smile widen slightly as she answered, "Yes."

Those grey eyes flashed almost silver as he bared his teeth in a savage smile. Bending until he could brush her nose with his, his growled response was full of relief and pride, "Good."

"Tell me your name," she murmured, spellbound and breathless with his nearness.

Some of the anger in his eyes vanished, replaced with surprise and pleasure. "Fearson."

"Fearson," she repeated softly.

His eyes went hooded at the sound of his name on her lips, a low, rumbly purr of approval vibrating his chest.

Turning her face into his hand, she brushed her lips across his palm, then stepped away. He took a single step toward her but stopped himself, nostrils flaring, eyes flashing with hunger.

With slow, controlled movements that spoke to how much he wanted to advance on her, he turned back to the container and loaded the crate onto the hand lift.

Taking it from him, she caught his gaze and murmured softly, "Still holding you to that promise." Before he could respond, she looked at Viper and the dark one. "Boys."

She started to walk away only to turn back when she heard one of them following her. For some reason, she wasn't at all surprised to see it was Viper.

Cocking a brow and holding back a smile, she questioned, "What are you doing?"

He widened his eyes innocently. "You said you were going to keep me, so I'm going home with you."

Chuckling, utterly charmed by his playfulness, she corrected, "No. *You* said I was going to keep you."

His smile became wicked. "Ah, but you didn't say 'no.' We both know you want me." Under his breath, he added, "Almost as much as I want you."

He was right. She did want him, badly. She wanted all three of them. Arawyn had never experienced such an immediate and intense attraction as she had with these men, and she didn't know how to deal with it.

"And how do I know you wouldn't turn on me? I've got a feeling you bite."

"Oh, I'd definitely bite you, but I wouldn't ever turn on you, Pretty Loon."

Smirking, she shook her head. "I've already got one feral pet. I don't need another."

His teasing expression twisted into something dark and possessive, his amber eyes flashing gold. Arawyn read the murderous thought passing through his captivating gaze with surprising ease.

She shouldn't be turned on by the knowledge he was contemplating killing her nonexistent boyfriend.

"I'd be a better pet," he hissed softly.

"Oh, I don't doubt that, at all," she whispered.

Why did that look of jealousy in his eyes excite her so much?

Biting her lip, she made herself leave before she did something reckless, feeling the stares of all three on her back every step of the way until she rounded the corner.

Back at her SUV, Arawyn loaded up the crate, then moved to the driver-side door. Standing there, keys in hand, she gazed back in the direction of the docks, curiosity making her hesitate.

Next appointment.

Hers had been the only crate of dakaryian steel. She

would've sensed if there'd been more when she'd used her power. So, what were they buying?

Don't do it. Don't fucking do it. Just get in and go home.

She looked down at the keys in her hand, willing herself to get in the vehicle and leave.

Fuck it.

Cussing herself the whole way, she crept back on silent feet.

Chapter Fifteen

Rathe

The fearless little vixen watched him. Rathe felt the brush of her inquisitiveness like a light caress against his skin, a subtle electricity that tingled and teased.

As intrigued as he was by her, he was becoming more and more suspicious.

He'd thought she was just a mark, but the red flags were beginning to tally up, one right after another, until there were too many to ignore—Fear letting her go from the club, Viper 'losing her,' how taken they'd been with her since the moment they laid eyes on her.

That she'd shown up here, on the one night they were scheduled to meet with Orin, tipped the scales from coincidence to full-blown skepticism. She'd appeared genuinely surprised to see them, but it seemed entirely too suspect to be happenstance.

Her motives, however, were a mystery to him. Perhaps, she was a fawner trying to get close to him because of his position. But, maybe, it was something more devious.

Sensing his brother was becoming increasingly tempted to leave his post and go to their pretty little stalker, he unleashed a sliver of his power and jolted Viper with it.

"Focus," he warned softly.

The jolt hadn't been enough to hurt, just a nudge to redirect his brother's attention, but the glare Viper sent his way spoke to genuine irritation.

Surprise flickered through Rathe. He couldn't remember a time when his brother had been this preoccupied with a woman.

Obviously realizing he'd given too much away, Viper's expression changed in a blink. With a coy grin, he stuck his tongue out, yellow eyes flashing with a brotherly promise he'd reciprocate when Rathe least expected it.

Resisting the urge to shake his head, Rathe glanced at Fear. There was a dangerous stillness to the man, and though his friend didn't waver, didn't turn and seek out the woman, he could tell Fear wanted to.

Rathe knew they could feel the draw to her as intensely as he did, but that the vixen had gotten under their skin to this degree concerned him.

Did they not harbor the same suspicions he did? Were they already so deeply under her spell?

Feeling the weight of his stare, his stoic friend peered down at him from the corner of his eye and arched a single thick brow, the expression a clear warning not to try the same jolt on him.

The corner of Rathe's mouth pulled up, and he gave Fearson a small nod before turning away.

Mollified they weren't going to give in to the draw, he pushed the worries still swirling through his mind aside, for now.

They had a job to do, and they all needed to stay focused on the deal, not the suspiciously tempting woman who called to him like a *Siren*.

"Ya said yer interested in some of me product?" Orin questioned, rubbing his greedy little hands together with anticipation of making another sale tonight.

Bauchan were excellent peddlers, their penchant for making deals, and trying to bleed you dry in the process, a gluttonous artform.

Luckily, that was the only thing they ever tried to bleed. For as gruesome as Orin appeared in his fully unglamored form, his kind rarely resorted to violence unless provoked, making him one of the safer dealers operating along these docks.

Pushing aside the disconcerting realization he was concerned for the little vixen's safety, he narrowed his eyes on the small Fae. "You're mistaken."

Orin glowered, his browless skin wrinkling across his forehead. "Ah," he grunted angrily. "Don' be wastin—"

Rathe arched a brow, holding up a hand to silence the man. "You misunderstand me. I'm not here for *some* of your product. I'm here for all of it."

Orin's tiny eyes widened, and his entire demeanor changed to something far more accommodating as he picked up a crowbar and went to work prying off the top of the crate.

Rathe crossed his arms and waited, keeping a watchful eye on the man while he let his senses expand.

Unable to keep from drawing another deep inhale of musty air, he sorted through the scents of rusted metal, dried seaweed, and the rotten stench of fish until he found the one he was looking for—an intoxicating blend of moonlit lilies, spring thunderstorms, and warm vanilla.

It belonged to the problematically captivating woman hiding in the shadows, trying to remain inconspicuous.

As if she weren't alluring enough, her power called to him, as well, the sweet taste he'd detected when they arrived at the docks lingering like electricity in the air before a rainstorm. Though she contained it well, he could trace it directly to her, now that he'd savored it not once, but twice.

And it tasted just as sweet and tantalizing as her unique scent on the breeze.

That she thought she could hide surprised him. Surely she wouldn't be foolish enough to expect his senses to be dulled like those of the banished Fae. She felt strong and was undeniably fresh to this realm. She should know better than to think the High Prince of the Light Court would be weakened like that. He may not be at full strength, thanks to the years spent away from Faery, but he was still the most powerful being in this realm.

Fuck, he was the most powerful man in Faery, aside from his father.

Rathe was not a man to be trifled with. Far larger, stronger beings had fallen to his intensity, bending to his will like a willow in the wind without him having to lift a single finger. He'd earned every ounce of that fear and respect, had committed atrocities to garner that reverence and trepidation, necessary evils to placate his father in order to keep his brother and friend safe from the man's cruelty.

Yet, unlike all the Fae in this realm, and the next, Arawyn didn't cower in his presence. She didn't wilt like a dying flower in autumn.

She'd bewitched his best friend, held his brother at gunpoint—not that he blamed her, he'd often been tempted to do the same—and didn't shrink under his own steadfast, rather intimidating scrutiny.

This type of boldness was exactly the trait sure to catch his attention.

Which was another red flag.

He had never been around someone who didn't bow or curtsey, who didn't quake in fear when they saw him coming. Even his allies welcomed him into their Kingdoms, Queendoms, or Clans, with tentative wariness.

Why then, did she appear so unfazed by him? Moreover, why did she so pointedly favor his brother and guard?

Did she think the way to him was through his friends? Or did she believe they would be easier targets to seduce and glean information from?

Before he'd seen how bewitched his friends had become with her, he never would have given the possibility a second thought, but her power was unquestionably strong.

It hit him then—in the five days since he'd seen her, her power hadn't diminished in the slightest. How?

The only people who could keep their power from rapidly fading in the human realm, and extend that ability to those around them, were rulers of Faery.

Fear and Viper both bore his royal mark, the small brand woven into the ink decorating their skin.

Someone had to have marked her for her power to remain mostly unfaded in this realm... and there was only one other person he knew who had the mastery to bestow such a gift with the Night Court still technically rulerless.

His father, High King Ehrendil of the Light Court.

There was only one reason he could think of as to why she'd suddenly appeared in his city, why she watched him, why she didn't kiss his ass or tremble in his presence.

She must have already known what to expect. She'd been briefed, warned, sent in undercover.

The hunch she was here to test him, to spy on him and report back to his father about what she found, grew.

A muscle ticked in his jaw. He'd foolishly thought the three of them were safe from his father's machinations here, that they would have some small measure of freedom as long as they did the King's vile bidding and fed his insatiable hunger.

That, even here, so far removed from the Court, Rathe still had to worry about his father's spies pissed him off.

The only place he could truly be himself, where he could remove the callous facade and breathe, was around Viper and Fear, and only when they were home or in private.

They were the only ones who truly knew him.

The appearance of the treacherous little vixen might be even more worrisome than he'd first thought. If she were a spy, did that mean they'd done something to arouse his father's suspicions? Or was the King just descending further into madness?

The part that disturbed him most was he was still drawn to her, had to consciously keep himself rooted to the spot, despite his suspicions. Rathe knew if he crossed to her, he'd kiss those perfectly bow-shaped lips. He'd lick across the soft seam of her mouth and demand she part for him so he could thoroughly taste her.

And that absolutely, without a doubt, could not happen.

Chapter Sixteen

Rathe

The possibility of how much worse her pull would be, if he lost control and touched her, shot through Rathe in a burst of icy unease. He let that coldness envelop him, let it harden into the imperious exterior he needed to portray during this transaction with Orin.

The peddler finally removed the top and reached into the crate to procure a brick of white, powdery substance wrapped in clear cellophane.

"You won' find better product this side o' the realms." Orin waved Rathe forward until he could see the stacks of drugs lining the crate. "Already got several buyers I be sellin' ta." Orin grinned, flashing yellowed teeth at Rathe. "A'course it can all be yers for the right price."

"I won't be offering any price until we check the contents for ourselves."

Orin jumped to comply, slicing the product open with one taloned claw, then handing over the brick of *Pixie* dust meant for the streets of this city.

Rathe's fucking city.

Bending his head slightly, Rathe lifted the brick and took a whiff of the product. His nose tingled, the effect of the Pixie dust strong even from a distance.

Fuck. Where the hell did he get this shit from?

Somehow, he doubted the Pixies had willingly sold it to this man. Pixie dust was a prized possession, and there was no way Orin procured the amount he'd offloaded from his ship legally.

"It's the very best from the Lilium Meadows. As fresh as you'll find on this side, I can promise ye that." Orin's beady little eyes flashed as he waited for Rathe's reaction.

Rathe couldn't deny the product was legit, but it only increased his desire to lay into Orin for daring to sell this veritable poison in his city, knowing full well the dust wouldn't stay in the hands of the various Clans. It would undoubtedly end up being sold to the humans, whose systems would never be able to handle the potent magic of the Pixies.

For banished Fae, dust was as strong and addictive as cocaine was for humans. Tensions were already high between the Clans. If he let this shit hit the streets, it could push them into full-out war. They'd fight over every ounce like hungry *Minotaurs*, uncaring about the blood spilled in their efforts to feel even marginally like they used to back in Faery.

Normally, he'd just put an end to Orin and his entire

operation, but finding another dealer as well connected would be difficult. He'd worked too long and too hard to get a man like this in his pocket, a direct line to the seedy underbelly he was often given wrongful credit for running.

Rathe, Viper, and Fearson were dangerous—that much was true—but despite their reputation, they operated with as much integrity as possible, only engaging in the dirty work necessary to keep this city, and the beings in it, safe.

He passed the brick to Viper, who dipped his pinkie into the white powder and dabbed it on his tongue, releasing a low, throaty moan.

The slightest feminine gasp floated on the sea breeze, hardly perceptible to anyone not actively listening for it, and Rathe felt her retreat.

To any outsiders, it would look like they wanted the product for their own desires, whether to sell it or use it themselves. It was a good cover, and one he made no effort to correct. His true motivations were safe, as far as the little blonde minx surveying them was concerned.

If she were a spy sent from his father, her wrongful assumption would play into his hands nicely.

Then why the fuck did his heart fall the farther she crept away?

Finally, he heard the faint kick of an engine and a dull roar as it disappeared into the night.

Viper's head whipped around, and he tossed the brick to Fear who caught it effortlessly. Both men gazed toward the shadows. Rathe read the regret mixed with the longing written across their faces.

Prodding them both this time with another jolt of power, he ignored the glares they gave him and nodded pointedly at the product in Fear's hand.

He held Fear's stormy gaze while his friend tested the powder.

"Fuck, that's strong," Fear cursed the moment the dust hit his tongue, and his demeanor changed as they all came to the same conclusion.

This shit couldn't get onto their streets, or they'd be too distracted cleaning up the mess for the next few weeks to have any extra time to sort out the appearance of their mystery woman.

Orin practically hissed his pleasure, his beady eyes gleaming in the dark, dancing with dollar signs. "Only the best for the Prince."

"Is this crate all you got?" Viper asked, his gaze darting to all the other crates stacked inside the container.

Orin banged his small fist against the wooden boards. "There'd be no reason ta hide it from ya. Them other crates hold other valuables. The Prince wants all me dust, and this crate be what I got. It's a mighty lot more than anyone else be carryin'."

Already tired with the exchange and ready to get on with it, he reached into his suit jacket and pulled out a small bag of coin.

"You'll take *banálch* of Faery, I presume."

He tossed the bag at a sputtering Orin, who had undoubtedly expected some form of human currency. The man's mouth dropped open as he dumped the contents into his palm, the excess coins falling to chime against the dock. The pure-gold currency was embossed with the royal crest and worth far more than the Pixie dust.

"I believe that's a generous offer," he said flatly, watching Orin scramble for the fallen coins, tucking them all back into the black bag and holding it close.

"Aye, your highness. 'Tis all yours." Orin waved toward the crate with a satisfied grin.

"Excellent." Rathe straightened his suit jacket before stalking forward slowly. "And while we're in negotiations, let me make something very clear. While I prefer relics and lost artifacts, if you ever find yourself with another elusive shipment of dust, though I assume it's not something you will carry often, you sell it to *me*, do you understand?"

Without having to look, he knew his brother was grinning, the smile feral, his sharp teeth visible in the dark, a manic promise from the assassin there wasn't another choice but to agree to Rathe's terms.

"A- aye." Orin nodded, the grin he'd worn bleeding from his face as the excitement of the sale he'd just made dulled.

"If I find out you've been selling to anyone else, you won't live to regret it. Do I make myself clear?" He tilted his head, staring through a narrow-eyed gaze at the dealer.

"As ye command, Sire." Orin had the good sense to bow, showing his allegiance to the crown.

"Wonderful," Viper snickered, clapping like a child on Christmas morning, his grin growing wider while Fear mumbled something about getting the fuck out of there. "I so love a good deal, don't you? I do. I *really* do."

"You sure you're not high from that tiny hit?" Fear grumbled, lifting the crate with Viper, their strength supernatural for this realm.

"I don't think so. Why do you ask?" Viper tilted his head like a curious cat, blinking at Fear.

"You know better. He's always like this," Rathe deadpanned, giving his brother a raised brow, who responded by waggling his own. Shaking his head, he waved his friends down the dock while smoothing a hand down the expensive line of his tailored suit.

Realizing he had an opportunity to learn more about the vixen, he turned on his heel to face Orin once more as Viper and Fear continued on in the direction of their vehicles.

"Tell me. How long have you been selling to the woman who was here before us?" he questioned, ensuring the authority he carried in both realms came through clearly, so Orin would know not answering wasn't an option.

"Arawyn?" Orin asked, scratching at his chin and glancing at Rathe with wary eyes.

"Mm," he hummed, unwilling to speak her name. He didn't want to know what it felt like on his tongue, passing his lips, filling the night air.

Would it contain the suspicions he harbored about the woman? Or would the notes hint at the way he'd devoured the sight of her? The way his cock hardened when he'd watched her dance? The way he touched himself at night to the memory of pleasure playing across her beautiful face as she came for his best friend?

"This was our first deal. She be lookin' for a type of metal. Dakaryian steel, ta be exact." Orin said with a shrug, obviously unsure how the additional information would help.

He expected the answer, but it didn't stop his stomach from clenching at the realization the doubt he harbored about the little vixen was correct.

"For your trouble. And your silence." Rathe reached for another coin and flicked it to the peddler. Orin snatched it from the air as he turned and stalked away to where Fear and Viper had paused, waiting for him with twin, narrowed gazes.

"What was that about?" Fear grunted, hoisting the crate into the air, carrying it himself while Viper walked backward, keeping a knowing gaze on him.

"You asked about her." Viper knew. There was no sense in hiding it. His brother's hearing was too sharp, his senses too honed, to lie.

Fear glanced at him a little too quickly, his gaze a little too eager, and questioned, "What did you find out?"

"Exactly what I expected."

He opened the back of the SUV he'd driven, waiting while Fear loaded the contents of their deal, and then shut it. The finality of the sound echoed through the darkness, accentuating his next statement.

"She's working for my father."

Chapter Seventeen

Fearson

Fear stared out the floor-to-ceiling window, leathery wings arched around him, eyes narrowed to block the painfully bright light blazing from Rathe's palms as he destroyed the Pixie dust, burning it to ash with concentrated sunlight.

He could feel her out there, calling to him. The need to go to her was a thrumming in his bones, an ache in his chest getting increasingly harder to resist.

There was something about her, something... lost that called to him almost as much as the draw. She was a fierce little thing, strong and brave, but there was a vulnerability there, too. What had she lived through to have such a haunted, wary look in those beautiful green eyes?

When the light faded, he turned back around to find Rathe staring at him. Fear hadn't made much effort to hide his preoccupation with Arawyn, so he'd been expecting his friend to say something. He was just surprised it had taken this long.

"You know we can't trust her, Fear."

"Do I?" he challenged mildly.

Rathe narrowed his eyes. "If you weren't so fucking infatuated by her, you'd see what I see. It's too much to be a coincidence."

Rathe's declaration at the docks that Arawyn was working for the King had been echoing in Fear's mind all morning. He'd considered it, analyzing what he felt over and over again, but he came to the same conclusion every time. It didn't mean he didn't understand Rathe's suspicion. If he hadn't felt from her what he had, Fear likely would've thought the same.

He knew why Rathe's first instinct was to assume the worst of people. That way of thinking had kept not just Rathe, but Viper and himself, alive all these years.

But, this time, he was wrong.

Fear may think of Rathe and Viper as brothers, but they were from very different Courts. As he stared at his Prince, that difference was clearer to him than it had been in a long time. Fear's people still remembered the Old Ways, still knew of the draw one felt for their *Firláh*, their Fated.

The Light Court no longer waited for the draw to show them their soul's match, hadn't since Ehrendil's father, Manon, ruled and convinced them that it was just another way for the Old Gods to control them. In reality, Manon was the one who wanted control. Now, they married for power, to seal alliances, using their children as pawns in their endless greed for more control.

But, the 'lesser' Courts remembered and continued to secretly follow the Old Ways.

Fear had never experienced the draw before, and as such, he couldn't know with one hundred percent certainty that's what this was, but it felt exactly as the stories foretold.

So, yes, he'd expected Rathe's suspicion. What intrigued him was Viper's apparent trust in the draw.

Being a son of the Light Court, bastard or no, he wouldn't have been taught about it. However, Fear could see no doubts in the man's eyes. *That* surprised him. Viper had more reason to doubt Arawyn than Rathe. He, more than any of them, should have been wary of any kind of draw toward a woman after what he'd endured at the hands of the Court's ladies.

Viper stepped up to his side and elbowed him none-too-gently in the ribs. "He thinks we drank the Kool-Aid."

Blinking, he looked down at his friend, confusion furrowing his brows. "I don't like Kool-Aid."

Viper gazed up at him, a smile twitching his lips, the yellow eyes exposing his *Naga* blood and marking him as the Light King's bastard glittering with mirth. "It means he thinks we're under her spell."

"Am I wrong?" Rathe questioned.

"Yes," Viper answered before he could, his expression utterly serious. Before Rathe could reply, he kept going, "But, *you* think she's sketchy, so we should watch her. Fear and I volunteer."

Rathe gave him a droll look. "Why the fuck would I allow that? You're both already affected by her."

"Exactly!" Viper agreed. "We're already affected, as you say. This way, we're exposed to her, and you aren't."

Fear could see the thought moving behind Rathe's eyes, could see the question forming before he spoke, and Fear was still taken aback when he asked, "And how do I know you won't lie to protect her?"

Fear started to growl out a reply but stopped himself. Much as it chafed, he had to admit the question wasn't entirely unwarranted. Even so, it still pissed him off.

He'd been unfailingly loyal from the moment he'd been conscripted into Rathe's service. That he and Viper had both deviated from their loyalty, for the first time in their fucking lives, should have told Rathe there was something exceptional about her. Instead, Rathe was expecting the worst. This shouldn't have surprised him either, but he'd hoped his Prince would let go of his suspicion long enough to see her, truly see her.

Viper didn't share his restraint and scoffed irritably, "You've got more trust issues than I do. Under her 'spell' or not, you know we wouldn't do anything to bring Ehrendil's wrath down on us." He paused a beat and pursed his lips. "Well... not without a really good reason, anyway. And she's the best reason."

Rathe gave Viper a withering look and bit out, "If that was your attempt to convince me you're not compromised, you failed. Miserably. You're both blind to her."

"Or you are," Fear countered, holding Rathe's gaze steadily.

A tense beat passed before Rathe slowly blew out a frustrated breath. Obviously, his friend didn't believe he was wrong in this matter. But, it was exceedingly rare for he and

Viper to go against Rathe. That was finally sinking in and, perhaps, even casting a shadow of doubt, no matter how small.

It was enough.

Rathe held up a hand. "You're right. There's a chance, albeit a *very* small one, I'm incorrect about the girl and her intentions."

He watched silently as his friend began pacing across the room, a rare display of worry from the usually intensely restrained man. Finally, Rathe stilled and faced him, searching first his eyes, then Viper's.

"Fine. Viper, you take day shift. Fear, night. Follow her. I want to know where she goes, who she talks to, her Court, powers, and contacts. But, I want both your words: if the pull to her gets worse, you'll leave immediately. I won't risk either of you just to find out more about her."

Fear nodded once. "My vow."

"Aye aye, Captain!" With that, Viper disappeared down the hallway, no doubt headed to his rooms to pack supplies for a stakeout.

Fear watched him go with carefully hidden envy. Being that Fear was Night Court, it made sense to put him on night watch. Not only were his powers stronger then, but many of them, like *Shadow Jumping*, only worked in the dark.

Yet, logic did nothing to temper his impatience to see her again.

Turning, he descended the stairs to the garage and immersed himself in work, needing to keep his hands, and his mind, busy to make the time pass faster.

ARAWYN

Four days. It'd been four days since she'd been at the gym, since she'd gotten home and found her property had been invaded, since she'd gone to the docks only to be surprised by her three strangers. Four days since she'd learned the names of her devilish blonde and familiar stranger. Viper. Fearson. Four days since any of the delusions she'd had about those three men had been crushed by the sharp lens of reality.

She'd known they were dangerous the moment she saw them in the club, but drug dealers? It wasn't like Arawyn was a saint herself, but she generally tried to be a good person. Dealing drugs crossed a line, and she was still struggling to come to terms with just how wrong she'd been.

Unless… was it possible she hadn't seen things correctly? It'd been night, after all, and she'd been decently far away.

No. She had great vision at night, an oddity that set her apart from others. White bricks of some sort of product had definitely exchanged hands, and she knew better than to believe it was powdered sugar, especially after the throaty moan Viper had given when he'd tasted it.

How could I have been so wrong?

Being in Viper's arms had been... fun, and just as addicting as the cocaine or heroin they'd bought. But, there was no way she'd allow herself a repeat, if he magically showed up again.

Right?

Her heart gave a little squeeze at the thought of never seeing them again.

Dammit.

Huffing in frustration at her own circling thoughts, she turned into the lot and parked, hoping Braven was still there and would be up for a night of sparring. Hitting something was sure to help calm her mind and bring her clarity. It wasn't her usual night at the gym, but she didn't think her friend would mind, and she could really use the workout, if only to stop thinking about *them*.

Standing in front of the gym's doors, Arawyn read the note taped to the inside for the second time.

Gone? Gone where? The man doesn't know the meaning of 'personal life.'

Still frowning, she moved around to the back of the building. About three months after she started going to Braven's gym, he told her if he ever had to leave, he'd hide a key to the place and the alarm codes behind a loose brick.

It had been a long time since she'd had anyone truly care about what happened to her, and she'd been so stunned she hadn't questioned him about it. He never brought it up again after that, and he hadn't left, so she'd never had cause to wonder if he truly meant it.

Apparently, he had.

Using the tip of one of her daggers, she wiggled the brick free, slid her hand into the hole, and blindly felt around until she encountered metal.

Back at the front, she stared through the glass door into the dark building, key still clasped in her hand, but made no move to enter. If she were honest with herself, she hadn't truly come to spar. She'd wanted to question him, to find out why he felt even slightly like *them*. Maybe he knew them. Maybe he'd have insight to help her decide if they were trustworthy or simply men she needed to avoid, if she didn't want to borrow trouble.

She had so many questions, and suddenly it felt imperative she get the answers before she ran into the trio again, because something told her she would. She hadn't seen the last of them. Not even close.

Now, with Brave gone, that wasn't happening, and the thought of being in there by herself held no appeal.

Turning away as she pocketed the key, she made it a single step back to her SUV before movement had her jerking to a stop. There was a child standing there, staring at her. He looked like he couldn't be older than nine, maybe ten.

"Holy shi- oot, kid! You scared the fuc- er, fudge out of me," Arawyn gasped, trying to censor herself mid-heart attack.

She had zero experience with children, but she knew enough to know you weren't supposed to cuss at them.

Or point guns at them.

Wincing, she stopped her hand mid-motion from automatically reaching for her weapon.

Blinking, she realized the child, who'd somehow snuck up on her without her hearing him, looked like he was about three seconds from keeling over. There were dark circles under his brown eyes and his hair was tangled and matted to his head. The pajamas he wore, patterned with cartoon characters she didn't recognize, were smudged with dirt, and his feet were bare like he'd crawled out of bed in the middle of the night.

"Jesus, are you okay? How did you get here?" The closest neighborhood she knew of was a few miles away. "Where are your parents?"

She eyed the small, nearly deserted corner grocery store and gas station down the street. It was the only logical place he could have come from at this hour.

Late-night grocery run? Seems like a weird thing to do at ten o'clock, but what the hell do I know about parenting?

Arawyn scanned the street and dark parking lot, but her's was the only vehicle there. Looking at him again, waiting for an answer, she wondered if she needed to take him to the nearest hospital. There would be police there. If he'd been kidnapped, they'd be able to help, and if he'd sleep-walked, they'd have a better chance of finding his parents than she would.

The boy opened his mouth, but all that came out was a raspy, wet rattle that sent a chill down her spine and brought to mind every horror movie she'd ever watched.

Oookay, he's definitely sick with something.

Arawyn hadn't been ill a day in her life, and she still had to fight back the urge to cover her mouth and nose so she didn't catch whatever it was he had.

"Come on, buddy. We can go in here and call your paren—"

That was as far as she got before he scared the hell out of her a second time by slipping his hand into hers. His fingers were nearly as chilled as the cool metal of the ring he wore that pressed uncomfortably into her skin.

Instinct had her yanking back slightly before she stopped herself. Thoroughly unnerved she hadn't heard him move, but not wanting to traumatize the poor thing more than he clearly already was, she smiled tightly and let him keep ahold of her hand.

"It's okay, kid, we'll... whoa."

Arawyn braced herself against the door of the gym with her free hand as a wave of lightheadedness swept through her. Blinking rapidly, wondering if she'd forgotten to eat, she glanced back at the kid to reassure him she was okay only to be hit with the insane sensation she couldn't move. Her feet felt as though they were encased in concrete, and her arms suddenly felt sluggish and heavy.

"What the fuck?" she choked out, heart skipping a beat as adrenaline surged through her in a rush.

The sickly, innocent-looking child he'd appeared to be seconds before was gone. Where his face had been slack, expressionless and dull, it was now nightmarishly animated. His eyes were wide, feverish, and unblinking, glittering with something feral and greedy, and his teeth were bared in a hair-raising parody of a grin.

Arawyn tried to jerk her hand out of his, but her movements were slow and uncoordinated. He gripped her tighter, his hold unexpectedly strong.

Another wave of lightheadedness, stronger than the first, had her stumbling as she tried to move back, and she still couldn't shake him loose. He followed on silent feet, continuing to grip her hand painfully tight, mouth stretched in that eerie, hungry grin.

Black dots swam in front of her vision, coalescing until the world grew darker at the edges. Arawyn tried again to rip her hand away, but the child's nails bit into her skin, leaving long, bloody gashes behind.

Her skin heated suddenly, then rapidly became a tingling sensation like ants were crawling all over her. The unusual feeling demanded her attention, but she couldn't think clearly as another wave of mindless dizziness swamped her. All she could do was stare down at the strange, feral child with confusion and struggle to break free of his hold on her.

She could have sworn his eyes were glowing, a savage wildness gleaming through the darkness trying to drag her down.

Her head spun sickeningly. The ground felt as though it was moving beneath her feet, pitching her forward and back, an angry sea in the midst of a storm. She swayed and tried to stay upright while her skin continued to heat, like it had been doused in acid. Instead of clearing the haze enveloping her mind, the pain only seemed to deepen the disorientation and weakness.

Without warning, the well of power surged in her chest, rebelling against whatever was happening.

It simmered and sparked as the strangest feeling overtook her. It felt as though her power was being dragged out from within her, the sensation of it being yanked and pulled away, causing panic to rise in her chest until she could barely breathe.

Tongue thick, throat tight with nausea, she slurred, "Lemme go."

The heat in Arawyn's skin turned electric. Tiny zaps skated along her arms, shoulders, and back in a wave of knee-weakening agony. She swallowed a moan, the pain reaching almost unbearable levels. Then, the scent of burnt flesh filled her nose.

Renewing her struggles, Arawyn tried frantically to escape his grip, the feeling of the delicate bones of her wrist grinding together adding another layer to the torment.

Just as she was sure she was going to pass out, a power both hers, yet, somehow foreign, rose up, trying to protect her.

From a child?

Nothing made sense. Not the unhinged grimace the boy wore or the unearthly hiss he released as her power lashed at him.

Desperate, knowing she couldn't let herself lose consciousness, she didn't fight this new facet of her power. Gritting her teeth around a scream, she held on, the electricity coursing through her growing until it left her in a shockwave.

The pained, inhuman hiss of the boy almost matched the one escaping her own lips as her power immediately rebounded, crashing back into her chest like a wrecking ball.

As the endless well inside of her drank down her returning power, a wave of cold air washed over her like a soothing breeze a moment before a large shadow fell across the pavement. The boy's reaction to the coldness was vastly different. He recoiled like it physically hurt him, jerking away from her with a howl.

Her knees grew weak as he released her. Vision swimming, the darkness creeping in grew thicker. Through the limp strands of hair hanging in her face, she watched the hazy figure of the kid turn and run until the night cloaked him in shadows.

Arawyn tried to brace herself, to keep herself standing,

but her energy waned. She sagged backward on legs that refused to hold her any longer.

Darkness embraced her as she teetered on the edge of consciousness. Expecting to hit the sidewalk, she gasped when the scent of amber, oakmoss, and winter berries surrounded her like a warm hug a moment before strong arms wrapped around her.

Chapter Eighteen

Arawyn

"I've got you," a deep, rich voice rumbled through her. Comforting coolness wrapped around her just as softly as the strong arms holding her close, chasing away some of the desire to sink further into the darkness.

Prying her lids open, she blinked until Fearson's face materialized, his handsome features tight with concern.

"What happened?" he questioned, his voice a menacing growl but his eyes soft with a promise to keep her safe.

She opened her mouth to respond, but all that came out was a whimper, the lingering pain sizzling across her skin and throbbing in her chest, stealing her words.

Blearily, she watched him scan the shadows and pools of light from the evenly spaced street lamps, looking for her attacker, but everything was quiet now, the only movement that of the stop light on the corner bleeding from yellow to red.

With a tilt of his head, he drew a long, deep inhale, then released an equally deep growl.

"It's gone now," he murmured, gazing down at her with worry narrowing the skin between his brows. "Fuck, I should've been here sooner." When he caught the confusion tightening her features, he cleared his throat. "I was tied up with work or I would have found you at nightfall."

She tried to sit up, tried to question him, but a fresh wave of dizziness washed over her with the force of a tsunami, sending her dropping limply back into his arms. Fearson's hold tightened around her, pulling her back into his chest.

"Easy, now, Baby. Don't try to get up just yet. I've got you. You're safe."

Safe.

That she believed him was unexplainable, but her heart warmed as he held her protectively close. If this mountain of a man wanted to hurt her, he would have done so already. She was at her most vulnerable and couldn't fend off another attack if she tried, yet, he helped her. He'd scared off the creepy kid, held her like she were precious to him, and stayed vigilant, scanning the streets for any other threat to emerge from the shadows, ready to shield her, to fight for her, even though they'd only recently met. She had questions for him —a lot of questions—but they swam out of reach as she fought to contain the static rapidly growing in her mind.

Darkness crowded at the edges of her vision, and she knew she was going to pass out. Using the last of her strength, she dug the key to the gym out of her pocket.

In that moment, it didn't matter he was essentially a stranger to her. He was here, protecting her. That same familiar feeling of home washed through her, easing her mind as she pressed the key into his hand.

"Here," she managed weakly, hating how breathy and frail she sounded. "In there." Her head lolled on her shoulders just as she felt his fingers close around the key.

The last thing she remembered before the world went dark was Fearson scooping her up like she weighed nothing at all, cradling her against his chest, murmuring sweet reassurances she was going to be okay.

The first thing Arawyn noticed as she began to rouse was the scent of the gym—rubber mats and old sweat that never went away, despite the disinfectant—all clashing with the intoxicating mix of cedar, dark winter berries, and oakmoss.

Warm arms tightened around her, holding her against a hard body.

Still lingering in the space between wakefulness and sleep, she snuggled into the embrace, holding on tightly to her recurring dream. It was lovely here. She felt cared for. Safe.

These moments were the ones she held on to when she opened her eyes and found herself alone.

Arawyn didn't need a man. She could protect herself. She'd survived this long on her own, only occasionally scratching the itch with one-night stands. She was a strong, independent, capable woman.

That didn't mean it wasn't something she wanted. These men haunting her dreams hadn't just awoken the hunger in her for companionship and love, they'd intensified it a hundred fold.

But, she was equally as wary of them, equally as hesitant about the feelings they inspired. Experience told her nothing good would come of letting anyone get that close. It was only here, in her dreams, where she could embrace the fantasy.

"Arawyn," a deep voice called.

Jesus.

Her name in that deep, rich tone made her want to curl her toes.

Say it again.

She wanted to hear it. Wanted to wrap herself in it and carry it with her when she woke up.

Her lashes fluttered at the sound of a low chuckle.

"Arawyn." This time, the voice sounded more amused.

Her brows furrowed, her nose scrunching up as she tried to open her eyes.

It all came crashing back to her then. The gym, the note, the key... the creepy-as-fuck little kid.

She opened her eyes and gazed into Fearson's handsome face. His stormy grey stare was filled with concern, just the faintest tinge of mirth, and... Was he blushing a little?

"F- Fear?" The nickname slipped off her tongue without thought, but she immediately loved the taste of it, the intimacy of sharing something personal with the incredibly gorgeous mountain of a man holding her like she was precious.

He reached for her, running the back of his knuckle down the curve of her cheek. "Are you alright, *moín Firláh?*"

Was she? It was a damn good question.

She took stock of herself so she could give him an honest answer. Somehow, she knew it was the only kind he would accept. If she gave him some half-assed line about being fine, he'd never believe her.

"I don't know what happened," she answered honestly. "I'm still dizzy."

The fluorescent bulbs lining the ceiling were blurring in and out of focus, and despite how hard she tried to sit up, she felt like she'd just run a marathon, and then tried to climb a mountain. Her arms were useless things, her hands barely able to make fists.

Fear helped her until she was sitting beside him on the workout bench. She gripped the edge, keeping herself vertical.

Fuck.

She'd never been so incapacitated before.

She didn't like it, at all, and she especially hated looking weak in front of Fearson. She was also grateful as hell he'd been there. Which begged the question...

"What are you doing here?" She glanced sideways at him, watching the tension that pulled across his shoulders.

"I promised I'd find you," he said honestly. His grey eyes flashed with what she thought was self-reproach, but it was gone before she could be sure of what she saw. "A man never breaks a vow." His gaze dropped to her lips before returning to hers. "And I wanted to see you again."

Whether it was smart or not, a small smile curled her lips. "So, you're stalking me?"

First, she found out he and his friends were drug dealers, and now, she learned he'd been stalking her. There was no other explanation as to how he'd found her at the gym no one knew she frequented or how he'd gotten there in just the nick of time.

The real question was: why the hell was she feeling flattered he'd wanted to see her again?

Well, that's that. All the isolation has finally driven me insane.

She should've been mad, but insane or not, she wasn't the slightest bit upset to see him again. He'd been there for her right when she'd needed him, like an avenging angel. He'd kept her safe and taken care of her. She liked it. More than that... she liked *him*.

Fear reached up and rubbed a hand across his chest, his lips quirking in a small smile. "If following the draw I feel to you is called stalking, then yes. You could say that."

Arawyn gasped at his honest confession, the quiet, breathy sound filling the air between them. Her fingers trailed along her collarbone, palm grazing across her chest where the pull that never left her resided. Even as they sat at a small distance, she could feel the tug, the desire to move closer. It spanned between them, and she realized her intuition had been right.

He could feel it, same as she could.

A thought occurred to her on the heels of that one—he had to know she'd been watching them that night at the docks, had to have felt her there. Had the others felt her, as well? Had all three known she was there, spying on them in the darkness?

Why hadn't they said anything? Why had they let her listen in on their deal?

Maybe the dark one wanted her to see it, wanted it to scare her off. Oddly, it was starting to have the opposite effect. That they'd allowed her to spy on them intrigued her. They were mysteries wrapped in enigmas, and damn if that wasn't a draw all it's own, one just as strong as the tug in her chest. She wanted to learn more.

"Will you tell me what happened?" Fear asked, the demand to know barely contained, but he waited; he didn't press.

She liked that about him. Fear was very clearly strong and capable, but he didn't behave as though he were god's gift to women. In their few encounters, he'd always trusted her to hold her own, to be just as strong and capable as he was. Even after rescuing her a few minutes ago, he didn't look at her like she was weak or lesser than him. His desire to help was genuine, as was his desire to avenge her.

Her heart squeezed in her chest, because even though it likely wasn't warranted, she worried about the child who had seemed so lost and vulnerable when she first laid eyes on him.

Something wasn't right about the whole situation, but she couldn't make sense of it.

Despite her hesitation, Arawyn told Fear the whole story and watched his eyes darken until they were nearly black.

A dark curse fell from his lips in a language Arawyn didn't understand, and he pushed to his feet. Fear paced in front of her, only going a few steps before pivoting and starting again. He scrubbed a large hand down his face, then combed his fingers through the thick beard covering the strong line of his jaw.

She watched through narrowed eyes while he practically prowled across the linoleum. He knew something. The question was, what?

"What is it? What's going on?"

Her legs were still shaky when she pushed herself to her feet, and the room tilted on its axis. Her equilibrium was off.

Arawyn felt herself listing to the side before Fear was in front of her, his large hands clasping around her biceps gently. He pulled her into his body, and she placed her palms flat against his chest instead of pushing him away.

Jesus, this man is beautiful.

The moment she touched him, electricity shivered through her, making her breath hitch. The draw pulling her to him intensified until it felt the connection between them should be visible.

Fear was chiseled, his muscles sculpted and honed beneath her fingertips. The desire to explore became a visceral need, and she let her hands slowly drop to trail along the deep ridges of his abdomen hiding beneath the dark cotton of his shirt.

His low, growling purr spurred her on. She let her fingers graze across the valleys and plains of his stomach, each etched line a story of how hard he worked to keep his body in such incredible shape. It spoke to a dedication Arawyn herself had, and it warmed her to know they shared another thing in common.

It spoke to discipline, mastery, and years of hard work.

Somehow, she knew he was just as skilled a fighter as she was, if not more, and she found herself wanting to test that theory, to spar and fight, to dance across the mats and see just how lethal he was.

The thought of seeing him in action, of watching the corded muscles shift beneath his skin while he fought, became a thrumming pulse between her thighs.

Gently, so very gently, Fear guided her a short distance away to the mirror-covered wall, then helped lower her until she was sitting safely on the floor.

She swallowed back the protest making an effort to rise

when he turned away, curling her hand into fists to keep them from reaching out and grabbing him, from pulling him down to her, against her.

Despite the persistent weakness making her feel unsteady, and the questions swirling in her mind, she wanted him, *badly*. It took every ounce of control she could muster to keep from whimpering when he left her there, scolding herself internally that she wasn't desperate enough to have sex with him on the floor of her friend's gym.

Instead, she watched him.

As big as he was, his movements were surprisingly graceful, conveying his skills as a trained fighter. Not everyone would see that when they first looked at him, but she did. She recognized the tightly contained ferocity just below the surface, and the control he wore as a second skin.

Fear struck her as the type of man who used his strength and cunning carefully. He didn't flaunt his masculinity like most men she encountered, and that intrigued her.

Everything about this man called to her in a way no one had before... with the exception of his friends.

Chapter Nineteen

Arawyn

When Fear returned to her side, he swiftly took the spot beside her and pressed a cold cup of water into her hands.

"Drink," he ordered softly. "It will help restore your strength."

Arawyn nodded and did as she was told. The cool water trickling down her throat was heaven, and she took a moment to gather herself before turning to thank him for the thoughtful gesture.

The words died on her tongue from the untamed interest she saw reflected in his grey stare. This close to him, she could see the silver flecks within, and the nearly lavender starburst ringing his pupils. The color was so unique she caught herself staring, drowning in the intensity of his steadfast attention.

"Thank you," she whispered, leaning her head back against the mirrored wall so she didn't lean forward to kiss him.

Fear lifted his hand and cupped her face in one calloused palm. The pad of his thumb stroked along her jawline.

"Are you feeling better?"

"I think so." She nodded slightly, and nuzzled into his hold.

It felt good to be touched. She hadn't realized just how much she'd missed his hands on her body, and she welcomed the sweet caress.

"Good," Fear said, dipping his chin. A sliver of relief washed through his features, and his shoulders relaxed marginally. "Good," he repeated, releasing a weighted exhale, like he'd been holding his breath this whole time. "It didn't smell exactly right, but if that was an *Aswang* like I'm thinking, it can take time for the effects to wear off. You still feel strong. I don't think it took much."

He said the words so casually that it took a suspended moment for them to register. Trying to hide the shock and excitement flooding her in a rush, Arawyn sat a little straighter against the wall. Fear was right. With every passing minute, she felt better.

And that left her with the strength to question what the fuck he was talking about.

'I don't think it took too much.' He had to be talking about her power? Right? He truly was like her, wasn't he? The questions circled through her mind like vultures, but a more pressing concern shouldered its way to the forefront, one she couldn't ignore even if she wanted to.

If she revealed her ignorance, would he explain, or would he shut down and play it off? Worse, would he leave? Arawyn wanted to believe he would answer her questions, but she couldn't take the chance. Still, she couldn't let go of the opportunity to learn more entirely.

Hoping against hope the being he'd named wasn't something all her kind knew about, she asked as casually as she could, "Aswang?"

Fear's dark brows drew together, creating a rather adorable crease in the center of his forehead, just above the line of his nose.

"Aye. We don't see them often in this realm, but there are a few of them in the human realm."

Realm? Human? Fuck me, so I am *an alien?*

Arawyn nodded like it all made sense, but she was silently freaking out. What was happening to her life? Ever since that surge nine days ago, it seemed like every possible alien in the city was coming out of the woodwork. That may not have been such a bad thing, except most of them were hellbent on coming after her.

Fear tilted his head, studying her as though he could read her thoughts. Maybe he could. That was damned disconcerting.

Changing the subject, she tried to cover her blunder with more questions. "What will happen to the child... er, the Aswang?"

"I put Viper on it. He'll track it down and make sure it doesn't harm you or anyone else, again."

The vision of her devilish blonde tracking down the

threat like some psychotic Sherlock Holmes was oddly comforting.

And, yet...

The lost look on the boy's face haunted her, as did the vicious change in his eyes—from innocent to predatory. Something didn't sit right, but no matter how hard she tried, she couldn't put her finger on it.

The more she mulled it over, the more she could have sworn the boy was sick. He'd seemed almost gaunt. Ill.

Like a freight train, it hit her: it was the same look her neighbor had. The same look on the homeless woman who'd stared at her in the gym's parking lot not five nights before. The same look on the man she'd caught staring at her across the street when she'd run to the Post Office earlier that day.

A cold chill wormed its way through her chest.

No. It wasn't possible. The situation with her neighbor had been her fault. She knew that. But, that had happened because of the surge. She'd kept her power tightly fisted ever since, only letting it out in tiny, controllable tendrils. There was no way she could've drawn these people to her like she had Peter.

Looking inside herself, she double-checked her power but found it just as leashed as it always was.

Whatever happened to her the day her power burst from her was a one-off. An oddity. A mistake she wouldn't allow to happen again.

But, the notion this was all somehow her fault wasn't easily shaken, snaking through her mind like a poison vine.

The child was just a few years younger than she'd been when her life imploded. When the curse that followed her like a bad omen first appeared. When her powers changed everything.

If she were somehow responsible for ruining the life of a child, she'd never forgive herself.

She wanted badly, so very badly, to believe the boy had been an Aswang like Fear presumed. She wanted to believe in the tales he spun, if only to stop the dread collecting in the pit of her stomach, but she just couldn't be sure.

Arawyn needed time to think, research the foreign names of the creatures both Fear and Orin had mentioned to her, and come to her own conclusions, outside of the watchful eye of the steady, sexy mountain man.

Arawyn stared up at Fear. She wanted to trust him more than anything, but she just couldn't. Not yet. This close to him, it was hard to remember the last time she'd seen him, he'd been buying what looked a hell of a lot like drugs from Orin.

There might be a perfectly logical explanation...

She couldn't deny it was a possibility, a very slight possibility, but she wouldn't lie to herself either. Getting involved with a bad boy was a terrible idea, no matter how much her heart, and her sex drive, wished otherwise. The last thing she needed was to borrow trouble. She had enough of that all on her own.

Still, there was a part of her that didn't want to inherently distrust him, that wanted to prove her first impression correct. From the moment she met him, Fear felt familiar and safe.

Maybe if I followed him...

The thought bloomed like a spring flower bursting open in the first rays of sunlight, only to quickly die away. No. There was no way she'd be able to trail Fear. The connection he'd acknowledged they shared was too strong and would ruin any chance she had at remaining inconspicuous.

But, once it entered her mind, she just couldn't shake it.

She wanted to find a way to prove to herself, once and for all, he was worthy of her trust, that he wasn't a drug dealer or something far worse. If she could trust him, maybe, just maybe, she'd feel comfortable revealing her own secrets and asking the questions she couldn't bring herself to voice.

Unfortunately, what she truly needed right then was space. There was no way she could think clearly and rationally when every breath of his scent made her want to lean closer, to press her body against his, and have a repeat of the night they met.

Downing the rest of her water, she let it fortify her for what she had to do next.

"I have to go," she whispered, regret coloring her words even though she tried to hide it.

"Arawyn," he pressed, her name rolling off his tongue like a song as she rose to her feet.

She praised herself for not falling right back on her ass and for resisting the desire to heed his unspoken plea that she stay. It took everything in her to turn her back and stride away to throw the plastic cup into the trash can near the door, and it took even more not to turn around when she felt Fearson warm her back, trailing after her like a protective shadow.

With a resigned sigh, he flipped the lights off, casting them in darkness as she opened the door. The light breeze filtered past them, and she instantly missed the strength of Fear's scent as they stepped into the cool night.

The encroaching autumn air stole some of her warmth until Fear brushed against her as he exited the gym, standing close, guarding her while she locked up.

Like a true gentleman, he walked her to her car, the soft

thud of their footsteps the only sound between them. Every step felt like a decision she had to consciously make over and over again, one that would take her away from Fear.

Arawyn knew what she had to do, knew she was making the right choice, but it didn't make it any easier. As much as she needed the down time to process everything on her own, she hated to leave him.

How is it possible to care so much so quickly?

She didn't know, and a part of her didn't want to question it.

The fact was, she did care about Fear, about Viper, and, hell, even about the dark one. Just as she'd felt comfortable the first time she met Braven, she felt infinitely more so whenever she was around Fear and his friends.

Reaching for her keys, Arawyn unlocked her SUV, and Fear pulled open the door for her. She could feel his eyes tracing over her curves when she climbed into the vehicle like it was a physical touch coaxing her to change her mind.

"Arawyn." Fear's deep voice broke the silence, rumbling into the night like a purr. His hand landed gently on her leg as she sat in her seat, daring her to look at him.

When she did, her breath caught. In the moonlight, his eyes appeared silver, and his pale skin almost glowed. He was even more beautiful under the stars. Oh god, she was tempted.

She wanted to stay, to sway forward and taste his full lips. She wanted to tease the seam of his mouth until he opened and devoured her like he had on the dance floor all those nights ago.

"You tempt me," he all but growled, repeating the words he'd whispered in her ear that night, his gaze dropping to her mouth.

Sitting in her car as she was, their height difference was lessened, and it would take almost nothing for him to swoop down and make good on the way he looked at her.

"You tempt me, too," she said quietly, owning the attraction thrumming between them.

"Tonight didn't go as I'd hoped, though I'm very glad I was here," he started. "I'd like to see you again. Will you meet me back here one night hence?"

Arawyn smiled at his question and the strange way he spoke. "Tomorrow?"

He hummed his agreement, the vibration of it settling low in her belly.

Arawyn looked at him. Really looked at him. Her mind rebelled with all the reasons why saying 'yes' was a terrible idea. But, her heart? It gave the answer she longed to give freely.

"Okay."

Fear's smile was dazzling. Dizzyingly so. Her pulse skittered like a schoolgirl reacting to her first crush. She reached for the steering wheel, just to have something to hold onto, wondering if she were truly okay after the incident earlier.

The flash of his perfect, white teeth was as bright as the genuine relief and happiness glimmering in his far-too-captivating eyes.

I'm a goner. What have I gotten myself into?

"It's a date, *moín Firláh*."

Date.

That simple word set butterflies fluttering through her stomach as she settled into her seat and let the gentle man shut her door. The feeling followed her as she left him behind and drove down the dark country roads, warming her all the way home.

Fearson

Fearson's thumbs fumbled over the ridiculously tiny phone in his hands. Seven years in this realm, and he still wasn't used to the technology they used. It was the largest one on the market, and it was still too damn small. Spellcheck fixed the numerous errors where his large fingers pressed the wrong key, or worse, multiple keys, while he sent a quick text to Viper, demanding an update on the search for the Aswang.

With dawn on the horizon, it was his friend's turn to tail Arawyn, but watching her taillights disappear sat like a lead fucking weight in his stomach. He didn't want her out of his sight.

For a Fae from the Night Court, that was disconcerting on many levels. Women of the Night were known for being exceptional fighters. They were cunning and brave, strong and swift. Though Fear still hadn't been able to discern which Court Arawyn hailed from, a fact that increasingly bothered him, she unquestioningly displayed all the characteristics valued in Night Fae women.

Yet, even knowing she could take care of herself, that she

could and had, protected herself all these years without him, he still wanted to be by her side, to guard her and keep her safe.

Worry raged like the strongest winter storm inside his chest at the thought of what she'd been through tonight.

If I hadn't been here...

His hands clenched into tight fists at his sides, the muscles in his forearms straining from how much strength he used to hold himself back from pummeling the brick exterior of the gym Arawyn frequented.

Everything inside him rebelled at the thought of what could have happened if he'd arrived even a minute later. That he could have been there sooner had he not been hunting down a rogue Fae with Rathe to send to the King ate away at him like acid. He'd just found Arawyn, and just as quickly could have lost her.

The ding of his phone drew his attention, alerting him of an incoming message from Viper saying he hadn't found the vile creature yet. Anger the threat was still out there shot through him.

Needing to find an outlet for his rage, he narrowed his gaze in the direction the creature had disappeared. He'd wanted to track it, to hunt it down, and kill it the moment it had released his *Firláh*, but attending to Arawyn and guarding her while she was vulnerable was far more important.

Now, with her safely on her way home and Viper leaving to watch over her, he was free to take over the hunt, exact his own revenge, end the threat, and guarantee her safety.

Lifting his nose into the air, he drew a long, deep breath, sorting the various scents filtering past his senses. Gasoline fumes were the most prevalent, followed by the lingering scent of sweat seeping past the locked glass door of the gym. The secluded area on the outskirts of the city wasn't the cleanest, and a foul stench leaked from a nearby dumpster. A dog hiding behind the neighboring building was in desperate need of a bath, and if he were a betting man, he'd wager someone had pissed in an alleyway just down the block sometime earlier in the evening.

None of that interested him, and he quickly discarded them in favor of Arawyn's signature: moonlit lilies, spring storms, and warm vanilla.

The combination wrapped around him and refused to let go. It captivated him, seeping around him as he drew another breath, needing more of it inside his body. A groan rumbled past his lips unbidden, arousal firing his blood.

By the Gods, but he wanted her. Never in his life had he been so intrigued, so utterly bewitched by a woman.

Moonlit lilies reminded him of the mountainside meadows of home, awakening a longing in him akin to the pull in his chest that had flared to life when he met the gorgeous little temptress. He knew he'd never be able to sit through another thunderstorm without thinking of Arawyn, without wanting to hold her through it while they watched the rain fall and the lightning flash.

Fuck, he'd never been so taken with a woman before, but Rathe's warning wouldn't quite leave him.

One thing was clear: Rathe wasn't entirely wrong. Something more was going on with their little Arawyn, though exactly what was frustratingly elusive.

Was she a spy for Ehrendil?

The possibility was remote—very, very remote—but he trusted Rathe with his life, and wouldn't cast his concern aside completely.

But, if he followed his gut?

Arawyn was many things—a mystery, a beauty, a fucking challenge—but he highly doubted she was out to deceive them.

He had the overwhelming sense she needed them. All of them.

She'd been attacked tonight right in front of his eyes. The rage that swamped him when he saw her silhouette in the distance struggling, fighting, falling... He'd seen red. The need to protect her, to eradicate the threat, overtook everything else. He'd sent a wave of power toward the Aswang to weaken it, then used his abilities to Shadow Jump across the distance and reach her side before she hit the pavement, catching her lithe little body in his arms.

Regretfully, he moved past her signature, drawing in one last inhale to take in the sickly sweet scent of burnt marshmallows, the woodsy aroma of pine, and a hint of sour cherries.

The Aswang's wasn't quite right, but it'd been ages since he'd seen, much less smelled, one, so it was possible he'd forgotten their exact signature. They were rare in the human realm. In fact, he hadn't been aware of any near their city, a concern he'd have to raise with Rathe when he checked in next.

For now, he let his power loose and used it to trail after the being like a haunting nightmare.

Chapter Twenty

Arawyn

Arawyn had a startling sense of déjà vu when she pulled into her driveway. Right away, her hackles rose, and the tiny, fine hairs on the back of her neck stood on end.

Someone had been there.

She couldn't see anything amiss, had no proof, other than the tingling awareness and the intuition she trusted above all else. But, those were enough. They had never steered her wrong before, and she wasn't about to start doubting herself now.

She unfisted her power and let it unfurl outward, sending tiny tendrils in every direction to search out the threat.

Nothing.

The only thing she sensed was the lingering feeling of something... bitter. She could almost taste it, almost smell it. It was acrid, like rotting lemons, and repulsive, akin to spoiled garbage with an undertone of wet dog.

Chasing away the shadows of the night, the moon waned as the first rays of sunlight crept into the twilight sky the way she crept her SUV up the driveaway, slowly and with purpose. She kept her eyes peeled for any movement in the lingering darkness, scanning her yard, her house, her windows.

It only took her a moment to park and draw her gun. Fingers tightening around the weapon, she stepped from the car, gaze constantly on the move, while she swept her way toward the front door.

Just like the other day, she backed up the steps, refusing to give the tree line her back, and aimed into the forest beyond. Her focus narrowed on the swaying trees at the edge of her yard, staring, watching, waiting for the threat she knew was out there somewhere to emerge.

A soft, fluttering sound, as soft as the flap of a butterfly's wing, caught her attention, and she spared a quick glance over her shoulder to see another image pinned to her front door.

Déjà-fucking-vu.

Her brows drew together, confusion dawning as she reached behind her and yanked the picture free.

What the fuck? Again?

Her heart didn't slow the rapid pace it beat in her chest, but her arm didn't waver as she held the gun outstretched, trained into the distance while she spared a quick moment to study the glossy paper in her hand.

The photo was fuzzy, the image clearly not high-resolution. It was pixelated and dark, the brightness increased only enough to make out the figures who'd been captured. But, she didn't need any help recognizing the subjects.

The moment frozen in time was also one she'd never forget.

Being wrapped in Viper's arms on the dock, his nose buried in the crook of her neck as he drew in her scent, her gun pressed against his ribs. A smile wanted to curl her lips at the memory, but wariness and anger prevented the emotion from fully developing.

Because Viper's face had been scratched out with something sharp.

The gloss and ink had been scraped away, leaving nothing but white marks where his devilishly handsome features should be.

The first photo had felt like a taunt—whoever left it got a thrill from letting her know they were watching her. A cat playing a dispassionately sadistic game with a mouse. This time was different. There was a distinct sense of anger and jealousy emanating from the picture. What had changed? She hadn't lost control, her power hadn't surged again, and her neighbor was dead. Why, then, was someone stalking her, leaving her these pictures like ominous little gifts?

It didn't make any sense.

Was it possible that this had something to do with Viper, Fear, and their dark friend, rather than being connected to her directly? Had she been caught up in a mafia feud? Was she being targeted by one of their enemies? It was possible, but she had to admit the images felt personal.

This is really getting out of hand.

Arawyn shoved the image into her back pocket where

she'd been keeping the first, refusing to spend another second even partly distracted.

Something wasn't right.

Who would have taken the picture? Someone had been watching them. Following her. And she had no earthly idea who. Or why.

What the hell is going on? Why am I being targeted by everyone and their fucking alien cousins all of a sudden?

That magnetism she'd struggled with her whole life had been under tight rein. She'd even given up practicing her powers since the incident with her neighbor.

Better safe than sorry. Not that her precautions were currently doing her any good.

This is bad. This is really bad.

The ominous feeling surrounding her since she pulled onto her property grew. The sense someone was watching her here and now suddenly crawled over her skin like a million tiny ants. A chill raced down her spine, despite the warming rays of the morning sun.

If someone was still here, there had to be a reason for it. They wanted something. Or they wanted *her*.

Either way, she was ready to end this now. She wouldn't run. She wouldn't hide. Unlike her neighbor, this threat seemed worse. Whoever was out there was intent on toying with her, trying to get inside her mind with every picture they left, and she was over it.

As much as she hated the idea of adding another life to her tally of sins, she wouldn't allow whomever was targeting her to continue their little game until it was her life on the line. Besides, her aim was impeccable, and she could always shoot the prick somewhere that would merely incapacitate, rather than kill. Then she'd question the hell out of them until she got some answers.

Let them come to you. Keep the house at your back.

Carefully avoiding the creaky spots on her front steps, she crept down them and crossed into the yard, scanning for any sign of movement.

She felt like a sitting duck out in the open like this, but maybe that would draw whomever was watching her to make a move. Being the bait was never fun, but Arawyn would do what she had to do, if it would guarantee her safety when all was said and done.

Resting her finger against the trigger, there was no hesitation. If it came down to life or death, she'd do what needed done, in order to keep breathing.

Gun held in both hands, she let her power loose, sending out more than last time to search. Her heart beat faster, the rapid thump of it filling her ears.

Calm down, she scolded herself. *Stay level-headed. Just breathe. Stay focused.*

Inhaling deeply, she steadied herself, honing and sharpening her senses.

Pushing the tendrils out farther, she sent them into the woods, searching, hunting. There, dead ahead, not eighty feet away, she felt something. It was too big to be any of the forest animals inhabiting the woods around her property, but that wasn't what had her stiffening.

It was the sense of menace and a sadistic kind of covetousness radiating from them that had the fine hairs on the back of her neck standing on end.

Though she couldn't see the threat through the shadows, her intuition flared as the sinister sensation she'd been feeling increased tenfold. Realizing whoever was out there knew she'd spotted them, and enjoyed the hunt, she narrowed her gaze and aimed her gun low. As if the game had officially begun, the fucker took off through the trees, heading straight for her. She waited for a good shot, then fired twice.

The low, masculine grunt of pain told her her aim was true, but it didn't stop or even slow them down. Before she could fire again, the faint sound of a shot rang out, echoing through the trees a moment before she felt a sharp prick in her neck like she'd just been stung by the world's biggest fucking wasp.

Re-aiming before the pain had even fully registered, Arawyn pulled the trigger in quick succession. She got off two more shots on pure instinct before she removed a hand from the gun and reached for her neck. Her fingers grazed the feathered end of a dart.

Oh, shit!

A motorcycle revved in the distance as Arawyn yanked the dart out.

"Fuuuuccc..."

The curse trailed off as a crippling wave of dizziness washed through her, spreading like warm water through her limbs. Weighted and heavy, her arm dropped and the gun slipped from her suddenly useless fingers to clatter against the ground.

No.

It was the only word able to reverberate around inside her head.

Arawyn had been drugged before, knew what it felt like, but being tranquilized? This was so much worse.

She'd never considered being drugged from afar, but she should have.

The image of Fear's handsome face filtered through her mind, the image as unsteady as a mirage in desert heat.

Unbalanced, she stumbled backward. The world spun, and the trees in the distance blurred into unrecognizable shapes.

At that moment, the sun crested the horizon, the light shining brightly through the forest. The golden rays nearly blinded her, but even as her legs wobbled, the bright sunshine reminded her of Viper. His amber eyes and manic smile swam before her, but it didn't stay, sliding away like sand through her fingers.

A distressed noise slipped from her throat as she collapsed, falling to her knees before listing onto her side. She tried to catch herself, but her arms wouldn't cooperate and she hit the ground hard. Green blades of grass swayed in front of her eyes, and her vision grew dark at the edges.

It took all her strength just to roll onto her back. The unfocused sky above was so blue, the color deep and rich. It reminded her of the fallen angel's eyes. Even in the dark club, they'd been stunningly vibrant. She couldn't hold onto the picture, and it melted away like ice on a summer day.

Despite the fear almost lazily running through her veins as she tried to fight off the effect of the tranquilizer, she just couldn't bring herself to regret staying. To regret learning more about herself, though she had a million more unanswered questions she couldn't quite recall at the moment.

To regret meeting *them*.

Thick fog descended over her mind, obscuring any further thoughts and making it hard to process what was happening.

Just as her eyes slid closed, she swore she saw a bright flash of light before a pair of motorcycle boots appeared not inches from her nose. Darkness swallowed her to the tune of a menacing, distinctly male growl.

A rawyn rose slowly through the heavy fog enveloping her mind, the faint sense something wasn't right pulling her out of the depths of slumber. Prying open bleary eyes that didn't want to focus, she tried to look around, but all she could see were indistinct shapes and shadows.

Swallowing a pained groan, she tried to reach up and hold her head, but her arm refused to move. It felt like gremlins had taken up residence in her brain and were having an absolute blast stabbing it with ice picks. Everything was fuzzy, her thoughts sluggish and disconnected.

She knew this feeling.

Drugs may not work well on her, but there had been a few idiots who pumped her with enough they knocked her out. Had she been different, the doses likely would've killed her.

She couldn't remember what happened before she was tranqed, but the realization she had been was enough to send a spurt of adrenaline through her, helping clear her head just enough she got her body to cooperate. Movements sluggish and clumsy, she rolled over on a bed definitely too soft to be hers.

Keeping panic at bay by sheer force of will, knowing it wouldn't help her, she squinted at the room around her. It was surprisingly well decorated, a damn sight nicer than the dank basements and abandoned buildings she'd woken up in in the past.

Find a weapon. Look for an escape.

Finding a weapon was easy, considering the walls were decorated with them. Guns, ancient-looking swords, daggers, and some things even she didn't know the names of artfully adorned the walls. Turning, her gaze landed on the bedside table where a gun... no, *her* gun was sitting, simply waiting for her to wake up and take it.

What the fuck kind of game is this?

Confusion and distrust compounded the haze in her head.

At least I'm dressed, thank fuck.

Not only was she fully dressed, minus her shoes, but immensely relieved someone had ever-so-thoughtfully covered her in a blanket.

So, a considerate kidnapper. How delightful. Gotta remember to thank them before I shoot them.

Body still feeling disconnected, arms shaking with the effort, Arawyn pushed up far enough to grab the gun before letting herself collapse back to the mattress. Blinking hard to make her eyes focus, she dropped the magazine, then stared at it for a long second. It was full.

Why...

Nothing made sense. Feeling like she was in some kind of surreal dream, she popped the magazine back in and chambered a round.

Once she thought she could walk without falling on her face, giving away she was awake, she pushed up until she was sitting and swung her legs over the edge of the mattress.

A wave of dizziness had her swaying the moment she was upright and almost sent her falling back to the mattress. Arawyn sucked in a deep breath and shook her head, blinking hard until the blackness crowding in on the edges of her vision receded slightly.

As quietly as possible, she crept to the open door and pressed her shoulder to the jam. A quick peek showed a wide, thankfully empty, hallway. Hearing what sounded like the faint clatter of pans coming from the right, she turned in that direction.

As she slowly tiptoed along, she catalogued what she could of the place, looking for an escape, even as she got closer to the source of the noise.

Beautiful hardwood floors polished to a high shine, ceilings at least fourteen feet high, and the glimpse she could see at the end of the hall of an open space told her she was likely in some kind of retrofitted warehouse loft.

That meant she was probably in one of the many warehouse districts, which also meant, if she could get out of there, she should have plenty of cover to run.

Or places to hide, more likely, considering the worsening lightheadedness.

Stopping a few feet before the end of the hallway, she leaned against the wall and scanned the massive, open space beyond. There was a kitchen just ahead on her left, from which the noise was coming, partially blocked from view by the wall. Ahead was a living area complete with a truly gigantic flatscreen, a pool table and bar area to the left of that, and a staircase leading to an upper level on the far right.

The space was bright with the golden rays of the mid-morning sun streaming in through the floor-to-ceiling windows lining the entire back wall. That brightness stabbed at her eyes, compounding the headache throbbing in her temples.

Squinting through the pain, she took in the multitude of guns, stacks of cash, and what looked like ancient artifacts carelessly scattered throughout. Zeroing in on the artifacts,

Arawyn could feel the tingle of them even from thirty feet away and briefly wondered if they were made of dakaryian steel.

It looked like she was in a mafia boss's den, one who had a penchant for collecting antiquities.

A door she thought would lead either outside or downstairs was on the left side. The problem was she would have to get past the kitchen to reach it, and there was no way she'd be able to do that without being seen.

The dizziness was getting worse. Knowing she was on the verge of passing out again, she needed to make a decision: make a run for it or take out whoever had kidnapped her.

Pushing off the wall, feeling how unstable she was on her feet, she gauged the distance to the door.

Take them out, it is.

Arawyn peered around the wall and into the kitchen to find two tall, very fit, blonde men cooking what smelled like... pancakes? The tug in her chest that had been faint, dulled from the drugs, snapped into place the moment she laid eyes on him, er, them?

Huh. Viper has a twin. That's nice.

Leaning against the door jam, she raised the gun that felt like it weighed a hundred pounds, fought to aim at the closest twin through the vertigo making it feel like she was on a rollercoaster, and fired.

The bullet whizzed past him, boring a hole into the wall not six inches from his head.

Hm, aimed at the wrong twin.

Viper didn't jump at the loud report, didn't yell or drop to the floor or even peer at the hole she'd just put in his wall. He simply turned to her with a wide grin, dangly, silver dagger earrings glinting in the bright lights, wearing an apron reading 'May I suggest the sausage?' with a hand pointing downward.

Finger tightening on the trigger, squinting one eye shut so two Vipers turned into one, she took aim again only to hesitate when he asked, "Do you like pancakes?"

Arawyn didn't have time to answer before she lost the fight with unconsciousness.

Chapter Twenty-One

Arawyn

The second time Arawyn woke up, she was sitting at the table, drooling on the polished wooden surface. Pushing upright, groaning when her head swam sickeningly, she squinted at Viper regarding her sympathetically from a seat on the other side.

"How are you feeling?" he asked on a breath of sound.

Swallowing thickly to try and wet her desert-dry mouth, she croaked, "Why are you whispering?"

He cocked his head, then answered as if it were obvious, "Because your head hurts."

That... was actually kinda thoughtful.

"Where's my gun?"

"I took it. Sorry." He winced apologetically and scratched at his eyebrow.

Focus zeroing in on his fingernails, she frowned slightly. They were black, but they didn't have the shine of nail polish which struck her as odd. Were they naturally black? Was that an alien thing? Blinking to focus when he spoke again, she tried to concentrate.

"I figured you'd shoot at me. I just didn't think your aim would be so good with the tranq still in your system. Impressive."

He was smiling at her like he meant it. Another oddity, though she was beginning to see most everything about Viper was odd.

Her mouth was moving before her brain could tell it to shut up. "Not my first time being drugged."

At that, rage twisted his handsome features, turning him from charmingly crazy kidnapper to coldly dangerous psychopath in a heartbeat.

Suddenly feeling much clearer, Arawyn jerked back in the chair and eyed him warily. Noticing he'd unnerved her, he made an effort to hide his reaction.

As much as she appreciated the attempt, it was a needed reminder he'd tranquilized and abducted her. Thoughtful or no, she couldn't trust him.

Keeping the movement subtle, she slipped a hand under the table and felt for the other weapons she always wore. The hope he'd missed some was replaced with shock.

He hadn't taken any of them.

She wrapped her fingers around the hilt of one of the throwing knives strapped around her waist under her shirt but hesitated before unsheathing one.

She should go on the offensive. She should make her escape. Instead, she found herself asking, "Why didn't you take my weapons?"

The anger melted away like it had never been there. He smiled knowingly and shrugged, his amber eyes as soft as his voice. "I thought it would make you uncomfortable."

The honest answer, paired with the earnestness in his pretty eyes and his open expression, relaxed some of the wary tension in her body. He was right. It would've made her damned uncomfortable, but it begged the question...

"Why? What's to stop me from slitting your throat?"

As though she'd just suggested they make out instead of threatening his life, his gaze went hooded. "The thought of having a knife fight with you is hot as fuck, Babe, but we should probably wait until you're steadier on your feet."

Arawyn just kind of... blinked at him. He never seemed to say what she expected him to. If she weren't still concerned, and more than a little pissed off, over him kidnapping her, she might have smiled.

Before she could come up with a response, he clapped. "Speaking of, I made food! I was gonna bring you coffee and donuts in bed, but then I worried you would stab me in the face. That shit hurts more than you'd think! Also, I don't actually know how to make donuts." He grimaced in apology then brightened just as quickly. "But, I can make pancakes! You passed out before you could answer, but you like pancakes, right?" He waved like he was erasing the question. "Pfft, of course you do! Only assholes don't like pancakes."

He chuckled like he'd just told a joke, pushing to his feet and walking to the counter to gather the plates stacked high with pancakes, bacon, eggs, and fruit. Mildly impressed he managed to juggle it all without dropping anything, she just watched, speechless, as he set the table.

Casting a quick look around again, since he clearly

wasn't going to attack, her gaze lingered on the stacks of cash and the assortment of weaponry before returning to him.

He met her eyes with a smile which struck her as almost nervous. Settling back in his chair, he began making her a plate, like they were on a date where he wanted to make a good impression.

"I don't know if you noticed, but I took the liberty of packing some things for you. I don't know if I got the right things, but we can always go back for anything I missed. Or we could just buy new things! I like shopping. Do you like shopping?"

Choosing to ignore the insane ramblings spilling from his mouth, because she couldn't, for the life of her, think of anything to say, she peered at the food. That was when she noticed the long scratches and dried blood covering both of his forearms.

What did it say about her that the first things she felt were concern and anger he'd been hurt?

That I'm just as batshit crazy as he is. I should be concerned he cooked while bleeding.

Taking the plate he handed her, she nodded her chin at his arm and demanded, "What happened?"

He followed her gaze, then grimaced, a faint blush coloring his cheeks, making the scar slashing down the left side of his face stand out starkly in contrast. "I, uh, tried to bring your cat. He... resisted. Vigorously."

She tried, she tried so hard to hold the laugh in, but he just looked so put out that Asshole hadn't fallen for his charms.

Coughing to try and cover her snicker, she murmured, "Don't take it too hard. Asshole doesn't like anyone. Not even me."

He dipped his chin in affirmation, like that made him feel better, punctuating a wink with a smirk. "See? Definitely not a pancake lover."

That surprised a chuckle out of her. Viper grinned with her, looking delighted, his eyes sparkling.

"I filled up his food and water dishes before we left."

"Thank you," she murmured, then frowned at herself.

No thanking your kidnapper. Jesus, I really am losing my mind.

She still didn't understand what the hell was going on here. Had he abducted her to... woo her? That didn't actually seem that far-fetched for him. He hadn't made any move to hurt her, and hadn't threatened her in any way. Instead, he'd cooked her breakfast, fed her cat, and packed her an overnight bag like this was a sleepover.

Cheerfully lying to herself that the feeling in her stomach was disconcertment, and most definitely *not* butterflies—because who the fuck got flustered over being kidnapped—she focused on the food.

Conversation quieted as they ate, but despite the circumstances, it was almost... comfortable.

VIPER

Viper watched her as she wandered around the loft, trailing her fingertips over a couple of the Fae artifacts they had laying around, gazing at the books filling the wall of shelves.

He was trying to give her some space, not wanting to freak her out, but Godsdamn it was hard. He wanted to be close to her, wanted to touch her and talk to her and ask her why the fuck the prick in the woods beyond her house shot her.

He wanted to ask why she felt like home and smelled like his dreams, why there was a magnet in his chest drawing him to her. Why she, and only she, intrigued him, where every other woman he'd ever met inspired only apathy, at best, but, more often, a bitter kind of resignation.

He wanted to find out what all her favorite things were.

He wanted to kiss her and touch her hair and sink his teeth into the delicate, pale column of her throat.

Instead, he stayed where he was, leaned back against the wall of windows, and watched her. Catching her gaze darting around, making note of all the escape routes, he smiled.

Fuck, but he liked her. Hadn't, in fact, found anything he *didn't* like about her.

Feeling his phone buzz in his pocket for the third time in as many minutes, Viper grimaced and pulled it out. A glance at the screen showed two texts from Rathe demanding an update on Arawyn and one from Fear also wanting an update on her and relaying that the Aswang was still eluding him.

Typing out a quick reply to both, he tucked his phone back in his pocket. He should probably feel guilty for not telling either of them he'd brought her home, but he didn't. He'd have to let them know eventually. He knew that.

But, he wasn't ready. He wanted time with her first. Time before Fear got here and stole her attention away. Time before Rathe showed up and lost his shit.

Time to try and figure out who'd sent the Aswang and the man he'd killed, who smelled like a *Virika*, after her.

The memory of seeing her go down, not knowing at the time it had been a tranq dart and not a bullet, and being too slow to stop it sent pure fucking rage burning through his veins. He'd called off the hunt for the Aswang as soon as he got a text from Fear saying he was on the creature's trail, but even pushing his Ducati to top speeds, it still took him forty-five minutes to reach her house.

She'd been unguarded for less than an hour. Whoever was sending these beings after her was fucking relentless.

As though she could sense his anger, Arawyn stopped scanning the books and pivoted on her heel, pinning him from across the room with those stunning glass-green eyes.

"What?" she asked, frowning at him.

"What what?"

She raised a brow at him. "Don't play me. I can sense you're upset. Why?"

Stunned she actually had sensed his anger, Viper couldn't answer for a second.

He took pride in being able to hide what he was feeling when he wanted to. That she could see through his mask when not even his brother or best friend could should have disconcerted him. Instead, it made something warm and soft unfurl in his chest.

Clearing his throat so he could speak past the tightness, he asked, "Why did he shoot you?"

Arawyn frowned sharply before her eyes went hazy. Reaching up, she touched the deep purple bruise marring her neck, wincing at the light contact. Blinking, she focused on him, her examination sharp and searching.

"He?" she repeated.

Taking a calming breath so he didn't sound as murderously fucking livid someone had hurt her as he felt, he nodded. "Mmhm, definitely a he. You don't have to worry about him anymore, but I'd like to know—"

She cut him off. "Why is that?"

Viper squinted at her warily, wondering if this was a trick question. "Because I killed him?"

Her eyes went wide, and her jaw dropped. He wasn't one hundred percent certain what that expression was, but it definitely wasn't appreciation. Realizing she must think he'd left a mess behind, he held up his hands.

"It's okay, I cleaned up after myself. Even buried him, though I was real fucking tempted to let the wildlife have him. The humans won't find his body, I promise."

Her eyes were still worryingly wide, but she nodded slowly. "Oookay."

Viper smiled and let out a relieved breath. "I'm glad you're not upset. I did think about *not* killing him, so you could question him. Buuut... I'd kind of already killed him by the time I thought of that."

At that thought, his lip curled in a snarl and his eyes burned, telling him they were glowing yellow.

"And anyway, he hurt you." Hearing the guttural sound of his voice, he cleared his throat and forced his expression into something bright and happy to relax her. "Obviously, he couldn't be allowed to keep breathing after that. That would just be... ridiculous!"

Arawyn stared at him for a long moment, something soft, almost vulnerable, passing through her eyes before she turned away and hid the emotion from him. He instantly wanted her eyes back on him, needed to see her, to see the feelings she hid.

Unable to help himself, he pushed off the window and took a step closer. "Will you tell me why he was hunting you?"

She glanced at him sideways. He could see her hesitation, could see her wondering if she could trust him. He wanted to tell her she could, that she could trust him with anything—everything—but he knew she needed to come to this conclusion on her own. So, he waited, standing still and quiet, watching her unblinkingly.

After a long moment, she let out a sigh. He could hear the longing in her breath, could almost feel the weight of being alone pressing down on her shoulders. Faster than he expected, her expression cleared.

Viper wanted to cheer but contained it, in case it startled her, and she changed her mind about trusting him.

"I don't know why." She turned back to the bookcase,

staring blindly at the spines. "I don't know why any of this is happening."

That last was said softly to herself, but he heard.

"Any of this," he repeated, taking another step closer, but only one. She still felt like a wild animal, skittish and wary. "What else has been happening?"

She glanced at him with a hint of fear in her eyes, then walked to the couch, curling herself into the corner, intentionally positioned so she could see the door.

Looking at her made his chest hurt. She looked so fucking tiny there, so small and vulnerable he almost couldn't stand it. He knew he'd have to let her leave eventually. Rathe would insist. But, the thought of her being out in the world, alone, made something sharp and almost panicky fill him.

Following hesitantly, Viper settled on the couch with her, unable to bear her sitting by herself any longer. Much as it pained him, he made sure there was a full cushion between them, the paranoia he would scare her away still riding him hard.

Eyes focused on nothing, voice almost emotionless, as though she were reading off a grocery list, she detailed everything that had happened in the last twelve days.

He could sense she was still holding back, leaving out pieces of her story. He could see them like little shadows in her guarded eyes, but he didn't push her. Someday, if he worked hard and proved himself, maybe she would trust him with those secrets. But, that day wasn't today, so he sat quietly and listened as she shared what she was willing.

That she could talk about someone harassing her for days, covering her porch with a dead animal, being stalked, and repeatedly attacked so calmly pissed him off so badly he could barely breathe through the need to kill things.

It wasn't even the things she listed off. It was that she was so composed. That meant it wasn't the first time shit like this had happened to her. The haunted, scared look in her eyes told him it wasn't even the worst of what she'd survived.

And it gutted him.

He knew that look. He saw it in his own eyes every time he caught his reflection in a mirror. She'd lived through unspeakable horrors, just like he had. Was that why he felt so inescapably, irresistibly drawn to her? Maybe that was part of it, but it wasn't all of it.

Viper had never felt protective of a woman before, had never wanted to be close to one, to touch one, to let one touch him. But, by the Gods, he was ravenous for her touch.

The need to be near her, and keep her near him, was a compulsion, one he had no desire to fight.

When she finished, Viper swallowed back the emotions roiling through him and raised his face to hers. For a moment, a brief second in time, she let him see past the shield she kept steadily in place, and the vulnerability he saw, the invisible scars of a horrible past he could more than relate to, stole his breath away. "Thank you for trusting me," he whispered softly, afraid to break the moment of trust by speaking too loudly.

He wanted to reach for her, to pull her into his arms and hold her. He settled for staring at her.

"You're safe with me, Pretty Loon. No one will hurt you here. That, I swear."

She gazed up at him, her eyes moving back and forth between his. "Why?"

Viper frowned and cocked his head. "Why... what?"

"Why would you care? Why do you want to protect me?"

"Because I like you."

Seeing that saying this wasn't enough, he drew in a slow breath and let her see the pain he usually kept so carefully hidden.

"Because I know what it is to be haunted. I know the toll of fighting your demons alone. And I know how much it helps to have someone in your corner, to know that someone has your back. Let me be that for you, Arawyn. Please."

Her lips parted on a sharp exhale. The look in her eyes stabbed at him, a heartbreaking mix of shock and a fragile, wary kind of hope. She wanted to believe in him. He could see it. But, she was scared.

Viper nodded and smiled at her softly. "I understand. I'll prove it to you, my Loon. I'll prove you can trust me with your nightmares." Seeing she was feeling overwhelmed, he changed the subject. "Wanna play Scrabble?"

Arawyn blinked rapidly, a smile quirking her lips. Eyes flicking to her mouth, he gritted his teeth.

Fuuuck, she smiles pretty.

Realizing he was leaning toward her, he straightened quickly and clenched his hands into fists.

No, no. Don't pounce on her, she'll run away. Shh, restraint. I have restraint.

Pushing to his feet before he made a liar of himself, he turned away and adjusted his cock, cheerfully prepared to lose the last of his questionable sanity and wait until she didn't look like a cornered animal before he pounced.

Chapter Twenty-Two

Fearson

Fearson gripped the steering wheel tightly and pulled into the converted garage of the warehouse. The large metal door slid down with the press of a button. For just a moment, he sat in his car and released a frustrated growl.

He'd spent hours chasing the Aswang's signature trail through the city, closing the distance between them a little more with every passing minute. Just when he was sure he was about to have the bastard within sight, the signature had simply vanished, fading into the mundane aroma of perfume and heavy-handed cologne the humans were prone to wear.

He'd searched for hours more, trying in vain to find even the smallest hint of the Aswang's stench, but there'd been nothing, and he had eventually been forced to admit defeat.

It chaffed and pissed him off that the threat to Arawyn hadn't been extinguished.

He wasn't quick to anger—never had been—but failing a mission, even a self-appointed one, especially *this* one, made him want to punch something.

No, not just punch, fucking *pummel*.

Maybe a trip to their in-home gym would help ease the tension in his shoulders. He could use a few rounds on the bag or maybe lifting. It might help him relax enough to keep him from snapping at Viper or Rathe tonight. Probably Viper.

Who was he kidding? It was always Viper.

He might love the guy like a brother, but his friend also irritated him on a regular basis. On purpose. Viper loved to needle him, to draw a reaction out of him. Or try to, at least.

The thought didn't even bring a smile to his face. How could he have any fraction of happiness when Arawyn was still in danger? When he'd failed to secure her safety?

You're totally fucking gone for this girl.

Fearson shook his head, unfolded himself from the car, and slammed the door harder than necessary. Most of the time, he did it by accident, but tonight had been purposeful, a small token of his frustration.

The faint melody of a feminine laugh trickled into the garage, making Fearson stiffen and stop mid-step. The pull in his chest that was usually a steady presence was now alive with energy, drawing him up the stairs two at a time like a strong magnet.

He moved swiftly until his hand was on the doorknob which he nearly broke off in his haste to investigate, to see if she were truly here in his home.

Fearson burst into the loft to find *her*, sitting in the living room with Viper playing... was that Scrabble?

The picture was completely odd, yet, somehow felt completely normal. It was undeniably *right*. A sight he wanted to walk into every day when he got home.

The realization startled him, but he decided to lean into the feeling. She was quickly overtaking his thoughts. She already owned his dreams. And, now, his beautiful little *Firláh* was here.

He barely had time to take in the platinum blonde hair cascaded down her back before she whipped around, eyes wide with fright, and threw herself in front of Viper like she was his guard. Despite the fear in her eyes, her movements were smooth and practiced as she pivoted in her seat, reached for her boot, whipped out a throwing knife, and hurled it in his direction with flawless accuracy. It cut through the air with precision, perfectly balanced and weighted, a lethal slice of aerodynamic metal.

She was fast. Faster than he'd expected, and that shocked the hell out of him, but it also pleasantly surprised him.

Seeing her defend herself was sexy as fucking hell, even as his stomach twisted at seeing that look on her face.

With speed and precision of his own, he reached up and slammed his hands together, snatching the knife out of thin air just as it sliced into his lower lip, damn near cutting it in half.

The tang of blood burst over his tongue and immediately began to pour over his beard. His palms stung just slightly from the cuts now marring his skin, but the brief pain did nothing to stop the arch of a brow or the corner of his lip from tugging up in a crooked smile.

"Well done, *moín Firláh*," he praised.

Viper's confused gaze shot to him upon hearing the endearment, clearly trying to figure out what the words, common in the Night Court but unknown in the Light Court, meant. Fear ignored him, entirely focused on the shock filtering across Arawyn's beautiful face at the realization of what she'd done. And who she'd done it to.

"Oh my god, Fear!" Arawyn gasped, her eyes widening now that she registered who had walked through the door. "I- I didn't mean to do that."

"Of course you did," Viper replied happily, just as impressed as he was. His friend's eyes glittered with amusement, taking in the blood he could feel beginning to drip off his beard.

Fear studied the unique Fae markings decorating the blade before tossing it into the air, effortlessly flipping it, then catching it, swiftly but carefully.

"I'm so sorry." Genuine regret laced Arawyn's sweet voice. She was already on her feet, crossing the living room to him.

Early afternoon sunlight streamed through the window to backlight her, a golden halo surrounded her pale hair and made her look like an angel. Caring and, somehow, innocent, yet, incredibly fierce. That was his *Firláh*. A contradiction of a woman. Godsdamn, but she couldn't have been more his type.

"Shit. You're really hurt." She reached up for him, her small finger touching the edge of his lower lip. With a wince, she murmured another apology.

Fearson blinked down at her. He couldn't remember a time when anyone worried about him. He'd suffered far greater injuries, and no one had ever batted an eye.

"I'm fine, Baby," he reassured her. "It'll heal soon, and I've had worse."

Much worse, but he kept that part to himself, not wanting to further worry her.

With a light stroke from her thumb, she gazed into his eyes, then looked to the blood now wetting his shirt. He was sure he made a rather gruesome sight, though the injury was minor. Some areas bled worse than others, and the mouth was always a sieve. If it wasn't staining his teeth to transform his smile into something feral, he'd be surprised.

"I think this belongs to you." Opening his palm, he offered the throwing knife back to the little temptress and watched the slight hue of a blush stain her cheeks.

She sheepishly looked up at him from under her lashes. "Thanks," she murmured, quickly taking the knife from him and tucking it away before frowning down at his hand. She reached for the other, checking the wounds she hadn't noticed at first.

"Dammit." The curse was quiet, meant only for her, but he heard it just fine. "Where's your first-aid kit?" Arawyn asked, throwing the question over her shoulder to where Viper lounged on the couch, completely unfazed by the sight of blood on his face.

Viper had seen him in far worse shape, and his friend seemed happy to sit back and watch Arawyn fuss over him.

"'First-aid'?" Viper cocked his head in confusion.

"Yeah, you know... antiseptic? Gauze? Band-Aids?"

"Uh, nope. Sorry, Little Loon." Viper frowned, unhappy he hadn't pleased her by giving her what she'd requested, but it quickly evaporated and he brightened like a lightbulb had gone off over his head. "But, I do have Windex!"

Arawyn snorted, the small sound making the pink staining her cheeks deepen to a far rosier shade.

"Windex?" she questioned with an amused lilt. "Nevermind. Good ol'-fashioned water and soap will have to do."

Clasping his hand, Arawyn pulled him after her like she owned the place. Almost as if she owned *him*.

Fuck, why did that sound so Godsdamn good? He'd missed her touch, her smell, her voice in his ears. Hell, he'd even missed the sight of her ass as she walked away from him.

Thankfully, this time she was taking him with her.

Arawyn led him into the kitchen, and he followed obediently. She'd never be able to move him, if he'd decided to stay put. She was all of five foot three, her body barely half the size of his own.

While her delicate frame was far shorter than an average Fae woman's, he found her short stature endearing.

Entering the kitchen, he found it permeated with lilies, spring storms, and vanilla, telling him she'd been in here earlier. Just having her signature mixed with theirs settled his previous agitation some.

Hell, having her here so he could protect her pleased him in a way nothing else had before.

It wasn't something he had time to analyze, because she shoved him instantly into one of the small kitchen chairs he always hated sitting in. While Viper or Rathe looked fine on the custom-made chairs, he always felt like a Giant in a child's seat. More than once, he'd thought of commissioning his own chair, but their time in this realm was limited.

That thought had always soured both his stomach and his mood, but it held even more gravity, now he'd met the woman he suspected was the other half of his soul.

Fearson watched Arawyn as she rummaged through their cabinets and drawers, searching out supplies to patch him up. He took the time to study her, truly study her.

Her blonde hair was so light it was practically white, falling in soft waves over her shoulders and down to the small of her back. She tucked it behind her ear, and he saw the slightly abnormal shape of it. The tip was clearly more defined than most humans he'd encountered and, yet, much more blunt than that of a Fae. If he hadn't known what to look for, it would have been easily missed, but he noticed. He noticed everything about her.

If he didn't know better, he'd think she were a half-blood, but her power said otherwise.

Even as suppressed as she seemed to keep it, he could sense it just below the surface. In the confines of the kitchen, it brushed gently against his own, tingling lightly, like the tip of a feather brushing against bare skin.

The line of her delicate neck beckoned him to move to her back, lean over her shoulder, and trail a line of sultry kisses up the column of her throat until he reached her jawline. The desire to nip at her sun-kissed skin, to taste her, to bite the shell of her ear and hear her release a breathy little gasp nearly had him clenching his hands into fists.

Arawyn tried a different set of cabinets, stooping over to search the drawers of the island, giving him a perfect view of the generous globes of her breasts.

Fearson suppressed a groan at the erotic sight. He couldn't see much more than the top swells, but somehow, her clothing only made the view more enticing.

He wondered what they would feel like in his palms, and what color her nipples would be. Were they a soft pink, like her beautiful bow-shaped lips? Or were they a light sandy brown?

He shifted in his seat, the wood creaking beneath him, subtly trying to adjust the tightness growing within his jeans. The zipper strained already, but he couldn't stop his eyes from continuing their downward path, prying his attention from her gorgeous tits to the dip at her waist and the flare of her hips.

Without even trying, his *Firláh* tempted him, and though he knew he shouldn't, he looked his fill, his eyes roaming over her hourglass figure.

Her ass was ripe, round and toned. Hoisting her up by those curves was becoming a growing ache inside of him. Would her shapely legs even be able to lock around his waist?

Gods help him, but he wanted to test the theory.

Chapter Twenty-Three

Fearson

Arawyn sighed as she returned to him, dropping her haul on the table with a crease between her furrowed brows.

"This was all I could find. I can't believe you don't have a first-aid kit," she scolded, waving toward the meager supplies she'd pulled together.

Her concern warmed him, even while his cock hardened further from the fresh wave of her scent that followed when she brushed closer.

Fuck.

The reminder of how good she'd felt against him when they'd danced, of how incredibly sexy she'd sounded as he'd muffled her cries of ecstasy when she'd come for him, only increased the uncomfortable tightness in his pants.

This isn't the time to get turned on.

Too bad his better sense fled the room. He was pretty sure Viper's had gone, as well. Because Arawyn was still here in their loft, it only meant one thing.

Rathe didn't know she was here.

Shit was going to hit the fan when he got home, but for now, he pushed that concern to the background.

"This might sting," Arawyn warned, holding up a cloth that smelled of vodka.

"I'm not worried."

Instinctually, Fearson opened his knees, allowing her to step closer. Accepting the unspoken invitation, Arawyn gingerly moved into him and cupped his face in one palm while the other hand gently dabbed at the cut splitting his lip. He watched her while she worked, fully captivated.

No one had ever cared about him enough to tend to his hurts. It was a little... disconcerting, but infinitely touching. This was a moment he knew he'd treasure.

Taking her time, she cleaned him up and ensured the bleeding had stopped. With each dab, she seemed to move closer, and when she hummed her approval, signaling she was finished, she glanced up only to realize just how close she'd drawn.

Breathlessly, she stared straight into him with those fathomless glass-green eyes. This close to her, he could make out the darker flecks interspersed throughout and the barest hint of a lighter ring around her pupil.

Her breath caught in her throat at his low, rumbling purr of thanks, and she released an airy gasp that drew every ounce of his attention.

Fearson couldn't resist the temptation to glance down at her mouth. Peeking over her full bottom lip, her tongue darted out to wet the pink flesh. Hunger blazed to life in her eyes, and she unconsciously swayed forward until her stomach brushed along the hard line of his chest.

Chasing her would be so very easy. The slightest lean forward, and she would be his.

The light flush mantling her cheeks told him she knew it as sure as he did. That color on her was addicting, and he decided he wanted to put that look on her face every damn day.

One hand gripped the plate-laden table while the other clenched the edge of his stupidly small seat. It took everything in him to keep himself planted, to stop himself from closing the last few inches between them.

As if she knew the Siren's effect she had on his body, Arawyn stroked her fingers through his thick beard, and he fucking lost it.

Godsdamn.

His grip tightened like a vice until the keen sound of a crack infiltrated their moment like a needle to an overfull balloon.

An audible curse slipped out as he surveyed the damage he'd done to the table. A long crack snaked its way down the smooth wood, irreparably fracturing the custom furniture.

Honestly, Fearson couldn't bring himself to care much. Now, he could commission something to accommodate them all. Just like the ridiculous human fairytale about the little blonde who infiltrated a bear's den, they'd all have a seat to fit them comfortably, if he had anything to say about it.

He almost smirked at just how accurate the story fit. Arawyn was his little Goldilocks, though he wasn't so sure she'd wandered into their den of her own accord. Viper must have had something to do with why she was here, in their home.

A chuckle from the doorway infiltrated their moment even more than the cracked table Arawyn was currently staring at with wide eyes and parted lips.

Glancing first at him, then back at the split wood, she drew in a breath to say something but exhaled without uttering a word.

Fearson could see the questions swirling in her pretty green eyes, could feel her desire to say something more. What he wouldn't give to know what she was thinking, but he didn't press.

For Fae banished to the human realm, it was rude, and incredibly forward, to speak of such things openly. Arawyn hadn't brought up her power or abilities. Neither had she chosen to drop her Glamor at all around them, which was telling.

He hoped she came to trust them enough to do so soon, but he understood, despite the connection between them, they were still essentially strangers to her. The last thing he wanted to do was pry and scare her off, so he would follow her lead and let her set the pace.

Besides, he could admit he wasn't in a rush to reveal his true form to her just yet either. He wanted her affection, and perhaps, even needed to build more trust himself, before he exposed the... *unique* features of his mixed blood.

"It's okay. I'll replace it," he reassured her, extracting his hands from anything breakable.

He didn't want her to worry about such trivial things when she had much larger problems on which she needed to concentrate.

Like the being who had tried to steal her power the night before.

Fearson glanced to where Viper leaned against the doorframe, seeing him grinning and tracking Arawyn with a fervent stare. Feeling his attention, Viper slid his eyes to Fear, and the two of them shared a heavy look.

Spending these last number of years together in such close quarters had allowed them a certain closeness which helped them communicate without words. The trick came in handy, now, as they shared a silent conversation while Arawyn bustled around the kitchen, cleaning up from her brief stint as his nurse.

With that one look, Fear knew his friend was thinking the same as he was: they needed to work together to keep her there. In complete agreement, Viper nodded, one sharp dip of his head.

Flicking his eyes toward the front door, and then back, Fear lifted his brows at Viper, communicating his concern of Rathe's reaction to finding Arawyn in the loft when he got back.

Viper shrugged, clearly deciding to cross that bridge when they got to it.

Fear scrubbed a hand down his face, the cuts on his palms already scabbed over and healing nicely. He was careful not to reopen the wound on his lip Arawyn had so sweetly tended to, though his expedited healing was already knitting the injury back together, as well.

Didn't matter. He wouldn't have traded having her caring touch for anything. The selfish part of him wanted to reopen the damn cut a million times just to have her standing in front of him with that worried little crease lining her forehead as she fawned over him, but he knew she wouldn't appreciate him bleeding all over the kitchen and didn't want to see him hurt. So, he left it alone and contented himself with simply having her close by.

Watching her find her way around his space, his home, changed something in him, and for once, he was in complete agreement with Viper's train of thought.

Keeping her safe was their number-one priority, and that included finding a way to convince Rathe Arawyn wasn't a spy or in any way working for the King. Then, they needed to sway him to allow her to stay.

The connection in Fear's chest pulsed, almost as if in solidarity with his plan. More and more, he was convinced she was his *Firláh*, though he reminded himself, uselessly, he needed to proceed with caution.

But, it was simply one more reason to keep her close. He wanted time with her to figure it all out.

Speaking of...

"Why are you here, *Firláh*?" he asked, unable to contain his curiosity any longer, now the weapons were safely sheathed.

Arawyn tilted her head, scanning past him to his friend who was still holding up the doorframe. A small smile curled her lips. "Your friend kidnapped me."

Appalled, he whipped around to look at his friend, who was about to shed some blood of his own, if he didn't have a damn good explanation.

"The fuck?!" he barked.

Viper playfully glared at their beautiful house guest, ignoring Fearson's wrath entirely. "You pronounced 'saved my ass' incorrectly."

Fear raised a brow, a clear demand for someone to explain, and explain now. Where he came from, women were respected and revered. That one of his best friends would be foolish enough to kidnap Arawyn, and that she hadn't cut his balls off and fed them to him already, was confusing the fuck out of him.

Arawyn shook her head at Viper's antics, then turned to address Fear. He didn't even have time to marvel at the way she could read him, at how she seemed to know his barely contained fury was building, at how she understood his need for answers.

"Someone shot me with a tranq dart," she started, as though that was going to help ease his level of pissed off.

She was mistaken. Red bled into his field of vision.

"Viper," she eyed his cheeky friend, "my knight in shining armor, apparently killed the guy, buried him in my woods, and brought me here. I woke up in what I'm pretty damn sure was his bed." Arawyn peered at Fear with an arched eyebrow. "Unless your favorite color is bright yellow and you have weapons decorating your walls?" It was a rhetorical question, so he didn't bother answering.

Fearson ignored everything except the 'shot me with a tranq' part, more livid than he'd been in a long-ass time.

His eyes heated with his rage, and he knew flecks of purple would be shining through with his fury. His eyes swept over to Viper, as sharp and cutting as the knife she'd launched at him earlier.

"You took a moment to make it hurt, I hope."

Whether the statement would scare Arawyn, he hadn't thought to consider. He hoped not, but the sooner she understood there were dark parts of their life, the better it would be for all of them.

"Pfft," Viper sounded. "Don't insult me. 'Course I did."

A miniscule amount of the rage he felt subsided.

Arawyn shook her head, but he could make out the smallest smile playing at the corner of her lips when she whispered under her breath, "That should not be flattering."

He didn't try to contain his smug smile in return and shared another weighted look with a wickedly grinning Viper. Because he'd been right all along.

There was no doubt their little temptress fit in just fine with their deadly band of misfits.

Chapter Twenty-Four

Rathe

Rathe stood outside the door to his loft listening to his brother and guard chatting like old friends with *her*.

The white-haired, green-eyed vixen. Arawyn.

They were supposed to follow her, not bring her back to their fucking home. He was absolutely furious they'd disobeyed orders, but within the anger was worry. He'd been questioning the wisdom of allowing them to tail her for the last three days and, now, his doubts were proven right.

Keeping his power drawn tightly into himself so they wouldn't detect him, Rathe eavesdropped, hoping against hope they didn't do, or say, anything dangerous but needing to know just how far gone they were.

Her entirely too-appealing voice filtered through to him over the sound of movie credits rolling on the TV, her words as clear as though she were inches away instead of what was likely fifty feet.

"You knew I was watching that night at the docks."

"Yes," Fear answered honestly.

"Why didn't you say anything?"

"Pfft, a gentleman never interrupts a lady's appreciation of his ass. That's just common courtesy," Viper scoffed playfully.

Arawyn choked on a laugh. Rathe bared his teeth, irritated by how much he liked the melodic little sound.

"It's not going to work, Viper. I want a real answer." There was a short pause. Her voice was quieter when she asked, "Why were you buying drugs? And what's with all the guns, cash, and antiques?"

Rathe stiffened, wondering if they were going to give away what they were really doing that night, wondering if they were too infatuated with the little vixen to keep their heads.

Hands curling into fists, he almost burst in before they could answer. If she was using a power, or magic, on them, it wouldn't be their fault, if they told the truth.

He knew that.

But, he also knew it would feel like a betrayal, regardless, knew it would splinter something in him to hear the only two people he trusted in this realm, or any other, betray him.

Closing his eyes, he waited, forcing himself to remain still. For better or worse, he had to know how lost they were to her.

"We can't answer that," came Fear's deep voice, sounding apologetic but unyielding.

The relief surging through Rathe almost staggered him. In that relief was contrition he'd questioned their loyalty, even if briefly, and a quickly squashed flicker of gratitude he wouldn't have to hold her hostage. He would, without hesitation, but she would hate him for it, and that, for reasons he wouldn't acknowledge, bothered him.

Arawyn seemed to pause, to think over what Fearson had said before pressing for more. "Can't answer, or won't?"

"Both."

Clearly trying a different tactic, she asked simply, "Are you mafia?"

Rathe could practically feel the sly smile filling Viper's smooth voice. "Depends. Do you like mafia men?" his brother asked.

"I... don't know that I've ever met any."

"Oh. Well, then, maybe. Maybe not. If you decide you like them, yes. If you decide you don't, no."

The answer was so typically Viper that Rathe rolled his eyes.

Having heard enough, he released his power and entered the room, immediately zeroing in on her. He caught Viper's knowing look from the corner of his eye, telling him he'd known Rathe was listening in, but that wasn't what held his attention.

Arawyn whipped around faster than he anticipated, a blade in one hand, her other pressed against Fear's chest as though to hold him back.

Or protect him.

Rathe quickly dismissed the thought, forcefully reminding himself she was a spy. He couldn't trust her words or actions. Everything she said and did would be tailored to lure them in.

Scanning the three of them, he cocked a brow. Despite the abundant seating options available to them, they were all piled on the couch, seated as close to her as he suspected she would allow.

Fear was sitting sideways, watching her instead of the movie that had just ended. Something told him it wasn't a recent repositioning, that his guard had been like that for a while.

Viper was on her left, one arm stretched over the back of the couch, the other actively twirling a lock of her long hair.

Ignoring the way she was warily eyeing the blood splattering his shirt, he addressed Viper and Fear. "What the fuck is going on here? You were supposed to follow her, not bring her home like a stray fucking cat."

Arawyn's eyes widened with outrage, a look he found entirely too attractive on her, and sputtered, "Who the fuck are you calling a stray- wait, follow me?" She eyed first Fear, then Viper.

Fearson, the same man who'd faced half a dozen enemies singlehanded, unarmed, without flinching, shifted uncomfortably in the face of this tiny woman's anger.

Viper, in direct contrast, nodded enthusiastically. "For three days!" He rubbed his chest and added, "Couldn't get as close as I wanted." Meeting and holding her searing glare, Viper winced, his expression full of regret. "I would've gotten there sooner, otherwise. I'm sorry, Pretty. I tried."

Arawyn's anger melted in the face of Viper's remorse. Reaching for him, she trailed her fingertips over his chest. Rathe didn't miss the way his brother's eyes brightened almost feverishly at her touch, or the way he swayed toward her.

"I'm just glad you were there, at all." She glanced over her shoulder at Fear, including him in the sentiment. Her lips twisted in a wry smile. "Even if you were stalking me."

Eyes narrowed nearly to slits, wondering exactly what had transpired, and why the hell neither of them had thought it worth mentioning to him, Rathe drew in a calming breath and wordlessly stalked to the kitchen.

Steps faltering for a moment at the absolute disaster greeting him, he glared at the pancake batter splattered on his countertops, then at the veritable feast covering almost every available inch of the table. The *broken* table.

Turning on his heel when he heard Viper and Fear enter behind him, he looked at both men, brows raised, only to frown when he saw Fear's bottom lip had recently been sliced open.

"What happened to your face?" he asked, somehow knowing the woman staring at them from the living room was at fault.

Fear confirmed it by gazing at her with a besotted look, but it was Viper who answered.

"Fear came bursting in and startled her. She tried to protect me and threw a knife at him." Viper leaned forward, his expression bright with amazement. "He wasn't fast enough to catch it before it cut him."

Rathe cut a sharp look at her, impressed in spite of himself. Still staring at her, he asked, "And why is she here in the first place?"

They took turns quietly telling him about the incidents they'd witnessed and the ones she'd told Viper about.

"You should've questioned him before you killed him," he admonished when his brother finished filling him in.

Viper grimaced and looked away for a moment. "I know. I was... upset. If I'd gotten there just two minutes sooner—"

Rathe bit back a sigh. Viper could be cold and calculated, thoughtful in his actions and capable of planning five steps ahead of his prey... so long as he wasn't emotionally invested. It was when he lost that detachment that he sometimes became impulsive.

In this instance, Rathe could admit, if only to himself, he might not have reacted all that differently, had he been there to witness her fall. He couldn't quite stop the rage burning through him at the knowledge she'd been hurt not once, but twice, or the dark pleasure that Viper had killed the being who shot her.

His surety that she was a spy wavered for a moment. He wondered if he'd been wrong, if she actually was what she appeared to be.

He wanted to believe she was authentic, but it was the very intensity of his desire to believe it that had his suspicions rising again.

Rathe may be fighting it harder than his brother or friend, but he was far from immune to whatever spell or power she was using on them.

That an Aswang and a Virika had both attacked her, and within such a short span of time, was odd, to put it mildly. It wasn't impossible that she'd hired them, but Aswangs weren't known for being particularly interested in money, of any kind.

No. This had to be a setup, a ploy to get herself closer to them. She was playing the damsel in distress to make them want to protect her.

Peering at the others, he had to admit it was working beautifully.

Mentally bracing himself for a fight, he faced them again. "She can't stay here."

A soft sound from the doorway had him whipping his head around to find Arawyn standing there. Surprise that he hadn't heard her approach was quickly outweighed by the feeling of being punched in the stomach when he saw her pretty eyes shutter and the happiness which had lightened her face disappear, replaced with an expressionless mask.

Viper and Fear both started to argue but cut short when she held up a hand.

Staring directly at him as she spoke to them, Arawyn said flatly, "He's right. I can't stay here. I can handle my own problems."

Looking away from him, she glanced at Fear, then Viper. Something entirely too close to jealousy fired through him at the way her face softened for them.

"Thank you, both, for... " She trailed off with a small shake of her head and left it at that.

Rathe watched her disappear down the hall. The urge to go after her was instant, but he refused, standing firm under the combined glares of his friends and the memory of the quickly hidden look of hurt in her eyes.

Moments later, she returned with a bag slung over her shoulder and an expectant expression, the sting from seconds before hidden now, locked away.

Viper made a low sound in his throat and jerked like he wanted to go to her. "We should eat dinner before you go! We could have leftovers," he offered quickly. With a pointed look at him, Viper muttered to her, "Rathe doesn't like pancakes, but he can go hungry."

Pretending her muffled laugh didn't have his cock hardening in his slacks, he gave his brother a droll look, knowing he'd just called him an asshole. "No. We're leaving now."

Viper glowered at him through slitted eyes. "Killjoy. I actually made a roast!" Walking to Arawyn, he muttered,

"Slaved over a hot Crock Pot for literal minutes! No one appreciates my efforts. Except you, Pretty."

In front of her now, Viper pulled her into a tight hug and whispered something in her ear too low for even him to make out. Whatever it was made her blush, an enchanting flush of pink painted across her high cheekbones.

Fast as a snake, Viper pressed a quick, mostly chaste kiss to her lips, then danced out of reach before she could take a swing at him.

Grinning, Viper promised, "I'll see you soon, Pretty Loon. And I look forward to our knife fight."

Frowning between her and his brother, Rathe resisted the urge to pinch the bridge of his nose.

Just when I think his insanity can't catch me off guard anymore...

Viper raised his hand like he was in a classroom and volunteered, "I'll take her."

Rathe gave him a look. "Not fucking likely." Glancing at Fear when he opened his mouth, he spoke before his guard could offer the same. "Both of you have proven you have shit for control around her. I'll take her."

Moving to a particular drawer, he pulled it open and withdrew a black bag from within, then held it out to her.

Arawyn was eyeing the drawer with something akin to shock. "You just keep bags to put over people's heads in your kitchen?"

Rathe cocked a brow. "Never know when you're going to need one. If you would," he prompted, still holding the bag out to her.

According to his brother, she'd been unconscious when he brought her here, so she didn't know where they lived.

That, at least, was something to be grateful for, and he intended to keep it that way.

She took it from him to the sound of Fear and Viper making simultaneous noises of upset and anger, but she, again, silenced them with a raised hand.

That she could command his men better than he obviously could both irritated the fuck out of him and was reluctantly impressive.

Neither of them were exactly known for being obedient or docile.

Peering at his friends, he amended.

Before her, anyway.

Chapter Twenty-Five

Rathe

Rathe took in her small, run-down house with something entirely too close to anger. Why the fuck hadn't the King provided her with enough funds to afford something less... decrepit? Other than a few obvious security upgrades, the house didn't look like it had seen any repairs in the last twenty years.

Arawyn pulled the bag off her head and scowled at him through the tangled strands of her hair. "Did you just audibly sneer at my house?"

"Yes," he answered simply, sweeping the house and the land around it.

Her little growl of irritation made his cock twitch. Being locked in a vehicle with her for the last hour and a half as he navigated the congested city streets and headed past the suburbs had been torture. Being unable to escape her intoxicating scent, the sight of her small, curvy little body in the passenger seat of his car had tested his control in a way he found both unwelcome and unexpected.

Parking near her front entryway, he got out and rounded the vehicle to open her door. The look of startled confusion she sent him had a frown flickering across his brow.

Has no one ever opened a door for her?

The thought was oddly upsetting.

The expression remained as he walked her to the porch. Holding her keys in one hand, she hesitated before unlocking the door.

She tilted her head back just enough to give him a cold look. "You can leave now."

Oh, but he liked her fire.

Rathe bit back a smirk and stayed where he was, standing ever-so-slightly too close to her, masochistically enjoying the way her scent wrapped around him. "Open the door, Arawyn."

As he expected, she made no move to obey, instead holding his gaze in a silent battle of wills. Finally, with a sigh and a grumble, she broke eye contact first.

"At least there's not another picture," she muttered under her breath.

Rathe's gaze sharped on the top of her head. "What picture?"

Arawyn blinked up at him, appearing startled he'd heard her, though why she would be was puzzling. Even if she were operating, or pretending to operate, under the assumption his time in the human realm had lessened his powers, it wouldn't have any effect on his senses.

When she didn't answer, he cocked a brow and repeated, "What picture?"

Huffing a breath, she finally began unlocking the numerous deadbolts. "Someone has been leaving pictures of me and your friends taped to my door."

"Show me," he demanded.

"My god, you're bossy," she sassed but did what he wanted and pulled two photos from her back pocket.

Taking them from her, he stared at the first. His cock gave another hard twitch at the pleasure written on her delicate features as Fear brought her to release on the dance floor of the club. He remembered it vividly, even without the picture as a sinful reminder.

There was nothing arousing about the second, however.

Someone had snapped a picture of them at the docks. Viper's face being scratched out of the photo was mildly concerning, but it was the fact that someone had followed them, without any of them sensing the being, that had his hackles rising.

"What the fuck is this, Arawyn?"

She exhaled sharply and shook her head, not reacting to the clear threat in his voice. "Your guess is as good as mine. I thought either you or Viper sent the first one. When I got the second, I realized I was wrong. Now? I don't have a damn clue."

She opened the door then, his reply cut short when the destruction beyond came into sight. Glancing at her quickly when she made a sound, he took in what looked like genuine shock and horror on her face. It was gone in the next breath, replaced with hard-eyed anger as she drew her handgun.

Drawing his own weapon when the faintest scent of wet

stone, stale blood, and rotten meat wafted to him, he scanned the space ahead.

A Redcap?

The smell was slightly wrong, but it was close enough to put him on high alert. Redcaps were nasty fuckers, known for eating their victims while they were still alive and screaming.

Whether this had been arranged by her as a last-ditch effort to worm her way into his protection or not, Rathe had no desire to be caught off guard by one.

"I'll go right," she whispered on a breath of sound.

"I've got left," he murmured just as quietly.

A thorough sweep of the house showed the destruction continued into every room, but the being who had caused it left at least six hours ago, by his guess.

Working his way back through the house, he took in the boxes stacked haphazardly in the corners, covered in a layer of dust that spoke to them having sat there for months, if not years. Aside from the boxes, the house had a lived-in feel to it, her personal belongings scattered throughout.

Either her eye for detail was truly fucking impressive… or his theory that she was a spy might possibly be wrong.

He found her in a back addition that had been converted into a workshop, sitting in front of a computer. Pausing in the doorway, he took in the chaos.

This room hadn't been spared. It wasn't the mess that held his attention, however, it was the weapons, most scattered on the floor, though some were still affixed to the walls.

They were exceedingly well made, crafted with obvious time and care, the weapons' names meticulously carved into the metal in ancient Fae. There was no question they'd been forged by her hand. The tingle of her power radiated from them, filling the room and washing over his body like warm water.

Curious.

He hadn't heard there were any *Druiach Nihr* still living. It was an ancient calling, forging weapons of power, a practice usually passed through a bloodline, but the last ones he knew of died out twenty or thirty years ago.

Gazing at her through assessing eyes, Rathe joined her at the workbench in time to hear her whisper.

"How..."

"How what?" he asked as he took in her security system. It was impressive, damn near as good as his.

Arawyn jerked, peering up at him as if she'd forgotten he was there. Her face was pale, and she looked shaken, more so than he'd seen her. Frowning sharply, he was on the verge doing something foolish, like asking if she was okay, when she answered.

"There's no evidence of a break-in." Turning back to her computer, she shook her head slowly, fingers flying across the keyboard. "That's impossible."

Still frowning, he watched the screen. "Odd. Redcaps can't Ride Shadow or Light. They use brute force."

He'd assumed she had found the point of entry during her sweep, because he hadn't on his. There'd been no broken walls or windows. Realizing she was staring at him wide-eyed, he raised his brows questioningly.

"I don't know what the fuck that is," she murmured shakily.

Rathe was so taken aback by that he almost missed what she said next.

"Whoever these people are, they're fucking relentless. Should've known they'd figure out a way to break in eventually. I just don't understand how they did it without being seen." She sighed deeply, shoulders slumping. "What the fuck is going on?"

The look on her face—a gut-wrenching mix of anger, loss, and fear—almost more than her words, had an unexpected and wholly unwelcome surge of protectiveness rushing through him.

Tamping it down ruthlessly, he kept his expression blank. The doubts whispering in the back of his mind might be growing, but until he knew for sure she wasn't a Trojan Horse, he'd damn well keep them to himself.

At the sound of a meow, Arawyn pushed off the stool. Back in the living room, Rathe sneered at the sight of the feline. Seeing him at the same time, its back arched sharply as it hissed.

Intending to question why the fuck she had a cat, the only animal that universally hated High Fae, he turned to her only for the words to die unspoken.

Standing there, she looked... small. Vulnerable. Not helpless or defeated. Never those, because right there within the vulnerability shining from her eyes was fury that someone would do this to her.

Suspicious of her though he may be, Rathe could admit she was an admirably fierce little thing—brave and bold. But, at that moment, standing amidst the destruction, knowing her home had been invaded, she looked so fucking alone.

The worst of it was that, real or feigned, she was clearly trying to hide what she felt from him, but he could see it in her eyes, in the slight slump of her shoulders.

He tried to hold on to the surety this was another ploy, another bid to get close to him, but it just didn't feel quite right. Not anymore.

Perhaps, this was a warning from his father that he was losing patience with her. Perhaps, this was a deal gone bad. Perhaps, it was exactly what it appeared to be, and she was in real danger.

Either way, he should leave. It wasn't his fucking problem.

He couldn't afford to invite a traitor into their midst. He'd done horrible things to keep Viper and Fearson safe, things that stained his soul and haunted his sleep. Those deeds would be for naught, if he gave in to the need thrumming in his bones: the need to protect her, to bring her back to his domain where none would dare touch her.

Rathe felt the cold exterior he'd put around himself to fight her influence crack a little even as he turned toward the door.

He made it a single step before every atom in his being rebelled.

Chapter Twenty-Six

Rathe

Cursing himself for a fool, but knowing he couldn't leave her there, Rathe pivoted to face her again.

"Grab your shit. You're coming back with me," he growled, his voice coming out harsh and angry.

Arawyn, much to his irritation, didn't look at all thrilled. Much the opposite. Her brows were pulled down, forcing a small crease between them, and she was shaking her head just slightly, staring at him with suspicion in her glass-green eyes.

"I thought you didn't want me at your house."

"I changed my mind. Unless you want to stay here?" he challenged.

She frowned at him harder, a spark of anger he was glad

to see, even if it was directed at him. "I don't need your pity. I can handle my own problems."

Rathe walked to her silently, pinning her in place with his fixed look, only stopping when they were damn near chest to chest and he could almost feel her breasts brushing him.

She didn't give any ground, and Godsdamn if that didn't make him want her more.

Leaning down, his voice unexpectedly soft, surprising even him, he murmured, "I know that, Little Vixen. But, I'm not leaving you here. So, you either get in the car of your own volition, or I'll tie you up and carry your sweet ass there myself." Straightening, he cocked a brow. "Choose."

"What makes you think your place will be any different?" she fired back. "How do I know this won't keep happening there?"

Rathe felt his lips curl in a darkly anticipatory smile. "I'd like to see these motherfuckers try. No one fucks with me, Princess." He paused, eyeing her pointedly. "Or with what's mine." Before she could voice the outrage he could see on her face, he cut her off, "But, if you want to stay here, all alone, and hope you truly can handle your own problems... "

He trailed off and shrugged, as though it were no concern of his. That was quickly becoming a lie, however. He did care, and that bothered him as much as it worried him.

Was he falling under her spell as much as his friends? Or had they been right about her all along?

Eyes narrowed to slits, she snarled, "Asshole."

Going perfectly, dangerously still, he questioned softly, "What did you call me?"

Arawyn widened her eyes innocently and called out in a

sing-song voice, "Asshole." A meow answered her. Smirking, she peered at the cat. "There you are—" With a look up at him she added, "Asshole."

Rathe felt the smallest flicker of a smile curl his lips. But, it faded in the next second when she blew out a defeated breath and looked around her home, shoulders drooping.

As much as he hated to see the fight go out of her, he savored the win. Watching her walk toward the back of the house, he wondered if she'd have the same fire in bed, and if she'd eventually submit. Something in him hoped she wouldn't yield, that she'd meet him as an equal.

After loading his car and her SUV to capacity, he got the fucking feline wrangled, though not without sustaining wounds. Rathe eyed the claw marks scoring both his arms and the torn sleeves of his shirt irritably. He'd sustained far worse in battle, but the damn things stung like acid.

Glaring at the feline hissing at him from its small enclosure, he slung off the blood dripping from his fingertips and closed the door a little harder than strictly necessary.

Returning to the house, he found Arawyn gazing mournfully at all the tools and equipment that wouldn't fit in their vehicles and had to be left behind. He'd noticed she packed very few clothing and toiletry items, using the space they would've occupied to bring more weapons and tools, which surprised him. She hadn't made any comment or complaint either.

Rathe was accustomed to dealing with females of the Light Court, ladies known throughout Faery for being high strung, manipulative, and high maintenance. Whether that was a change that came about under the rule of his infamously misogynistic father or not, he couldn't say, but it was all he'd known of women.

Arawyn was as different from those pampered, simpering ladies as night to day. He wasn't quite sure how to deal with it.

With a sigh, she left, leading the way to the door where she set the security system and locked the excessively numerous deadbolts, not that it had stopped the being who'd ransacked her home.

He could see how much it bothered her to leave the place in such a state, but they'd lingered too long as it was. While Rathe welcomed the intruder returning so he could question them, painfully, he didn't want her with him if, or when, that happened.

With that in mind, he waited for her to turn away, then drew a small amount of power into his fingertips and drew a rune on the door. It was a subtle, but strong, bit of magic that would alert him if anyone, human or other, came near her home.

Alert, eyes sweeping the deep shadows cloaking the property with the setting of the sun, he walked her to her SUV, ignoring the faint headache building at the base of his head as the cost of the conjured magic sank in.

"Follow close. And watch for a tail."

A wry smile curled her lips as she gazed up at him. "I've kept myself alive for twenty-six years. I know how to spot a tail. Besides, I'm wearing more weapons than you are."

Reminded, again, of the stark difference between her and the women to which he was accustomed, Rathe made a low sound in his throat, shut her door, and got into his car.

On the way back to the warehouse, he found himself watching her in the rearview mirror more than the road. Without her close to him, clouding his thoughts, doubts filtered back in.

He justified his choice with the pragmatic argument that with her under his roof, she'd have a hell of a time passing any information she had gathered to her contact.

As the humans said, keep your enemies closer.

On the way back to the warehouse, Rathe intentionally drove at least twenty miles over the speed limit until he hit the city and had to slow out of necessity. Driving at high speeds meant anyone trying to follow them would stick out. Thankfully, he hadn't seen or sensed anyone. He'd worried briefly her vehicle wouldn't be able to keep up but, impressively, she stayed right on his bumper.

Parked in the ground level of the warehouse they'd turned into a garage, he moved to help her carry some of her things upstairs, only to pause when he caught her staring at him oddly.

"What?"

"I just realized I still don't know your name," she remarked.

Rathe blinked, thinking over their interactions, sure she must be wrong, but a quick run-through of their brief interludes told him she was right.

That didn't account for her being a spy, however. Did she truly not know his given name? Or was this simply another deception?

It didn't feel like one, yet, he couldn't quite shake the wariness.

The way she cocked her head, her eyes searching him like she was trying to guess what it was, made him pause.

She seemed so... honest. So genuine in her interactions,

in her interest in him and his friends. It made his thoughts circle all over again.

Setting down the bags he'd grabbed, he stepped close and held out his hand. Heeding his hand, then his face, she slid her palm into his.

Tightening his fingers, feeling how small her hand was in his, he brought it to his lips and pressed a light kiss to the back, murmuring against her skin, "My name is Rathe."

Her lips parted slightly, those striking eyes of her darkening as she took him in. "Nice to meet you, Rathe."

Heat flared at the sound of his name on her lips in that breathy voice of hers. His was deeper, rougher when he whispered, "The pleasure is mine, Arawyn."

Her lips quirked in a small smile, a faint blush warming her cheeks. She swayed toward him before she seemed to catch herself. Slipping her hand out of his, she gave him a wry look.

"Liar."

With that, she turned on her heel and ascended the stairs like she owned the place.

Sliding his lower lip between his teeth, he followed, allowing himself to enjoy the view as he climbed the stairs behind her, even as he wondered if he'd just made a decision he would come to regret.

Chapter Twenty-Seven

ARAWYN

Arawyn was focused on Rathe behind her, and the absolute surety he was staring at her ass, when the sharp crack of something shattering from above pierced the air. Not a second later, Viper came flying down the stairs, his steps silent, despite the reckless speed with which he came at her.

Eyes wide, she barely had time to brace for impact before he scooped her up into a tight hug, lifting her like she weighed nothing and spinning her around. Still frozen with surprise, she didn't dodge him when he lowered his face toward hers. Hell, if she were being honest, she probably wouldn't have dodged him, even if she'd had time to.

Instead—like the touch-starved idiot who was unhealthily fascinated with the endearingly psychopathic blonde she was—she melted into him the moment his mouth pressed against hers.

The shock she felt melted away in a mere second. His lips were soft, the foreign smoothness of his lip rings adding a new sensation, one with which Arawyn was immediately enamored.

Carding her fingers into the silky length of his hair, she slanted her head and opened her mouth just far enough to graze her tongue over one of those rings that had been driving her to distraction.

Mmm, he tastes like cookies.

Viper gave a strangled groan that shot straight to her center, then went perfectly still at that little flick, arms still wrapped around her, mouth still pressed to hers. She was pretty sure he wasn't even breathing.

Opening her eyes, she met his very wide ones and smiled against his mouth, whispering, "Hello, Cookie Monster."

He made a sound like a half-swallowed giggle, higher pitched than she would've thought him capable of, considering his voice was naturally deep and smoky.

Still not moving, he whispered back hoarsely, "Hi, Loon. I missed you."

Finally pulling away so she could see him clearly, she arched a brow. "I've only been gone for like four hours."

He nodded slowly. "Five hours and twenty-seven minutes. Felt like forever. I was gonna give you thirty-three more minutes before I came after you."

The butterflies in her stomach fluttered to life, a slow smile curling her lips as Rathe made a low sound of irritation behind her.

Who are these guys?

She'd never understood the idea of swooning before, but she was pretty sure her reaction to these men came close.

Flattered Viper knew how long she'd been gone down to the minute, Arawyn's grin widened.

Her house was still wrecked, people were still hunting her for reasons she didn't understand, she was potentially an alien, and the man holding her was more than likely not human either. Yet, he had a way of making everything seem... better. Lighter. Like her problems weren't all that bad, after all.

Footsteps sounded behind Viper, and she leaned to the side to smile at Fear, only momentarily worried about what he'd think of her being in Viper's arms. Her worry vanished at the warm smile he gave her.

Tapping Viper on the shoulder so he would set her down, she laughed softly at the small pout that pulled down his sexy mouth as he reluctantly released her.

Noticing the bag still clutched in her hand, Viper took it from her, then flicked his gaze to Rathe.

"She's staying?"

"Mm. For now."

Sounding as suspicious as a kid being offered candy for dinner, knowing it was too good to be true, Viper narrowed his eyes and warily questioned, "Why? What changed? Did something happen?" He frowned darkly and scanned her, looking for injuries. "Are you okay? Are you hurt? Did someone shoot you again?"

"She's fine. We'll discuss it shortly. After we get her things unpacked."

Cutting Rathe a look for answering for her, she glanced up at Viper, then over at Fear. "I'm okay. My house, not so much. But, Asshole and I are fine."

Fear made a low sound, like a half-swallowed laugh and cleared his throat to cover what noise escaped, but the slight curve of his lips gave him away. Shaking his head, he repeated, "Asshole?"

The fact that he was looking at Rathe when he said it had her snickering. "Not Rathe. My cat's name is Asshole."

Fear eyed her. "You have a cat?"

"I- yes? Why? Are you allergic?"

"No. It's just odd."

Before she could question him as to why, he moved to the step above hers. Arawyn tilted her head back, breathless at his nearness, and let him cup her cheeks, instantly lost in those warm, grey eyes of his.

"You sure you're okay?" he asked softly, his deep voice a vibration she could feel in her chest.

She leaned into his warm, calloused palm. "Yeah. I'm okay."

He searched her face intently, only relaxing when he saw she meant it. "Good."

The stroke of his thumb across her bottom lip sent a pleasant shiver through her, but he released her a second later. Settling a hand at the small of her back instead, he ushered her upstairs.

"C'mon, then, Baby. Let's get you set up."

Viper led the way, bounding up the stairs like an overly excited puppy. In a move she probably should've seen coming, he tried to put her bags in his room. Fear made a sound almost like a growl and gave him a look, then retrieved her bags and led her farther down the hall.

"I just wanted her to feel safe, is all!"

Arawyn hid a grin and shook her head. She had a feeling

staying with these men would be a lot of things, but boring wouldn't be one of them.

It took two hours to unpack everything and get her belongings set up in the guestroom Fear showed her to, telling her it was hers for as long as she wanted it.

That had surprised her, to put it mildly.

She'd been operating under the assumption she would be expected to leave as soon as she found a new place. That still might be true, if Rathe had anything to say about it, but oddly enough, Mr. Dark and Brooding had clearly overheard the invitation and hadn't disputed Fear's words.

Fear had gone on to shock the hell out of her by carrying Asshole up the stairs. In his arms. Arawyn had watched on, slack-jawed, as he cradled the imposter who looked like her cat but couldn't be, because Asshole hated everyone.

When Fear finished setting up food, water, a litter box, and even a window perch, she'd asked simply, "How?"

He just shrugged. "Cats don't hate all of us."

Okayyy? 'All of us.' So, cats hate most aliens but not all. Cool, cool. Explains a lot.

She'd just nodded like that was a completely normal thing to say, not wanting to give herself away.

Arawyn settled in, putting her clothes away in a beautifully carved dresser and hanging a few articles in a closet the size of her old bedroom all while convincing herself she should simply accept their hospitality for tonight instead of voicing any of the questions building in her mind.

There'll be time for that later.

Turning once she'd finished her task, she found Viper

and Fear working together to stock the attached bathroom with toiletries and towels.

It struck her, then, just how much her life had changed. Having two large men in a room with her, especially one as giant as Fear, should've made her feel crowded. Would have, if they'd been any other men. Instead, it was kind of nice.

She glanced toward the door when she heard a noise in the hallway and found Rathe looking in. He made no move to enter, and not for the first time, she got the impression he held himself apart, even from the men she suspected were his only friends.

It wasn't hard to recognize the behavior. She, too, had been holding herself apart for so long. So very long.

He met her gaze, his own narrowing sharply before the emotion in his eyes disappeared like it had never existed. Realizing he'd seen the empathy on her face and didn't appreciate it one bit, she tried to hide it, but it was too late. He was gone, vanishing down the hallway. She heard water running a moment later.

"Are you hungry, *moín Firláh*?" Fear asked, ducking under the door frame as he stepped out of the bathroom.

"I kept the roast warm!" Viper's amber eyes warmed as he slipped past his friend. "There's plenty. I can make you—"

"No, thank you. Both of you," she murmured, peering up at them with a tired smile. "I think I'm just going to rest, if you don't mind."

Fear frowned. "You sure?"

Viper stepped up next to him and added, "You haven't eaten since breakfast."

Her smile widened, becoming something more genuine

in the face of their concern. Food was tempting, but she needed time to just... breathe.

"I'm sure."

Fear gave an understanding nod and clapped Viper on the back. "Let's give the lady her space."

"But, but... I wanted to—"

"Tomorrow," Fear interrupted. "Patience."

Viper visibly recoiled. "What the fuck is patience? Sounds awful! Besides, I made cooki—"

The rest of Viper's words were cut off with the closing of the door. She debated locking it behind them but dismissed it after a second. Something told her if they wanted to get in, a locked door would do less than nothing to stop them or slow them down.

Letting out a deep breath, she gazed at the room. It was massive and beautiful. Floor-to-ceiling windows took up the rear wall, giving her an uninterrupted view of the vast, moonlit ocean beyond. A king-sized bed was positioned in the middle of the room with a sitting area and a vanity on the left wall next to a door that led to the walk-in closet. On the right was the door leading to the attached bath.

The huge, walk-in shower hiding within called to her like a Siren. Stripping as she went, she cranked the water to something just shy of boiling, then stepped under the spray.

As the water sluiced over her, she tried to make sense of the chaos her life had suddenly become. Her power had first emerged when she was sixteen. That was ten years ago, so why, now, were all these... beings coming out of the woodwork? And why the fuck did the majority seem hellbent on hurting her?

What changed?

As hard as it was to believe that pulse of power was at

fault for all the strange occurrences, she couldn't convince herself it was unrelated. Too much had happened right on the heels of her unleashed power to be coincidental.

Finally shutting off the water when her skin was bright pink, she dried off and threw on the oversized t-shirt someone had laid on her bed—Viper's, if she wasn't mistaken.

Something mouthwatering wafted past her nose, making her stomach growl demandingly. Turning toward the scent, she spotted a plate that had been placed on the small table set beside the door. Under the plate was a note that read 'In case you change your mind.'

Swallowing past a lump in her throat, she took the sandwich and cookies to the sitting area. Arawyn ate on autopilot, her mind blessedly blank as she stared into space.

As soon as the hole in her stomach was filled, exhaustion swept over her in a wave. Climbing beneath the incredibly soft sheets, she tried to pull sleep over her as easily as she did the blankets, but almost the moment she laid down, tears built behind her eyes.

The unfamiliar shadows on the walls blurred when her eyes filled, then overflowed, the salty trails slipping over her temples to soak into her hair.

She didn't even know why she was crying. She'd lived through much, much worse without breaking down.

She just felt... overwhelmed.

The emotions making her chest feel like it was caving in weren't all bad, though. A lot of it was gratitude. There was confusion and wariness in there, too, and a jaded kind of skepticism.

She didn't understand why they cared. Why would they protect her, take her in, feed her? That was hard enough to reconcile with the life she'd lived and her experience with people, but that they didn't seem to want anything in return?

Alone now, without their presence filling her mind, *that* felt too good to be true.

There was just so much roiling through her that it needed an outlet, so she gave herself this moment. She let herself cry in the dark quiet of a strange room. She let herself break down, just a little, with the shadows of night hiding the weakness like it was their secret.

Arawyn could feel how close she was to answers. More than once, she'd opened her mouth to ask what she desperately wanted to know, but she stopped herself every time. She wanted them badly, but while there was a part of her that was excited to learn about what she was, there was an equally strong part of her that was hesitant, that whispered there might be bliss in her ignorance.

That part said, once she began asking the questions, nothing would ever be the same again. And that scared the shit out of her. Her life wasn't perfect. To most, it might not even be considered good. But, it was hers, and she'd fought like hell for it.

Despite the hardships, despite her power and her past, she'd made her own version of normalcy, and she was proud of the life she'd created.

Asking questions was sure to change everything, and she needed to be prepared for the harsh bite of reality that might tear apart all she'd worked for.

Deep down, she knew finding the truth would be worth it, even if it upended her world. She could handle it, whatever *it* was. Right?

Yes. She was sure she could, but showing her vulnerability wasn't easy. What if they stopped being so open with her, once they realized she knew nothing of what she was—or... what *they* were? There were too many unknown variables at play to give her any kind of comfort in making a decision about how to handle herself.

A ragged breath slipped past her lips, and she tried to gather herself while the wet trails cooled on her warm cheeks.

Viper's voice sounding through the wall startled her enough that she jerked. "Goodnight, Pretty!"

Huffing a watery laugh, she swallowed the tears still clogging her throat and called back, "Goodnight, Cookie Monster." She paused then yelled, "Goodnight, Fear."

She heard a distant, masculine chuckle before he responded faintly, "Sweet dreaming, *Firláh*."

Arawyn almost didn't... but then she remembered the look in Rathe's eyes when he'd stood outside her room, holding himself apart. Voice quiet, she spoke into the darkness. "Goodnight, Rathe."

There was no answer. She hadn't expected one, but some sense told her he'd heard.

Chapter Twenty-Eight

Rathe

Rathe lay awake for a long time, listening to the rhythmic sound of her breathing. He'd more than half-expected her to get up when she thought them unaware, so he waited, but she never did.

Instead, she cried, then fell asleep.

Many thought him to be a cold, uncaring son of a bitch. And they were right. The only people he gave a fuck about were his brother and friend. But, the sound of her suppressed tears, and the image of her in that room, alone, tore at him.

Just as his resolve to ignore it, and the surety it was a ruse, began to fracture, just as he was on the verge of going to her, his brother yelled a good night's wish and transformed her tears into laughter.

She'd returned the sentiment, calling out to Viper, then Fear. When the soft melody of her voice filtered through the walls to extend a good night to him, as well, surprise and a flicker of confusion had his brow tightening with a frown even as his lips curled in a small, involuntary smile.

Rising when the sun was a couple of hours from breaking the horizon, he dressed quickly and woke his brother. With the roads empty, the skies still dark, and Arawyn safely asleep in his home under Fearson's watchful eye, he and Viper returned to her house.

VIPER

Viper frowned as he drew in another deep breath, searching again through the plethora of scents to find the one that didn't belong, but it was frustratingly elusive.

Cutting a look at his brother, he murmured, "You said you smelled a Redcap earlier?"

"Mm. Why?"

"That's not what I'm getting." Dropping his Glamor enough that his tongue returned to its natural forked shape, he flicked it out to test the air. "Tastes like a *Troll* to me, but something about it is off. And it's dissipated more than it should've."

Rathe's gaze sharpened on him. "Redcaps and Trolls don't work together. Ever."

"Exactly. Fear said an Aswang attacked her at the gym, and what I killed tasted like a Virika." Holding Rathe's gaze, he waited for his brother to come to the same conclusion he had.

Rathe narrowed his eyes at him. "You think someone is sending assassins after her."

"Only assassins bother to use magic to change their tastes—or scents—and only those who don't have enough power or aren't strong enough to handle the cost needed to hide it entirely." He shrugged. "Changing it to cover our tracks is the next best option."

"Then why did the one you killed here use a tranq dart? If they had a clear shot, why not just take her out?"

Viper grit his teeth. The memory of seeing her go down had played a prominent role in his nightmares last night. Even Light Jumping, he hadn't been fast enough. As absolutely fucking murderous as it made him, Rathe was right. If the assassin wanted to take her out, he had a clear shot.

Killing her wasn't the goal.

"Whoever hired them must want something from her," he answered.

Rathe made a low sound. "Or they're being sent to harass her as a warning from my father."

Viper barely resisted the urge to roll his eyes. "You're still on about that?"

"Yes," his brother said flatly. "Until I've got definitive proof to the contrary, I can't rule it out. And neither can you, so watch what you say around her."

"What happened to 'innocent until proven guilty,'" he fired back.

He knew Rathe felt it: the draw to her, the inescapable sense she was important to them. He wasn't naive enough to think that meant she couldn't be a spy, but you only had to look in her pretty green eyes to see there wasn't a scheming bone in her body.

There was no doubt she was dangerous. He had sensed there was some blood on her hands, but he also had the distinct feeling there was more to her story. The shadows buried in the depth of those eyes told him as much.

She had a past, one he wanted to delve into and learn more about. But, was she plotting against them? Was she a pawn for the King? No.

On that, Viper was absolutely fucking positive.

A muscle ticked in Rathe's temple, a sure sign he was getting pissed. "We don't have that luxury, and you damn well know it." His brother's gaze dropped pointedly to the countless scars visible below Viper's tats, scars he usually kept hidden beneath his Glamor.

Ignoring the look, he stepped closer and clasped Rathe's shoulders. "You've always trusted me before. Why can't you do that now? Why can't you trust in what I feel? In my instincts. I know you have to think this way, that you have to be suspicious of everyone. I know you do it to keep Fear and me safe. But, this time... This time you're wrong."

Rathe let out a breath, his expression softening slightly, but his eyes stayed hard. "And if *you're* wrong? What then, little brother? If we let down our guards, and she betrays us, what then? This time, you may not escape with a few scars. This time, I may actually lose you."

"I understand your fear, but I need you to trust me now.

She's not what you think she is." When Rathe started to argue, he cut him off, "Just try. Watch her. Look at her actions. Listen to what she says. Everything about her is genuine. It's the way she moves, the way she speaks and holds herself."

Viper could see the doubts in Rathe's eyes, could see the refusal to trust an outsider, no matter how drawn to her he knew Rathe was. Chest tight with regret, gratitude, and sorrow for what his brother had to do to protect him from their father's wrath, he grabbed the back of Rathe's neck.

Pressing their foreheads together, he rasped, "The scars I wear aren't your fault. No matter what happens to me, it's not your fault. It never has been. You're not the one who picks up the lash."

At Rathe's scoffing sound of disagreement, he straightened and squinted. Deciding on a different tactic, he shrugged and turned away.

"Fine. If you're that convinced she's untrustworthy, keep on making her dislike you. Fear and I will woo her." He peered back over his shoulder. "But, don't come crying to me when she falls madly in love with us and wants nothing to do with you."

And there it was. The realization of exactly how serious he and Fear were about her, and the glint of understanding they were playing for keeps.

Good.

He didn't want to leave his brother behind, but as the humans say, 'all is fair in love and war.'

Chapter Twenty-Nine

ARAWYN

Arawyn stretched as wakefulness seeped into her, chasing away the nearly dreamless night's sleep she'd had. She hadn't slept that well in years. Surprising, considering she was in an unfamiliar place surrounded by men who, regardless of the connection between them, were practically strangers.

Throwing back the covers, she padded into the bathroom, halting mid-step when she caught sight of her reflection in the mirror. Her green gaze seemed brighter, there were no dark circles under her eyes, and she had a healthy glow in her cheeks.

Staring at herself, she realized she felt as good as she looked. There was an energy coursing through her, a lightness she couldn't explain.

Arawyn frowned and leaned into the mirror, studying her reflection for a second longer before shaking her head. Blaming the change on getting a decent night's sleep, she carried on with her morning routine.

Taming her hair into subtle waves, she quickly dressed in a pair of leggings and a slouchy tunic, then slipped from the room and quietly made her way down the hall.

The loft was silent, the early sunlight just beginning to glow warmly through the windows. She half-expected the guys to be awake already, but the living room was empty, save for Asshole curled up in his window perch, and a glance told her she had the kitchen to herself.

Impulsively deciding to do something to say 'thank you' to Viper and Fear—and even Rathe—for all they'd done, she rummaged through the cabinets, pantry, and fridge, acquainting herself with the kitchen, as well as the stash of food they had on hand.

Breakfast. All men like to eat, right? Even aliens.

Pulling a full carton of eggs from their freakishly large fridge, she wondered if aliens ate more than usual. Then again, with three large men living beneath one roof, she could understand the need for all the large appliances. Even the stove was professional, an eight burner Viking she was excited to use.

She pulled out the bowls and pans she'd need to cook, staying quiet so breakfast would be a surprise when they woke.

Taking stock of her ingredients, her first inclination was to make pancakes, but since Rathe wasn't a fan, she decided to make biscuits instead. Arawyn followed the recipe, then doubled it, letting her mind wander while she worked.

She was surprised by just how relaxed she felt in the loft,

cooking for three men she barely knew. Yet, the more time she spent with them, the more comfortable she grew, the more she settled into that familiar feeling each of them gave her.

If her intuition was correct, and it usually was, they were like her... or perhaps *she* was like *them*.

I can't believe I'm actually entertaining the idea that I'm an alien.

But, it made sense. The power, the magnetism, the intuition. She was stronger and faster than everyone else, with the notable exception of Braven. Her senses were sharp, and her night vision was very, very good. *Inhumanly* good.

She'd always known those weren't human traits, had always searched for answers to what she was, often entertaining the idea of beings that were decidedly supernatural. She'd researched everything from shifters to vampires, mermaids to fairies, and even entertained the idea that other worlds existed beyond her own.

At least aliens are hot, she smirked to herself. *If women knew the males looked like these guys, they'd be begging to get abducted.*

Popping the trays in the oven, she went to work scrambling eggs, frying bacon, and making coffee while she mulled over the questions circling through her mind.

Refreshed after a full night's sleep, she didn't feel quite so overwhelmed in the light of day, but she still wasn't sure if she was ready to question the very fabric of her life. Deciding to play the morning by ear and follow her intuition, she relaxed and lost herself to the mindless task of cooking.

When she was done with the meal, she eyed the chocolate chips she'd meant for the pancakes before she'd changed her plans. Needing to keep her hands busy, and her mind distracted, she set to work making a batch of cookies for Viper. Somehow, she just knew he'd appreciate the effort.

Scooping neat little balls of dough, and trying vigorously not to pop any more into her mouth, she almost missed the sense of someone moving in behind her.

Arawyn whirled, wielding the cookie scoop like a weapon while her free hand went to the knife holster she'd strapped to her thigh.

"Holy shit, Viper! I swear, I'm going to get you a bell, if you insist on sneaking up on me," she scolded him.

His only response was a sleepy smirk she found entirely too sexy. The crooked way it pulled at his lips made her soften, relaxing from the fighting stance... which was when it sank in that he was naked.

Well, mostly naked.

Viper ate up the sight of her with a long, lazy glance. She could practically feel the way his gaze traced down her neck and bare shoulder before skimming over the curve of her breasts down to the flare of her hips. His eyes glittered at the sight of her weapon before journeying down her shapely legs and back up again just as slow and purposeful.

"I could get used to waking up to you in my kitchen every morning." The grin on his lips grew downright mischievous. "Even better, if it were in my bed," he purred.

Every molecule in her body tingled at the open hunger in his eyes. For a moment, she felt like prey beneath his stare. Except, she was fairly positive bunnies weren't tempted to cuddle up with the tiger looking at them like they wanted to eat them.

Jesus. Who knew aliens could flirt so damn well. I think my fucking elbows are blushing.

Arawyn may be unwillingly accustomed to being the

object of people's obsession, but standing there, lost in the frank admiration and desire shining down at her from Viper's handsome face, she realized she was not at all accustomed to being flirted with, at least not without being accompanied by a manic, grasping kind of desperation.

It was intoxicating. At least, coming from him.

Over and over again, these men surprised her, awakened parts of her she'd never had the opportunity to explore before.

Restraint finally breaking, she slowly let her eyes drop down his body, taking in his state of undress. Bare chested, the imposing breadth of his shoulders and every defined ridge of his stomach was on lusciously rugged display.

The man had abs for days. It was almost unfair. She wanted to count them, wanted to study every colorful tattoo inked across his skin.

Entirely unable to help herself, she let her gaze continue south to the mouthwatering, very impressive *V* of muscle angling past the black waistband of his boxers.

A laugh burst out of her without warning and quickly devolved into an uncontrolled giggle the moment her gaze dropped lower still.

Displayed right over the bulge beneath his boxers was a warning label.

"'Choking hazard'? Really?"

"What?" he teased, prowling forward a few steps until he was just over a foot away. Too close, but not nearly close enough. "You nearly choked already."

"On a laugh," she drawled, trying her damndest not to blush any harder.

"I call that a success." Viper waggled his brows before

running his hand through his sleep-mussed hair, pushing the blonde strands away from his forehead.

His muscles shifted and bunched with the motion, the images displayed on his body rippling deliciously.

That her cookie monster looked that good after just waking up made her a tiny bit jealous. She had to work to make herself presentable in the morning, but Viper appeared to have just rolled out of bed looking like a damn underwear model.

It took serious restraint not to move closer and lessen the space between them.

"You cooked? For us?" he questioned, eyeing what was clearly too much food for just her. His voice was oddly soft, his attention unexpectedly intent on hers.

"Yes? Is that okay?" she asked, worried she'd overstepped.

"No. I mean, yes! Yes, that's- it's uh... " He trailed off, looking flustered and, weirdly enough, almost shy. Before she could wonder too much about it, he spoke again, effectively distracting her.

"Are you making cookies?" he asked suddenly, his voice still husky from sleep, though his face was lit up like he'd just walked into a kitchen full of presents.

"Yeah. Chocolate chip."

He peered down at her with wide, excited eyes. "How did you know those are my favorite?"

Arawyn arched an eyebrow, but her voice was warm when she said, "I have a feeling all cookies are your favorite."

"You're not wrong." His grin made the butterflies in her stomach flutter.

Smiling in return, she eyed the tattoos decorating his corded forearm and strong, defined bicep, seeking out the chocolate chip cookies amidst the design. "If I'm being honest, though, your tats gave you away."

"How observant of you," his grin turned playfully predatory, like he knew she'd checked him out on more than one occasion and found him sexy as hell. She couldn't even deny it was true. Reaching for her wrist, he grasped her lightly and brought the cookie scoop closer, holding it between them. "I like things that are sweet and delicious."

Those startlingly gorgeous amber eyes never left hers while he dipped his head. The color brightened, appearing almost golden in the morning light.

Tongue flicking out, he licked the scoop. The flash of a metal piercing caught her attention, and she stared, riveted, as he stole a taste of cookie dough.

Her heart beat a little faster, and her breathing became shallower.

Because watching him lick... well, anything, was hot as fuck.

After their kiss last night, she was eager to taste him again. This time, she wanted to know what his tongue piercing would feel like as it grazed her lips, explored her mouth, brushed against her own tongue.

"Mmm," he hummed appreciatively, and Arawyn swore the sound went straight through her, settling low in her belly. Her clit thrummed with newly awakened want, and she almost gave in to the need to kiss him. To really kiss him. To feel the smooth metal of that tongue ring.

Viper grinned, and she clenched her thighs, shifting on her feet.

The sharp beep of the oven timer startled her, and she nearly jumped, cursing it's impeccable timing. Damn the thing.

Viper chuckled, and released her wrist to not-so-subtly readjust his growing hardness.

Arawyn nearly choked, for real this time, to see the blatant evidence of how much he wanted her tenting his boxers. She tried so, so very hard not to stare... or lick her lips at the sight.

That would be rude, right?

But damn, it was tempting, because holy shit... 'Choking hazard' was an understatement.

"What can I do to help?" Viper asked, moving to the oven to turn off the timer.

You could take me back to the bedroom...

She almost said it. Almost.

Except he opened the oven and pulled out the perfectly golden biscuits. Seeing him standing there dressed only in his boxers and an oven mitt while he helped her with breakfast just made her fall that much harder.

Who is this man, and where the hell did he come from?

She'd never met anyone like Viper before. She'd never met anyone like Fear or Rathe either.

She shook her head, standing motionlessly in the kitchen, just watching Viper juggle the biscuits and the cookie sheets, easily shuffling them around and resetting the timer.

Together, they baked, set the table, and chatted easily until Fear crossed into the kitchen.

Oh my god...

Wearing only a pair of grey sweatpants, she nearly drooled at the sight of his muscles covered in those white, swirling tattoos. His arms were huge, corded and powerful, and his abdomen looked like it was made out of bands of steel, the hard planes cut to perfection.

Mahogany hair hung loose around his shoulders, tempting her to cross to him, climb him like a tree, and run her fingers through it.

With wide eyes and parted lips, she tried to force herself back into a semblance of normal.

Why was she so affected by these men?

She had seen plenty of attractive guys in her life, but none of them had called to her like this. Attracted her so deeply, so desperately. Her whole body thrummed from the combination of their intoxicating scents and the light brush of their power whispering against her own.

Arawyn basked in it, the electrifying, yet infinitely comforting, feeling of it stunning her to stillness for a handful of seconds.

"Good morning," Fear rumbled, his voice deep and rough, his gorgeous grey gaze eating her up like she was his breakfast instead of the spread Viper was placing on the table for them. It did funny things to her stomach, those butterflies working double time simply to keep up.

To distract herself from doing something foolish—like throwing caution to the damn wind and kissing both of them, right here, right now—she spun on her heel and headed to the coffee pot, determined to keep her hands busy and off of the men behind her.

Did these men realize she was attracted to both of them?

The real question is: what the hell does it say about me that I can't determine which of them I'm more attracted to?

She wasn't ready to look too closely and find out, not over what was supposed to be a pleasant breakfast. Shaking the thoughts away, she raised the carafe, the dark liquid sloshing against the glass.

"Can I get you coffee?"

"You don't have to do that," Fear mumbled, already moving toward her.

Arawyn waved him off, turning back to grab a mug before filling it. The warm, rich scent of an expensive brew wrapped around her, but it wasn't nearly as mouth-watering as the scent of Fear that stole every ounce of her attention.

A large hand gently settled on her hip. Just as tentative and questioning as he'd been at the club, Fear waited for her response, for her permission.

As though her body had a mind of its own, she was leaning back against him before she could decide if it was wise. The moment her shoulder blades brushed his chest, he relaxed, drawing a full breath and releasing it slowly, like he'd just wagered a huge bet and won.

It warmed her how much he valued her space, how he asked instead of just assuming he could take like most men she'd met. That same familiar feeling stole over her, and she realized just how safe she truly felt with both Fear and Viper.

That protected feeling she'd gotten at the club had increased tenfold in the days since.

Rathe was a different subject, but that he'd all but hauled her back here told her beneath his cold, authoritative exterior, he cared.

If she closed her eyes, she could still feel the brush of his lips against her hand, could still feel the warmth of his skin.

This might be a problem.

Deciding not to borrow trouble, she set the mug down and watched as Fear filled it with milk until the color was a warm caramel. He took it with only two sugars while Viper wanted his as sweet as he could make it.

When Fear was finished, she stirred his coffee, their

movements coordinated like they'd done this morning dance a million times together.

Turning in his arms, she tipped her head back, unable to stop her lips from curling as she gazed up at his ruggedly handsome face.

"I hope you're hungry, because we made a ton of food. Maybe too much." Peering around his bulk, she eyed the plethora of dishes.

Never in her life had she cooked this much. They'd gone through two entire cartons of eggs, at Viper's insistence, and the biscuits were piled into an unstable tower. An array of jams and jellies were spread across the table, and the bacon... well, you could never have too much bacon, so she relented on that one. Especially since it had already taken a substantial hit thanks to Viper's snacking.

"No such thing as too much food, Pretty Loon." Viper pulled her chair out and swept his arm toward it in a playful little bow.

"Such gentlemen," Arawyn teased as Fear led her to the chair, and Viper pushed it in when she sat.

Apparently, chivalry wasn't dead, and it made her giddy.

When had she ever felt so light? So excited for the day ahead?

A scoff sounded behind her, and she tensed, only relaxing into her seat again when she noticed Rathe entering the kitchen dressed in a set of golden silk pajamas.

"Don't let them fool you. These two haven't been called gentlemen since they were old enough to talk."

Arawyn couldn't respond, too busy trying to keep her jaw from dropping as Rathe crossed to the coffee bar.

His pants hung low on his hips—teasing her with the promise of one hell of a view, if they slipped just another few inches—while the top hung open, completely unbuttoned as though he'd just thrown it on before leaving his room. His hair, unlike his friends, was tamed back with only one dark lock escaping haphazardly across his forehead.

He looked like gilded sin, a walking temptation.

"Speak for yourself, Brother. I'm always a gentleman." Viper winked at her, the long scar bisecting his left eye wrinkling with the gesture, while Rathe raised one dark brow in return, a hint of a smile tugging the corner of his lips.

Seeing the two of them interact, she could tell they were close, and she wondered what the story was between them. While there were many visual similarities between the two, she couldn't get over their dissimilarities.

Their personalities were so different. Where Viper was light, Rathe was dark. Where Viper hid behind his humor, Rathe hid behind his authority.

Even their ink spoke to the differences between them— Viper's colorful tats to Rathe's monochrome. Black and grey tattoos blazed across Rathe's bronzed skin, covering nearly every inch in elaborate images and patterns she wanted to trace. She ached to study each one and learn the story and importance behind them.

Rathe caught her studying him. Refusing to turn away and pretend she hadn't been watching, she held his unwavering focus while he joined them at the table.

Chapter Thirty

Rathe

Most women would flirt with him or drop their gazes only to glance back up coquettishly. It was a move he'd seen over and over again, one he'd become increasingly impervious to.

Yet, this little vixen held his heavy stare boldly. Those beautiful glass-green eyes of hers held no shame for the way she'd watched him. Once again, he'd felt the weight of her gaze upon him like a light caress when he entered the kitchen. It was a nearly physical sensation, and he warred with himself over how much he enjoyed her attention.

"I need you to trust me." Viper's words from last night resonated with him.

He trusted his brother with his life. But, he also felt responsible for both Viper's and Fear's safety.

His father had done terrible things to both of them, ruined each of their lives in ways Rathe could never fix. Throughout all the years they'd spent together, he'd been trying to make amends, providing for them and sheltering them from the worst of his father.

If his initial suspicions were correct about Arawyn, she was just the latest in a long line of deception and treachery from the King.

But, what if he was wrong?

Or what if Viper was?

The war within him waged on as he fought his growing attraction to their little vixen. He needed to know her, needed to find out if he could truly trust her or if his wariness was warranted.

Finally letting her out of their staring contest, he spared a moment to scrutinize his brother, who was watching her with an intensity he hadn't seen in him for far too long.

Viper had a devil-may-care attitude about many things, but Rathe knew it was a shield, his humor donned like armor. He saw it for what it was: Viper's way to protect himself.

That his brother was lowering that shield for Arawyn spoke to just how much he liked her. Just how much he trusted her. He couldn't remember a time Viper had ever taken such keen interest in a woman.

While they ate, Viper and Fearson carried on the conversation, leaving Rathe to simply observe the way she interacted with his friends.

More and more, he wondered if he'd been wrong. She seemed so genuine.

For his brother's and friend's sakes, he hoped he'd jumped to conclusions about her.

Because if she were a snake, a treacherous spy sent from his father, it might break Viper. No one else could see the pain his brother lived with daily, and suffered from at night, but he could. So could Fearson.

They were the only family he cared about, and he wouldn't, couldn't, stand by and let her destroy another part of Viper.

As for Fearson, the man was fierce and strong. A powerful warrior, if he'd ever met one, but even he had endured much in his twenty-nine years. Rathe knew how private his friend was, how long it took the man to trust him and his brother. That Fearson let Arawyn in so easily concerned him. If she betrayed them, any of them, he'd have no choice but to end her.

Given how bewitched his brother and friend were, he didn't know if they'd ever forgive him for it. He didn't know if he would be able to forgive himself, for that matter. He'd done dark, horrible things, but killing her...

The sharp ding of his phone blessedly cut through his dark thoughts to interrupt breakfast, and the conversation hiccupped while he dug into his pocket and pulled it out.

Clearing his throat, he cut a look at Viper, whose smile bled from his lips as they exchanged a long, knowing look.

Often, the Fae Clans would reach out when they had a problem, and the rogue blood sucker they'd been getting reports about had struck again, this time taking out a small group of humans, leaving their bodies in the streets, fully drained.

Viper nodded once in understanding.

"Gotta go, Pretty Little Loon." Viper's chair scraped along the floor as he stood. Swooping down, his brother kissed the top of Arawyn's head, then gave her a cheeky grin. "Try not to miss me too much while I'm gone."

Rathe could see the desire to question where they were going in her beautiful green eyes. He stood swiftly, smoothing a hand down his stomach while he pushed his chair in.

"Thanks for breakfast, Viper."

"Nope. Uh, uh." His brother shook his head, a secretive smile dancing across his features. "This was all Arawyn's doing. I just helped." Viper all but skipped from the room, leaving him with that little bomb of knowledge.

Hiding the shock from his face, he tried to relax the furrow of his brows.

She'd cooked for them? The significance of that stunned him so much he froze in place for a beat.

She waved off Viper's comment, a light blush warming her cheeks. "It was nothing. I just wanted to do something to say thanks for... you know... everything." She tucked her long, pale hair behind her blunted ear, the shape not quite human but not quite Fae either.

Was this a way to get him to let his guard down? Or was she being sincere?

Not for the first time, he wished his powers included the ability to Discern: deciphering lies from truths.

Rathe said the only thing that came to mind, "You didn't have to do that."

The little vixen cocked her head, studying him gently. "I know," she said softly. "And you didn't have to bring me back here last night." She shrugged her shoulders.

Rathe nodded, trying to make sense of her as he took his leave and headed to his room.

Rumpled, twisted sheets greeted him, reminding him of his restless sleep.

Blowing out a breath, he changed quickly and left the loft with Viper, looking forward to a day of relative normalcy. Tracking down rogue Fae was typical for him, and if he were lucky, the fucker would make a perfect meal for his father.

He looked forward to the hunt—thrived in serving justice where he could.

Yes, it promised to be a damn good day… if only he could keep his mind from returning to the little minx he'd left behind.

FEARSON

His little temptress watched Viper and Rathe leave without a single question. He knew the need to know where they were going and what they were doing burned on the tip of her tongue. It hadn't escaped his notice that she observed everything with rapt attention to detail. She'd seen their weapons, the cash, and antiquities littering various surfaces.

She'd asked as much from them yesterday, and it had taken a small piece of him to deny her the answers she was looking for.

He wanted to share his world with her. If she knew the truth, she'd understand the things they did, while not always wholesome acts, were for the greater good. In their own twisted way, they helped people and made it a mission of theirs to serve and protect just as much as, if not more than, any harm they caused.

A ruler could ask for no more. He may not be on the path to ruling any longer, his Clan long-since fallen to High King Ehrendil, but it would always be a part of him, a heritage he'd been set to fulfill, if the tide of war had gone differently.

The familiar stab of anger and pain at what his people, what his parents, had suffered hit him. The atrocities Ehrendil had wrought upon his Clan and the memory of blood-soaked bodies littering the ground of their mountainside home still haunted him.

Focusing on Arawyn, he swallowed down the old rage, unwilling to let it sour this moment with his Fated.

For now, he needed to subdue his fury and follow orders, no matter how hard it was to do the King's bidding. There would come a time for revenge, for justice, but it wasn't this day.

Arawyn stood and began clearing dishes, stacking their plates and gathering the utensils. Fearson knew she lived alone and had cooked and cleaned for herself for years. Hell, he knew things were different in the human realm—the women carrying much of the burden of the household, child rearing, and even maintaining a job to support their families —but his heart nearly stopped when she moved to wash his dirty plate in the sink.

Women of the Night Court were highly revered, and there was no greater honor than to serve your *Firláh* in all things. Hunting, cooking, cleaning, and helping with the young were all duties of the males in his Clan, as well as maintaining their own training as warriors and protectors. In his case, he would've had the added responsibility and privilege to rule alongside his future Queen.

"No," he stood quickly, crossing to Arawyn and lightly touching her wrist to stop her. "Don't worry about the dishes. I'll take care of them."

"Don't be silly," she said, and peered up at him. Her lashes were dark, despite her pale hair, and they framed her confused, pale green eyes. "I don't mind washing the dishes, Fear. You've all done so much for me. It's seriously the least I could do."

"You made breakfast." Something that still had his heart feeling as light as a fucking feather, even knowing she hadn't done so with the intentions the gesture normally carried. "I'll do the dishes. But first, I thought you might want a tour of the place." He shrugged, hands slung into the pockets of his sweats. Belatedly realizing they'd inched down when Arawyn tracked their downward progression, he smirked, his eyes crinkling at the corners with his smile.

It was good to know she was as attracted to him as he was to her.

Last night, he couldn't get her out of his mind. Just thinking of the sounds she'd made when he got her off in that club got him hard. Having her just one door away, sandwiched between his room and Viper's, had been torture. The desire to go to her rode him hard. Harder still with her scent permeating the loft, driving him to distraction.

He'd barely been able to sleep between lustful dreams.

It was like he was an adolescent all over again—a 'teenager,' as the humans called them—struggling to control his urges.

It was damned embarrassing. He'd fought an erection all through breakfast, enjoying the little hums of enjoyment she made when she ate something delicious, and he made a note not to wear sweats around her until they were more... familiar. Afraid of scaring her off, he tamed the beast in his pants, his heart finally settling when she caved and set his dish in the sink.

"I'd like a tour. Thanks," she smiled while wiping her hands dry.

Fearson wondered if he should change, but a masochistic part of him wanted her gaze on him, wanted to see that same lust in her eyes all morning.

He took her through the basics, showing her the rest of the rooms on the second floor before taking her downstairs. There wasn't much to see outside of storage and his haven—the multi-bay garage where they kept their vehicles.

"This is impressive," Arawyn beamed, easily noticing the interest he had in the cars and bikes filling the space.

"We like our vehicles," Fearson said, rubbing a hand along the back of his neck.

While most women fawned over their expensive taste in cars, he wasn't sure if Arawyn would see it as ostentatious.

"I think you more than like them." Arawyn pointed toward the organized wall of tools and car parts, then eyed the restoration of a vintage 1964 Pontiac GTO he'd been filling the past few months with.

Surprisingly, he felt no rush to get back to his project, now that he had her in his life. Spending time with her was a far better way to fill his days.

"I like to rebuild them. Gives me something to do with my hands."

There were a few other activities he'd like to do with his hands, but he kept that thought to himself. For now.

"You like to create. That's how I feel about weapons." There was an almost lustful note in her voice as she ran her fingertips lightly over the shiny black surface of Viper's Hennessey Venom GT. "Working with metal, shaping it, and creating something from nothing"—she sighed wistfully—"it makes me happy."

She told him about her workshop and how she'd started a small business. A backlog of work waited for her, and she worried about keeping her customers when her workshop had been destroyed. Watching how her face changed just talking about her work, he knew their plan would be timed perfectly.

"We're the same that way, *moín Firláh.*" Fearson looked around proudly. "Rathe noticed my affinity for vehicles and converted most of the main floor into a garage where I could work."

"He did all this?" She glanced around, taking it in with new eyes.

A spark of hope filled his chest. Arawyn and Rathe had started off on rocky ground, and he wanted nothing more than to see the two of them break down their walls, see each other for who they truly were. The more time he spent with her, the deeper the need to unify their group became.

Because he had the distinct feeling she wasn't meant to be only his.

Viper was just as taken with her, and if Rathe would let the tight walls in his armor slip, even just a little, he'd see what they saw in her. His friend would undoubtedly fall every bit as fucking hard.

"Come on." Fearson held out his hand, an open invitation for her to take. "Let me show you the rest."

Careful with his initiation of touch and familiarity, he waited for her to slip her palm into his own. When she did, his world immediately felt right. She filled a piece of him he'd always known was missing.

He'd waited for her, and now, she was here.

Fast cars and motorcycles used to be the only things he thought he'd miss about the human realm when they returned to Faery, but now, he knew that wasn't true.

Every encounter he had with his *Firláh* deepened their connection. He'd never be able to leave her behind.

The realization was startling, but also, so damn right.

He was falling for her. Deeply. And there wasn't an ounce of doubt left.

She was his, and he was undeniably hers.

Chapter Thirty-One

Arawyn

Three more days passed in what felt like the blink of an eye, due entirely to the guys and the fact that they kept her days full. Of course, it was often full of chaos, but it was an addictive kind of chaos, one she was growing to enjoy more and more with every minute she was around them.

She wasn't used to so much human—or non-human, as it were—interaction. She'd spent most of the first day after the tour with Fear waiting for claustrophobia to set in or to feel suffocated by the constant company.

It never came.

Perhaps, it was how long she'd spent alone or, maybe, it was just them, but in the short time she'd been around them, she'd come to crave their presence.

Viper decided keeping her entertained was his job, and

he took it seriously. When he was at the loft, and not off doing whatever it was he did, they cooked together, watched movies, and danced around like crazy people to blaring music. It, admittedly, took quite a bit of coaxing on his part to get her to dance with him, but he'd been determined and eventually won her over.

That was becoming a problem, actually. They were all winning her over. Even brooding, suspicious Rathe.

She didn't know whether to blame her rapidly growing attachment to them on the years of isolation or the ever-strengthening connection drawing her to them, but either way, she was becoming undeniably comfortable with the new direction her life had taken.

When Viper wasn't keeping her busy, she and Fear were in the gym working out together or in the garage trying to get a makeshift workshop set up for her to use during her stay.

All the while, she watched them, listening to everything they said, soaking up any little bit of information they dropped.

Despite her increasing fondness for the three men, she was still wary, still kept her secrets close to the vest, careful to keep her questions as innocuous as possible.

It took those three days of subtle questioning, and cautious wording, to give the impression she knew what they were talking about, to figure out that an Aswang was like them. Sort of. It was a type of whatever they were, anyway.

A secret Internet search from her phone while hiding in the bathroom revealed more information, informing her that an Aswang was a type of shape-shifting vampire. After having a silent meltdown over the possibility that she, too, was a vampire, she eventually calmed herself with the potentially incorrect assurance that she hadn't ever craved blood before, so it was likely she wouldn't start to.

That explained why it had looked like a child and the draining sensation she'd felt on the well of power inside her. It must have been trying to eat it.

She also gleaned that the man who'd tranqed her was what Viper called a Virika. She hadn't figured out what the hell that was and the Internet wasn't any help. She did, however, find out that Viper thought he was an assassin.

To say that little bomb of information had freaked her the fuck out was putting it mildly.

Why the hell was someone after her? And who, or *what*, was he?

Unfortunately, no matter how she phrased her questions, she hadn't been able to garner any further answers from them.

Used to taking care of herself, she wanted to hunt down whomever sent the assassin and eradicate the threat. But, even if she had the information necessary, to have any hope of finding them—which she didn't—she fully acknowledged she was in way over her head. Humans twisted by her power, she could handle. Whatever this prick was? She wasn't so sure she'd make it out alive, if she tried.

They did, at least, try to reassure her by telling her they were on the case. Well, Viper told her *he* was on the case. Fear's exact words were, 'I'm sorry, Baby. If I could tell you more, I would. I know you're used to handling your own problems, but try to trust us.'

Maybe she was crazy, but that did actually make her feel better.

Viper was cheerful, flirtatious, and charming around her

the vast majority of the time, but she'd seen his eyes go cold, had seen his expression become predatory.

Fear was sweet, thoughtful, and gentle. To her. Arawyn was under no delusions that he was just as dangerous and deadly as Viper. The only difference was, where you'd never see her cookie monster coming unless he wanted you to, Fear would walk up to you boldly and slit your throat.

Rathe didn't make any promises, didn't ask for her trust or offer reassurance. He simply met her eyes, and in that one look, she knew he wouldn't rest until he'd erased the threat, no matter what it took.

Arawyn knew that if whoever had sent the possible assassin after her could be found, they would find them.

That understanding, more than the connection she felt to them, more than the way they made her feel, solidified her choice to stay.

There was something about knowing she had three men, with no compunction against killing those they deemed worthy, watching her back that made a girl feel safe. That one of them was definitely psychotic didn't hurt either.

Every day, she found her trust in them growing. Fear and Viper made it easy. The jury was still out on Rathe.

Sometimes, he looked at her like he was contemplating tying her up and interrogating her while other times, she found him watching her with untamed heat in his blue gaze. She didn't know what to make of him, but she was beginning to understand his suspicion of her came from a place of protectiveness for Viper and Fear. Somehow, that understanding only increased her fondness of the brooding, temperamental man.

She'd just made the decision that morning it was time to face the music and ask her questions as soon as they were all home. She was as nervous as she was eager, and she practically vibrated with anxious energy. Luckily, this morning it was only her and Fear, and she had a date with him in the gym where she could work off some of her growing tension.

Arawyn ducked under the jab Fear released, popping up on his inside, getting in two quick hits to his stomach, then dancing away before he could return fire.

The mats beneath her gave a little with every step, letting her bounce on the balls of her feet easily.

Arawyn had nearly squealed with delight when Fear had tugged her up the spiral staircase leading to the third floor loft the other day during their tour, claiming he had a surprise for her.

She'd fully expected another seating area, or perhaps an office, to fill the space, but instead, there was a fully equipped gym. Made sense. These guys were all ripped, gorgeous specimens. Of course, they worked out.

It made her giddy to see the top-of-the-line equipment. Treadmills, ellipticals, stationary bikes, a rowing machine, punching bags, and a slew of weightlifting machines and free weights lined one side of the space, while thick mats covered the rest of the flooring, an obvious arena to train.

When he'd offered to spar with her, she'd jumped at the opportunity and hurried off to change into something to allow better movement.

Every day since, they'd worked out together before ending with a sparring session. The normalcy of the routine had easily become addictive, and she woke up each morning looking forward to their time together.

Just this morning, she'd stood before the mirror in her room trying on the new workout clothing Fear had surprised her with: black yoga pants and a forest-green tank top. The green brought out the mossy color of her eyes, and the fabric clung to her curves in a way that made her look both strong and feminine.

But, hidden beneath her white, lacey tattoos, pale scars slashed across her left bicep and shoulder blades, left visible by the sleeveless top.

Usually she kept her scars hidden away beneath layers of clothing. She'd debated changing before discarding the notion. No. If she were going to live here for any length of time, the guys would eventually see them. Besides, she'd liked the way she felt in the outfit. Casual. Sexy.

A part of herself she'd denied for far too long enjoyed seeing the appreciative looks Viper, Fear, even Rathe gave her. Just being around them soothed the loneliness she'd lived with for so long.

Refusing to hesitate any longer, she went to meet Fear, taking her place before him on the mats.

Fear's eyes had raked over her form-fitting clothing with a molten heat that made her want to squirm, but just as she'd feared, his gaze halted when he caught sight of the scars. Breathless, she'd waited for his reaction. Would they lessen her beauty in his eyes? Would he see them as weaknesses as she once had?

Turned out, she needn't have worried. Crossing to her, Fear had simply reached out and lightly grasped her bicep before brushing his thumb across the marks. Swirling in the depths of his light grey eyes was a wealth of emotion: anger that she'd been hurt, tenderness, as though he wished he'd been there to care for her when she was injured, and a fierce protectiveness that made her feel utterly and blissfully possessed by him.

Somehow, and she wasn't sure exactly how, she felt the depth of his belief in her. His need to protect and care for her wasn't the least bit smothering, because alongside it, he encouraged her, he nurtured her independence, and he acknowledged her ability to take care of herself.

Even now, as they sparred, his lips curled gently while he nursed his ribs.

"You're quick," Fearson praised, rubbing a large hand over the tattooed ridges of his abs where she'd scored those punches.

"And strong if that wince was any indication," she smiled sweetly, enjoying their banter.

Sparring with Fear was so different from sparring with Braven. She was keenly aware of the way Fear moved, how he watched her, how he tracked her movement with both anticipation of her next move, as well as pride at her skill level.

"You're holding back, though," she challenged. "Don't."

Fear arched a brow, and a flicker of emotion worked through his handsome grey eyes. She knew he didn't want to hurt her, but he also didn't want to snub her talent by refusing. Both concerns warmed her, making her heart expand in a way she didn't know it was capable.

The debate was short, his resolution to use full strength hardening his features slightly. Taking up a fighter's stance, he grew more serious.

Something inside her beamed. That he trusted her skills and training enough to let loose thrilled her.

They moved like water, flowing and dancing around each other. Soon, the gym was filled with panting breaths from their exertion. For such a big man, he moved with a gracefulness that must have taken years of training and hard work.

The sun gleamed off his glistening skin as he worked up a sweat, and Arawyn couldn't keep her gaze from trailing a droplet down his hard chest and sculpted abs. She'd never been so envious. The desire to kiss her way down that salty trail settled like fire between her thighs.

Momentarily distracted, Fear threw a punch, but she recovered quickly and slipped his jab. Shifting her weight, she kicked out, her foot making solid contact with Fear's ribs.

Faster than lightning, he caught her ankle and twisted, being careful not to wrench her leg too hard when he threw her off balance, twirling her and sending her careening to the mat.

Breath whooshed from her lungs as she hit the ground hard, barely catching herself with her palms, but she was only down for a second, a mere blink of time.

Bouncing to her feet, refusing to give him a chance to come at her before she had her balance back, she reacted as quick as a cobra, striking at him with two quick punches to his jaw and his ribs before she leapt away.

Fear grinned, the half-feral look on his face more of a turn-on than it should be.

Why does fighting him feel more like foreplay?

Chapter Thirty-Two

ARAWYN

Arawyn wanted to fan herself, to stop long enough to fully appreciate the vision Fear made—hot and sweaty, energized from the fight, his beautiful grey eyes dark with the same lust she felt.

With the white tattoos swirling over his skin, his full beard, and his long, mahogany hair hanging loose around his shoulders, he appeared every bit a warrior, like he'd walked right out of the pages of a romance novel.

They wore a path in the mat, circling each other, both tempting the other to make a move, until Fear lunged for her in a blur, so fast she barely saw the movement, barely realized his intention until his strong arms locked around her body like a vise, and he took her down.

Faster than she anticipated, he knelt over her and pinned

her to the mat. With her wrists firmly in his grasp, he held her hands above her head, trying to incapacitate her. It was clear he thought he'd won, given his sheer size and strength, and Arawyn bit back a grin as she reacted quickly.

Locking her foot around his ankle for leverage, she threw herself sideways with considerable strength, enough to move his broad, muscled frame. Shock widened his eyes, and he grunted when his back made contact with the mat as she reversed their positions of power, but it was all soon replaced with a look of pride and approval.

Fear grinned widely, the white flash of his teeth bright as she settled on top of him, her legs framing his waist. The moment his large hands came to rest on her hips, the mood changed, and she became intensely aware of her center pressed against the hard lines of his abdomen.

Deep, panting breaths had her breasts heaving against the fabric of her tank top, and every graze felt like a little spark of electricity shooting down through her belly.

"Well done, *moín Firláh*," Fear praised, his voice a rumble she could feel beneath her palms as she braced herself against his chest.

A lock of hair fell past her cheek, loosened from the messy bun she'd thrown her pale blonde locks into.

Tentative, so gently it was a stark contrast to the fierce fighter he'd been not a minute earlier, Fear reached up and brushed it back, his fingertips lightly tracing the path along her cheekbone before he tucked the strands behind her ear.

"You're beautiful," he murmured, those arresting grey eyes tracing her features before meeting hers.

The flush of exertion in Arawyn's cheeks deepened. "So are you."

For an extended moment, they locked eyes with one

another, silent but for their rapid breaths. Her gaze slowly dropped to his mouth and her pulse sped until it felt like a hummingbird was trapped in her chest. God, but she wanted him. She wanted to taste him, to feel his hands on her again, to experience the bliss he'd so skillfully given her in the club.

Without letting herself overthink it, she leaned down and kissed him, her lips a soft, tentative graze over his own.

The low groan he gave had heat rushing through her veins. His hand dropped back to her hip, those strong fingers tightening on her, digging into her ass deliciously. It was all the incentive she needed to deepen their kiss, darting her tongue out to lick at the seam of his mouth.

"Fuck, Baby. You taste as sweet as the fruit from the moon trees," Fear muttered against her, then devoured her whole.

He kissed her passionately, driving her to distraction. Their tongues danced together as easily as they had sparred earlier, fighting for control and dominance, yielding and playing and taking.

Every stroke turned her into liquid fire.

Dragging her up the hard line of his body, Fear broke their kiss to trail his mouth along the column of her throat. His beard tickled her skin with every graze.

"Do you know how many times I've dreamt of you since I last had the honor of touching you, Little Temptress?"

A delicious shiver caressed its way along Arawyn's spine from the need in Fear's hoarse voice. Her pussy clenched, and her nipples hardened to points.

"I've thought about you, too," she admitted.

"Have you?" Intrigue filled his baritone voice. "Have you touched yourself, *Firláh*? Have you thought about me while you came around your fingers?"

Arawyn could barely believe he'd been audacious enough to ask, but she couldn't deny the effect his rumbling words had. She was more aware of her body in that moment than she'd been in... maybe ever.

She could feel the rapid rush of her pulse, mindful of each lungful of air she drew, intimately aware of how her clit thrummed to life, begging her to let the man she had pinned to the mat touch her again.

"Yes." The whispered confession was soft in the stillness of the loft.

Fear's groan quickly followed it, breaking the serene quiet. A thrill shot through her from the rough sound. She was already wet for him, and she had no doubt he was just as ready for her, hard and aching.

"Let me touch you again." As much of a demand as it was, it was also a question.

Arawyn felt safe with her gentle giant of a man. If she so much as uttered a rejection, he'd back off, no matter how much it pained him to do so.

Of this she was absolutely positive.

Fear was as respectful a man as she'd ever met.

But, a different hunger flared to life, one she had no desire to deny. "Maybe I want to touch you," she whispered, trailing her eyes up to his.

Smiling at the way his pupils dilated, she slowly slid down his body and settled over the steel-hard evidence of his desire. His hands never left her hips, and they tightened on her flesh when she rocked against him.

Holy hell, he's bigger than I remember.

Pleasantly surprised, Arawyn enjoyed teasing them both a moment longer before she slid farther down his body.

"*Firláh*," he growled, and the hungry note in his voice gave her all the confidence she needed.

Her hands moved over his stomach, worshipping him slowly, her steadfast attention devouring his chiseled abs. She leaned down and kissed the hard planes, enjoying the taste of his skin.

Fear sucked in a harsh breath at the teasing graze of her tongue over his white tattoos. Ever since she'd seen them, she'd been dying to trace them, to study them. She wanted to take her time and become intimately familiar with his body, but she didn't stop, the hard thrum of need making her impatient.

Instead, she focused on the taut muscles of his lower abdomen as she kissed her way to the waistband of his sweats.

"Baby," Fear gasped when she curled her fingers beneath the fabric. "Let me please you."

A sweet smile curved her lips. "You are. Now, shush. It's my turn."

His chuckle broke on a low groan as she slowly tugged his sweats down.

Arawyn bit her lip when she saw the tattoos continued below his pants. They trailed off to points low on his pelvic bone, almost seeming to frame his groin.

Within moments, she had him bared before her, his cock jumping when her fingers grazed the sensitive flesh.

Poised above him, she froze at the sight that greeted her. Questions immediately flooded her mind only to get stuck on her tongue. Soon, she'd ask them, of that she was sure, but for now, she pushed them away in favor of studying the erotic sight before her.

Fear wasn't human. Of that, she was suddenly and absolutely positive.

She'd known or, at the very least, seriously suspected it, as much as she could without definitive proof, but it had been in an abstract way. Now, staring at the very real, very tangible confirmation of his inhumanness, Arawyn thought she should be unnerved, maybe even freaked out. But, the feelings uppermost were curiosity and a stunned kind of wonder.

And lust. Intense, fervent lust.

Fascinated, breathless, she took a moment to study him as she reached out tentatively to touch the velvety length.

Instead of being skin toned, his shaft was almost lavender in color. The pale skin stretched over aching flesh as hard as steel, but it was the large knot at the base that had her eyes growing wide.

Oh my god... What would that feel like inside of me?

Was it odd that was her first thought? She didn't know, but she owned it.

The shape of his cock was unlike any she'd ever seen. It was thicker at the base than it was at the top, and the head was more triangular in shape with a flare at the bottom that almost seemed to pulse. Rigid veins ran through the length, creating a texture better than any dildo she'd ever purchased.

Fear lay perfectly still beneath her, his muscles rigid with the restraint it took to be patient while she looked her fill, but he never once rushed her, didn't shift or sigh.

Rather than scaring her, his differences excited her, making her core slick with need. She bucked against his legs. Her thighs, spread as they were while she continued to straddle him, couldn't get any purchase. The ache in her clit intensified with the denied pressure she needed. It was like the ultimate tease, and she whimpered.

As she stared, a rivulet of precome glided thickly down his pulsing shaft. Entranced, she followed its path, her mouth watering with the sudden need to taste him.

Watching him intently, she leaned down and licked him in one long swipe, moaning when his sweet flavor burst in her mouth.

Chapter Thirty-Three

Fearson

Her mouth was like fucking heaven. Her warm, wet tongue worked expertly over his aching, needy flesh.

"Oh, fuck." He released the human curse, finding it fitting for the exquisite torture Arawyn was giving him.

When she'd peeled away his clothing, she stared at his cock with a wide-eyed, curious gaze. At first, he wondered if it was his size that intimidated her, or the rather large knot at the bottom not all Fae were endowed with, but as her gaze traced every inch of his length, it eventually dawned on him why her breath caught. To realize it was the unglamored sight of his cock that had astonished her.

Unsure of what to do, he let her study him and watched her reaction carefully in return. Her shock quickly blossomed into interest and curiosity, but he'd caught her utter surprise upon that first glance, and it was then the suspicion began to form that she may not know about her Fae heritage.

Was that possible? It was damned hard to believe and, yet...

Her unfamiliarity with Aswangs had been odd, but on its own, not enough to raise any doubts. However, when he considered how strong, yet muted, her power felt—and the fact that, other than letting it brush against him when they'd danced at the club, she'd never once used it, not even when Viper took her off guard at the docks—it raised questions.

Seeing how stunned she'd been when she'd uncovered him—more so than he thought she would've been, if she just hadn't been with his kind before—only served to string his growing theory together.

It was almost too unbelievable to consider, but the suspicion niggling at the back of his mind wouldn't be dismissed.

Just as he was going to say something, the look in her eyes darkened, changing from astonishment to heated passion. When she put her pretty mouth on him, he couldn't have spoken in more than grunts and curses, if his life depended on it.

With each lave of her tongue, he thanked the Gods that while his anatomy may have been strange to her, she found him attractive regardless. Fear knew his cock was inhuman, but just like his tattoos, it had been the one part of himself he couldn't bring himself to glamour.

It never mattered until now. He hadn't been attracted to a woman in years, hadn't even looked at one since coming to the human realm.

Now, he knew why. The moment he entered this realm, something inside of him had sensed his mate. He just hadn't known it consciously, until this moment.

He truly believed he'd been unwittingly honoring his *Firláh* by remaining chaste.

Staring down at his beautiful Arawyn, he was amazed that she'd accepted him between one heartbeat and the next, and he reveled in the lust, desire, and undeniable attraction that darkened her glass-green eyes to something more mossy.

He barely had time to growl, to moan, to hiss a breath at the feeling of her licking up the trail of precome before her lips wrapped around the head of his cock. The pressure of her hot little mouth closing around his length had him cursing under his breath as she slid down his shaft, and then back up.

The moment her tongue touched his sensitive tip, he could no longer keep from tangling his large hands in her silky hair.

Arawyn hummed in appreciation as he wrapped the pale locks around his fists and guided her gently over him, setting a deliberately slow pace. He watched her lashes flutter closed as she savored his flavor, her hums and moans of pleasure vibrating down his cock to settle in his balls.

His little *Firláh* surprised him. Her body was so tiny, her mouth just as small as the rest of her in comparison to his much larger size, but she never gave up her quest to take him deeper and deeper into the recesses of her throat and mouth, determined to please him.

With each bob of her head, she took another inch, then another, and another. He was mindless with passion, his vision glazed. All he could see was her beautiful face, her small hands roaming over his sides, abs, hips, thighs. He craved the light bite of her nails as they scraped along his skin, and he hissed when she boldly cupped his balls in the palm of her hand.

Fear didn't know if he should pray to the Old Gods or the New for the strength to hold on, but it took every ounce of his concentration to hold back, to enjoy her exquisite torture for just a little longer.

Arawyn's beautiful green eyes flicked to his face as she stroked up and down, and a hint of a smile curled her lips when he bucked like a wild man at the feel of her hand venturing to his knot. That spot, that swollen ball at the base of his cock, was reserved solely for his mate. For *her*—his *Firláh*.

If he hadn't already known she was his Fated, his knot swelling for her would have confirmed it.

Never in his life had he dreamed it would feel this good, and he released a needy groan as she wrapped her lithe fingers as far as she could around the girth of it and squeezed. Molten fire licked along his cock, heating him with a passion so intense he could barely see straight.

"Oh, fuck," he rasped, the accent of his Night Court ancestry bleeding more heavily into his voice from how distracted she had him.

"Does that feel good?" she whispered, pulling her lips from him as she played with the most intimate part of his body.

"More than you can imagine, Baby."

He hadn't known how good that knot could make him feel, and thus, wasn't able to brace himself for the moment her mouth latched to it, sucking on the bottom of the knot gently. Her fingers grazed over it, teasing him mercilessly.

"Arawyn," he groaned, unable to contain the warm tingles crawling up his arms and legs. Jolting down his back like bolts of warm electricity, they settled low in his spine, and his heavy balls drew tight.

His cock throbbed and swelled, the veins becoming more pronounced as he neared release.

His little temptress moaned as she felt him grow larger in her hand, and her fingers tightened like a warm, cozy vise around his pulsating knot. Wetting her palm, she stroked it down his shaft and over the knot, mimicking what he wanted her body to do when he had the honor of burying himself inside of her.

Will her gorgeous little pussy be able to take me? Will it be able to stretch over my knot as her fingers do now?

It was a dream he couldn't wait to bring to reality. How many nights had he fallen asleep dreaming of her on top of him? How many mornings had he awoken only to wish she were beneath him? How many times had he fisted himself, squeezing that very knot her hands now blissfully strangled, only to wish it were his mate taking him inside her tight, hot little body?

Between the combination of her swallowing him back inside her sweet mouth, her tongue swirling over his aching flesh, and her hand stroking the swollen base of his cock, he lost himself.

"Baby, I'm... fuck, I'm..." He couldn't finish the sentence as she stole his breath, pushing him over the edge as her mouth, hand, and tongue worked in unison.

He came on a long, loud groan. His hands grew more demanding as he fell, holding her head down as he came into her mouth. Hips jerking, he filled her with jet after jet of his seed, and she swallowed it on a greedy moan, lapping at him like she'd never tasted anything so good.

Her power swirled with his own in the aftermath, the light tickle of it intensifying the headiness of his release.

"Holy shit, woman," he grunted as he released her, and she sucked him clean.

Bright green eyes stared back at him when she lifted her head, and her beaming smile lit up his entire world.

"You taste good," she said, licking her lips and making him grunt from the intoxicating sight.

Though he was sated, spent to within an inch of his life, a new desire flared and demanded attention.

"I bet you taste as good as you smell." Making his point, he drew her scent into his lungs, enjoying the way their combined signatures mixed together until he couldn't tell where one ended and the other began.

Arawyn's eyes visibly darkened as he groaned from the alluring aroma, and his hands landed on her hips a moment before he dragged her up his body.

"Fearson!" she scolded, using his full name as he slipped his arms under her thighs and used his hold to pull her farther up his chest until her wet center was poised above his face.

He kissed her inner thigh, then the other, unashamed of how very much he wanted her.

"Oh god," Arawyn breathed as he pulled her even closer, lifted his head, and nipped her, directly over her center.

Chapter Thirty-Four

Fearson

He was dying for a taste of her, yearning to please her as she'd just done for him.

"Should I taste you?" he asked, unable to hide his desperate desire for her to say 'yes.'

Nodding her head, giving him permission, her breathing became ragged and her scent increased. She'd never be able to hide her bodily reactions to him or his friends, and the thought delighted him more than it should.

He always knew finding his *Firláh* would bring joy to his life, but he hadn't realized just how much fun it would infuse into every day they spent together.

Already, he was addicted to her, desired to spend all his time with her, and they'd only just met about three weeks ago. Getting to truly know her would only make him fall harder, and he craved how much deeper their connection would grow with time.

Deliberately slowly, he drew her closer to his mouth, nudging her sensitive core with his nose as he breathed her in. This close, her scent was mouthwatering. Every moment that passed without her taste on his tongue was torture, and he quickly grew tired of teasing her. The fire burning through his blood demanded he have her.

"Are you particularly attached to these?" He gazed up Arawyn's frame until he found her eyes, his cock flaring to life once more at the sight of her hands cupping her full breasts.

Cheeks flushed, she shook her head. He smiled at just how distracted he already had her. That she was flustered this thoroughly brought him joy.

Before he was done with her, he wanted her writhing, panting, and breathless.

"Good," he growled, unable to waste another fucking minute. Grasping the fabric, he flexed and ripped her yoga pants in two.

His mate gasped, and he smirked as he peeled her leggings and underwear off, then threw them away.

"I'll buy you a new pair."

"I... I'm not sure I care," she mumbled, while she surveyed the damaged articles of clothing lying on the floor in a heap somewhere above his head.

"Good, because I plan to do that whenever I need you bare before me."

Arawyn arched a challenging brow. "Then maybe you should buy me more clothing, after all. I didn't bring all that much with me, and I don't want to walk around this house naked all the time."

His cock twitched at the image she described, and a wicked smile curled his lips. "On second thought, maybe I shouldn't replace the clothes I destroy. Having you naked sounds like a damn good idea." He knew Viper and Rathe wouldn't mind either.

His *Firláh* slapped him lightly, and he chuckled. Still smiling, he raised his head and swiped his tongue along her seam.

"Oh my god," she gasped.

Fear didn't wait. He licked her again, humming as he got a taste of her essence on his tongue.

By the Gods...

She tasted just as delicious as her signature: as sweet as flower nectar, as fresh as spring thunderstorms, with just a hint of vanilla.

He buried his face into her pussy, licking and sucking. She cried out, her hands burying in his long hair as she held herself up while simultaneously holding his mouth to her center.

"Holy shit." The airy curse spurned him on.

He nudged her clit with his nose before angling his head and circling it with his tongue, not touching it directly. Teasing her, he continued the leisurely pace, enjoying how she wiggled above him.

Wrapping his arms around her thighs, he dug his hands into the curves of her ass and held her still for him.

He touched her everywhere with his tongue, kissing every inch of her except the place she needed him most.

"Fear." His name was a song on her lips. "Fear, p-please."

Her fingers curled sharply into his hair as she tried to drag him to the right spot. He grinned beneath her, turned his head, his beard tickling her thighs, and nipped her inner leg.

"Stay still," he warned.

"No." Her defiance only made him want her more.

"Mmm. Then someone won't get what they so badly need," he tsked, having too much fun playing with her.

Moving one of his hands, he placed it between her thighs and thrust a large finger into her opening. Her pussy clenched around him, and he groaned as he moved it in and out of her, only curling it into the sweet spot inside her every now and then, easily keeping her on the edge without sending her over.

He loved the sound of her gasps, and the way she rocked into his palm, but he was careful. He didn't let her have that pressure where she wanted it.

"Dammit, Fear," she cried, and finally stilled.

"Good girl," he purred, and curled his finger into her just right. He followed it up with a strong, slow lick right over her clit.

"Yes! Oh, thank fuck," she cried, her hands digging into his hair as she continued to hold still for him.

He loved how responsive she was, how she glistened with her excitement.

Latching his lips around that little bundle of nerves, he sucked and lapped at her, fucking her with first one finger, then daring to stretch her with two. Finally, he let her move, and she rode him with abandon, her initial hesitance dissipated like smoke in the wind.

She bit her lip to try and hold in her moans, but he

wanted to hear her. Wanted those sweet noises to fill the air around them.

Sex was normal, even praised, in the Fae realm, and he wanted everyone in this realm and the next to know he'd claimed her. That she was *his*.

"Make me come, Fear," she ordered.

His cock throbbed from the clear demand, and the faint wash of power behind her request. "As you wish, *moín Firláh*."

Teasing her clit mercilessly, he sucked and nipped and licked until she was screaming his name. He felt the moment she lost control, her pussy fluttering wildly around his fingers, squeezing him so strongly he wanted to curse and worship the ground she walked on every day for the rest of her life.

He ached to know what she'd feel like clamped around his dick. Just imagining it had him dripping precome. Tongue circling right over her clit, she broke apart and soared for him.

He half expected her wings to sprout from her back as she flew, and he relentlessly licked her, pushing her higher and higher, wanting to see them arch above her.

"Oh my *god!*" she keened, rocking her pussy against his tongue.

Curling his fingers, he worked that swollen spot inside of her, refusing to quit until her thighs were quaking. Cheeks flushed a rosy pink, eyes bright, yet dazed, he finally slowed so she could breathe again.

Air pumped in and out of her lungs. Her beautiful breasts heaved and strained against the shirt she wore. He wanted to peel the rest of her clothing from her body, flip her onto her back, and thrust inside of her, but he knew as badly as he wanted to, she wasn't ready for that step yet.

Closing his eyes, he licked her clean, savoring the flavor of her on his tongue, and willed his own dick to settle.

When she was ready, he helped lift her, and set her down beside him.

Small fingers intertwined with his as they lay next to each other, and when she smiled at him, he knew his whole world had been set right.

She studied him then, looking deeply into his grey eyes, searching, perhaps, for expectation or pressure to take things a step further. It made him want to pummel whatever men she'd been with in the past, and he made sure there was nothing but genuine happiness for what they'd just shared together.

Someday, when they were ready, they'd take their relationship further, but he was sated and more than happy to just be in her presence. He hoped she knew she could trust him, that he'd never push her to do anything she wasn't ready for, and that included so much more than just the sexual part of their relationship.

She was his to protect, to cherish, to care for. To love.

"Come on, Baby," he prompted when he caught the quiet sound of her stomach growling.

While lazing around with her all day sounded like his version of heaven, he couldn't have her hungry. Providing for her brought him just as much joy.

Sitting up, he quickly hiked up his boxers and peeled off his sweats. Helping her to her feet, he held his pants out for her, and urged her to step into them. Chuckling from how they swallowed her whole, he spent an extra minute or two rolling the waistband and the hem of each leg, but she still had to hold them up as she walked.

The grin was permanently plastered to his face as he led her back down the spiral staircase. However, he couldn't help but notice the way she somewhat nervously searched the apartment, looking to see if any of the others were home, if they'd seen her and knew she'd just been with him.

While she hid it well, he could sense her apprehension and wondered what it stemmed from.

Does she think they'll be upset? That they'll think she's chosen me?

It wasn't difficult to deduce she had feelings for each of them. Honestly, it made him happy to know the three of them may share a mate. Both Viper and Rathe were like brothers to him after all the years they'd spent together, and being separated by different matings didn't appeal to him.

If his inkling were correct, she was their Fated, and belonged to all three of them.

He needed to talk to the others before broaching the subject with Arawyn, but he didn't like her feeling even slightly anxious about her reactions.

What she felt for each of them was completely normal. Hell, it was expected for a woman to have multiple mates in the Night Court, and it was doubly celebrated if the matings were Fated. That practice had fallen out of favor among the higher classes in the Light Court, discarded in lieu of matches made for power and prestige, but it wasn't completely out of the ordinary. Fear didn't worry about Viper following conventions, but Rathe may be a different story.

As the Prince, his friend's role in the Light Court complicated things. It was expected for him to make a marriage of prestige and alliance, and his future wasn't his to choose. But, even with his duty to the Kingdom, Fear knew Rathe would never reject his Fated mate.

If Arawyn was truly Rathe's Fated, as well, having someone in his life who would love and care for him instead of manipulate, control, and punish would be a welcome change. He just needed to pull his head out of his ass first and realize Arawyn wasn't the least bit deceptive. She was genuine and pure, not a spy working for the King or whatever shit Rathe believed.

Pushing those concerns to the background, Fear led Arawyn down the hall to his bedroom.

He watched as she studied the forest-green walls with minimal decoration, took in the rumpled grey sheets and the few potted plants scattered around the room that reminded him of home. Unconsciously, she drew in his signature, and it made him happy to know she was just as affected by him as he was by her.

Tugging her gently into the bathroom, he went about running her a bath, dropping in some soothing bubbles that smelled of the forest with an underlying tang of berries. Having her smell like sex and him for the rest of the day appealed greatly, but his own bath products would do just as well, and he knew she'd be more comfortable if she could bathe after their activities.

"You're the sweetest," she beamed at him and popped onto her toes to kiss the scruff of his cheek.

"I think that title belongs to you," he replied, boldly leaning down to kiss her.

She moaned when she got a taste of her own essence on his lips, and deepened the kiss. For a long moment, they devoured each other until, like the gentleman he tried to be, he pulled away.

"Careful, *moín Firláh*, or we'll end up starting all over again."

With more strength than he realized it would take to walk away from her, he slipped through the door.

Just as he was closing it, he heard her sweet, happy murmur, "I can think of worse ways to spend an afternoon."

Chapter Thirty-Five

Arawyn

Arawyn felt Fear staring down at her and glanced up with a smile, happiness sparkling in her chest like effervescent bubbles. That happiness was foreign, but she loved it, loved how he made her feel light and carefree.

If she weren't careful, she could easily become addicted to the feeling. That she felt this intensely after only having met them less than three weeks ago probably should've alarmed her, but she couldn't muster any concern.

It was more than just having companionship, more than just sating her loneliness. Being around these men filled a hole inside her, one that had been there for as long as she could remember. Being with them felt right in a way she couldn't put into words.

"Picnic on the roof?" Fear rumbled, his curved lips framed by his thick beard.

She could still feel the tickle of it on her thighs, if she closed her eyes.

Smile widening, she leaned over and brushed a light kiss across his bicep, unable to reach the towering man's lips without him bending to meet her halfway. "That sounds amazing."

When they finished making a late lunch, Fear held out a hand, silently offering to carry her plate. He did things like that a lot: carrying this, cleaning that. She liked it, but she still shook her head 'no.'

"I've got it, but thank you." When he looked like he was going to insist, she cut him off. "It'd be hard to open doors for me with both your hands full."

She could see him weighing which was more important to his gentlemanly sensibilities: carrying her plate or opening doors.

He narrowed his eyes down at her, but the smile tugging at his lips widened. "I think you're underestimating my juggling abilities, but as you wish, *Firláh*."

Grinning from her victory, Arawyn gestured for him to lead the way. "Someday you're going to tell me what that means."

She could hear the smile in his voice when he answered, "Someday."

Halfway to the stairs in the corner of the living room, her steps faltered as an odd sensation washed over her skin. It felt warm and almost tingly, like standing in full sunlight when you were already sporting a burn.

Frowning sharply at a spot near the door where the feeling was emanating, she cocked her head, peering at the shaft of light cutting across the floor there. For a moment, she could've sworn the light... glittered.

Right on the heels of that odd shimmer, a whooshing sensation like air being sucked into the vacuum of space almost made her stumble forward. That was weird enough, but what had her on high alert was that it wasn't a physical feeling.

She felt that whoosh with the well of power in her chest. *Oh, fuck...*

Eyes flying wide, she opened her mouth to warn Fear something was wrong.

She never got the chance.

Between one heartbeat and the next, Rathe appeared in the shaft of light. Just fucking appeared like a magician. Except there was no trap door beneath him, no puff of smoke to conceal him running back on stage, no misdirection.

One minute he hadn't been there and the next, he was.

Arawyn choked on a sound somewhere between a scream and a gasp. The plate fell from suddenly numb fingers, shattering against the wood floors with a jarring crash, shards of glass flying everywhere. She didn't even feel the nicks as pieces cut her shins, ankles, and the tops of her bare feet.

Fear, who'd glanced almost casually at Rathe, spun on his heels at the crash and rushed back to her.

"What's wrong?" From the corner of her eye, she saw him glance down at her legs. "Fuck, Baby, you're bleeding," he growled roughly. "Where else are you hurt?"

Arawyn stood perfectly still, frozen with shock, as he dropped to his knees and carefully patted her down, looking for any other injuries. Her mind was in chaos, her thoughts moving too fast to hold onto or she would've told him there weren't any others.

Fear sounded pissed when he snapped at Rathe, "You startled her."

"I announced I was coming," Rathe clipped shortly, stepping from the beam of sunlight. Despite the pique in his voice, he was looking at her with something that appeared a hell of a lot like concern. "My apologies. I didn't intend to scare you," he murmured, almost gently, as he started for her.

In answer, Arawyn held up a visibly trembling hand, halting Rathe mid-step and Fear mid-pat.

"Somebody better explain to me what the fuck just happened. Right now," she rasped shakily.

Is this some kind of alien power? Teleportation?

Suddenly, all the questions she'd been holding back flooded to the forefront, warring for a place on her tongue, begging to slip past her lips and demand answers.

Rathe couldn't have looked more confused, if he tried. If she hadn't been frozen with shock, she might've laughed at his expression, because he was looking at her like *she* was the crazy one.

"Surely you've seen someone Light Jump before," he almost scoffed.

"No," she said flatly. "I most surely have not."

Frown deepening, Rathe stalked closer. It wasn't until then that she noticed the tear slashing through his black button up and the bleeding gash beneath it.

What looked like claw marks scored the flesh of his right forearm, and there was blood splattered on his sleeves and pants, though whether it was his or someone else's, she didn't know.

She wanted to know what kind of creature was capable

of making the deep, scoring marks, but she couldn't move past the worry she felt at seeing him injured.

"You're hurt," she pointed out, concern edged in her voice.

Fear looked over his shoulder at Rathe who blinked and glanced down at himself, then back up at her.

"Yes," he said simply.

Arawyn nodded slowly, unsure what to make of his nonchalant response. She felt oddly detached, like she was underwater, kicking and swimming, trying to reach the surface, but didn't know which way was up.

Fear's big hands wrapping around the backs of her thighs brought her attention to him, where he was still kneeling before her. He tipped his head back to stare up at her, but his words were for Rathe.

"She doesn't know what she is," he murmured, his voice gentle.

That quiet declaration cut through some of the shock. She'd been trying to keep her ignorance of what she was, and they were, to herself, worried they would clam up and stop dropping little bits of information, but apparently her giant had seen through the front.

Conflicting emotions ran through her.

Just how long has he known?

Rathe's frown deepened as he peered between her and Fear. "What the fuck do you mean she doesn't know what she is?"

Fear stood and snatched a bottle of liquor from the bar, then guided her back into the kitchen and gently sat her down. She went along easily, still too stunned to do much else. Kneeling again, Fear propped one of her feet on his knee and set to cleaning the nicks on her lower leg.

Rathe followed and stood at Fear's back, regarding the cuts the big man was cleaning with the liquor through narrowed eyes, tracing his lower lip with his tongue.

"That's a three thousand dollar bottle of bourbon," Rathe commented mildly.

"Mmhm," Fear hummed back.

Arawyn hissed softly when Fear got to a particularly deep cut. Glancing back up at Rathe when he sighed, she saw some kind of decision pass through his eyes.

"Move," he directed shortly.

Fear, instead of looking irritated at the command, smirked slightly and got to his feet, moving back to lean against the counter. Arawyn started to ask what was going on when Rathe knelt in front of her, stunning her to silence.

Those bright blue eyes, framed by thick, black lashes, locked onto her. His voice contained an odd mix of anticipation and resignation as he asked, "May I?"

Blinking past the unexpected arousal of seeing him kneel at her feet, she frowned slightly. Arawyn glanced at Fear before meeting Rathe's gaze again.

"May you what?"

There was that look again: distrust and a hint of astonishment, like her not knowing what was going on was too outlandish to entertain and he was trying to figure out her angle.

"*Heal* you," he clarified after a pause.

"Heal me," she repeated, beginning to feel like a parrot, but he was speaking in riddles.

How the fuck is he going to heal me? Is this another alien thing, like the teleporting?

If it were, and if she were alien and had the ability

herself, it would have been damn good to know about years ago.

Eyes narrowed, he didn't try explaining again. Instead, he watched her closely as he bent, raising her leg at the same time.

If Arawyn had known what he was about to do, she might've dodged him. Then again, maybe she wouldn't have. As it was, she just stared at him as he drew closer.

The moment he dragged his tongue—his very *long* tongue—over one of the bigger cuts on her leg, pleasure shot through her with such sudden force she cried out.

Eyes wide with shock that a lick on her shin had her nipples hard and her panties damp, she opened her mouth to ask what the hell he'd just done.

He didn't give her the chance.

Staring at her steadily, blue eyes glittering with heat and a touch of intrigue like her pleasure had been unexpected for him, as well, he licked her again. A moan slipped past her lips.

"What are you doing to me?" she gasped, lashes fluttering.

His only answer was to hum low in his throat and lick her again. Over and over, he laved her with his tongue, and with every swipe, the pleasure intensified. By the time he'd licked almost all the cuts on her left leg, Arawyn was on the verge of climaxing.

With one hand clamped over her mouth to muffle the moans, and the other gripping the seat of the chair so she didn't fist his hair instead, she squeezed her eyes shut, trying to fight off the orgasm steadily looming closer.

Her thighs were slippery with need, her nipples hard

buds under her shirt, rubbing teasingly against the soft cotton with every rapid breath.

"Oh god, Rathe, you have to stop. I'm... I can't," she panted.

"Can't what, Little Vixen?" he purred roughly with another slow drag of his tongue.

She didn't answer, knew she wouldn't be able to speak again without moaning.

Arawyn didn't have time to feel relief, or disappointment, when he set her leg down, because he immediately picked up her other. Groaning, she gritted her teeth. She should reach down and push him away, should stop him before this went any further.

She and Fear had just had sex in the gym. It was a terrible, awful idea to let Rathe continue. Her relationship with the brooding man was already tenuous. This—letting him do whatever the fuck it was he was doing that felt so goddamn good—would only confuse her more.

But, she didn't stop him. Couldn't.

Because when she opened her eyes and looked at Fear, her gentle giant, her protective mountain of a man was watching on hungrily from his position leaning against the counter. His grey eyes were greedily taking in her flushed face and his lips were curled in a wicked smile.

For some reason, instead of being shocked, knowing Fear was watching released her inhibitions. With a moan, Arawyn stopped fighting the orgasm.

Hand still covering her mouth, she let her head fall back and shuddered with bliss as she fell over the edge with the next lave of Rathe's tongue.

When the last tingles of release trembled through her,

she opened her eyes and gazed down at Rathe where he was sitting back on his heels between her legs.

Swallowing to wet her mouth, she whispered, "What the hell was that?"

His voice was hoarse and gravelly when he lifted her leg, revealing smooth, unmarred skin and replied, "I healed you."

Jaw dropping, Arawyn stared at her leg as if she'd never seen it before. Jerking upright, she ran a hand over her skin, but it wasn't an illusion. He really had healed her cuts.

"Godsdamn, that was hot."

Startling, Arawyn whipped a look behind her to find Viper leaning on the counter separating the kitchen from the rest of the loft, his eyes molten.

Still staring at her, he addressed Rathe. "I didn't know your healing caused pleasure, Brother."

Rathe's voice was still rough with arousal when he answered, "It hasn't. Before."

Viper's brows lifted, eyes sparkling with intrigue. "Interesting."

"Mm, indeed."

Turning back, she watched as Rathe absently licked his palm and rubbed it over the gash on his chest and claw marks on his forearm. Eyes wide, Arawyn watched the skin knit back together until it was perfect and golden once more, leaving only smudges of blood behind.

Heart fluttering a little too quickly, Arawyn pushed to her feet only to immediately wobble on legs still tingly and weak from pleasure. She would've fallen right back into the chair, if Rathe hadn't caught her, his hands gripping the backs of her thighs, right under her ass.

Heat rushed through her at the contact. A glance down into his eyes told her she wasn't the only one who felt it.

Stepping out of his hold before she did something more ill-advised than letting him magic her into a climax in front of everyone—like kissing him—she made her escape.

"We're going to talk about whatever the hell you all are when I get back," she declared over her shoulder.

After a quick trip to her room to splash water on her face, change panties, and try to convince herself there was no reason to feel shy or embarrassed without success, Arawyn started back to the kitchen.

At the sound of their low voices, she hesitated. She knew immediately they didn't want her to hear what they were saying. Which meant it was definitely something she needed to know.

Quieter than she'd ever moved in her life, Arawyn crept down the hallway until she could just see them around the wall. The second she looked at him, Viper's eyes darted to her.

Her stomach dropped.

She expected him to say something, to alert Fear and Rathe, who hadn't noticed her, that she was there. Instead, he winked and looked away, appearing for all the world like he hadn't seen her.

If she hadn't already had feelings for him, that right there would've had her falling.

Barely breathing, she listened in as they discussed Light Courts, Night Courts, and a half-dozen other things that sounded like made-up words. Rathe argued that she couldn't possibly *not* know what she was while Fear and Viper both insisted she didn't have a clue. When they began discussing how strange her power felt, Arawyn decided she'd had enough.

Head spinning, she stepped out of the hall and cut in, "What the hell are you talking about?"

Rathe and Fear spun around, Rathe's countenance severe, Fear looking impressed she'd snuck up on them. Eyes narrowed to slits, Rathe scowled back at Viper.

"You knew she was there."

"Yep!"

"And you didn't think to mention it?"

Viper shrugged unrepentantly, his features steady and unapologetic. "She deserves to know."

Chapter Thirty-Six

Viper

Viper watched Arawyn's face intently as he closed the distance between them and cautiously ran his hand down her arm, trying to gauge how she was feeling. He couldn't begin to imagine how hard her life had been not knowing what she was or what she must be feeling right then, knowing they'd held the answers to all her questions and seemed to be keeping them from her with their whispered conversation.

He wouldn't blame her, if she were pissed, wouldn't be surprised if she didn't want to be touched.

That moment of not knowing how she would react to his tentative caress, not knowing if she would shrug him off and spurn him, had his pulse speeding and anxiety shooting through him.

He could've made her feel whatever he wanted her to feel. He wasn't what anyone would call particularly empathic, but inflicting emotions on others? Making them feel what he wanted? That *Influence* was one of his strongest abilities.

And, yet, the thought of manipulating her like that was repellent.

Instead, he waited, anxious and tense, to see if she would welcome him or shove him away.

The moment she relaxed into him, swaying forward to rest her forehead against his chest, the breath he'd been holding burst out of him. Wrapping his arms around her, he pulled her in tight, bowing over her small frame.

"I'm sorry, my Loon," he whispered.

"Did you know I didn't know?"

"Not until today."

She turned her head and pressed a kiss to his chest, then tipped her head back to peer up at him. "Then, there's nothing to be sorry for."

Gods, but he could stare into her eyes forever and still never get enough. The way she looked at him, as if she were truly seeing him, and liked what she saw, was fucking terrifying.

He was already addicted to it.

Viper made himself release her when she straightened, despite it being the last thing he wanted to do. When she turned to pin Fear with those piercing eyes though, he was glad he had.

"You knew."

Fear held her gaze steadily, which Viper thought impressive as fuck. If he'd been in the big man's place, he didn't know if he would've been able to withstand that hurt look in her eyes without crumbling.

"After earlier, your reaction... I suspected," Fear replied honestly.

"Why didn't you say anything?"

The flicker in Fear's eyes was slight, so much so even Viper almost missed it. But, Arawyn didn't.

She followed that flicker to Rathe. Arawyn stared up at his brother for a long moment, silent, searching, then nodded. "I understand."

"Do you?" Rathe challenged, staring down at her with a frown tightening his brow.

"Yes." She glanced pointedly at him and Fear before turning her attention back to Rathe, her pretty green eyes soft, the anger and betrayal that had filled them moments before easing. "I do. It took me a minute, but I see you, Rathe."

Viper watched on as she took a step closer, standing almost toe to toe with Rathe, fearlessly holding his gaze.

"You come off as cold and dangerous. And you are, in a lot of ways. I've seen you come home with blood on you more than once, and I know you won't hesitate to get your hands dirty," she murmured dryly.

Viper let out a soft breath at that, not because she'd noticed the blood, but because she didn't sound horrified by it. That wasn't to say she sounded particularly happy about it, but he would take *not horrified*.

"But, that's not who you are, not really. You're a protector. I may not get why you needed to be suspicious of me, but I understand now—it was to protect Fear and Viper."

To others, he was sure his brother looked impassive while he stared silently down at Arawyn in the wake of her shockingly insightful speech, but Viper could see disconcertment and the sharp glint of covetousness warring in his eyes.

Being seen was a hell of a thing. Terrifying, thrilling, and addictive all in one.

Viper didn't make any attempt to stop the smile stretching his lips. That she understood Rathe's distrust of her wasn't because of her, not really, but because he was trying to protect him and Fear was just more evidence she was perfect for them. And he took particular glee in watching his brother join him and Fear in falling for her.

'Bout fucking time.

With a last, piercing look up at Rathe, Arawyn turned and took a seat at the table, then waved for them to join her. Which they did. Even Rathe.

Viper wondered if she realized she'd just commanded three of the most powerful Fae in this realm, or any other, as casually as one would order room service.

Once they were all seated, she set her hands flat on the table, drew in a breath, and met each of their eyes. "So. Are we aliens?"

There was a moment of stunned silence.

Fear's deep voice came out shaky and strangled, "What?"

Arawyn's eyes narrowed as she peered between the three of them. "Aliens," she repeated slowly as if they hadn't heard her the first time.

Viper tried really damn hard to swallow back the laughter, knowing she likely wouldn't appreciate it, but he failed miserably. It burst out of him in loud, shoulder-shaking peels. By the time he got himself back under control, sitting up to wipe the tears from his eyes, she was looking at him drolly.

Fear was chuckling as he answered, "No, Baby. We're not aliens."

"Vampires, then, right? And I'm either some kind of half-vampire hybrid, or the whole non-aging thing is bullshit."

Viper saw the smile twitching at the corners of his brother's mouth as Rathe shook his head and answered, "No. We're—"

"Demons," she finished with a sigh and a grimace. "I knew it." She squared her shoulders. "What kind? Am I a *Succubus*? Some kind of sex demon?"

Viper had to hold his breath to keep from bursting into laughter again. Why she thought she was a 'sex demon,' he had no idea, but he would cheerfully cut off someone else's foot to discover the answer.

"'Sex demon'?" Rathe choked out, brows raised. "By the Gods, woman, where are you getting this information?"

She narrowed her eyes on him, as if his disbelief was suspect. "The Internet."

"'The Internet,'" Rathe repeated, looking like he wanted to rub his temples.

"And the library," she added.

"We're Fae, Arawyn, not 'demons' or whatever the hell else you've looked up."

"Fae. As in Fairies? Like Tinkerbell?" she asked, an adorable frown creasing her brow.

For the next hour, they did their best to answer her questions: explained what they were, where they were from, and why they were in the human realm.

Well, not them in particular, of course, but Fae, in general.

Viper had no desire to see her look at them with disgust, if she learned they were there to find victims to feed to the

King. She would find out eventually. He knew that. But, he planned to wait until she was madly in love with them first, so the chances of her hating them were slightly less.

Even among their kind, who didn't have many of what the humans called 'morals,' what they were doing was monstrous.

Chapter Thirty-Seven

Arawyn

Trying to sate a lifetime of questions in the course of one conversation, Arawyn let them fly at will.

"Why do people become obsessed with me?" she asked, the question one she'd been harboring for the last decade.

Sitting back in her seat, she braced for the answer, nervously playing with the hem of her sleeve while she tried to listen past the abnormally loud beat of her heart.

"All humans experience that magnetism toward Fae. It's called Allure. You evidently just haven't been taught to keep it in check," Rathe answered.

"Oh."

That it was something she could have controlled hit her in the chest like a ton of bricks, stealing her breath and making her head spin. How long had she tried to contain her power? To change people's reactions to her? And all along, it was apparently an easy fix. If only she'd known what she was, she could have saved herself a lifetime of hardship. It was almost painful to swallow.

Fear must've caught the stricken look on her face, because he reassured gently, "I can teach you how to control it, Baby."

"Thank you," she murmured softly, lips curling in an affectionate smile. Pulling in a breath then letting it out slowly, she tried to center herself. "Where do we come from? Orin mentioned realms during our deal."

Viper beat the others in answering. "We're from Faery. This realm and ours, and quite a few others, are connected. Sort of. It's basically a different dimension."

"Okay," she said slowly, blinking a couple of times, trying to wrap her head around the concept of entirely different worlds somehow connected to this one. It was a lot to digest, so she moved on to another question and filed it away to mull over later.

"So, what exactly are Fae?" She glanced at Rathe, raising a brow. "Since apparently the Internet isn't always to be trusted."

She could've sworn he almost cracked a smile, but the faint curve of his lips was short-lived and quickly replaced by his usual watchful suspicion.

Fear's deep voice cut through her and Rathe's stare-off, explaining, "Unlike humans, there are many different kinds of Fae, though all are divided into two Courts: Night or Light. The number of species is so vast it would take days to describe them all, but I can tell you they can look like almost anything from what humans would call 'monsters' to those of us who look more humanoid. Our lifespans are longer, closer to three thousand years, and—"

"I'm sorry, what?"

Jesus, have I been lusting after men that are old enough to be my grandfathers?

He chuckled lightly. "Don't worry, Baby, we're not too old for you. I'm the eldest at twenty-nine, Rathe is twenty-eight, and Viper is the youngest at twenty-six.

For a moment, she wondered if she'd said the 'grandfather' comment out loud but realized he'd just read her expression.

Hiding her relief, and wishing she could hide her hot cheeks just as easily, she cleared her throat. "You said 'Courts.' What are those?

Fear's smirk told her he knew she was trying to change the subject, and why, but he responded anyway. "It depends on species and bloodlines, but all Fae are born either of the Light or of the Night. In the past, there were many Courts and Clans in each, left to rule themselves autonomously."

"And now?"

His expression hardened briefly before he smoothed it back out. "Since the War, there are only two Courts. Everyone in Faery has been conquered and is now under the control of King Ehrendil and the Light Court or the throneless Night Court, overseen by Regent Malgath."

"Which one am I?"

The three men exchanged a weighted glance with each other.

"We don't know," Fear answered honestly, a hint of regret in his otherwise deep, soothing timbre.

"What? Why? Is it hard to tell?"

Arawyn studied Fear, then Viper and Rathe, trying to discern if she could suss out which Court they were from.

Viper seemed easy. She'd often thought of him as a golden god, and he'd always reminded her of sunshine. It was his styled blonde hair, those amber eyes often gleaming with mischief, and the sunny, manic energy he had. That she'd also witnessed his dark side, the violent storm raging beneath the surface, carefully contained until he called upon it, didn't change her guess. Viper was from the Light Court. She'd bet her favorite set of daggers on it.

But, the other two? That was much harder to guess.

Since Viper and Rathe were brothers, it was easy to assume Rathe was also of the Light Court. But everything about the brooding man was dark and dangerous without an ounce of sunny disposition or humor.

Fear was even harder to guess. There was something predatory about him, something ruthless and deadly. But, to her, at least, he was kind and caring, thoughtful and attentive.

Distracting her from her musings, Fear replied, "Not usually, no. Your power, however, is difficult to discern."

She didn't know what the hell that meant. Arawyn started to question him further, but Rathe cut in before she could.

"Let's finish covering the basics before we delve into that." His tone didn't encourage continuing down the path of questioning.

Narrowing her eyes at him speculatively, she considered ignoring him and asking anyway, but a knee bump and subtle head shake from Viper stopped her.

Swallowing a growl, she let it go. For now. They would definitely be revisiting why her power, in particular, was hard to 'taste,' but she had more questions she wanted answered before she pushed Rathe into turning back into a brick wall.

"Since there are Fae here, I take it that means we're able to go back and forth between... realms?" It felt strange as hell to talk about other dimensions like it was perfectly normal.

Viper nodded. "Unless they were banished, yeah. Those just visiting can use one of the gates. Or Portal to jump back, but only royals have that ability."

"What stops the banished ones from using the gates?"

Viper snickered, "Ha! I'd pay to see someone try. The guards would eat 'em while they were still kicking and screaming."

Arawyn felt her eyes go as wide as saucers and gave him a horrified look. Seeing it, he bit his lips like he was trying to suck his smile back in and scratched at his neck.

"Er, just kidding! That would be... not funny." He paused and gave her a questioning look. "Right?"

"Right," she confirmed.

"Yeah, no, of course! Definitely not funny," he proclaimed with a wave of his hand, though his eyes skittered away from her.

Shaking her head, she focused on Rathe again. "Were you all banished here? Wait, was I?"

"No." For the second time, Rathe made it clear that line of questioning wasn't open.

Sighing, loudly, she made a face at him, but his expression remained immovable. Arawyn went quiet for a moment, trying to pick which of her many questions she should ask next.

"Not all Fae look human," she surmised, remembering how shocked she'd been when she'd arrived at the docks and met her new metal dealer. "So, how do the ones like Orin avoid being seen by people, or captured and turned into lab rats by the government?

"Glamor," Fear said. "All Fae are born with certain features, depending on their bloodline. I mentioned earlier there were hundreds of types of Fae, and each species looks different. Glamor is an ability that can be used to hide those traits from sight."

"Like an invisible cloak," she murmured. It would have been hard to believe, if she hadn't experienced the tangibility of her own power before. But, she knew power, magic, Fae... everything they spoke of was real.

"Exactly. Except instead of actually making us invisible, it only cloaks the characteristics that make us *other*. This is what we look like without the... extras." Viper's eyes flashed a deeper gold, as if showing her the smallest glimpse of what he kept hidden beneath. And it made her want to see more.

"Takes a little practice, but it becomes easy to pull into place," Fear assured her.

"Does this mean you don't actually look like this?" Her curious gaze darted from man to man, trying to see beyond their beautiful exteriors.

"At the heart, we look the same, just more inhuman." Rathe tapped the shell of his ear. "Things like our pointed ears and wings would draw far too much attention in this realm, so we hide them away in favor of this rather mundane appearance." He peered down at himself as if he weren't jaw-droppingly gorgeous.

"I don't think 'mundane' is a word I'd ever use to describe you," she admitted.

The man had shockingly electric-blue eyes, a toned, cut physique, and tattoos inked across his bronzed skin. He looked incredibly sexy, and that didn't include the possessive air about him that curled her toes and made her pulse beat just a little faster.

Other men would kill for what Rathe had going on, yet, he saw himself as mundane? It made her question what he would look like without the Glamor. Somehow, she just knew he'd be even more spectacular, and she was just wrapping her mind around the possibility of things like pointed ears and wings.

Holy shit.

"Wait, wings?"

He'd definitely said 'wings.'

"I was wondering when she'd circle back to that," Viper grinned mischievously.

"Many Fae have them." Rathe shrugged, but she felt like he'd just told her unicorns were real. Who knew, maybe they were.

"Do you think I have wings?" The question seemed as fantastical as this conversation had been, but she leaned into it, embracing her new reality. If it came with wings, that would be a serious bonus.

"We're not sure," Fear said honestly, leaning his crossed arms atop the broken table, being careful of the crack he'd placed in the wood the other day. "It's highly likely."

Arawyn nodded, feeling equal parts overwhelmed and greedy for more.

She almost asked to see Rathe's wings, but didn't want to deter from the conversation. Seeing them would probably blow her mind, and she needed to focus. There was so much more she wanted answers to, and so much more she wanted to learn.

Head spinning, she leaned back in her chair and let out a

long breath, letting her gaze wander. Doing a double-take when her eyes passed over one of the strange antiques lying haphazardly around, she abruptly remembered seeing them buy drugs. Knowing what she knew now, the guys buying what had looked like cocaine or heroin made little sense.

Peering at Rathe, she wondered if this was going to be another question he wouldn't answer, but figured it wouldn't hurt to try.

"Why don't human drugs and alcohol affect me much?"

"Our metabolism is much faster and our bodily systems have had millennia longer to learn how to more efficiently eliminate toxins and poisons of all kinds."

Arawyn nodded nonchalantly, but continued to hold his gaze. "So, why were you buying drugs that night at the docks?"

For just a moment, he looked approving, those vibrant blue eyes glittering with a mixture of mirth and appraisal.

"Ask something else, Arawyn," he directed, those kissable lips ever so slightly raised at the corners.

Huffing, she pretended the expression on his face wasn't as panty-meltingly sexy as it was infuriating, and continued with her questioning, peppering them with everything she could think of for the next hour.

Chapter Thirty-Eight

VIPER

When they finished, Rathe broke the strained silence that had descended over the room.

"Arawyn." He waited until she looked up at him. "I have questions for you, but I need to be sure you tell the truth."

She seemed to blink free of the daze she'd fallen into, enough to give him a dry look. "Are you about to pull a polygraph machine out of one of these drawers now?"

Viper and Fear both chuckled. Even Rathe couldn't stop a smile.

"No, Smartass. We're not human, if you recall," Rathe drawled. "We have other ways of discerning the truth."

Wariness flickered through her gaze, and fairly so. His Little Loon was smart. To have survived this long on her own in the human realm with the amount of power that lived within her, alone and unaware of what she was, she'd had to be.

"How?" she questioned.

"Magic, of course."

Her brows rose, her expression impressed, "Is that one of your abilities?"

"No. I'll need to use conjured magic, but I know the invocation, and I'll take the cost."

"Cost?"

Rathe started to wave away her question, but Viper cut him off. "If someone doesn't have enough power, or the right kind of power, to do something, they can conjure magic. But, it'll cost 'em."

"Cost them what?"

"It varies. The price it extracts is always equal to what's asked of it. So, if I wanted to magic myself a stack of human cash, I'd probably have a headache for an hour. But, if I wanted to magic myself a dragon, it may cost me three years of my life," he finished, throwing a taunting look at Fear who just snorted in return.

"It'd cost you more than that," Fear fired back.

"That's terrifying," she breathed.

Rathe sent them both a look for interrupting, then caught her gaze. "Yes or no?"

He watched as she blinked free of whatever imagining she was lost in and frowned worriedly at Rathe. "Will it hurt you?"

Glancing at his brother, Viper saw the surprise flash over his face before he hid it.

"I'll be fine, Little Vixen."

"Will it hurt me?"

"No," Rathe assured, looking encouragingly perturbed at the thought of her in pain.

Viper smirked.

That's right, big brother. Fall a little further.

"Okay. Do it," she murmured.

For just a moment, Rathe's face showed surprise at the trust she was putting in him, and then his eyes brightened as he whispered the incantation under his breath. They changed until they were no longer a dull, human blue, but vivid cerulean with a sunburst of fiery orange encircling the pupil, a mark of his royal lineage and proof he was the first-born Heir of the Light King.

Viper pushed back the familiar surge of envy at seeing them. His own eyes were yellow, a sign of his Naga blood, proof he was a bastard and a reminder of the horror the King had committed upon his mother.

He pushed that old rage aside, locked it back in the box with the rest of his demons, when he felt the magic settle over Arawyn like a blanket.

It wouldn't hurt her, wouldn't even make her tell them things she didn't want to. It would only prevent her from lying. Rathe, however, would have a wicked headache for the next couple of hours...

"Are you here to gather information on us?"

"Partially."

Viper saw Rathe stiffen slightly from the corner of his eye, but he kept his gaze on Arawyn, knowing she didn't mean that the way Rathe was thinking.

"For whom?"

"Myself."

"And who else?"

"No one else."

His brother went very, very still. Viper could feel him tasting the magic, prodding and testing it, but he knew she was telling the truth.

"You said 'partially.' Why else are you here?"

"Because I want to know what I am."

"Is that the only reason?" Rathe pressed.

Arawyn's voice dropped to a soft murmur and the faintest blush colored her cheeks. "No."

Viper grinned widely, feeling his scar crease with the motion but not caring. "She's here because she likes us, isn't that right, Pretty?"

"Yes," she admitted, cutting him a slitted look, but he just waggled his brows at her, entirely unrepentant.

Rathe cleared his throat, bringing their attention back to him. "Are you a spy?"

"No," she repeated, her gaze steady and open.

"Are you working with or for Ehrendil in any capacity?"

"No. I don't even know who that is."

"Told you so!" Viper crowed.

Rathe rudely didn't acknowledge his victory, just leaned back in his chair and gazed at her thoughtfully for a long, quiet minute. Viper leaned back in his chair, too, stretching his legs out and lacing his fingers behind his head, feeling smug as fuck.

That changed to impatience quickly when Rathe continued to just sit there, but he contained it, making himself sit equally as still, pretending it was a competition in his head.

"Will you tell me about your life?" Rathe coaxed, his voice surprisingly gentle.

"I—" She blinked, appearing a little thrown by the change of topic. "It's not a pretty story."

Rathe nodded. "None of ours are. You won't be judged or pitied here, Little Vixen. The pain you've survived is yours, and yours alone, but we all know horror. If you're willing, I'd like to know your past."

Viper saw the shadows pass through her eyes, saw that same haunted look he'd recognized before. She was quiet for so long, he didn't think she was going to answer, but then she did.

She paused to clear her throat, her lips tightening, eyes still focused on nothing. And then, she retold the story she'd relayed to him, but in greater detail.

He listened about how her parents had changed, pulled her out of school, and eventually lost their jobs because they refused to leave her alone. When she spoke of how her father used to sneak into her room to watch her sleep, he felt his stomach twist because he knew, he fucking knew what was coming.

He could see the fear in her eyes, the pain and betrayal. And the guilt.

It was the last that had him gritting his teeth so hard his jaw ached.

"And then, one night, my father didn't just watch. He didn't manage to- I fought. I think I broke a couple of his ribs." Arawyn inhaled slowly. "I ran away that night. I lived on the streets for a while, but I didn't know... I hadn't realized, yet, that it wasn't just my parents. It was me. Everyone I was around too often changed. They became obsessed." She huffed a mirthless laugh, her eyes hollow. "You'd think people would be kind to the person they're so fixated on, but most weren't."

Viper didn't think she was aware of tracing her fingertips

over her upper stomach, but *he* was. He knew, suddenly, that there were scars under there.

Murderous rage had everything inside him going quiet and still.

Memories of his father ordering the Royal Guards to whip him flitting around in the back of his mind like poisonous shadows. Sometimes, he still felt the sting of the iron-tipped lash flaying his flesh open, still heard the crack as it split the air.

Fae healed fast—Viper faster than most—and they didn't scar easily... unless the weapon is made of iron.

What had they used on her to inflict those scars she traced?

A Fae's Allure was powerful. She hadn't known how to control it, and the humans around her wouldn't have been able to resist. But, that wasn't going to stop him from gleaning the names of those who'd hurt her and hunting them down.

Everyone had a monster inside them, something capable of horrible things. For some, it would only ever come out in protection of others. For others, it was a predator, a hungry thing that relished inflicting pain. A Fae's Allure, unchecked and unguided, brought out that monster in people. The problem was, once it surfaced, it didn't sink quietly back into the depths.

The ones who'd hurt her would have to die, mostly for hurting her, but also, to ensure they didn't hurt others.

"I learned to stay away from people, to limit my contact with everyone. It took years before I figured out how to control it, even a little bit, years before I figured out how to contain the power inside me so it didn't leak out so badly." She blinked, clearing some of the distant look from her eyes, then met their gazes. "It was actually only a couple weeks before I met you all that I started trying to work with it, instead of just keeping it locked up all the time. Just little tendrils, tiny bits I was pretty sure I could handle." Her lips twisted. "Should've left well enough alone. I lost control that night."

Viper nodded, understanding why he'd felt her power so strongly then when he hadn't before. "I felt it."

Arawyn looked up at him sharply. "What?"

"When your power pulsed. I felt it. I'd been feeling hints of it for weeks, when you were working with it, but that night I got enough of a taste to *See*. I knew you'd come to that club, if we went." He smiled down at her, the memory of seeing her for the first time, one of his favorites.

Rathe made a low sound, his eyes narrowed with realization. "So, you didn't lose her."

Smirking, he gave his brother a look. "Of course not. You should've known better than to believe that."

Arawyn cut in before Rathe could respond to that. "What do you mean 'see'?"

"I've got the Sight. Premonition. Sometimes it comes through as visions, sometimes a feeling." He paused, his lips pulling up at the corners. "Or, recently, as a draw."

Her eyes widened and her hand flew to her chest. "It was you? You caused this pull I feel? But then, why—" She glanced at Fear.

Viper shook his head. "No, Loon. I didn't create it. That's not one of my abilities." He paused. "That'd be cool as fuck, though. Would make hunting a hell of a lot easier if I could make my prey come to me..." He trailed off, lost in the possibilities.

Arawyn lightly flicked his arm. "Focus, Cookie Monster."

"Hmm? Right, yes. No, I didn't create it. Wouldn't have been able to make Rathe and Fear feel it, too, if I had. I just followed it to you."

Her eyes widened slightly and flicked to Rathe at Viper's intentional revelation that his brother felt the draw, as well, but she kept her thoughts on that to herself, asking instead, "Then, what's causing it?"

Viper sighed happily. "Fate."

Arawyn blinked up at him, a slow smile blooming. "You're a romantic."

"For you, Pretty, always," he purred, leaning forward to nuzzle his nose to hers.

He wanted to kiss her, badly, but he had plans for their next kiss, so he settled for flicking his tongue against her upper lip. Just a little taste to tide him over.

That was the idea, anyway, but then her breath hitched and, from this close, he saw her pupils dilate with arousal.

Need was an electric rush through his veins, so intense he felt his scales trying to surface through the layers of Glamor he had over them, felt his own pupils tighten briefly into slits.

Groaning, he snapped his teeth at her. "You keep lookin' at me like that and I'm gonna forget my plans."

The faint pink blush warming her cheeks shot right to his heart. And his cock. By the Gods, but he was lost for her.

Rathe cleared his throat, stealing her attention away before she could respond. Viper glared at him, not appreciating having his moment with Arawyn broken, but his brother ignored the look entirely.

"Do you have the Sight, Arawyn?"

"I don't know. I don't think so? I get feelings about things, but I've always just assumed it was intuition."

"Did your intuition tell you to go to the club that night?"

"No."

"So, why did you? As you said, you'd learned to stay away from people, yet, you went to a place with at least a hundred of them."

Viper scowled. Rathe didn't sound particularly accusatory, but he didn't like that he was still questioning her.

Without looking away from Rathe, Arawyn set a calming hand on his knee. His focus immediately returned to her, the tension melting out of him like she'd used magic to drain it away. She hadn't. He knew that. It was just her. Gods, but her touch soothed him. He wanted to wallow in it, wanted to hold her against him, wanted to tote her around so they were in constant contact.

For a moment, his mind wandered off, contemplating if he could convince her to let him carry her, then working out the logistics of it, in case she said 'yes.' She was small. He could probably fit her in his hoodie with him. That would help hold her against him so she didn't get tired. He might have to cut the neck hole so both of their heads would fit, but that was fine. If they were chest to chest, and she wrapped her legs around his waist...

Blinking out of his distraction when she began speaking, he set the hoodie idea aside for now to focus on what she was saying.

"When my power pulsed that night, it, uh, drew my neighbor to me," she cringed, her eyes shadowed with sadness and guilt. "The magnetism... " She trailed off for a moment. "He was lost to it. I tried to stay quiet, hoping he'd go away, but he didn't. So, I left. I hoped distance would help the effects fade quicker." She went quiet for a moment, then lifted her head, returning Rathe's gaze steadily. "I was just driving, killing time. Then, I felt something, like there was a string in my chest, drawing me somewhere. I'd never experienced anything like it before, but it felt... " The blush in her cheeks returned. "It felt good. Warm. Like home. I decided to follow it. And I found you all. That was the first time I'd ever been around people who felt like me."

"And your neighbor. What happened to him?"

There was that guilt again.

"He died," she rasped. "He stuck around for a few days, trying to break in, then lure me out, when that failed. I think he was sick. He looked gaunt, like the life was being sucked out of him." Her gaze went distant and her brows drew together. "His eyes were bright, feverish. I remember thinking they almost seemed to glow."

Viper cocked his head at that. Something in what she'd said had a thought fluttering around in the back of his mind, but he couldn't quite catch it.

She shook her head. "I guess his body couldn't take the strain. I don't know if you saw it on the news, but the man they found dead in the woods outside town?" At their nods, she sighed, "That was him."

"And everything that followed?" Rathe pressed. "The various Fae we've all sensed hunting you?"

"Your guess is as good as mine," Arawyn shrugged. "I don't know if it was that pulse or meeting you three, but it seems like ever since that night, your kind, or *our* kind, I guess, have been coming out of the woodwork. And they don't seem to like me much," she drawled wryly.

Viper stared at his brother when Rathe leaned back in

his seat. He knew that look. Rathe had figured something out. The question was, what? He didn't have to wait long to find out, thankfully. He wasn't known for his patience.

"Arawyn," Rathe started. When he had her attention, he sat forward, resting his elbows on the table. "Have you ever heard the term *'Changeling'*?"

Chapter Thirty-Nine

Rathe

Rathe kept his gaze focused on Arawyn, but he caught Viper's brows shooting up in shock.

"You don't think..."

Fear sounded just as stunned when he questioned, "Are you sure? We stopped doing that, what, two hundred years ago? How would she have surv—"

He held up a hand to silence them, still staring at Arawyn. "Have you?"

She shook her head, gaze bouncing between the three of them before returning to him. "No. What is it?"

He saw Viper reach out and lay a hand on her knee, twisting the fingers of his other into the long strands of her white blonde hair. He knew his brother had to be feeling the urge to prevent her from experiencing the horror they all knew she was about to feel. To his relief, he didn't sense any of Viper's Influence ghosting over her.

She wouldn't appreciate having her emotions manipulated, but more importantly, it would muddy the magic he'd evoked and make judging her reaction impossible.

For Viper's and Fear's sakes, he was still trying to hold onto his suspicions about her, but after hearing nothing but truth in her voice, that distrust was rapidly crumbling to dust. Even if it hadn't been, he was nowhere near immune to her. He could admit, to himself at least, that if he'd been able, he would've been sorely tempted to supplant her emotions with something softer, something less... painful, regardless of the effect it would've had on the spell already making his head ache.

Drawing in a slow breath, he held her gaze. "A Changeling is a Fae child who is taken to the human realm and left with a human family. The human child is taken back to Faery, our realm, in their place."

"You're not serious. They just abandon them? I- why the hell would someone do that?"

"The reasons varied. For a time, it was thought new blood was needed to strengthen failing magics. It didn't, so the practice fell out of favor."

"And the Fae babies? Did they give a fuck what their lives would be like, growing up not knowing why they were different?" she demanded, her delicate features twisted with outrage and no small amount of hurt.

Rathe shifted slightly, wishing to hell he didn't have to tell her. The betrayal and grief he could feel from her tore at him. That she was trying to conceal them behind anger was salt on the wound. Her first instinct was to hide any weakness, even here with them, and he knew, without question, that she trusted them more than she had anyone else in a long time.

"No, Little Vixen. The Fae child was left in the human realm to die. They were babies that were either born sickly, deformed, or had broken magic. They would've died anyway. It was thought kinder to let them fade slowly under the love of a human mother. And it was easier on the Fae mother to be spared the pain of watching their child pass, to instead have a different child to nurture."

Arawyn reared back. "W- what? What about the ones who didn't die?"

"To my knowledge, there haven't been any who survived being denied the magic of Faery. Eventually, all Fae cast out will fade and die."

"Then, how did I survive? If I'm a 'changeling' like you think, why didn't I die?"

"That is the question, isn't it?"

"I don't understand."

"The fact that you survived twenty-six years outside of Faery is strange enough, but that none of us can sense from which Court you hail... " Rathe shook his head. "Your power feels different, Arawyn. I can sense its strength, we all can, but it's muffled."

He felt Fear's and Viper's gazes zero in on him when he hesitated. He knew they were wondering if he was finally going to decide to trust her.

Even with the truth spell, it was a risk. Though the chance that she could outwit a truth spell was small, so small it was nearly impossible, he had to admit the tastes he'd had of her power told him she was strong. That he didn't know which powers she possessed, or from which Court she hailed, was unsettling. As a Prince, he was usually always in the know, and the mystery surrounding this woman drove him to the brink of distraction.

While he hadn't sensed a flare of power, that didn't mean it was completely impossible that she might be using an ability or conjured magic of her own. If that were true, it would make it feel like the spell was working, when in reality, it wasn't. She *could* be lying. She *could* be a spy.

But, it was a remote possibility... and he wanted to believe her. He wanted to stop battling back the draw he felt to her.

"I thought you were a spy sent by the High King of the Light Court, to glean information from us," Rathe admitted.

"About fucking time," Viper muttered under his breath.

Rathe spared his brother a look, then focused back on Arawyn. "I assumed you were muting your power intentionally, to make yourself feel like a banished Fae."

"And you don't think that anymore," she surmised.

"Mm," he hummed noncommittally. "When you said you were working with your powers, you mentioned only releasing it in tendrils. Have you ever tried to release more than that?"

She immediately shook her head. "No. I was—am—afraid it'll flood out, and I won't be able to pull it back in."

Rathe nodded. "Try now."

He saw her stiffen. Before he could reassure her, his brother smoothed his hand up and down her leg, gaining her attention. "You're safe, my Loon. We won't let it get out of control."

She frowned up at him uncertainly. "How can you be sure?"

Viper winked at her and tipped his head. "Because Rathe, here, is the High Prince of the Light Court."

She made a startled sound and gave Rathe wide eyes. "You're kidding."

"Nope!" Viper said cheerfully, but the look his brother gave him was taunting.

Rathe didn't know what he expected her reaction to be, but the slow grin she gave him wasn't it. Wary of the delight sparkling in her eyes, he narrowed his own.

"Something amusing, Little Vixen?" he murmured.

"You're a Fairy Prince," she chuckled. "I thought you'd be much smaller and more... fluttery. You mentioned wings earlier. Are yours little sparkly things?"

Rathe lifted a brow, his own slow smile decidedly predatory. She couldn't know the breadth of a male Fae's wings were associated with his size in other areas or that asking a male to flash his wings was a rather bold come on.

"I have wings, yes, but they don't sparkle. And they're not small," he purred.

Her expression progressed from startled to interested before it settled on fascination.

"Would you like to see them, Arawyn?" he coaxed, his voice a low, seductive invitation.

By the Gods, but if she kept staring at him like that, he was going to show her exactly how big his wings were.

Before she could say 'yes'—and she most definitely was about to—Fear chuckled and shook his head.

"Come on, *Firláh*, before you tempt Rathe any further. A male can only take being looked at like that for so long, my Little Temptress."

Arawyn blinked and looked up at him with a confused frown. "Tempt?"

Fear muttered something under his breath, then smiled down at her and helped her to her feet. "Come. We'll go to the basement to test your power. It's shielded, so if you lose control, it won't pulse past the walls."

Her expression faded back into one of uncertainty and worry. Turning, she pinned Rathe with a searching look. "Can you really help, if it goes haywire?"

Pushing to his feet, he rounded the table to stare down at her. Unable to fight the need to touch her, he caught the ends of her hair with his fingertips.

"I can. You'll be safe," he promised, marveling at how soft and silken the strands were before he made himself release her.

The trust in her eyes as she gazed up at him was more seductive than the wide-eyed fascination, and infinitely more detrimental to his self-control.

"Okay. Let's try, then."

Chapter Forty

ARAWYN

Arawyn followed Rathe as he led them downstairs, her heart beating a little too rapidly, nerves buzzing through her like a swarm of angry bees. Part of it was the lingering shock over everything they'd told her, but part of it was good old-fashioned fear of the unknown.

She believed Rathe when he said he could contain her power, if it got out of hand, which eased some of the fear; but not all of it. The what-ifs were circling around and around in her mind. He'd said her power felt different, so what if it were broken? What if he were wrong, and he couldn't contain it?

What if he could prevent it from escaping the room to which he was leading them, but he couldn't stop it from hurting him, Fear, or Viper?

What if they became obsessed? What if her power finally began to affect them like it did, well, humans?

That's going to take serious getting used to.

Sure, she'd kind of, sort of, thought she might be an alien. Now, after having confirmation she definitely wasn't human, she realized she hadn't truly believed she was... *other*. Different, yes. But, in the back of her mind, she'd been holding onto the belief she'd formed years ago: that she was just mutated or a freak leap of evolution.

Leaning to the side to see around Rathe's bulk when he opened the door at the bottom of the stairs, Arawyn caught sight of a dark, underground hallway, at the end of which was a massive, steel door.

Arawyn slowed to a stop. "Umm, guys? Someone tell me you're not leading me into some kind of dungeon, because that looks a hell of a lot like the door of a torture chamber."

"Oh. Uhhh," Viper faltered.

Whipping around to face him, she gave him wide eyes. She caught the look Fear gave Viper and the elbow he threw into her Cookie Monster's ribs.

"Ouch! What was that for?" Viper yelped, rubbing the spot with a look akin to a wounded puppy, the scar cutting through his eye creasing with his tented brows.

Fear shook his head at his friend, then smiled reassuringly down at her. "It's not a torture chamber, *Firláh*."

"Oh! Riiigghhtt," Viper's expression changed to one of understanding. Looking down at her, he nodded with exaggerated agreement. "Yeah, no, definitely not a torture chamber." His eyes flitted to the right. "Or... not *exclusively* a torture chamber. It's a multipurpose room, really."

A garbled sound escaped her throat, and she was sure if

her eyes got any bigger, they were going to be in serious danger of popping out.

She felt Rathe's heat a moment before his deep voice whispered in her ear, "If torture was on the menu for you, we would've done so by now."

Viper held up a finger and added, "Let's not be rash here. I don't think we should cross it off the menu entirely. Some torture is fun!"

Arawyn gave him a look that clearly said he was crazy, which she thought was more than fair. Catching it, he bent and brushed the tip of his nose across hers, eyes flashing gold in the faint light.

Voice a low rasp, barely a breath of sound, he purred, "Denial, biting, being tied up... Torture doesn't always have to be unpleasant, my Pretty Little Loon."

Seduced by that low purr and the way his eyes held her captive, Arawyn swayed forward. Before her lips could brush his, Viper straightened. He glided the tip of his tongue across his lower lip, giving her a teasing peek of the barbell piercing it, then grinned widely, looking smug as fuck.

"See? Lie to me and tell me you don't wanna kiss me even more now."

"Ooh, that was dirty! You're going to pay for that later," she growled, but the threat was ruined by her smile.

His eyes went hooded, and his grin became anticipatory. "Promises, promises."

The quip she was about to fire back was cut short when Rathe slipped one thickly muscled arm over her shoulder and across her chest. The touch, which was more contact than they'd ever had, stunned her to silence.

And, apparently, to docility, because when he used that arm to guide her around, it didn't even occur to her to resist.

He held her lightly against his front, not so close walking was difficult, but close enough she could feel his hard body brushing hers from the back of her head down to her ass. Close enough she felt small, delicate, safely enfolded by his big frame, and drowning in his intoxicating scent of sunshine, smoke, and bourbon.

"Flirt later. We have more important things to do at the moment," he prodded.

Viper snorted as if that were the most ridiculous thing he'd ever heard. Even Fear made a skeptical sound low in his throat.

Snickering, she shook her head at their antics. That was when it hit her they were distracting her on purpose, trying to calm her by taking her mind off of obsessing about what was coming. Even Rathe—dangerous, deadly, brooding Rathe—cared enough to try and make her feel better.

Careful guys, you keep this up, and I'm going to fall in love.

Once inside the room, still standing in Rathe's arms, Arawyn quickly scanned the space as either Fear or Viper secured the door behind them. It was weakly lit with a single, bare bulb hanging from the ceiling.

Nose wrinkling at the faint scent of copper and damp earth, she eyed the drain directly under the bulb warily. To the right was a long, metal table covered in dents and scratches—the only furniture the room boasted.

Cutting Fear a look when he stepped up to her side, she drawled, "Not a torture chamber, hmm?"

He had the grace to look slightly guilty, but she knew it was for the fib and not at all over the fact that they had a dungeon.

"As Viper said, it's not *exclusively* a torture chamber, and it's not used as such all that often. Only when we're left with no other recourse," Fear soothed with a small smile.

Her gentle giant, the man who touched her with such tenderness and care, was talking about torturing people with about the same amount of contrition as confessing he didn't always take the time to recycle.

That wasn't actually what shocked her, though. She knew they were on the dark grey side of the morality scale.

When she continued to frown up at him, he lifted a hand and cupped her cheek, looking suddenly unsure. "Does that bother you, Arawyn? Would it help to know we don't hurt the innocent?"

She noticed Rathe was very, very still at her back. He hadn't pulled away from her physically, but she could sense him closing off, could almost feel him pulling the cold, unfeeling mask back into place.

Viper, who'd strolled farther into the room, snorted. "Of course she knows that!" He stopped walking when she didn't immediately agree with him and peered at her over his shoulder, amber eyes searching. "Right? You know we're not the bad guys. Villains, sure, and not the good guys, per se, but... "

Stepping out from under Rathe's arm, she moved so she could see all three of them.

"I trust you," she said softly.

That was what shocked her.

It wasn't just that she believed they wouldn't hurt her. It wasn't just that she believed they would be as honest with her as they could.

The trust she had in them was no longer broken up and parsed out in small, specific instances. She simply trusted them. And that astonished the hell out of her.

Arawyn hadn't trusted anyone since she was a teenager.

Despite the questions that still surrounded what it was they did when they left at all hours, despite seeing all of them come home with blood on their clothing more than once, despite standing in what was unmistakably a room used to hurt people, she trusted them.

At her softly spoken words, all three of them zeroed in on her, going perfectly, predatorily still. She'd thought Rathe was stiff before; now, he could've been a statue. She wasn't sure he was even breathing. But, his eyes, those bright blue eyes, were so intense on hers they almost glowed.

Fear was the first to speak. "Say that again."

"I trust you."

Fear grunted as if she'd knocked the breath out of him, his beautiful, expressive grey eyes sparkling with emotion.

She met Viper's gaze. "And I do know you're not bad guys." Pausing, she gave them all a small, wry smile. "Despite all"—she gestured to the bloodstained concrete around her—"evidence to the contrary."

The smile her Cookie Monster gave her was brilliant. Sniffing, he wiped away the single tear trailing down his scarred cheek and proclaimed, "That decides it. I'm getting your name tattooed on me."

"Don't you dare," she warned with a giggle, sternly pointing a finger.

He shrugged. "I already made the appointment. No take-backs."

Rathe caught the ends of her hair once more, tugging gently as he ran his fingers down the length of them.

"Come, my Vixen. Show us that trust you profess to have. It's time to play with your power."

Chapter Forty-One

Arawyn

Arawyn blew out a nervous breath. "So, what happens now?"

She peered between the three of them, brows raised, containing the urge to anxiously wring her hands or something equally as telling that she was nervous as hell. It wasn't that she didn't feel comfortable showing her apprehension, it was just her go-to reaction to appear unrattled.

"Do you have a magic wand? Do we do a little woo-woo dance? Blood sacrifice?"

Please don't be the last one.

If it were just pricking a finger, that would be fine, but if they wanted to go full-on animal sacrifice, she'd have to draw the line. She could maybe be convinced to sacrifice a bad human, like a serial killer or something, but no animals. That would just be too far.

Rathe's lips twitched. "No. We're not Blood Fae."

"And thank fuck for that," Viper said, giving an exaggerated little shiver. "Creepy fuckers."

Brows raising, she eyed him with surprise. "I didn't think you knew how to be afraid."

She'd held a gun to his ribs, and he hadn't so much as twitched. Whatever these Blood Fae were, they must be the stuff of nightmares to make her Cookie Monster flinch.

Viper waved a dismissive hand. "They don't scare me, they weird me the fuck out. Anything that drinks blood to survive is freaky. I mean, really…. Have you ever drunk blood? It's gross."

Fear, to her surprise, rumbled in agreement, "Like liquid pennies."

Arawyn gave them both a look and drawled, "No, I can't say I've ever drunk blood."

Viper's face scrunched up like he'd just been force-fed kale, something she'd come to learn he hated. Passionately. "Well, take my word for it. Nasty as fuck, I tell you."

"Wait." Arawyn held up a hand as realization hit. "They're like vampires?"

Fear hummed and nodded. "That's what the humans call them, yes. We said earlier that banished Fae have limited power."

"Because they're separated from the magic of Faery," Arawyn recited.

He sent her an approving smile. "What they do retain becomes susceptible to collective human influence. They begin to change, physically, to reflect human beliefs about supernaturals. Blood Fae become 'vampires,' as you call them. Those capable of shifting forms become 'shifters' or 'werewolves.' Those particularly skilled in conjured magic or with elemental affinities: 'witches.' High Fae of the Night: 'demons.' Of the Light: 'angels.' Water Fae become 'merfolk.' The list goes on."

Arawyn gave him wide eyes. "Whoa. That's some quantum entanglement shit, right there. So, which Clan is strongest?"

Rathe answered, "The strength of the Clans and which is considered the strongest is fluid. Usually, the amount of power a Fae possesses depends on the severity of their banishment. Some are stripped of the majority of their power before being banished—an ultimate punishment— while others' powers are left to wither over time. Eventually, all banished Fae will devolve to their baser powers, and from there it becomes a ruthless game. There's only so much excess magic left in the human realm, and as such, it often depends on which Fae have the most control of the entertainment industry at the time."

Cocking her head, she frowned up at him. "I don't unders—" Her eyes went wide as it hit her. "Oh my god, I get it. So, if they make vampires popular in movies and books, that Clan becomes stronger, because more humans are glorifying them. Same for witches and werewolves and everything else, yes?"

"Exactly."

"Holy shit. I wonder how much I affected them in my Twilight phase as a kid."

Viper growled, "Those fucking movies! The 'vamp' and 'werewolf' Clans were out of control. The 'demons' were pissed. They'd been top dogs for most of, what"—he glanced at Fear—"like the last thousand years?"

"Mm, thereabouts, yes."

"Wait. Did I hear you say 'merfolk'?" she asked, ignoring the demon thing in favor of something more important: mermaids.

"*Water Fae,*" Fear nodded.

"Spiteful little fuckers, really. And always hungry!" Viper pointed to a few thin white scars crisscrossing the back of his hand, scars she'd somehow never noticed before. "They like people meat, and they are not against a little cannibalism. They look all innocent, but lemme tell you, their teeth are sharp as fuck."

And there goes that fairytale.

"This is all a lot to process," she said, head already spinning from the overload of information.

"We'll explain the Clans here in the human realm in more detail later. It's time, Arawyn," Rathe directed, catching and holding her gaze. "How about you try to open your power to us first? If that doesn't work, I'll draw it out of you."

Arawyn arched a brow at the bossy man, er, Fae standing across from her.

Fae.

It sounded far-fetched and fantastical, but it also felt right.

Hesitant to unclench the fist she kept around her power, she closed her eyes and let out a long, slow breath. She tilted her head to the right, then the left, stretching her neck, then shook out her arms like she was warming up for the fight of her life.

"Relax," Rathe prompted, like this was an easy ask, one she was making a bigger deal of than it was.

Bristling at his dismissive tone, she opened her eyes and

sent him a look. Maybe she was making a mountain out of what they saw as a molehill, but she hadn't grown up knowing how to control her power. The opposite, actually, and it wasn't innate to release it. She'd spent the last ten years trying to contain it, to dampen it.

To make it disappear so it would stop ruining her life.

It was only these past few weeks she'd even dared to try to loosen her hold, and look where that had gotten her?

One dead guy, two attempts on her life, three stalkers, and now she was in hiding. Granted, she wasn't hating her seclusion, and it came with an impressive silver lining. Or three. But, letting down her guard and releasing her power went against every instinct she had.

Catching the look she gave him, Rathe smirked slightly, appearing pleased with her open show of irritation. She'd caught that look from him before, but she hadn't understood it then. She did now. He was a Prince. As such, he was likely used to being treated with deference and having people kowtow to him.

Holding up his hands in surrender, he soothed, "I wasn't trying to condescend to you. You need to relax or your power will sense danger and be on alert. Have you ever felt it trying to protect you?"

She took a moment to think about that.

"Yes." The answer surprised her. All this time she'd thought of her power as something working against her. In many ways, it had, but there'd definitely been times it had reacted defensively.

Just recently, it had come to her aid when she'd been attacked by that creepy-as-fuck kid, er, Aswang, and had helped her fend it off. That'd been helpful.

At least it was something.

Trusting herself, and Rathe, she leveled out her breathing and slowly, so very slowly, reached inside of herself, where the well of power lived, and loosened her hold. It gradually rose, then slipped out of her in those familiar, little tendrils. She felt them beeline for the guys, felt them prod and caress the men like they were trying to coax their power out in return.

She heard Fear groan softly before he cut off the sound and almost opened her eyes. Did being touched by those tendrils feel as good for them as it did for her?

"Good," Rathe murmured, his voice sounding slightly rough. "I can feel it. Well done, Arawyn. Now, more." Rathe prompted.

Relaxing her grip further, she tensed, waited for it to surge out of her, resolving to not instinctively try and cut it off. Except it didn't surge. Eyes still closed, she frowned and reached for it, trying to draw it out. Strangely, it felt like she encountered a barrier.

That's new.

She reached again, trying to coax it out, practically cooing to it like it were a timid animal she was trying to lure out of its cage with yummy treats, but she couldn't quite reach it.

Scrunching her nose and furrowing her brow, she tried again, and again.

"Nothing's happening," Viper whisper-yelled.

Fear growled, literally growled at him, which was oddly sexy. "Give her a few minutes. She's doing great."

A smile pulled at her lips, then quickly fell away as she focused, yet again, trying to draw it out. And once again, it refused to cooperate.

Blowing out a short breath, she grumbled, "It'll flood out

when *it* wants to, but now that *I* want it to, it's playing hard to get."

"Breathe, Vixen. Center yourself," Rathe pressed calmly. "Now, try again."

"I... can't. It just won't cooperate." Frustrated, she popped her eyes open and sighed.

Narrowing his gaze, Rathe studied her inquisitively, like she was a puzzle he'd very much like to solve. "Explain it to me. How does it feel?"

"It feels like there's a barrier between us. I can coax out a little, but that's it. When I try to pull more, the barrier flexes enough that I can touch it, but it's preventing me from actually drawing it out. I don't understand. It's never done this before. Something's changed."

The guys shared a look. Fear rolled his big shoulders and speculated, "Perhaps, this is a defense mechanism. She's been away from Faery almost all her life. Maybe her power sealed itself off so it didn't fade. That might be why she survived."

"It's a good guess, but doesn't explain why it's suddenly unreachable." Viper's amber eyes were practically glittering with intrigue. He seemed like a man who enjoyed puzzles and was intent on figuring her out. "Something recent must have triggered the change. You said her power flared when that little fucker of an Aswang attacked her. Maybe it's a new development? A defense mechanism from being nearly drained?"

Rathe hummed pensively. "Perhaps. But, why wouldn't it have responded in kind any other time she was hunted, attacked, or hurt?" He let the question hang in the air, and for a heavy moment, none of them spoke. "Maybe someone bound her power." He shook his head. "That could explain why it feels almost muted and would account for the sensation of a barrier, but why they would bother is beyond me."

"Fuck. If someone bound her power, that could also explain why she's survived for so long. With it sealed away, it was protected from fading. It would also explain why shit changed when she was sixteen." Fear glanced at each of them in turn.

"Wait. Explain," she demanded, feeling like she'd been dropped in the middle of a conversation that had no context.

"Fae powers mature at age sixteen," Viper shrugged. "Think of it like puberty. We're born with innate powers, but they fully emerge and strengthen upon our sixteenth year."

Focusing on her, Rathe mused, "Let's start with the easiest explanation. If your power is simply reacting from the Aswang's attack, you should be able to coax it back out with practice and patience."

Arawyn made a face that clearly said how little she liked the idea of waiting for who knew how long. She wasn't especially impatient, usually, but what if it took months to lure her power out? Or years?

With the number of Fae who had already targeted her, she wasn't sure she could afford to wait that long. Not knowing how to defend herself from them put her at a hell of a disadvantage. One that could easily turn out to be deadly.

The memory of the creepy, child-looking Fae and the sensation of it sucking the power out of her, remembering how weak she'd felt afterward, sent a shiver down her spine and hardened her resolve.

All her martial arts and self-defense training had been useless against the thrall it had used on her. She'd spent too long and worked too hard to not be a victim to give up on this now.

Rathe smirked at her for the second time that day, setting a new record. His eyes shone with approval at the resolve in hers. "I can force your power out of you. If you'll allow me to try," he tacked on at the end.

Arawyn appreciated the effort he was making to be more polite, now he knew she wasn't a spy sent to surveil them. She just wasn't sure how to react to this new Rathe. He'd gone from cold and dangerous to interested and almost nice.

Almost.

It was a jarring change. Seductive, dangerously enticing, and intriguing as hell, but still jarring.

Arawyn glanced at Fear, then Viper, gauging their reactions to his offer. Seeing no hesitation in their open expressions, she turned back to Rathe. She meant what she'd said earlier. She trusted them, and that extended to him, as well.

She nodded once, giving him permission.

"Brace yourself."

"Whoa. Hold up." Arawyn took an unconscious step backward.

Okay, maybe I don't trust him fully *yet.*

"Communication is key, you know. What are you going to do, exactly? You're not going to try and release all of it, are you?"

They'd promised her the walls were reinforced, that none of her power would be able to leak out, but they'd also never experienced her power before. Were they sure—really sure—nothing would escape this room?

The last thing she needed was more stalkers, more obsessed men coming after her, more strange beings trying to kill her.

Rathe shook his head, and a lock of dark hair fell across his forehead before he brushed it back into place. She almost wished he'd have left it there. Somehow, that one out-of-place lock softened his appearance and made him feel less intimidating, not that she'd ever admit he had that air about him.

Arawyn wasn't the least bit scared of him, and she wasn't intimidated by him either. Well, not much, anyway.

But, Rathe was powerful. There was no questioning the strength that poured off of him, or the self-assured way he held himself. He exuded confidence and authority.

Maybe it came from being a royal. The High Prince of the Light Court, to be exact.

Or maybe it's just him.

She shook the thought away.

It was in all their best interests to learn more about who she was, why she'd been exchanged at birth, where she belonged, and perhaps, most importantly, what she was capable of.

"I'll keep it simple for now. I can unglamor you," he offered.

Since they'd explained Glamor earlier, she knew what he was talking about, but she'd been thinking about it in relation to them and how they looked without it. It hadn't truly sunk in that she may not look how she thought she did. For a moment, the concept was almost too outlandish to digest, even after everything else they'd revealed.

After a moment of stunned disconcertment, curiosity bloomed, intense and irresistible. "Do it."

A few moments later, Arawyn was surrounded in warmth as Rathe's power enveloped her, licking at her skin. She shivered from the sharp change in temperature and the soft, tingling feel of it against her, letting her lids fall closed in pleasure.

"That's it, Arawyn," Rathe praised, the earlier roughness in his voice more pronounced.

It had barely settled in that her appearance was going to shift. The idea she didn't actually look how she'd always known herself to look was both disconcerting and intriguing.

Fingers crossed I don't look like Orin. I don't think I can pull off those shark teeth as well as he did.

Arawyn bit her lips to hold back hysterical laughter of the unstoppable variety. The kind that purged you, cleansed everything, and left you feeling whole and centered by the time it died away.

But, underneath the bubble of hysteria, she was wildly, untameably curious about what she looked like as a Fae.

What do the guys look like?

She'd wondered since the moment they told her what Glamor was, mentioning pointed ears and wings. Once the thought had popped into her mind, she couldn't remove it. Now she was focused on it, she knew she'd been seeing glimpses all along. Viper's eyes turning more golden than amber, Rathe's flashing an inhuman blue with that shock of orange. When she first met them, she'd thought those were tricks of the light but now she knew them to be little peeks of their true appearances.

What else were they hiding behind their magic? Rathe said he had wings. Did Fear and Viper? Did they have horns? tails? scales? Did Fae even have any of those things? Or did they simply look like prettier versions of humans, the way vampires were depicted in almost every movie she'd ever watched about the creatures?

Thinking back to Orin, she knew that wasn't true. He was Fae, and he definitely wasn't prettier than a human. He'd been strange looking, his features inhumanly different.

Horns had sprouted from his head, he'd had bumpy wrinkles on his forehead, and pointed ears.

Oh no. What if I'm hideous?

It was a vain thought, but a serious worry. What if the guys didn't find her attractive once they saw her true form?

An infinitely more concerning thought hit her. What if they couldn't put her glamour back in place, once it was gone?

She didn't have another second to worry about it—or call this whole experiment off—because the heat licking her skin grew almost unbearable.

"Rathe?" she gritted out.

"It's fighting me," he answered, sounding slightly strained.

"That... shouldn't be possible," she heard Fear murmur.

Rathe grunted and pushed more power at her, changing gears from gentle coaxing to brute force.

Arawyn gasped, the heat becoming almost painful, the sensation of his power trying to tear a hole in the barrier taking her breath away.

Before she could tell Rathe it was starting to hurt, her power did what she'd feared—it rose suddenly with the force of a tsunami and lashed out before she could stop it.

To her surprise, she could feel that it wasn't doing so with the intention to harm. It felt... defiant. This was a warning more than an attack, a refusal to bend to Rathe's will.

That sense was confirmed when she felt her power gather Rathe's own and reflect it back into him.

Left shivering in the wake of all that heat, she stumbled forward a step. Her eyes flew open in time to see a bright light envelop Rathe, rushing over his skin and up his body before vanishing just as quickly.

What it revealed left her gaping.

Rathe was gone. In his place stood a stunning, beastly man with skin of melted gold and massive, black-feathered wings.

Chapter Forty-Two

Arawyn

Speechless, Arawyn gaped at the beautiful monster before her. Drawn like a moth to flame, she took a step closer, wanting, needing to see him, to touch him. She managed a single step before Rathe cursed, eyes wide and dark brows furrowed, as he stared down at himself.

"How the fuck did you do that?" he demanded, pinning her with a stunned look.

God, but his eyes were unreal. Vibrant, cerulean blue with a sunburst of bright orange around the pupils. They were the eyes of a predator. She wanted to get lost in them, wanted to stare into them until she'd mapped every facet.

"I have no idea," she admitted with a slow shake of her head. At the disbelieving expression he gave her, she tried to think past the shock of seeing him and explained, "The heat of your power was starting to get painful, and then, all of a sudden, it felt like mine got pissed off and threw yours back at you."

"You shouldn't be capable of that," Rathe muttered, but it was said almost absently.

His focus had returned to his appearance, head bowed as he stared down at himself. She had the sudden and distinct feeling he was intentionally avoiding looking at her.

Arawyn felt the tingle of his magic flaring and knew he was about to reverse whatever she'd just done and disguise himself from her again. That she could now feel his magic with such ease was a distant thought, far outweighed by the refusal to let him hide.

"Stop!" Arawyn gasped, throwing out a hand. "Wait!"

Rathe froze at her command, his gaze moving sharply to hers.

What she saw there surprised her more than his inhuman appearance. His face was as coolly forbidding as it always was, but shadowing those gorgeous, cynical eyes was wariness at how she'd react and a bracing expectation that she'd reject him. That shocked her, but it wasn't what stole her breath.

There, behind the wariness, hidden like a secret, was the quietest glint of hope that she *wouldn't* reject him.

It suddenly hit her—under all his confidence and authority, beneath the cold calculation and danger, Rathe was simply a man who wanted her to accept him as she had Viper and Fear.

Arawyn took another step toward him, locking with his eyes, letting him see everything she was feeling: wonder, awe, fascination, desire.

"You're beautiful," she whispered, hoping he could feel

the truth of her words without the special magic he'd used earlier.

Rathe had always been sexy as hell, but seeing him like this? She didn't have the words to describe him. She'd once thought of him as a fallen angel, and she could almost laugh at just how correct she'd been.

He was lethal, dangerous, powerful. Stunningly otherworldly.

Huge, black, feathered wings protruded from his back, the tips arching at least three feet above him, the bottoms brushing the floor. Each feather was so black it gleamed with a purple sheen, like an oil slick.

She wanted to reach out and touch him, to stroke her hands down the huge, sleek-looking feathers.

With a flex of his shoulders, he stretched those wings wide, leaving Arawyn gaping at his impressive wingspan. Her gaze caught on the middle of his wing. Located at the joint was a sharp, hooked talon that looked like it could disembowel her with a single, careless swipe.

These weren't the pretty, useless appendages she'd been imagining. They were fully functional. More, they were as much a part of him as his arms or legs. She could see it in the way he moved them, as though doing so was as natural as waving a hand.

Curiosity burned bright inside her. Had he felt bereft with them Glamored and hidden away? Were they as soft as they looked? Could he fly and carry her at the same time?

Rathe's gaze was intense, and the smallest smile was flirting with the corners of his lips. He took a step closer, wings now tucked neatly at his back. Feathers rustled with the movement, making her pulse race with both his advance and the exotically inhuman sound.

Voice a low, pleased purr, he asked, "You think I'm beautiful, Little Vixen?"

Arawyn lifted a brow and huffed lightly, ignoring the heat in her cheeks at the flirtatious look and triumphant sparkle in his eyes. "Don't play coy. You know I always have."

His smile grew just a little, revealing canines too long and too sharp to be human. "Even like this? Inhuman. Exposed as the monster I really am?"

"Yes," she breathed, trapped in his stare. "Even more like this."

Tearing her gaze away from his dangerously alluring one before she did something impulsive, she let herself scan his body.

His shirt had been torn from him with the sudden emergence of his wings, revealing hard muscle covered in dark tattoos. Under the ink, his normally tanned skin had taken a metallic sheen, making the etched lines of his abdomen, his corded arms, his strong neck, his angular, gorgeous face all appear as though they'd been carved from the purest, richest gold.

Catching movement, her eyes zeroed in on his hands. His neatly trimmed nails were now sharpened claws. At her wide eyes, Rathe's hands flexed and those deadly claws retracted, becoming almost normal looking nails again.

Envy was instant. "Oh, I want some of those," she whispered.

At Viper's snicker, she turned to look at him and Fear, her pulse speeding with excited realization.

"You two look different, as well, don't you?"

Fear's expression was still frozen with shock, his brows

sharply furrowed as he toggled between her and Rathe. His answer was a distracted, "We do, yes."

He opened his mouth to say something else, likely to question how she'd unglamored Rathe, judging from his speculative look, but she beat him.

"Will you show me?"

At that, he gave her his full attention. Beside him, Viper's smile vanished, and tension crept into his body.

Arawyn winced when she saw their reactions. "I'm sorry. Was it rude to ask?"

"No, *Firláh*, not rude. It's just—" He exchanged a look with Viper. "Viper and I don't look like Rathe. We're not... pure."

"I don't know what you mean by 'pure,' but you don't look like Rathe, now, so I didn't expect you would unglamored."

Viper shifted on his feet, the tip of his tongue peeking out to briefly play with one of his lip rings before he answered, "Pure-blooded. We're mutts, Pretty."

Arawyn frowned. She picked up on that being apparently a bad thing easily enough, but why he thought she would care was beyond her. When she voiced as much, he just blinked at her like she'd stunned him speechless, a first she was sure.

Peering between the two of them, she took in the tense set of their shoulders and the tightness in their expressions that lingered, despite her assurance she didn't care about their lack of pureness.

Deciding to fix the problem she'd inadvertently caused, Arawyn smiled softly at them. "I don't care if you're pure or as mixed as a Long Island Iced Tea, but I've obviously stepped on a sore point, so I rescind my invitation." Hoping to lighten the mood, she ended with a haughty sniff and an imperious wave of her hand.

Viper's eyes narrowed to suspicious slits. "Well! Now that you don't want to see, I want to show you. What is this witchery?"

Fear made a low sound and nodded, mimicking Viper's suspicious expression, though his grey eyes were dancing with amusement. "I've heard of this. Reverse psychology. Devious stuff, that."

Arawyn sputtered, "I didn't—"

"It's too late!" Viper interrupted. "I've already decided. Prepare yourself!"

With that, he whipped his shirt over his head, giving her a lovely view of hard muscle and colorful tattoos before he was enveloped in a soft, golden glow. When it faded away, the real Viper was standing before her, shoulders set, eyes nervous.

Lips parting with awe, Arawyn stared. She didn't know what she'd been expecting, but it wasn't this.

Chapter Forty-Three

Arawyn

He was... magnificent.

Pale gold, leathery wings arched high above his head, the hooked claws in the middle as black as his fingernails. Patterning the insides of those wings were scales in every shade of gold from the lightest champagne to the darkest bronze.

Like Rathe, his skin had become gilded gold, metallic and shimmery. Scattered across his chest and shoulders were more of those beautiful scales, glinting like polished copper in the weak light. She thought they were textured at first before realizing what she was seeing were his tattoos faintly patterning the scales.

Letting her admiration travel farther up his body, she went still when she met his eyes.

Like molten gold, they almost perfectly matched the color of his wings, and the pupils were no longer round, but slitted. Like a snake's.

"Say something," he rasped.

She wanted to say something eloquent or, at the very least, something reassuring to erase the insecure look she hated seeing in his eyes.

What came out was a breathy, "Oh my god, I hope I have scales."

"What?"

"What?" she echoed.

She tried to focus on his face to read his expression, but her envious gaze kept sliding back to those pretty scales. She wanted to slide her hands up his chest and across his biceps so badly her fingers tingled with it. Then, she wanted to journey farther to touch the insides of his wings.

Would the scales on his chest feel different from the ones decorating his leathery wings? Or would they feel the same? Would they be hard like armor or supple like a snake's? Tempering her wild curiosity, she held herself back from reaching out to explore, to find out if they'd be warm or cool beneath her fingers.

It'd be rude to paw at him... right?

Not that she truly believed Viper would object. She had the keen feeling he'd welcome any and all advances she made.

As she stared, he flexed his wings and gave them a little shimmy, making the scales glitter brilliantly in the dull light of the single bulb.

"Ooh," she exhaled, eyes wide and transfixed.

Viper gave a low, pained groan and whispered not quite

softly enough, "If you were prey, I could totally eat you right now, and you wouldn't even run."

Blinking free of her daze, she whipped an alarmed look up at him. "What?!"

He blinked back at her, eyes wide. "What?"

"You just said you could eat me."

"Pffft. No, I didn't." He paused a beat and glanced at Fear. "Did I?"

Fear had the side of his fist pressed to his lips to hide his smile—not that it was working—and coughed, "You did."

"Oh. Well, shit." Eyes wide and guileless, he lied, "I didn't mean the chompy kind of eating. What I had meant was the uhh, the sexy kind of eating." He nodded quickly, agreeing with himself and smiled a little too widely, showing off suspiciously fang-like teeth.

Arawyn gave him a raised brow, but chuckled, "You most definitely did not mean the sexy kind of eating."

"You've got no proof," he sniffed haughtily then waved a hand. "Anyway! Back to the important stuff." Tilting his head down, he gave her a look halfway between coy and shy as he twisted the toe of his motorcycle boot on the floor. "You think I'm pretty?"

"I think you're gorgeous," she grinned, charmed by his adorable insanity. "Gold is my new favorite color."

If hearts could have flown out of his eyes, she was sure they would've.

Viper stage-whispered to Rathe, "She called me gorgeous." Expression changing from delighted to devious, he added, "She only called you beautiful. I win."

Rathe didn't seem to take exception to that. The opposite, in point of fact. He was smiling, watching her like she'd just done something he found incredibly pleasing.

Looking away before she got lost in his eyes, Arawyn turned to peer up at Fear, trying to keep her expression open, but neutral, so he didn't feel pressured. If he chose to show her his true self, she wanted it to be wholly his choice, not because Rathe and Viper had done so.

"You don't have to—"

"Oh, but I want to, *moín Firláh*," he rumbled softly, his focus steady and intense on hers. "I can't let these two receive all those ego-boosting, doe-eyed looks of yours, now can I?"

That was all the warning he gave her. His grey eyes and wicked smile were the last things she saw before darkness cloaked him.

Having expected the golden glow Rathe and Viper had, the darkness caught her off guard. Just as she took an alarmed step toward him with her heart in her throat, thinking something had gone wrong, the shadow receded.

Stopping as quickly as if she'd run into a wall, Arawyn tilted her head all the way back, eyes as wide as saucers.

"Oh my fucking god," she choked out as she gawked, unabashedly, at what her Fear had become. "You said sex demons weren't real!"

The words escaped without thought, but she didn't have the mental capacity to regret them, even when the room was suddenly full of low, masculine laughter.

"Does that mean you think I'm pretty, too?" Fear rumbled, his eyes, now a vivid purple, sparkling—literally sparkling—as though they were dotted with a thousand tiny stars.

His voice had already been deep, but like this, it was even more so. The gravelly, bass sound vibrated through her like distant thunder.

Wordlessly, more than a little starstruck, she shook her head. Pretty wasn't the word that came to mind, but terrifying and erotically demonic had too many syllables for her to manage at the moment.

In an instant, Fear's whole expression changed, pulling down with a mixture of confusion and regret.

Oh, dammit. Did he not know just how beautiful he was in this, or any other, form?

Arawyn hurried to explain, not allowing another moment to pass where he doubted his decision to reveal himself to her.

"You're so much more than pretty, Fear. You're breathtaking and sexy as hell."

Fear's expression cleared until he was grinning down at her. Fangs flashing, he chuckled lowly, sending a shiver of delight down her spine. "Good."

Where Rathe and Viper had skin like molten gold, Fear's was silver, as though the moon was trapped inside him and shining through. Like them, he, too, had wings—huge, leathery, and black as night.

Unlike them, he had horns.

As black as his wings, they sprouted from his hairline and wrapped back around his head like a crown before the tips curled upward, ending in sharp points. Visions of holding onto them while he licked between her legs had her cheeks heating and her thighs clenching.

Movement by his feet caught her eyes. Leaning to the side to see what it was, Arawyn gasped when she caught sight of...

"Holy shit, is that a tail?"

The same silver as his skin and long enough to reach well past his ankles, it was undulating back and forth across the floor. It looked dangerous, the tip spade-shaped and very pointy, but that didn't lessen the sudden urge to touch it in the least.

Arawyn curled her fingers into her hands so she didn't make a grab for it, unsure of the etiquette on such a thing.

I wonder if it's considered rude to pet someone's tail?

Something of her thoughts must have shown on her face because Rathe's amused voice cut in, "Careful. It's got a mind of its own."

Not understanding, she threw a confused look over at him.

In answer, Viper grimaced and absently rubbed his shoulder. "It has a habit of stabbing people."

Fear snorted at the wide-eyed look she gave him, and she could've sworn smoke came out of his nostrils. "It wouldn't hurt you, *Firláh*. Them, sometimes. You, never," he promised.

As if it heard them talking about it, his tail went still, the tip moving to point at her like an arrow. Wariness had her sliding her right foot back, so she was ready to leap out of the way, if it took a jab at her. She trusted Fear, but after hearing them talk about his tail as though it had a mind of its own, like an octopus's arm, she thought caution was warranted.

Movements smooth and sinuous, it lifted higher, waving slowly back and forth. As she followed it with her eyes, the tension slowly drained out of her.

Closer and closer it moved while Arawyn just stared, feeling oddly relaxed even when it came within stabbing range. Thankfully, Fear had been right. It didn't poke any holes in her. Instead, it... pet her?

That was enough to snap her out of the trance.

Unsure if she was more freaked out about being hypnotized by a fucking tail, or charmed that it seemed to like her, she pet it in return, carefully stroking a fingertip lightly over the spade tip.

If it were possible, her eyes widened even more at the shiver working through Fear.

Did he like that?

Oh, how she wanted to play and find out.

Soon, it retreated, and Arawyn marveled at all three men as it really, truly sank in that they weren't human. They were predators and, unlike humans, had the features necessary to both lure in prey and kill it. Rathe's eyes, Viper's scales, Fear's tail—they were all mesmerizing.

"Like cuttlefish," she muttered under her breath.

Rathe zeroed in on her and cocked his head. "What's that?"

"Oh, nothing." Peering up at Fear, she prompted, "You wanted to ask something earlier?"

He gave her a look that said he knew she was intentionally redirecting the conversation but that he was going with it. "How did it feel when you rebounded Rathe's power?"

Arawyn immediately shook her head. "Not when *I* rebounded, when my power rebounded. I didn't even know I, or it, could do that."

Fear was quiet for a beat, a considering frown wrinkling the skin between his thick brows. "You're saying your power feels separate from you? Like its own entity?"

"Mm, like your tail, apparently. I take it yours doesn't."

"No."

Swallowing back a curse that her earlier fear concerning her power being broken had just been all but confirmed, Arawyn sighed, "Awesome. I get the feeling this is going to be a problem."

She could tell by his expression that Fear was about to say something encouraging and supportive, but Rathe cut in before he could. "It might be."

As much as she appreciated Fear's positivity, at the moment she needed Rathe's honesty. Turning to him, she echoed, "Might. Does that mean you have an idea of how to fix it?"

"Mm," he hummed, giving her a contemplative once-over before meeting her eyes again. "How opposed are you to getting naked?"

"Say again?" she croaked.

"This is a great plan!" Viper crowed.

Chapter Forty-Four

ARAWYN

Arawyn threw Viper a look in response to his unmitigated glee at her getting naked. While flattering, it wasn't how she imagined her first time being nude with him, not to mention it was cold as fuck down in the dungeon. And dirty. Not exactly a place in which she particularly wanted to strip.

To Rathe, she quipped, "I'm assuming you have a reason to want me to undress?"

She wasn't prepared for the wicked smile that graced his lips or the low, smoky, "Oh, yes. Many, Princess. So very many reasons."

Being flirted with by a shirtless, tattooed, winged Fae Prince with muscles for days and a smile so sinful it would tempt the devil? More potent than one hundred proof liquor. Panties ruined.

Jesus, I think I just orgasmed a little.

With that wicked smile still curling his lips, and a look in his eye that told her he knew exactly how much he affected her, Rathe coaxed, "You said your power feels good when you use it, yes? Pleasurable?"

"Yes," she breathed, pulse speeding, fluttering in her neck like a trapped bird as she caught on to his idea.

She felt, more than heard, Viper and Fear close in on her.

Anticipation blazed to life in Rathe's fiery, cerulean eyes, and his smile became hungry. "Then, perhaps, we can lure it out with pleasure where compulsion failed."

Fear and Viper stopped on either side of her, not touching, just waiting, their nearness and the yearning she could feel emanating from them, tempting her, enticing her to say 'yes,' but she hesitated.

She wanted this, wanted to find out what she was capable of, wanted to learn how to use her power—truly use it, so she could protect herself. But, in that moment, she wanted to feel their hands on her even more, both of them at the same time. She needed it so badly she ached. Yet, she hesitated, her mouth refusing to say the word they were waiting for.

What if they expected her to pick one of them? If she didn't, would they finally show the jealousy she'd been waiting for? And what if they didn't? Would that mean they didn't care about her the way she did them?

"Arawyn? Your consent," Rathe prompted when she was quiet for too long.

Bracing herself, she peered at all of them, dread at what she would see making her stomach clench.

What she found was anticipation, warmth, and a predatory kind of hunger. There was no jealousy, nothing detached or aloof to hint that this was only about lust for them. The opposite.

There was such tenderness shining down at her from Fear's inhumanly purple eyes. Viper's golden ones shone with adoration and desire he made no effort to hide or downplay. Even Rathe's fiery gaze was soft on hers, that hypnotic cerulean and orange sunburst stare holding an unexpected amount of affection.

Emotion tightened her throat, making her voice come out husky. "Yes."

Before the word had fully left her lips, their hands were on her, Fear at her front, Viper at her back. She'd half expected Rathe to join them, but he stepped back, his avid gaze never leaving her.

"Been so fucking patient. Finally get to taste you," Viper muttered under his breath a moment before he bent and sealed his lips to her neck, scraping the delicate flesh with sharp teeth, then sucking hard.

She felt that pull between her legs, as though he was sucking on her clit instead of her neck.

"Oh god." Moaning low in her throat, she let her head fall against his shoulder and looped an arm back around his neck, digging her fingers into his hair.

He released her long enough to whisper playfully in her ear, "You can call me Viper."

She would have playfully smacked him, but she was far too distracted.

Fear bent and stole her smiling lips in a drugging kiss, immediately sweeping his tongue inside to taste her deeply. He slid his palms up her ribs until he was cupping her right beneath her breasts, his hands so big his fingers were wrapped around her back, his thumbs pressed together on her chest.

Viper's hands were tight on her hips, flexing repeatedly as though he were trying not to jerk her back against him. Wanting exactly that, craving it, she arched her ass into him. Gasping into Fear's mouth when she felt the hard bar of Viper's cock, shivering at the sound of his low groan, she did it again.

Either that was the signal they'd been waiting for or their control reached its limit. With matching growls, they stepped closer and pressed their bodies tightly to hers, letting her feel their arousal. Arawyn slid her free hand up the back of Fear's head, carding her fingers through his long, silky hair until she found one of his horns.

Thighs clenching at the feel of it, so erotically foreign, yet so right, she writhed between them. In response, Fear coiled his tail around her leg, guiding her to widen her stance. He slipped a thigh between her legs at the same moment he cupped her breasts, and Viper sucked her earlobe into his mouth.

The multitude of sensations had her crying out into Fear's mouth. Pressing her breasts into his hands, she ground down against his thigh, needing the pressure where she was so wet and swollen for them.

Like an extra set of arms, she felt them wrap their wings around her, enclosing her in a cocoon of warmth, safety, and need. Even with her eyes closed, she knew they didn't surround her completely. She didn't have to wonder why. The knowledge that they'd left a gap so Rathe could watch unimpeded had a new rush of wetness slicking her core.

Lost to them, drowning in pleasure, the first tickle of

their power surprised her so badly her eyes flew open. They felt stronger like this, in their true forms, their power brighter, clearer.

Fear released her lips to stare down at her, his breaths harsh, pupils dilated so only a thin ring of purple could be seen. "Easy, Baby. We've got you."

Exhaling a shuddering breath, she let her lids fall closed again and relaxed back into Viper, trusting in him to hold her up while she gave herself back over to the pleasure.

Like vines, their power twinned around her: Fear's, cool and electric, whispering against her like a midnight breeze; Viper's, warm and sinuous, washing over her like sunshine in the spring.

The contrast of sensations was exhilarating, but more than that, it awakened the power inside her in a way nothing ever had before. As though it had been waiting for exactly that mix of cool and warm, it rose to meet them, escaping her in soft, little wisps to twist and play with theirs.

Fear's low groan was echoed by Viper's curse as her power danced with theirs. Hands tightened on her hips and breasts. Movements became more demanding, hungrier. Lips crushed to hers. Teeth set into the muscle of her shoulder, eliciting a sharp cry from her throat.

As the passion between them grew, her power became bolder, hungry and demanding. It wanted their pleasure. It wanted *them*. It knew what she didn't.

They were hers.

Arawyn's eyes flew open, and she sucked in a breath to warn them that her power wanted to bind them somehow. She didn't understand it, but the intention was clear.

She never got the chance.

Like a predator, it struck, taking a tiny piece of their power and pulling it into her, then blending a part of itself with theirs and pushing it back into them.

Fear and Viper simultaneously threw their heads back and dropped to their knees. Gasping, afraid she was hurting them, Arawyn tried to draw the power back inside herself.

Rathe's voice cut through the building panic, "No. Don't stop, Arawyn. You're not hurting them. Tell her."

Fear rolled his eyes up to look at her, his features harsh with need, voice guttural, "More, *moín Firláh.*"

Viper nuzzled his face against her hip, then nipped at her ass cheek through her leggings and growled, "I swear to fuck, if you stop, I'm never making you pancakes again."

A breathless laugh escaped her, but she immediately followed it with, "It wants you. It wants to bind you both."

"Gods, yes. I'm so fucking here for that," Viper panted.

Fear pulled her shirt up and dragged his tongue across her skin, leaving goosebumps in his wake. "It won't be permanent, *Firláh*. It can be undone. If you wish."

Peering down at him, she searched his face. Seeing only honesty and naked desire, she nodded and stopped fighting it. "Okay."

What she didn't say was she didn't wish for it to be undone, that there was a part of her, a dark, greedy part that wanted to bind them so tightly they wouldn't ever be able to leave her.

Rathe drew her attention back to him. "Release more, Arawyn. Draw it out. Push it to them. Focus on the feeling of their power. Light and Night touching you at once."

There was something in his tone, something curious, yet disbelieving, avid and incredulous in one.

What did he know that she didn't?

She didn't have time to question him, because just then, they pushed more power at her, and hers immediately responded, surging to meet them.

Pleasure was overwhelming, leaving her gasping at the intensity of it. In the same second, Viper's control snapped. With a hissed curse, he spun her around and buried his face between her legs.

Arawyn had just sucked in a sharp breath when he opened his mouth over her and bit her pussy through her leggings.

It wasn't pain that had the breath bursting out of her on a scream. The sudden, unexpected heat of his mouth against her core, the shock of feeling his teeth slide over her clit through the thin layer of her leggings, threw her into a shattering orgasm.

With it, the world exploded.

The first wave of pleasure-infused power threw Fear and Viper across the room, their big bodies making awful, stomach-twisting thuds as they impacted the concrete walls. Instead of crumpling to the floor, her feet left the ground, her body slowly lifting into the air.

The second wave shattered the bulb above her, sending sparks raining down as the concrete walls rumbled and cracked.

With the third, the color bled out of her eyes, leaving them perfectly white and sightless. The sound of distant thunder filled her ears, deafening her to the yells of the men around her. Her body felt both light as a feather and heavy as stone as she floated several feet above the ground.

The fourth wave of blissful power bowed her back and threw her arms wide. Blinding light erupted from her palms, scorching the walls and ceiling, narrowly missing Rathe. Inky shadows seeped from her skin. Above ground, a storm appeared over the warehouse, as if by magic.

Within the gilded shadows filling the room, electricity crackled threateningly, raising the hairs on her arms and biting at the men clawing their way through the waves of power, trying desperately to reach her.

Arawyn was aware of the chaos around her, but only distantly. It felt like a terrible dream or, perhaps, a beautiful nightmare.

It wasn't real. It couldn't be her who was hurting these men. It couldn't be her who had thrown Fear against the wall hard enough to split the skin on the back of his head. It couldn't be her who had burned Viper's palms when he'd shielded himself from the light beaming from hers. It couldn't be her who had shot lightning across Rathe's chest, leaving a jagged streak of black and blistered skin behind.

It's a dream, just an awful dream.

Except it wasn't a dream. She was actually hurting them.

These men who had shown her such kindness, who'd taken her in when she had nowhere else to go, who'd made her feel safe and accepted for the first time in her life were bleeding and bruised and burned because of her.

And they were powerless to stop her.

As though from far away, she could feel all of them trying to contain the surge, trying to tame it and urge it back inside her. She could feel that they were failing.

Ecstasy, horror, regret, and fear coiled inside her like poison.

She'd been right. Her power was broken. It was too wild, too strong to be trusted, and she was too weak to control it.

Gradually, bit by bit, the chaos erupting from her

quieted. Her senses returned in increments as her climax waned. The scent of burned flesh and the copper tang of blood hit her first, making her stomach roll and turn in on itself. Sight returned slowly, revealing the scorched ceiling and cracks running up the walls.

Shock at what she'd done had barely begun to flicker through her mind when she felt something heavy and oppressive build within her. A sudden sharp pain in her chest had her crying out as something foreign inside her pulled tight, stretching like a rubber band.

Oh god, it hurt.

It felt like every atom of her being was being simultaneously crushed and pulled to their breaking points.

The foreign sensation grew stronger, heavier, until it felt like she was being ripped apart. The agony was unreal. She tried to scream her pain, but her chest was caving in, and she couldn't breathe.

It was gathering her power. She could feel it, like a thorned vine, latching onto the tendrils, could feel it squeezing them, choking them.

With a violent, agonizing wrench, it yanked her power back into her, the cold, burning pain of it tearing a ragged shriek from her throat.

Like a hand swatting a fly, the whiplash of it folded her body in half and sent her hurtling toward the floor.

Strong arms caught her before she hit the concrete. She felt those arms pull her limp form against a broad chest, but it was a distant feeling, quickly overshadowed by the pain wracking her.

Wanting to escape the agony, she tried to sink into the blackness threatening to swallow her. It hurt so fucking much. Her body felt battered and bruised, torn apart and badly put back together. Her chest ached horribly, every breath feeling like her lungs were filled with shards of glass. And her power, the well in her chest, it felt cowed and beaten, and so far away.

As horrified by it as she'd been not minutes before, the distance left her feeling hollow. She wanted it back, needed it back. She tried to reach for it only to encounter a barrier, that same sensation she'd experienced earlier but stronger now.

Testing it, she pushed hard against it, harder than she had before, trying to break through. Just as she felt it start to give, it retaliated, sending searing pain through her body that bowed her back and tore another scream from her raw throat.

Panting, whimpering, she retreated and slumped against the warm body holding her so close. Oh god, the pain. She couldn't take it. She tried to will herself unconscious to escape the agony, but before she could a voice broke through.

"Arawyn! Look at me, Sweetheart. Open your eyes," it demanded.

Rathe.

She'd never heard him sound so agitated, almost frantic. She wanted to soothe him, wanted to smooth her fingers over the crease that formed between his brows when he was angry or upset.

But, she was so tired, and her eyelids were so heavy.

"Baby, wake up. Come back to us," came a second voice —deeper, rougher than the first.

Fear.

Her gentle giant. She wanted to do as he asked, wanted to open her eyes so she could look into his again. But, the darkness was thick now. It was pulling her down.

"C'mon, my Little Loon. I know it hurts, but you have to

wake up now." A hand, calloused, yet so very gentle, cupped her cheek. "Wake up. Now."

There was a compulsion in those words she couldn't resist. It made her fight against the peaceful, painless darkness. It made her swim to the surface and pry her eyes open.

Tears blinded her. Blinking them free, they trailed hotly down her cheeks as the men above her came into focus. She thought, at first, that her eyes were still blurry which was why everything seemed so dark.

And then she remembered. Everything.

Her relief at seeing all three of them was quickly smothered by the horror of what she'd done.

"I hurt you," she croaked, the words coming out as a nearly soundless, ragged whisper.

Everything ached, the pain so intense it left her shivering. But, that was secondary to the horror she felt at having injured them.

"We're okay, Baby," Fear murmured, his big hands warm and comforting as he gently held one of hers.

Viper, kneeling beside him, used his hand on her cheek to guide her to look at him and tenderly wiped away the tears wetting her lashes. His smile was as bright as ever, but his beautiful golden eyes were shadowed with worry.

"Don't fret, my Pretty Loon. Rathe already spit on us. Fixed our boo boos right up."

She was incredibly thankful for that. So, so fucking relieved she hadn't done lasting harm, but that didn't alleviate the guilt she felt at having caused their pain in the first place.

"What am I?" she rasped.

"Not what. Who," Rathe corrected, his voice hushed, as if he didn't want anyone to overhear.

Fear whipped a sharp look at him. "You don't think… "

"I do. And so do you. There's no other explanation, and you know it," Rathe cut in.

"By the Gods. We knew… But, to actually find her? This is going to change everything."

Arawyn frowned up at him, not understanding, the fear intensifying at the grave look in his gaze and the heaviness in his voice.

"What are you talking about?" Arawyn asked, peering between them. "Who am I?"

When she glanced at Viper, who'd been uncharacteristically silent during the exchange, her heart dropped at the look on his face. He was staring at her wide-eyed, his expression solemn and distant, like she'd just become something removed from him, untouchable.

"You're her. The lost Princess," he whispered as he slowly withdrew his hand from her cheek and let it fall limply into his lap.

The loss of his touch had panic skittering through her. "I don't understand."

He looked… devastated. His smile was a sad, lost thing. "The Daughter of Light and Night. The Heir of Gilt and Shadow."

Rathe tightened his arms around her, bringing her attention back to him. The look he was giving her had her pulse speeding and her stomach twisting into a knot.

Fear looked grim and calculating, like he was already trying to assess the fallout of this discovery.

Viper looked heartbroken and lost.

But, Rathe? Rathe was looking at her with a new light in his eyes, a possessive kind of fascination.

"You're the rightful Queen of Faery."

To be Continued in...

(A Court of Gilt and Shadow Series Book Two)

PRE-ORDER AVAILABLE NOW!

GLOSSARY

Terminology:

Banálch- pure gold Light Court currency

Changeling- term for a Fae child born sickly or with broken magic who has been taken to the human realm to replace a human child. This was done under the false hope that bringing in new blood, and preventing those with broken magic from breeding, would fix the magical imbalance in Faery following the deaths of High King Aodhan and High Queen Saoirse. The human child is then taken back to Faery

Clans- term for nations ruled by both a female and a male Fae. Can be a mated pair or two individuals chosen to rule together by their subjects

Dakaryian steel- a type of steel from Faery, mined exclusively from the Floating Mountains

Druiach Nihr- term for a person capable of crafting weapons or items and imbuing them with power. An ability passed down through bloodlines

Faery- the dimension from which Fae hail

Firláh- translates to 'Fated.' The term used among Night Fae for the other half of one's soul

Kingdoms- term for nations of Fae ruled exclusively by males, generally found in Light Court beings

Light Court- one of two classifications/denominations of Fae. Primarily consists of Spring and Summer regions. Home to the many Light Fae species. Following The War, the majority of Light Fae are now ruled by High King Ehrendil

Móirlhev- Light Court desert

Night Court- one of two classifications/denominations of Fae. Primarily consists of Autumn and Winter regions. Home to the many Night Fae species. Following The War, the majority of Night Fae are now under the rule of the Regent of the Night Court, Malgath, until Princess Nissa passes the Night Trials and ascends the throne

Old Gods- deities worshipped before Manon manipulated the denizens of Faery into casting them out upon the belief that the Gods were trying to control them. These deities are credited with the creation of Faery and were once entrusted with bestowing the titles of High King and High Queen to the two individuals they deemed worthy

Old Ways- the way of life in Faery before Manon manipulated the Fae people into no longer worshiping the Old Gods, believing in a caste system, and abandoning the practice of Fated matings

Portal- gateway between Faery and the human realm created with power or conjured magic

Lilium Meadows- a region in the Light Court which Pixies inhabit

Queendoms- term for nations of Fae ruled exclusively by females, generally found in Night Court beings

The War- following the sudden deaths of High King Aodhan of the Light Court and High Queen Saoirse of the Night Court, the Treaty of Gilt and Shadow, meant to unify the two Courts and bring peace to all of Faery, was dissolved, and a war was declared. The battle, perpetrated by the new, self-appointed rulers—Ehrendil, King of the Shining

Vale and Malgath, head advisor to Queen Saoirse—lasted a decade. After countless deaths and two Courts torn asunder, The War ended when Ehrendil and Malgath called a ceasefire. Amidst the ashes, Ehrendil declared himself High King of the Light Court—a title previously bestowed by the Old Gods—and Malgath became Regent of the Night Court. They created their own alliance, one that will be solidified upon the marriage of Prince Rathe, Ehrendil's son, and Princess Nissa, the orphaned daughter of Aodhan and Saoirse

Treaty of Gilt and Shadow- the alliance between the Light and Night Courts created upon the Fated mating of Aodhan and Saoirse, intended to unify Faery

Tribes- the different races of Fae beings. All belong to and are under the rule of either a Kingdom, Queendom, or Clan which are then ruled by either the Light Court or Night Court

Species:

Fae- a species of beings from a different dimension capable of wielding energy. All Fae are separated into two classifications—Light or Night—depending on lineage, race, and power.

Aswang- shape-shifting, vampiric race of Night Fae who feed on energy or power

Bauchan- a race of Light Fae and a type of Hobgoblin. They average at four feet tall, have nub-like horns at their hairlines, sharp, pointed teeth, and have hair that will often appear to be moving as though underwater during moments of high emotion

Blood Fae- broad term for races of Night Fae that subsist primarily on blood

Chimera- a race of Night Fae with the ability to shift into a winged, horned, creature

Dragon- broad term for a race of Fae. Can be of the Light or of the Night, depending on lineage and power. Shifters. Descendants of non-shifter, animistic Wyverns

Fire Wyvern- two-legged, draconic, winged Light Fae creatures capable of breathing fire

Giant- a race of Night Fae averaging twelve feet tall, generally found in mountainous regions

High Fae- a race of Fae once called Ísledair. Under the rule and manipulation of Manon, they are now referred to as 'High Fae,' making any race not Ísledair 'lesser.' Can be Light or Night Court

Ice Wyvern- two-legged, draconic, winged Night Fae creatures capable of breathing liquid nitrogen

Ísledair- a race of Fae now referred to as 'High Fae.' Can be Light or Night Court

Lesser Fae- any race of Fae not Ísledair. Were once equals, but under Manon's rule, have since been relegated to the status of inferior beings

Minotaur- a race of humanoid, horned Light Fae with facial features that vaguely resemble those of a bull

Naga- a race of Light Fae with the ability to shift into a half-human, half-snake form.

Pixie- a small, winged race of Light Fae. These mischievous descendants of Night Court Sprites predominantly live in the meadows and woodlands of the Light Court

Pixie Dust- magical dust that gives Pixies their various powers, but for other Fae is highly addictive, gives them a high, and increases their powers for a short time

Redcap- a race of Night Fae descended from Trolls known for their fierceness, warrior culture, and eating their victims while still alive. Notable by their blood-soaked caps

Satyr- a race of Light Fae with furred legs, cloven hooves, and human-like upper bodies

Siren- a race of carnivorous Light Fae who live in the water and are known for their beautiful, hypnotic song capable of luring their prey to them

Sprites- a small, winged, carnivorous race of Night Fae who are elf-like in appearance and extremely territorial

Troll- broad term for a race of Night Fae distinguishable by their appearance, though they vary in size and preferred local

Virika- a race of Night Fae, also referred to by the umbrella term 'Blood Fae,' who subsist primarily on blood

Water Fae- broad term for Fae that live in water, whether partially or exclusively

Wendigo- a cannibalistic race of Night Fae. They have long claws, shark-like teeth, solid black eyes, and are known for eating humans and other, weaker Fae

Abilities:

Devour- the ability to steal others' power or energy and absorb it into one's self

Discern- the ability to tell lies from truths

Heal- the ability to heal others, one's self, or both by a variety of methods particular to a person's bloodline and race

Influence- the ability to manipulate and control others' emotions

Light Jump- a Light Court ability to ride beams of light from one place to another

Shadow Jump- a Night Court ability to ride shadows from one place to another

Sight- Precognition; can present in a variety of ways from visions to intuition to crafting objects meant for specific people or purposes

Characters:

Asshole- Arawyn's cat

Braven- Night Court Fae of Chimera blood; banished to the human realm for practicing forbidden magicks; twin of Breac; friend of Arawyn and owner of the gym she frequents

Breac- Night Court Fae of Chimera blood; banished to the human realm for crimes against Regent Malgath following his twin, Braven's banishment

Ehrendil- once the ruler of the Shining Vale Light Kingdom; crowned himself the High King of the Light Court, following The War

Graeme- Light Court Fae of Satyr blood; banished to the human realm for crimes against High King Ehrendil; deceased

High King Aodhan- King of what was once the largest Light Court Kingdom: the Valley of the Lilies Kingdom; Fated mate of Queen Saoirse; deceased

High Queen Saoirse- Queen of what is the largest Night Court Queendom: the Shadowed Wood Queendom; Fated mate of King Aodhan; deceased

Malgath- once the head advisor of the Shadowed Wood Night Queendom; now acts as Regent to the Night Court

Manon- father of Ehrendil, grandfather of Rathe and Viper; was the ruler of the Shining Vale Light Kingdom before Ehrendil; deceased

Orin- Night Court Fae of Bauchan blood; peddler who smuggles goods from Faery to the human realm

Peter Harrison- human male; neighbor to Arawyn; deceased

Sneaks- raccoon that often visits Arawyn's home at night; proficient at sneaking past her motion sensors and cameras

AUTHOR'S NOTE

First off, thank you so much for reading! This book is pretty different from what we're accustomed to writing, but my goodness did we fall in love with this story and these characters!

Arawyn's strength and resilience hooked both of us, but it was her flaws and imperfections that made us fall in love. To have survived the life she's had, yet still be capable of trusting not just other people but also herself takes serious strength of spirit. We cannot wait to see how she continues to evolve in this series and to watch her take on the coming obstacles that will test her in ways she's never been tested.

And the guys. We are obsessed!

Rathe is so guarded in this book, his first and last thought always on protecting Viper and Fear, and we love him for that... even though he also makes us want to put cayenne pepper in his coffee sometimes. We're both sadistically looking forward to breaking through those walls of his, and we can't wait to see everything that's on the other side.

Fearson is and always will be the perfect book boyfriend.

Knowing, as the authors, that he was cold and unfeeling before he meets Arawyn in the club, then seeing the instant change in him to caring, protective, and supportive? We're irrevocably smitten. We hope that you've fallen in love with him just as hard as we have.

Last but never least, Viper. This man, here *insert all the heart eyes*. We just adore this batsh*t crazy, obsessive psychopath so much it's crossed the line into unhealthy. There's something about damaged men that, in any other story, would be the villain, that just makes you swoon when you get to see them in the light of a hero. Viper would do anything to protect and care for the few people in his life he deems worthy, and now that Arawyn has caught his rather manic attention, she's very much a part of that very short list.

There's so much more to come from this story and these characters and we hope you join us on their crazy, fun, addictive, dangerous, adventurous, romantic ride. We can't wait to bring you the next installment of A Court of Gilt and Shadow, which we are currently hard at work writing.

Through Illusions and Deceit will be here soon and is now available on pre-order with Amazon.

Until next time, may the books be addictive and the book boyfriends be sizzling.

So much love,
    Stacy and Harper

ALSO BY STACY JONES

*All ebooks available exclusively on Amazon and *free* to read with Kindle Unlimited*

CHOSEN UNIVERSE

CHOSEN SERIES

Chosen Series Collection: Books 1-3 with Bonus Scenes

Chosen (Chosen Series 1)

Tribe Outsider (Chosen Series 2)

Tribe Protector (Chosen Series 3)

Native (Chosen Series 4)

TAKEN SERIES

ARIA'S TRILOGY: Complete

Aria's Awakening (Taken Series 1)

Aria's Ascension (Taken Series 2)

Aria's Desire (Taken Series 5)

VICTORIA'S DUOLOGY: Complete

Victoria's Discovery (Taken Series 3)

Victoria's Embrace (Taken Series 4)

SHARED WORLDS

KHARGALS OF DURAS: Complete

Gravel and Grit (Khargals of Duras 1) by Stacy Jones

Hard as Rock (Khargals of Duras 2) by Stephanie West

Heart of Stone (Khargals of Duras 3) by Regine Able

Sticks and Stones (Khargals of Duras 4) by Tamsin Ley

Etched in Stone (Khargals of Duras 5) by Abigail Myst

Taken for Granite (Khargals of Duras 6) by Nancey Cummings

Rock my World (Khargals of Duras 7) by Zara Zenia

STANDALONES

A *Kiss of Madness* by Stacy Jones and K.B. Everly

Saving Merritt by Stacy Jones and CoraLee June

A Demon's Christmas by Stacy Jones and K.B. Everly

ALSO BY HARPER WYLDE

*All ebooks available exclusively on Amazon and *free* to read with Kindle Unlimited*

PHOENIX RISING

Born of Embers (Phoenix Rising 1)

Hidden in Smoke (Phoenix Rising 2)

Spark of Intent (Phoenix Rising 3)

Forged in Flames (Phoenix Rising 4)

Blaze of Wrath (Phoenix Rising 5)

Changed by Fire (Phoenix Rising 6)

Beauty from Ashes (Phoenix Rising 7)

Glimmer of Cinders (Phoenix Rising novella)

THE VEIL KEEPER

Shadow Touched (The Veil Keeper 1)

Blood Bound (The Veil Keeper 2)

Tethered Magick (The Veil Keeper 3)

Rising Darkness (The Veil Keeper 4)

THE HUNTRESS

An Assassins Death (The Huntress 1)

An Assassins Deception (The Huntress 2)

An Assassins Destiny (The Huntress 3)

THE REJECTED REALMS
Co-written with A.K. Koonce

Hell Kissed (The Rejected Realms 1)

Written solely by A.K. Koonce

Fire Kissed (The Rejected Realms 2)

Soul Kissed (The Rejected Realms 3)

STANDALONES

Goddess of Chaos (Blood Moon Rising)

Call of Magic (available anywhere ebooks are sold)

Printed in Great Britain
by Amazon